DAUGHTER
OF CROWS

Also by Mark Lawrence

The Broken Empire
Prince of Thorns
King of Thorns
Emperor of Thorns

Short story collection
Road Brothers

Red Queen's War
Prince of Fools
The Liar's Key
The Wheel of Osheim

Short story collection
The Red Queen's Ward

Book of the Ancestor
Red Sister
Grey Sister
Holy Sister

Short story collection
Tales of Abeth

Book of the Ice
The Girl and the Stars
The Girl and the Mountain
The Girl and the Moon

Impossible Times
One Word Kill
Limited Wish
Dispel Illusion

The Library Trilogy
The Book That Wouldn't Burn
The Book That Broke the World
The Book That Held Her Heart

Short story collection
Missing Pages

DAUGHTER OF CROWS

BOOK ONE OF
THE ACADEMY OF KINDNESS

MARK LAWRENCE

HARPER
Voyager

Harper*Voyager*
An imprint of HarperCollins*Publishers* Ltd
1 London Bridge Street
London SE1 9GF

www.harpercollins.co.uk

HarperCollins*Publishers*
Macken House,
39/40 Mayor Street Upper,
Dublin 1, D01 C9W8
Ireland

First published by HarperCollins*Publishers* Ltd 2026

1

Copyright © Mark Lawrence 2026
Map © Tom Roberts 2026

Mark Lawrence asserts the moral right to
be identified as the author of this work.

A catalogue record for this book is available from the British Library.

ISBN: 978-00-0-869610-8 (HB)
ISBN: 978-00-0-869611-5 (TPB)

This novel is entirely a work of fiction.
The names, characters and incidents portrayed in it are
the work of the author's imagination. Any resemblance to
actual persons, living or dead, events or localities is
entirely coincidental.

Typeset in Adobe Caslon Pro by Palimpsest Book Production Ltd,
Falkirk, Stirlingshire

Printed and bound in the UK using 100% Renewable
Electricity by CPI Group (UK) Ltd

All rights reserved. No part of this publication may be
reproduced, stored in a retrieval system, or transmitted,
in any form or by any means, electronic, mechanical,
photocopying, recording or otherwise, without the prior
written permission of the publishers.

Without limiting the exclusive rights of any author, contributor or the publisher of this publication, any unauthorised use of this publication to train generative artificial intelligence (AI) technologies is expressly prohibited. HarperCollins also exercise their rights under Article 4(3) of the Digital Single Market Directive 2019/790 and expressly reserve this publication from the text and data mining exception.

To my editor Jane Johnson. Who has through thick and thin, and the course of many years, skilfully hammered my work into something presentable.

Prologue

All of the people I hate are dead. Some of them I didn't even kill. Perhaps that's why I'm still angry. Perhaps if it had been my hand on the knife, my eyes the last thing they saw, perhaps then I would be at peace. Perhaps.

I am old. I have outlived my enemies and my purpose. Some people are hard to kill. I'm one of them. Whether that's a blessing or a curse can be difficult to tell. I've lived so often when I should have died. Lived when the better man or woman has stumbled into their grave. Lived when whole towns have burned. Even a city once. Twice. Three times if you count the Port of Laros, though that place catches fire every week.

Everything they said about age was true. That also irks me. All that the wordsmiths wrote, everything that toothless ancients mutter over long-nursed ales, all of it the gods' honest truth. And yet only as decades stacked upon me could I understand it. Same words, different ears.

Age took the beauty that I never recognized when it was mine. It dressed me in this tapestry of scars, and for each one of them sewn silver through my skin a dozen others lie too deep to see. Age stole my grace and left me stumbling on towards a final sunset. It exchanged a confidence born of ignorance, for a fear born of knowing that I do not know. And yet . . . and yet . . . it has gifted me a measure of peace I never thought to own. A breath of calm after a storm none of us expected to end. The fires of my rage are old coals now. Quiet, and banked against the coming of night.

I am older than anyone ever imagined I might become. Time's knife has pared away at me, revealing things I thought lost. And still I don't know if what lies ahead will be a death of a thousand cuts, or the gentle easing into the last bed I will ever lay my head in. Or maybe, at the end, the world will remember me again and we shall have a final reckoning.

One thing I have yet to learn in all this living is how to tell it. How understanding might flow from old tongue to young ear. Facts are blunt, awkward things, hard to miss, and yet the truths about how the years take from you, and what they give, are not ones that can be packed into a single sentence. They're too ephemeral, too personal, too subjective to be captured within the net of a single paragraph or page. Not even a chapter could hold them. But maybe an entire book could do it . . .

CHAPTER 1
Molly Plight

The calm before this particular storm had lasted ten years, much of which Molly Plight had spent knitting. Trouble had arrived in the shape of a man of no great height, road-dirty and weather-beaten. Save for the cruel curve of the knife at his hip and the dull glint of mail beneath his fleece, there would have been nothing to mark him. But when he paused in the inn's doorway and smiled that smile, Molly knew that the peace she'd thought would claim her final days was over. She knew what a predator's hunger looked like.

'That bull the Millers have won't last another season.' Jayne Clay, the tiny old woman on Molly's left, was given to predicting the death of prized livestock. That topic and regaling anyone who so much as paused in her vicinity with the doings of her two dozen tow-headed grandchildren constituted the majority of her conversation.

Molly's needles and ball of yarn lay on the table before her, abandoned in favour of a pipe and a drink. The village children said the pipe smelled like a burning midden heap, perhaps not unfairly, but good weed was hard to find so far from anywhere. The small, thick glass in her hand held ulik, a treacle-dark liquor the locals brewed from turnips. She watched the mercenary cross to the bar. 'Maybe.'

'Maybe?' Doubt was a slap in the face where Jayne's predictions were concerned. Her ability to number the days of anything with hooves was legendary. 'It's a certainty, girl!'

Molly sipped her ulik and made a face. Pipe smoke had numbed her tongue to the stuff's foulness, but she could still taste it. On her other side the third of their trio, Ambeth, hugged her ample belly and cackled at Molly being called a girl. Jayne and Ambeth might have a decade and more on Molly, but in no world that they knew of was anyone north of sixty summers a girl.

Cackled. Molly sipped again, winced again, and considered laughter. Age had blunted much of her sharpness but in turn it had put a harsh edge on her voice and turned laughs into cackles. Still, if that were the worst the years had done to her she would consider herself blessed.

'Another round, *girls*?' Ambeth patted her coin pouch. She'd sold all the cheeses she brought into Stones Corner on Davy's cart, even the blue that stank worse than Vale pipe-weed, and for once could back her generous instincts with funds.

A 'no' opened Molly's mouth but she bit down on it and shaped a 'yes'. One for the road. One to numb the aches before they walked the four miles back to Pye.

The tides that had left her stranded in the Vale a decade back had given no hint that her driftwood life had found its resting place. For the first few years everything had felt temporary – her pack ready by the door for a departure that never came. Instead, the slow and simple existence she'd picked up in the village of Pye had worked a strange magic on her. The steel spring that she had begun coiling in her chest at an age when she should have been chasing butterflies, or at least dreaming grand and empty dreams as she scratched a living from the soil, had started to unwind. The anger that she had for so many years bound ever more tightly at her core had somehow begun to seep away. The dark dreams, the watchful ways, the cynical poison that soured her days, all of it had started to leave her, worn away by passing seasons. Worn away by something as trivial as the community of peasants with no more learning among the lot of them than could be found in the head of any first-year acolyte of Kindness.

Ambeth struggled out of her seat and went to get the drinks, complaining of stiff legs. A mercenary wouldn't raise many eyebrows in the cities of the west, but out in the sticks where an oddly coloured pig could be the village's main subject of debate for several weeks, the man was drawing attention. Ambeth eyed him up and down as she approached, wrinkling her nose at the unfamiliar stink of him.

Molly stood, muttering something about the privy. It had been a long time since she'd been called on to do what had once been second nature to her. She had put all that aside, buried it both literally and figuratively. It had stayed buried so long that she had started to believe that that part of her life was over. She'd started to think that this was what her death might be, the slow setting aside of the things that had once defined her. A shedding of armour, one layer at a time. Until at last, she might go to her grave shriven of her burdens – stained by guilt but no longer defined by it.

She cursed as a second, larger man banged in through the street door, this one with a sword on his belt and a blackened iron breastplate. They had to be here for her. Nothing else made any sense. There wasn't anything a mercenary could carry away from the market of Stones Corner that would compensate the long ride to get to it.

CHAPTER 2

Rue

Age would have taken her if they'd just had the sense to leave well enough alone. Some problems are like that – if you ignore them long enough, they go away. Most problems, actually.

The crow hops from one foot to the other on the haft of a broken spear. The feast before it is reflected in the black beads of its eyes. An open grave in which bodies lie in their scores, layered carelessly, sprawled face down as if they might have fallen here rather than been tossed in from the edge of the cold slot in the ground.

The crow cocks its head, choosing. The mottled patchwork shows little exposed flesh: muddy homespun, bloody shawls, grey hair here, darker locks there. No warriors these, just peasants. Hard lives and easy kills.

Cawww? The crow looks up to where a figure looms at the grave's edge, dark against the sky's pain as the last of the sun's light bleeds away. Here stands a man of war, tall in the sharp angles of his armour, unbowed by the rain-laced wind that tugs at his cloak.

'Fly away, storm crow. There's nothing for you here.'

The crow doesn't challenge the lie. But its gaze flickers to the dead.

'Greater gods than you have run before me.' A low thunder edges the voice of this man who is more than a man. 'Their temples lie in ruin. Their statues are cast down. Their priests are crucified. Their faithful call my name.'

The crow caws but keeps its place on the broken spear that is anchored in the back of a child.

The man draws his sword, pale steel that looks like a cold flame in the last light of the day.

'Do you threaten me with that?' The crow is gone, and in its place a woman stands in the grave, her bare feet on the uneven ground of stiff limbs and narrow backs. 'I have no temples, no statues, no priests, no faithful.' Despite her newfound height the woman's head is still below the grave's edge.

'Play no games with me.' The warrior levels his blade at her.

'Games?' She smiles up at him, her face indistinct, flickering, perhaps from that of one corpse to the next as she picks her way among them. 'Are you going to jump down and poke at me with your little sword? I might enjoy that, Sunder.'

Sunder's teeth show beneath his helm's guard. 'I know your names too. Do not think I don't. Saraswati, Thalia, Woman of the Spiders, Morrigan, many others. You cannot hide from me. This is my empire. There is no space for you here, no souls to steal. Fly away.'

The woman's face hardens, ages, wrinkles spreading, eyes shading to pale, holding a cold and empty light. 'Knowing my names is not knowing me. You have nothing I want, little boy. It's not in my nature to take . . . only to test. You wouldn't want to go untested, would you? Older gods than I would be displeased by that.'

He throws the sword like a spear, swift and true. But the woman is gone, and the returned crow has fluttered skywards, snatched away by the wind. The man remains a few moments longer, sniffing at the air, scanning the blasted heath, peering into the grave's gloom as the shadows thicken. He does not, however, climb in to retrieve his sword. He leaves between one heartbeat and the next, as if he were never here, as if there had been no man, no woman, just a crow already too full of carrion to dip its beak. And of course, the corpses.

A night settled in, and later a grey dawn struggled over the horizon. But not until the first rays of the sun reached into the grave and found her outstretched fingers did the old woman draw in a sudden, unexpected breath, and raise her face to the world. If any other within the corpse heap were still among the living, then the cold light burning in her eyes would have persuaded them to play dead a little longer.

Rue had been born screaming at the world with an anger that took sixty years to fade. Even then her new neighbours had known that though she might look like them, she carried something else within her. *Hard as nails*, they said. *A mean streak. Something in the way she looks at you.* Had they known how deep that difference ran, they would have quietly left their homes in the night and never come back. She had told them a name that was true, though it had been so long since she had used it that it had felt like a lie.

The crow that had been following her since the grave landed close by.

'Stop following me, bird.' Rue wouldn't normally waste words on a crow, but she needed distraction from her pain. 'If I was going to die, I'd have done it back there.' Her head ached as if what had struck her had been an axe and the blade was still buried in the back of her skull. 'Fuck off!'

'I can't.' The bird's croak sounded like words to Rue's scrambled brains.

Rue stopped walking and finally reached back to examine the damage. Clearly the blow had fractured her thinking. 'Whoresons!' The oath escaped her through clenched teeth, but questing fingers had found no obvious fracture, just the tar-like adhesion of old blood in matted hair.

She turned on unsteady feet to examine the crow, now watching her from a rock five yards back along her trail. She had not expected a reply. Even on a day when she'd hauled herself from an open grave this was still the strangest thing to have happened.

'Don't test me, bird.' She eyed the ground for a suitable stone, though the thought of bending to pick one up made her teeth grind against the anticipated pain. Every part of her hurt and the sole advantage to the agony in her head was that it at least shut out the rest of her body's complaints – for the most part.

'Test *you*? That's not what I'm here to do.'

The crow's croaking was at once a human voice and also just a bird's chatter. Rue took it as more confirmation that the blow that had put her down, deep enough to be taken for dead, had rearranged her mind. 'Madness' was the word that suggested itself. With a groan, she bent and scooped up a stone from the side of the track.

'I can't stop following you!' Panic in the croaking now. The voice was somehow familiar.

More madness. Rue raised her arm to throw.

'She told me I had to!'

'She?' Rue knew better than to feed a delusion. But there had been a *she*. Somewhere in the depths from which Rue had hauled herself, a climb that began long before she could raise her head and contemplate escaping the grave, there had been a woman. A woman of uncertain age. Of uncertain everything. But the climb had begun with her touch. With the pressure of her bony foot between Rue's shoulder blades, perhaps a great enough pressure to squeeze out a reluctant beat from a still heart.

'She. You know. *Her!*' The crow hopped nervously from foot to foot, eyeing the stone in Rue's hand.

Rue did not *know*, but another thought possessed her. 'You sound like Senna Weaver.'

The bird said nothing.

'I don't like Senna Weaver.'

The bird shifted its feet.

'The only good thing about getting attacked was seeing that old cunt take an arrow in the—'

The crow launched itself at Rue in an explosion of feathers. She caught it around the neck, its beak two inches from her eye.

'I'm slow, but not *that* slow.' Rue snarled the words while tightening her grip on the fragile neck.

'Wait! Don't!' Everyone croaks when they're choking, but a crow double-croaks.

Rue squeezed a touch harder, then with an oath threw the bird away. It landed poorly and stared up at her, eyes black beads of malice.

'Killing you would be a waste of a good joke. Stay a crow.' She turned her back. 'I hope you like worms, Senna.'

'Why didn't you kill me when I was a person?' the crow cawed after her. 'She said you'd killed more people than the cholera.'

'I'm not a killer,' Rue muttered.

The path before her wound around a rise where thorn bushes and stunted trees huddled together, toughing out the wind. On the far side, sheltered by the ridge, the village waited for her. Her small house, her narrow bed, the peace that had become her normal far faster than she had ever expected it to. 'I'm not a killer.'

'Everyone said you were. Everyone said back in the day they called you—'

'The only person who said that was you, Senna Weaver. Stirring up trouble for me from the day I arrived. Starting rumours. You took against me—' Rue clamped her jaw shut to keep back the loose thoughts spilling from her rattled skull. She might not want to be a killer, but to say that she wasn't didn't make it so. She had to be again the thing she had once been, the one who wore this name. The Rue who succeeded in part because of skill, in part because of venom, but truly because she was part of that rare fraternity of individuals grouped only by a single characteristic. Namely that they were, for some gods-touched reason, hard to kill. That where others would fall or freeze or be overtaken by the horror of violence and adversity, Rue's kind evened the odds by stabbing someone in the throat. Rue was the sort that somehow washed ashore when everyone else from captain to cabin boy drowned. The kind found limping from the bloodiest quarter of the battlefield. The kind that crawled from the grave spitting earth and ready for vengeance.

She'd said more to this crow along a dusty mile of road than the old Rue would have said to any person in the course of a typical week. If death had kept her this time, Rue thought, it would have been an ignominious end, sucker punched from behind. Her time might be coming soon, but she planned to put on a show more in keeping with her reputation. Certainly, she intended to take a lot more people down with her when death came knocking again.

Another wave of pain flooded her head. Rue snarled and bared her teeth, challenging any more sentimentality to try its luck.

'You shouldn't go back,' the bird croaked. 'The sell-swords will have burned it all.'

'No smoke.' Rue nodded to the pale sky above the trees' reaching arms. 'Don't you want to warn your friends, Senna? Your boy? His young 'uns? That niece of yours?'

Senna had been quick enough to warn everyone when Rue came to settle in the village. The stranger wasn't to be trusted. She was dangerous. A witch perhaps. Children had started to avoid Rue in the main street within days of her arrival.

Senna made no reply. A talking crow wouldn't last long in Pye. Senna would have been the one to cast the first stone too. In a place where the young men had chased off a stranger for 'wearing foreign clothes', anything bearing even a hint of magic about it was treated with deep suspicion. Even the worthless healing charms they purchased at the grey markets were worn beneath their clothes, too shameful for the light to see.

On the long slow climb to the ridge, recent memories returned, images surfacing in Rue's mind every few paces: a horseman black against the sky as if seen from hoof height, Maddy Spinner's face twisted by terror, the pounding of Rue's heart becoming the gallop of mercenaries charging from the field.

Rue paused at the halfway point, shaking her head to rid it of the pictures. 'Shit . . .' The shaking was ill-advised. She put her hands to her temples and squeezed, trying to contain the hurt.

'Bad?' The crow could have been asking about the pain, or the memories, or both.

'Seen worse.' And Rue *had* seen worse. Worse than a band of hired blades cutting down peasants on their way back from market. But not for many years. Years spent trying to forget, trying to divert herself with the scratching of a living from unforgiving soil, raising goats, haggling for grain, all the dull, hard business of normal lives that can be lived without others having to die to make room for you.

Rue stopped again just shy of the ridge and whatever scene would be revealed to her on the far side. 'Why are you a crow?'

Her head still ached as if ten devils were trapped in her skull and wanted out in a hurry, her wits still felt loose and apt to spill from her if she made a sudden move, but she wasn't mad, she wasn't barking-at-the-moon mad, and this bird was Senna Weaver . . . which made no sense at all.

'I don't know.' The crow fluttered to the branch of a nearby tree where the buds were still green fists clenched against the last breath of winter. The bird managed to look guilty.

'You do know.'

'I think . . .' The crow pecked reflexively at some unseen thing. 'I think *she* sent it. This crow. And . . . I . . .' A shivering of black feathers. 'It picked me.'

'Picked *at* you, more like.' Nothing drew carrion crows faster than a heap of corpses.

'It was . . . I was . . .' Another convulsion and the bird took off, aimed at the sky. 'An eye. I was eating—'

The distance devoured the words, but Rue had heard enough. The crow had eaten Senna Weaver's eye and now it was Senna Weaver. That made no more sense than before, save now at least there was a reason for the connection, for the choice.

Rue walked on. She had been stupid, and she had been weak. How could she have fallen so easily? By rights she should be dead, still with the others rotting in the sun. Age: she blamed age. It had stolen all her sharp edges and paid her with aches, with grey hair, wrinkles, and confusion.

Fifty yards brought Rue to the ridge top from where Pye could be seen nestled in the bend of the river that wound its way down the shallow valley. The Rill – little more than a stream – and Aaron's Vale. It had been 'a' river and 'a' valley when she'd arrived ten years ago. Now they had names and characters. Characters she liked more than many of those she shared the village with. Even so, she had time for some of the inhabitants. Or at least the woman they'd tossed into the grave had. That old woman had had friends. Rue felt herself to have become something different now. Something both new and old. She had undergone a thing most unexpected in a person of her advancing years: change.

That other woman, the one she'd been, had had time for the children too, of course, even if they feared her. Children always eased her soul and tightened her heart, their chatter more soothing than the river's, but so much more vulnerable.

The chimneys in the valley below still smoked, but the thatch did not. She could see no fresh graves. Even so, there were a dozen horses in Steffan's field that had no business being there.

Overhead the crow circled, cawing alarms.

'I didn't want any of this.' Rue squeezed her head once more, never taking her eyes from the seeming peace of the village. 'I'm just an old woman. I only wanted to sit and stare at the fire until . . .'

She lowered her hands and made fists. A very long time ago a young girl had been taught three important lessons.

She had been taught not to care.

She had been taught not to get angry.

And she had been taught how to kill.

With a soft curse, Rue discovered that she had forgotten the first two lessons.

CHAPTER 3
Molly Plight

The signs that someone is about to commit an act of violence vary wildly. Those without the proclivity will need to build themselves up to it, like a horse galloping towards a high fence. They become loud, angry; their complexion may darken. Sweat and trembling herald the storm.

In those familiar with such acts, the indicators are smaller but just as certain for one with eyes to see. Only the broken-minded, in whom compassion, fear, and excitement itself are flattened to almost nothing, can surprise the wary. And even these ones may give themselves away by the necessary preparation, the positioning to gain advantage, the blocking of exits and the like.

Molly left one needle with her knitting, thrust up through and held in place by the ball of yarn – Jayne would know better than to mess with it. She angled past an old couple and their thickset daughter, all hunched together across their table, no doubt whispering about the newcomers.

The first mercenary was a boy of thirty, a child in Molly's view, but an old man when it came to the game of swinging blades. A short, dark beard hid a weak chin. Pale eyes spoke of a heritage in the frozen east. The rune tattooed on his neck looked like a target as he turned to glance at the second man, a frown furrowing his brow, half question, half irritation. Clearly, the easterner had intended to down an ale before commencing any of the other business that had brought him to the village.

'Quickly,' the second mercenary said. 'We need to get to it.' He nodded at the bar.

This one's height threatened the low ceiling. A younger warrior, more guarded than the first, two scars stitching an off-centre cross through his features. Lucky, then. Lucky or dangerous; or both.

Molly had been intending to be quick. But for a moment doubt seized her, its grip physical, arresting her arm, squeezing cold about her guts, bladder, and heart. She should be sure before she acted. There were other explanations. Maybe these men had just stopped to slake their thirst and would soon be on their way?

Survival depends on turning doubts into probabilities and playing the odds. Act or don't act. Hesitation will kill you more surely than an arrow. Already the larger man's eyes had settled on Molly, her quivering indecision separating her from the background of curious peasantry.

'Fuck...' Molly let her remaining knitting needle drop into her hand and drove it through the smaller man's neck, skewering the tattooed rune while deliberately missing his spine.

She jerked the needle back out before her victim understood what had happened, and with its crimson length in hand, launched herself at the swordsman. Her slowness shocked her. But for his surprise at having a grandmother rush at him, the grey tatters of her hair flying behind her, he would surely have impaled her on his blade.

Molly hit the man with less force than intended and he took only one step backwards. She had thought to drive her shoulder into his chest, but the breastplate changed her mind, and she ended up embracing him, legs locked around him, heels in the backs of his knees. The shock of the impact stunned her, and she had nearly bounced clear even as the mercenary roared in surprise and reached to pull her off.

As her opponent's right hand sought purchase in Molly's hair, she felt his other hand hunt for his knife. Thick fingers tangled and yanked, but Molly stayed put, thrusting forward to sink her teeth into neck flesh. Another step back. Cries of alarm rose around them: the inn's clientele only now catching up with events, their attention still on the smaller man stumbling behind her, trying to staunch the blood pumping from his neck.

The taller mercenary should have spotted the needle but somehow had not. Molly reached around and stabbed it into his back. She almost didn't pierce his jerkin and failed to reach his heart by a considerable margin. The knowledge that she was certainly dead now didn't stop her biting down, or from twisting her head, and struggling to force the needle past his ribs.

Any decent fighter would have ignored both needle and teeth and opted to stop the pain by stabbing her repeatedly. The fortune that forever evaded Molly in games of chance smiled on her now as the man instead grabbed her with both hands, trying to haul her off him.

There should have been no contest. Beefy soldier against old woman. And in truth the outcome of the struggle was never in doubt. Age hadn't laid a finger on Molly: it had wrapped its whole hand around her and squeezed until the juice ran out, leaving nothing but dry bones and venom. Her strength was a shadow of what it had once been, and even in her prime she wouldn't have defeated a large man in a simple contest of muscle against muscle. But a wiry tenacity had always run through her, capable of making an inexorable noose of her slim arms, claws of her fingers, and a rope of her body. Even now, some memory of that remained, and for several vital, agonizing moments she clung on, tightening her legs, tearing at his flesh.

One more step back. The low table where Jayne Clay still sat, frozen in astonishment, hit the backs of the man's legs. The table slid, jammed against the wall, and in the next moment the man fell backwards.

Whether it was the needle which Molly had set there that killed him as it punched through his neck, or whether the other needle found his heart as it was forced further in, Molly didn't know. What she knew with great certainty was that her knitting days were over.

Amid the screams, tumbling stools, and pushing bodies as Molly stood up, she saw that Jayne Clay's rheumy eyes had found her. The shrivelled little woman downed her ulik with a rapid motion, swirling her tongue around the glass, then gulped.

Molly had once been used to seeing that same look. The

recalibration as some familiar thing reveals itself to be something entirely new, something in opposition to its stated purpose. Like a knitting needle used to take a man apart rather than to fashion garments to keep him warm. The look had stung her before, and it stung Molly now, perhaps more deeply because this time she had also believed the lie. She had thought herself free at last of the awful truths of her life. Free at the very end to join in with everyone else, even if only in that final shuffle towards the horizon where the sun sets and never rises.

The exodus, that started with the opening of the door and a blast of fresher air, swept Molly with it, taking away her view of Jayne and of Ambeth. She would have resisted, twisted, kept her place, but her body felt broken, every muscle put twice through the mangle to squeeze out what little vigour remained in her withered limbs.

The bellowing and crashing of the first mercenary fuelled the panic. He would take his time to die. He could even have stopped Molly when she grappled the other man. But there's something about a fatal wound that takes the wind from the sails of most people. Anger and fear are what carry a person on at a time like that. Surprise is no help at all.

To begin with, it felt like an escape, from the inn's dim confines and the crashing of the dying man, to the brightness of a day still bitter with winter's trailing edge. It took longer than it should have for Molly to understand the new danger.

Ahead of her the beefy frame of Senna Weaver seemed to be ploughing into the emerging crowd, fighting the flow.

As the panic of the inn's patrons began to ease, an entirely new set of shouts and cries started to override their protests, underwritten by the thunder of hooves. The noise came from the direction of the market square. Senna, blocked by a farmer in overalls, turned her head to look back the way she'd come. The woman jolted, then fell like a discarded sack of grain.

As the crowd scattered, Molly saw the arrow jutting from Senna's eye and the loose line of horsemen charging from the square.

'Fu—'

Something hit her from behind.

CHAPTER 4
Rue

Two bodies lay on Main Street, which was about the only street Pye had. The pair of corpses were a reminder in miniature of the slaughter back at Stones Corner Market. Molly Plight had died a kind of death in Stones Corner and been reborn as Rue in a stinking hole a quarter of a mile from where she had fallen. The spot where ten years of peace had come to an unexpected but perhaps inevitable end. The market town had been on fire when Rue had clambered from the open grave they'd tossed her into. The mercenaries gone. So she'd walked back to the place she'd called home for the last ten years and that had, for the last few of those years, even felt like home.

'Padrick Tanner and Lorrie Smith,' Rue said to nobody in particular.

The old Senna knew them well enough to recognize both, even like this, though the new Senna would perhaps be more interested in their eyes. But the crow said nothing and made no move, only watched.

Padrick, who had once served in the town guard at Reddik, had been beaten. His thinning hair was thick with blood. The mud received his battered face, hiding the worst. He'd been loud, large, a bit of a bully, but hardly a bad man in the grand scheme of things. Lorrie had a single wound in her back, perhaps from a hatchet. She'd ended in an untidy sprawl of skirts and limbs. Rue wondered where the woman's daughter was. Soosa Smith had turned sixteen and flowered like a hedgerow primrose, breaking young boys' hearts left and right.

Senna hopped forward and landed on the blonde tangle of Lorrie's hair. She folded her wings, head cocking left and right in the quick, canny fashion of crows.

'Seriously?' Rue narrowed her eyes.

'What? I wasn't going to . . .' Could a crow look guilty?

The street stood empty, but Rue felt watched. The villagers would be hiding in their homes, except for the clever ones who had already left. Rue cricked her neck to the side, the bones making audible clicks.

Pye had no formal inn, but a bundle of hops always hung above Debban Tanner's door. He'd given up his father's trade and turned to brewing, selling sour pints in the cramped confines of his main room, or the sheds out back when custom was good.

'In there?' the crow croaked.

'Where else?' It wasn't as if Pye had a library or as if sell-swords would visit one while they still had grass to wipe themselves.

'You'll just get killed . . . again.' Senna's warning carried a note of panic. 'Isn't this just going to be a repeat of what happened before?'

Rue's cricked neck hurt. 'Maybe. But don't count me out. I killed someone with a candle once.'

The crow's croak was one of surprise this time. 'That's not possib—'

'I burned them. Not my finest hour. Hours. I'm not who you think I am.'

Rue wondered if she even knew what she was now. But it was time to find out. She walked slowly to Debban's door. Men's voices reached her through the shutters, loud and unconcerned. She paused, setting a hand to her ribs. The pain in her head had eased a fraction – enough for the rest of her body's protests to be heard. The years had washed over her and left her brittle, like driftwood. And the fight in the inn, such as it was, had broken what remained. She would not have won even that contest if she'd begun it in this state. She didn't have so much as a knife. Even her knitting needles were gone.

She stopped with her hand upon the latch. Did she want to die here? The two locals she'd best liked – Jayne and Ambeth, women she had called friends – were rotting in the grave she'd clambered out of. What did the rest mean to her? She could walk away. Start again. Just as she'd started here. Let the winds of chance blow her tumbleweed life to some new resting place.

The flood of years had swept her up and left her useless. Good for nothing but waiting for the end. She thought of waves now, imagining the distant sea as she stood in the too-bright street with her head aching like the devil, and the withered claw of her hand on the door latch. It seemed a stranger's fingers rested there, ringed in wrinkles. How had she let herself get so old?

Somewhere behind her a crow was cawing, crying warnings. Rue had seen the sea once, forty years ago. Seen waves wash upon beaches of hard, wet sand. Human lives, she thought, were like those waves. We rush into life, all fury and flow and a tumbling, churning hunger for the next thing. We smash ourselves upon that shore, and spread, and slow, climbing the gradient, starting to feel its pull for the first time. And then, either soon or late, but with the same inevitability, we reach our terminus and the sea and the slope start to pull us back into the whole. We leave a crescent of foam to mark the limit of our progress, a froth of bubbles, popping as they realize they're alone. And before the next wave comes, we're gone, taking all trace with us.

A shadow loomed across her. 'Who the fuck are you?' A rough voice, moments from anger.

Rue turned, took the knife from the man's belt and pushed it up into the softness where jaw meets neck, pressing it home with the heel of her other hand. She had not been fast, but she had been sure.

The mercenary staggered back, gurgling, then fell onto his arse, clutching at the knife's hilt, more confused than angry. Ill-advisedly he pulled it free, and a flood of hot blood painted his chest.

'A Durong,' Rue muttered. The man's skin was the colour of old oak, darker even than each summer's sun stained Rue's own. Whoever had assembled these mercenaries had cast a wide net, gathering every creed and caste.

She turned away and pushed through the doorway. She knew

she should have taken the knife, carefully wiping the blood from its hilt so that her hold would be true, but a strangeness had her in its grip. The imprint of a narrow foot seemed to burn cold between the blades of her shoulders, propelling her forward, and though Rue had long ago refused to let herself be pushed around, she decided to allow it this one time. After all, a failure to embrace change would truly be an admission of her age.

Her unexpected appearance stilled the conversation in the room. Perhaps ten of the newcomers crowded the space. Lorrie Smith's girl looked up from where she knelt between two of the mercenaries seated at Debban's rough-hewn tables, pale desperation on her face.

'I'm looking for whoever's in charge here,' Rue said.

It took several moments for the drinkers to swallow their surprise. Perhaps if a warrior with an axe had kicked down the door they would have reacted fast. Rue hoped for the sake of whoever paid them that they would have. She used the time to step to the side, removing her silhouette from the door and revealing the twitching collapse of their friend in the street. The light would blind them just as the gloom had dimmed her own vision.

One man, young with long hair in braids, pushed past Rue, his light mail rustling. He hung on the side of the doorframe, ignoring her, his gaze hunting the street for the killer, first left, then right. One of two women in their number, broad as an ox and with skin so red she might have been sunburned but for the season, came towards Rue, reaching with a sausage-fingered hand as if she were gathering up an errant child.

Rue plucked a knife from Long Hair's hip. If their underestimation of her wasn't so close to being deserved she would have been offended. As it was, she welcomed the opportunity it offered to slightly extend this final foolishness. Rue caught one of the woman's outstretched fingers and broke it. At the same time, with her other hand, she sliced open the side of Long Hair's neck, his blade proving keen enough to cut off three of his braids in the process.

'I've come about two deaths in Stones Corner Market.'

Rue's advantage was over. Good things never last. Rue had outlived a great many of them in her time. The burly woman's snapped finger quickly recalibrated her opinion of the ageing peasant before her, and ignoring the pain, she backhanded Rue, slamming her into the wall, before backing off to draw her blade.

As Rue slid to the floor, the thought bouncing between the front and back of her skull was that she'd seen the blow coming and that the woman she used to be would have ducked in time. She hit the ground feeling like a sack of broken bones and spat out a front tooth in a spray of blood. The force of the impact shocked her to her core. She had become brittle. And as she tried to curse the fact she became aware of her broken jaw.

'Wait!' The command, barked from the rear of the room, halted the thrust of a sword.

The mercenary drew her blade back, snarling, clutching the hilt in an awkward, broken-fingered grasp. 'The bitch killed Rakkar!'

That was a lie. Rakkar's eyes were still following the proceedings, though like Rue he was lying on the floor, and the increasingly sluggish pulse of crimson from his slashed neck indicated that he would not be getting up again, at least not of his own accord.

'The great Tabtha, shield-breaker, heart-taker . . . she needs a sword to finish off a grandmother?' The man doing the talking sat between two larger warriors, both wearing leather caps and sharing a blunt-featured brutality that suggested they were brothers. The speaker looked the more dangerous, though. Something about his lack of adornment announced it, that and the creases running the length of his wind-worn face from the corners of his narrow lips to the corners of colourless eyes that watched the world with curious hunger.

'Bitch had a knife . . .' Tabtha glanced around for the weapon.

Rakkar tried to speak but only managed scarlet bubbles and the faintest gurgle.

The man stood up from his stool, setting down his leather mug and wiping his lips, all without hurry. 'I'm a simple man. "Isik," they say, "go burn this shithole." I go burn it. "Isik," they say, "go slaughter the farmers and salt their fields." I slaughter and I salt. But there's no saying we can't enjoy ourselves first. This old girl's got a bit of fire left in her—'

'She broke my fucking finger!'

'And you were just going to run a sword through her?' Isik tutted.

'What happened to breaking *all* her fingers first? What happened to good old-fashioned entertainment? You're not going to let the little girl here' – he nodded at Soosa – 'carry that load all by herself?' He came to stand at Tabtha's shoulder, nearly as tall but half as broad. 'See how she's looking at us. All murder. No give. I'd sign her up if she were twenty years younger. Get up, Granny. Let's have a look at you.'

Rue made the effort. Grunting in pain and spitting blood, she got to her knees in slow, jerking movements, each punctuated by a gasp.

'Hurry. Up.' Tabtha loomed over her, reaching with her good hand to haul Rue to her feet.

Rue let the knife she'd taken fall from sleeve to hand and cut the woman's wrist, slicing veins and tendons, scoring a groove across the small bones. Tabtha's roaring retreat pushed Isik back, but not before Rue stabbed her in the meat of the thigh too, twisting the blade as she pulled it free.

She stood in the space cleared by Tabtha's exit, and showed what she knew to be a gap-toothed crimson smile. 'If I were twenty years younger, you'd all be dead already.'

CHAPTER 5
Bek

Year One

'Welcome to the Academy of Kindness.' The address came from a dumpy woman of middling years with an apologetic face. She seemed out of place on a platform that looked more like a gallows than a speaker's podium. 'Most of you will not survive the next ten years.'

Bek glanced at her cohort, one hundred children huddled on a windswept courtyard, still wearing the clothes their parents or their own cunning had provided them with. A mixture of emotions fluttered across their faces: fear, determination, some measure of defiance, even amusement. Surprise was the absentee. Whatever illusions they had carried through the gates with them, none were ignorant of the basics. The Academy graduated three students a year, three Kindly Ones, supposedly incarnations of the trio whose name you did not speak. The three who came for those who broke the oldest laws, the three who would hunt down any transgressor – mortal or god.

Some held that the Academy of Kindness trained nothing save assassins. Very, very good ones, but common murderers even so. Many more believed though, both in the promise and in the threat. Retribution and its embodiment were something that the servants of many different faiths could agree upon, an ancient, natural justice that cut through lesser laws, both the secular and the sacred.

Bek's mother, who had let her slip from tear-soaked hands, told her to believe. It was, her mother had said, belief that would carry her through the trials ahead. The same belief that the Academy's power rested upon. It was, after all, their reputation as much as their skill that opened doors for the Kindly Ones.

Bek listened as the unimpressive woman laid out a series of horrific truths before the children. The woman – Kindness Marta – stood wrapped in a dark swirl of cloak that the wind kept trying to snatch from her.

'The lichgate, there on the left by the sanatorium.' She pointed to a door so studded with diamonds of black iron that the wood barely showed. 'In a moment Kindness Undu will open it wide and until the sun sets all of you will be free to leave without repercussions.'

'Without repercussions *from them*!' A girl behind Bek snorted. 'My uncle has a man out there ready to kill me if I leave. The Academy takes its money back if we go, unless our bodies are returned by morning.'

Kindness Marta's address continued. 'Your last chance for a change of heart. Please do consider taking this opportunity. After sunset the gate will return to its purpose – to allow for the carrying out of any corpses to which families lay claim – and it will continue to be the only way to leave this establishment before completion of your training. Unauthorized departures from that point on will result in the miscreant being hunted down. And as you know, hunting miscreants is what the order does best.'

A figure, previously unseen in the shadow of the wall, now moved to open the lichgate. A fat, bald, fish-belly-pale woman also in the black cloak of a Kindness. Bek wondered how such poor specimens as Marta and Undu could have survived the training that would kill up to ninety-seven of the children huddled with her in the wind's teeth. Though, even as she wondered this, around ten of the candidates hurried shame-facedly towards the exit. Whatever threats or promises their families had made to get them through the front gate now proved insufficient to stop them slipping out of the side one while the chance remained. Perhaps in Undu and Marta's years everyone but them had had the common sense to leave at this stage.

Kindness Marta opened her mouth to speak again only to be interrupted by a shrill cry from the slopes outside. It seemed that it wasn't just the girl in the second row's uncle who had killers out there.

'The world that gives us one hundred daughters each year to spend in such a cause is not one that would tolerate the loss of one hundred sons. A hundred and seventy-three classes. A hundred and seventy-three years. Seventeen thousand three hundred children.

'It's a world that many of you would return to in a heartbeat to escape the death that haunts our halls. But in our early years the records say that we had no bars on our windows and that no threats of retribution were needed to keep the girls here. We did not hunt down those who left us.

'In those days the Academy paid only a token fee to the families of our acolytes, a loaf of black rye: daughters were unwanted mouths to feed. But payment is a necessary part of our Creed, whether a token or a burden. Money is older than our civilization and as old as any of those that have passed. Money is the salve that keeps the vengeance on which we trade from consuming the world. Some sins can be paid for only with blood; but naked murder, absent compounding crimes of hospitality, oath, or kin, is, according to the ancient lore something that may be atoned for by the paying of a wergild – the blood-gold that may comfort and sustain the victim's family.

'And similarly, when we take a child from a family, a price must be paid in compensation. When I came here the Academy paid my father one bronze mark. I paid your fathers nine, each bearing the Academy's three-whip stamp. Next year we are offering a silver mark for each girl. You can get a sturdy young donkey for a piece of silver!

'Try buying a hundred sons of Abrona for silver. Even for a gold mark you might struggle to find a healthy man-child for sale within a day's march of this spot. These facts are not a surprise to you. You know them to be true. You have been taught your value since the day of your birth. Likely by your own parents, and if not, then by the streets, by the institutions, the faiths, and the leaders of our society.

'Here, and here alone, can a woman take up a blade and slice away a life. Here and here alone does our world learn to fear us, and only through fear can respect be wrested from unwilling hands.

'If we merely trained you to be deadly. If all we did was to produce the most skilled assassins and sword masters, surpassing in their art, this would not be sufficient. We would be swept away, stamped out. Those who held power over us would have seen the danger, like the first flames flickering among the furniture, and they would have accepted the necessary cost to reverse what would suddenly have seemed like a foolish decision: that of allowing the triple-goddess her own house among the faiths.

'Fear was required. Terror. We needed to produce monsters and to be seen to do so with such reckless ferocity that our first Kindnesses would be accepted as the flesh-borne avatars of the three sisters who chastise the gods themselves.

'We are as vicious as we have to be. As loud as we must be. As cruel as is needed. What we do here is a dark prayer to the eternal. A threat carved into our own flesh. We say to the world that if we hold the lives in our care more cheaply than do you who sold them to us; what price do you think we set upon your life, be you priest or general, lord, duke, or king?

'The people know what we do here. They speak of it in whispers, but the unspoken part is deafening: if we do this to ourselves – what will we do to *them*?'

She paused her oratory and continued, in less theatrical tones. 'Once your training has begun you cannot of course be allowed to leave with those secrets save as a fully approved graduate. So please do think about the decision. And for now, that's all I have for you. Kindness Terra will take you to your chamber. Breakfast is served at dawn, lessons begin at sunrise. Miss the first and you'll go hungry. Miss the second and you'll get a strike.'

Kindness Terra actually looked the part: a lean, terrifyingly tall woman with scars seaming her hollow cheeks, and eyes like pieces of broken glass. She beckoned the children and set off towards a nearby door.

The Academy had been built in a great square, with fortress walls facing outwards, and castle-like chambers filling the space within, save for the central courtyard that accounted for perhaps half the area enclosed. Overhead, crows circled, black against the red stain of the sky. Others crowded the tower tops, and the stink of death rose whenever the wind fell.

Kindness Terra led them through unlit corridors of rough stone. The light pooling beneath infrequent wall slits made islands of illumination through which the bowed heads of children bobbed in her wake. She stopped at an arched door and unlocked it with a heavy key. The hall they filed into was large enough to accommodate the full intake of one hundred. Bek imagined that the chambers further down the corridor where Years Two to Ten were housed would be progressively smaller. The thought rekindled the mild panic that had seized her ever since the day her father had summoned her into the tiny room he called his study and explained that a great opportunity had opened itself to her.

As the last child shuffled into the room the door closed behind her. A long, still moment passed, broken only when a particularly large girl with a brutally blunt face declared loudly, 'We're allowed to kill each other, you know.'

'We know, Lucia!'

'You first!'

A wave of responses, mainly anger and outrage, bubbled through the hall as the girls nearest to the big one pushed back, seeking to claim more distant beds. Lucia just sneered and settled her mountainous form down on her blankets as if she hadn't a care in the world.

Bek sat on the nearest cot. A hard and narrow thing, bolted to the floor, the blankets grey and worn, the struts stained, scarred here and there by barely legible words or names carved into the wood. A covered bucket sat beneath the bed, the lid insufficient to hide the fact that someone had used it not so long ago.

Her father had called this a great opportunity, though primarily it was the opportunity to exchange the chore of having to watch her die for the handsome fee paid to the family of any girl sacrificed to the Academy. Providing of course that she didn't leave on the first evening. She was dead whatever she did: the visiting healer had pronounced her incurable and promised a slow demise.

For Bek it offered only the chance to cut short the suffering promised by whatever poison her blood had decided to manufacture against her body. Even so, though she knew that she should be crushed by the betrayal and terrified of what lay ahead, she found herself oddly intrigued at the prospect of being trained by the Kindnesses. This she knew to be a surer diagnosis that something within her lay broken already at the tender age of twelve than any of the healer's bleeding or their divining stones.

'I'm Einsa.' The girl on the bed beside her, solidly built, broad face framed by dark curls, grinned. Someone had broken her nose at some point and left it crooked. The small eyes that sat to either side of it, like black stones, held an unexpected amount of good humour – the warm infectious kind rather than the malicious type. She'd been the one saying her uncle had a man waiting on the slopes to stop her running. 'Maybe we should keep a watch tonight. Some of these bitches might want to tip the odds in their favour while everyone's asleep.'

Bek grunted noncommittally. Maybe it was Einsa who wanted to cut her from the list. Just visible past Einsa's wide shoulders a small girl, perhaps the smallest in the room, crouched in the centre of her cot, legs drawn in tight within the circle of her arms. A painfully thin and delicately featured child who Bek considered would be well advised to take her chances on the slopes no matter how many people her family might have set to watch them.

The girl looked up as Bek studied her, meeting her gaze with bright, pale blue eyes. Bek felt a faint shock of recognition, a moment of connection, though she didn't know her at all.

'Mollandra,' the girl said, barely audible above the conversations all around.

Was this how Bek was going to find her friends? Forming alliances with the very first girls to speak to her? It seemed too random, but perhaps that was just how life was. Maybe the three of them would be sisters. The only three to survive the nightmare years ahead. Bek found herself smirking at the idea. More likely they'd wake up dead, standing by the black river, waiting to cross. Certainly,

Mollandra looked to be one of the best bets for girl-least-likely-to-survive-the-night.

'Here.' Bek waved the frail, blonde child over and she came meekly, her feet bound in the cloth strips that the very poor pretend are shoes.

'Really?' Einsa looked the trembling girl up and down dismissively.

Mollandra, standing between the two girls' beds, said nothing, only looked from one to the other with those almost faery eyes of hers.

Bek shrugged. Her illness would get her if the other students didn't, so why play to win? She could be the sort of Kindly One where 'kindness' wasn't a stage curtain drawn to hide the horror. 'Small can be useful. Maybe she's fast too. Are you fast, little girl?'

'I . . . I don't know.'

Bek considered slapping her to find out, but remembered she'd aimed herself at kindness only moments before. 'You don't look fast.'

Einsa shook her heavy head. 'We should get someone else. The girl with the scar.' She nodded towards her choice.

The girl wasn't the only scarred face in the hall but this girl with the shaved head truly did have a magnificent scar that had torn open one cheek and healed pink against the smooth brown as if it were warpaint.

'We should stick to three. If there's four of us then we'll always be wondering which one isn't going to make it,' Bek said.

'None of you are going to make it!' said a wild-eyed girl with an untamed mass of red curls who perched on her bed like a bird of prey in some high place waiting to strike.

Einsa ignored her. 'So, we throw the minnow back and choose a better third.'

'Sometimes fate delivers a better choice than anything we can come up with ourselves.'

'Huh?' Einsa furrowed her brow. 'You sound like you've had tutors. Someone's been tipping gold down your throat.' Disapproval edged her voice.

'My father's a scribe,' Bek said. She kept the 'not a good one' to herself. 'And if he had gold, he wouldn't have sold me to this place.'

Einsa grunted. 'The little fish can stay then. I mean, if the gods have sent her . . .' She snorted and lay back on her bed.

'We'll watch each other tonight. Take turns. Sometimes the first night can get very murdery.' Bek looked around the room. The curly-haired girl flashed her a white grin that split her face like a wound. The scarred girl watched with dark eyes, statue-still. 'I'll take first watch.'

'How will you know when to—'

'I'll guess, I guess.' Bek cut Mollandra off and waved her back to her bed.

Heavy shutters covered the hall's tall windows, and the light came from a score of candles in niches around the room, ushering shadows to the centre. Already a few of them had guttered out, and none of those remaining alight had more than an inch of wax to burn. Slowly, but faster than Bek liked, the gloom thickened, and soon, despite her plan, she'd have nothing to watch save the blackness of the first night.

'How do you know?' Mollandra called. 'About the murdering?'

'Reading,' Bek called back. 'It often pays to read ahead. They've been doing this for years, you know. Nearly two centuries.'

'I don't know how—'

'They'll teach you here. They won't let you leave without knowing how to read.'

Einsa snorted and pulled her blankets around her. 'They will if you forget how to breathe first.'

Somewhere across the room a girl with her face pressed to the shutter cracks called out to inform them that the sun had fallen behind the ramparts.

A short while later, the low bubbling of nervous voices died away entirely as the door grated open. All across the hall girls sat up. Bek could see nothing past the crowding heads. She stood in time to see a shadowy figure slipping out through the gap.

'Two!'

'No three.'

Three girls taking their last chance to escape.

A fourth left some while later. Bek was sure that the sun must have already set but as she focused on listening now that the light had all but leaked away, she heard the clunk of a heavy key turning in the lock.

'Now you're mine.' Lucia's voice in the darkness. 'All of you.'

Shortly before dawn the shutters were drawn back from the outside without ceremony or any great noise, but it proved sufficient to wake Bek. Einsa's snoring identified her in the next bed. As dawn's grey fingers tested the night Bek raised her head. She could see that Mollandra was also sleeping.

Grinding her teeth, Bek slipped from her bed and went to poke the child awake.

'Ssssh. Sit up. Don't tell Einsa.'

Bek returned to her bed on quiet feet, followed by suspicious eyes both from the allegedly sleeping and those set to watch over other groups.

The light increased. Bek kept her place. She had no clothes to change into, no water to wash with, and until they unlocked the door the fact that she didn't know how to find the breakfast hall wasn't relevant.

Finally, a girl near the front stood up and tried the door. It had been unlocked without anybody noticing.

A mass migration towards the exit roused Einsa from what was a remarkably deep sleep given the circumstances.

'Come on.' Bek joined the exodus, Mollandra trailing her.

She turned at the door to wait for Einsa and they were among the last to leave.

Despite their fears only one girl had died in the night. She made a conspicuously large lump in the centremost bed. Lucia's head hung slightly past the top end of the cot, the discolouration of her face visible even in the gloom, as was the strip of cloth that had been used to throttle her.

CHAPTER 6
Rue

The mercenaries' leader stepped back, silently applauding Rue while Tabtha howled, clutching her leg and scattering chairs.

'Stop wailing, woman!' he barked. 'Jeron, get her leg bound.'

'My wrist—'

'Just stop her bleeding. And if she won't shut up, bandage her mouth too.' All the while he kept his eyes on Rue. The overlarge brothers in leather caps had come to stand at his shoulders while two men and the company's other woman brought Tabtha crashing down into a chair, still pouring crimson.

Soosa Smith looked more terrified than when Rue had come in, and now she seemed just as scared of Rue as she was of the rest of them.

Isik rubbed his narrow jaw, fixing Rue with a shrewd stare, his glance dropping briefly to the bloody knife in her fist. 'First Hobb out in the street, then Rakkar – though to be fair he was an idiot and was going to end up dead sooner rather than later – and now Tabtha. I have to say I didn't think I'd see anyone get the best of her. Certainly not in some dirt village out in the wilds. What are we going to do with you, Grandmother?'

'I'm here for Ambeth Potter and Jayne Clay.' Rue's words came out roughly formed, her broken jaw refusing to shape them properly.

Isik glanced left and right in amazement, the thugs gathered under his command returning his confusion. 'Who the fuck are Ammath—'

'Ambeth.'

'I don't give a shit.'

It hurt to speak, almost more than it hurt to stand. Somehow nearly a dozen pairs of hostile eyes helped keep her upright. 'You'll tell me who ordered the attack on Stones Corner, and if it wasn't you, I'll leave you to go about your business.'

That provoked a scattering of rough laughter, drowning out Tabtha's grunts of pain. Isik, however, only looked more confused.

'Wait, that's not Ammeth?' He pointed at Soosa Smith who sat frozen in her spot, eyes impossibly wide, a small trickle of blood running from one nostril.

'Ambeth. No. Ambeth and Jayne were both over seventy summers. I'm here for an account of their deaths. Tell me who ordered the attack on—'

'On Stones Corner. I get it. And what if it was me?' Isik grinned without humour, showing narrow teeth in surprisingly good condition for someone in his line of work.

'If it was you then I'll kill just you. Nobody else has to die.' Rue hesitated before adding reluctantly, 'Or you could pay the wergild. It's seven ounces of gold.'

A genuine belly laugh escaped the man. 'You want me to pay fourteen ounces of gold for two old peasant women? Fourteen for two hags?'

'No, I don't want you to pay. And it's seven. That's three and a half—'

'Well, we have two problems then.' Isik rubbed his hands together. 'First, it weren't my order. Second, I'm not telling you shit. Actually, three problems, because we still have the question of what to do with you.'

'You're their master.' Rue held her knife up. 'Try me.' She beckoned him forward. 'Show the children how it's done.'

'A duel, is it?' Isik's brows rose in mock surprise. 'Turning ten to one into one to one just by asking for it?'

To avoid further speaking, Rue raised her left hand, spread her fingers to show five, then folded two away. Five and three remaining. Eight to one now.

Isik glanced to where Tabtha sat huffing through the hurt as others bound her leg. 'Eight to one. I'll give you that.' He met her gaze. 'Does that work for you often? Just asking for a duel?'

'Hasn't worked lately,' Rue managed, dribbling blood, and sucking in a painful breath. 'But then I hadn't cut anyone for ten years until just now.' She leaned her back against the shack's wall. 'Thinking . . . your pride . . . all your crew . . . take the challenge.' She twisted her stolen knife back and forth as if in playful invitation.

Rue could see that Isik wasn't stupid. But most of his band probably were and he would lose face in their stupid eyes if he did the clever thing. Also, cunning or not, every man has his own pride. Common sense said to get a spear and finish her off . . . but a man's pride can always lead him into foolishness, even if you're telling him that's exactly what's happening. Pride's a strange thing. Long ago an alchemist had shown Rue that there are several parts to a lungful of air. One the alchemist had named oxygen – the invisible but vital stuff that fires the blood and gives flames the strength to burn. Too little of it and you die, but too much and you also die. Pride was like that too.

'My knife . . .' Rue slurred. 'Against yours.'

Isik considered for a moment, running his gaze the length of her body. He shrugged and drew his knife. He held it like a man who knew what he was doing. Who had taken lives with a short blade in tavern fights, dark alleys, and battlefields.

The mercenaries moved closer. Rue had their full attention now. Even Tabtha was glaring at her while applying pressure to her wrist. She would have mocked them, but her jaw hurt too much for wasted words. She hoped that Soosa would have the sense to slip out but couldn't risk a glance in the child's direction.

With a grunt of pain, she shrugged herself away from the wall. She had been overplaying her weakness to draw the man in, but not by much. She held her knife in a loose, bloody grip, and beckoned Isik forward with the fingers of the other hand.

Isik exchanged an amused glance with the brothers flanking him. Now he'd committed to the role he had to play it to the full. His humour didn't stray past his cheeks, though: his eyes held neither colour nor joy. They were the eyes of a man ready to do business.

He came forward, feinting as any knifeman will, looking to

prompt a response, make the foe twitch, gauge their speed. Rue kept still. Even the blood stopped dripping from her mouth. She gave him nothing.

Isik's hand flickered out and in its wake a hot line traced itself across Rue's cheek. He'd been so fast. He pricked her shoulder. A cat playing with its food. Making a show. Even so, he remained wary. The man wasn't stupid. He'd glimpsed her true self, enough of it at least to be waiting for a deadly reply if he gave her the chance.

The mercenary stabbed at Rue again and she stepped into the blade's path. That surprised him. Isik had enough experience to catch her knife hand as it descended in an amateur overhead blow. Anyone angry enough and lacking skill will go for the mutual destruction option, getting stabbed but stabbing back. Any fighter worth their salt will know to stop that.

Isik's blade slid easily between her ribs. It didn't even hurt. She felt the punch of his hand behind the hilt more than the deep kiss of the knife. It hurt when she twisted, but the fresh surprise on his face was reward enough, at least in the moment. He tried to pull his steel clear, but her ribcage trapped it.

In the same moment, not as fast as Isik could have done it, but fast enough to do the job, Rue dropped her stolen knife from fingers now all but nerveless in the ferocity of the man's bone-grinding grip . . . caught it with her other hand as it fell and stabbed him in the neck.

Isik let her go then, and she fell back against the wall once more, blood filling her left lung as she grinned at her audience's amazement.

'Who's next?'

They came at her together, still ignoring the common sense of the spear, crowding each other in their fury. Rue didn't imagine they were heartbroken over Isik. It was more that her defiance infuriated them – her refusal to comply with their expectations.

She managed to sink her blade into one of the attackers before she went down beneath a flurry of blows. The hardpacked earth received her and a rain of stamping feet kept her there. Rage isn't cruel – cruelty is a colder thing. All thoughts of torture had been washed away by the raw animal need to make an end of her.

Rue had hoped her last thoughts would be about something she loved, misplaced friends, the three daughters she'd lost, perhaps even the two Kindnesses who had once been her sisters. Instead, her mind emptied of everything, including pain, and she saw only a black sun in a bone sky, and heard nothing save the whispering rush of a river.

CHAPTER 7
Bek

Year One

Although the women who served breakfast in the Academy's great hall were variously maimed they all shared two mutilations. All nine had an ugly circular brand on their foreheads, and someone had taken their noses, leaving a wound that left Bek with little appetite for the porridge dumped into the bowl before her.

'Acolytes who nearly made it.' Einsa bent to the task of scooping oatmeal into her face at a rate that made it seem she must have been raised by wolves.

'I thought they all died,' Mollandra whispered on the girl's right.

'Almost all.' Einsa spoke through a full mouth. 'Some taken on as staff. Marked so they don't run off.'

Bek shuddered. The woman who'd served her had been wrinkled, grey-haired, and lacked a hand. A much younger woman, similarly noseless and branded, but with both hands, clumped along the aisle between the next two long benches on a wooden foot. It seemed a slow death to Bek. She hoped the Kindnesses had something quicker on offer for her.

The first years sat on their own four benches running the width of the hall. Sitting opposite Bek, Einsa, and Mollandra were the girl with the shaved head and pink scar, the red-head with the wild grin who had pronounced their mutual doom with such glee the night before, and a lean, dark-eyed girl with a seemingly permanent frown.

The red-head declared that she was Sharp – which sounded like a lie. She named her neighbour with the scar Tmanga, and the girl with the frown Wenda.

'Who killed Lucia?' Sharp asked as if this was everyday talk at the breakfast table.

Einsa waved the question away as if it were a fly seeking her bowl.

Bek noted that the acolytes in the second year and above all wore the same clothes: collarless tunics with loose sleeves, and trousers like the skilled men in the city wore. Those closest to her had white tunics, shading into greys as the years advanced, not from lack of washing but with proximity to the black of a Kindness.

Their numbers dwindled as their clothes darkened. Where the first years filled four benches, the second years occupied only three benches, the third years also three but more sparsely, the fourth years two, diminishing towards the far platform where the trio of Kindnesses sat together with six noseless instructors, black-robed but white-sleeved. These, Einsa supplied, must have failed during the last year or two, though even getting that far rarely meant earning a tutor's job instead of the axe.

Bek paused to watch the high table eat. All of them spooned what seemed to be the same bland porridge into their faces without conversation. All save Kindness Undu who didn't touch her food and instead let her gaze wander across the acolytes at their benches. Her eyes seemed to find Bek's and Bek looked down suddenly, paying renewed attention to the chatter around her.

'There's only three Kindnesses though?' Mollandra again, still with little more than a whisper. 'Don't they all come here to teach once they get old?'

'Old?' Einsa snorted. 'Kindly Ones don't get old.'

'How do you know all this?' Bek watched the big girl eat, wondering if she was one of those people who simply invented to cover their ignorance.

'My mother was a Kindness.' She didn't look up from her private eating contest.

Bek's brows rose of their own accord. 'I didn't think they were supposed to have children.'

'Who's going to tell them no?' Einsa shrugged. 'Also, why do you think I'm here? They did wait until she died though . . .'

Before the Kindnesses stood, signalling an end to the meal, Einsa further explained that while first-year acolytes were not forbidden from murdering each other – just as the unfortunate Lucia had announced the previous evening – it was forbidden to murder any acolyte in the years below your own. So the older, more skilled girls were not going to be slaughtering their way through ranks of twelve-year-olds. Self-defence and retribution were fine though if any overambitious youngster tried their hand against those above them.

The first year, the one hundred and seventy-third first year taken into the Academy of Kindness, began their formal education with a lesson taken by Kindness Undu. Because of the size of the class they remained in the dining hall after all the other years had absented themselves and the nine servants had cleared away the bowls, piling them in teetering columns.

Undu stayed on the platform where she had eaten. Bald and round, there was nothing about the Kindness to give away the fact that she was a woman, save that the Academy admitted only girls. The Kindly Ones of legend, the trio who even the gods feared, were women. Alecto – unceasing in her anger, implacable. Tisiphone – she who avenges, retribution made flesh. And Megaera, the trio's memory, keeper of grudges, custodian of feuds, jealous guardian of old fires.

'I am Kindness Undu.' She spoke in the fluting voice of a child rather than that of someone who looked to have eaten too many children. 'Let me echo the words with which Kindness Marta sent you to your beds last night:

'You are here to suffer and to die. And in this crucible, we will find the strength this order requires. Some few of you who prove worthy, those who survive the harrowing, will be woven into the whips that scourge the wicked of our world. You will join the ranks of the Kindnesses. We who guard the last glimmer of divinity that once sprinkled down from heaven upon the heads of mortals. We who uphold the oldest laws that stand between humanity and its descent into beasts. The guilty, be they peasant or prince, fear us, just as the gods themselves fear the Kindly Ones.' She smiled around at the girls as if she had just enquired after their grandmothers' health. Rubbing her plump white hands together she continued. 'My lesson is one that likely none of you will ever learn, and the only skill on whose mastery your lives do not depend. I am here to teach you about the river, and even among the Kindly Ones few have stood upon its banks. Fewer still, perhaps none that remain, have drunk its waters as I have and understood some portion of death's mysteries.'

'Shit . . .' Einsa muttered. 'Day one, lesson one: necromancy.'

Two of the servants in their grey tunics entered the hall carrying a stretcher that supported some heavy object covered with a bedsheet.

'Stand back,' the front one growled as she led the way between the first-year benches and those of the second.

Chairs grated and feet scuffled as girls tried to make room. Cold fear gripped Bek: the servants were coming towards her. They were going to deposit their ominous burden right in front of her in the very spot her bowl had occupied minutes before.

But no, the two servants stopped a few yards short and scattered more acolytes as, with some effort, the pair hefted the stretcher onto the long table. Neither sought instruction from the Kindness, just bowed their heads and departed. Bek detected a slight quickening in their stride as they left.

Kindness Undu levered herself from her chair and descended the platform. Acolytes cleared the path ahead of her as she came down between the benches towards the stretcher and its lump.

'Gather round,' Undu trilled. 'Gather round. Sit, stand, sit on the tables, stand on the tables. Tiers, you see? An amphitheatre of acolytes. How nice.' With a flourish she snatched the sheet away, clutching it to her in a small white hand.

Bek had already thought that it would be Lucia under there, but even so the shock of seeing the girl so close, without the mercy of the dormitory's gloom, drained the blood from her extremities. The dry, tingling cough that had started to plague her chose this moment to rise and wrap its scratchy fingers around her throat. She resisted, every part of her still, frozen in place. The healer had said the dropsy would claim her lungs before its other effects became too pronounced. She would die gasping for air, hauling her last breaths into ragged sacks. Perhaps she would look worse than Lucia at the end. She hoped not.

Lucia smelled, a sewer stench, and her discoloured features were frozen in a look that mixed fear and pain into something awful. Bloodstains and dried saliva around her mouth showed that she had fought. The ligature had been removed and the skin on her neck was mottled black, dark blue, a livid purple, nothing that looked natural, and yet what was more natural than death? The gouges were from her own fingers where she must have clawed at her throat, reaching everywhere but beneath the twisted strip of cloth that she'd been trying to get hold of.

'This young lady was Lucia Aqualas Divinanar. Daughter to General Aquinas of the Western Artan legions. I say *was* because she is currently elsewhere and only echoes of her remain.' Kindness Undu took Lucia's hand in her own soft, white grip, lifting the girl's arm. 'The corpse is cool but not cold. The limbs retain some of the stiffness that follows a couple of hours behind death's visit.' Undu let the hand fall and it settled with unnerving slowness. 'Lucia herself, the girl you probably did not find time to get to know, is standing by a river, one that few among the living can see or even hear, and yet it flows through all things, never more than a careless moment from any of us. Soon she will cross that river and answer to old gods whose names have been forgotten. She will carry their judgement into the sunless lands beyond. And this flesh, all of us, and even time itself, will be left behind her, forgotten and unmourned.'

Undu set her hand to Lucia's cheek: an almost tender gesture. Bek's flesh crawled at the thought of laying her own palm against that cooling, discoloured skin.

'But until she has crossed the river – whose name we do not speak within the hearing of the dead – she remains within reach for those who have the touch for it.'

Undu laid her other hand on the corpse's forehead. Lucia's eyes remained fixed on some distant point on the ceiling, glaring, her anger palpable, as if at any moment she might lunge upwards, seeking a mouthful of some enemy's flesh.

'She wasn't sleeping. She was ready to act. Ready to fight. The noose around her neck surprised her . . .' Undu closed her eyes as if looking for more answers in the darkness. 'Yes, surprised. Anger came next. She raged. If she had been able to make a sound it would have been threats, and then curses. The fear came only at the very end. There was a brief moment in which she would have pleaded. And at the last, in the heartbeats between knowing and unknowing, there was . . . sadness . . . a complicated sadness of many parts. Too many for her to . . . and then she was standing beside the river, gone from her flesh.'

Undu opened her eyes and withdrew her hands. 'I have amplified her last feelings to the point where some of you, those few with aptitude, might get a hint of them. Who would like to try?' She moved away, gesturing to the body on the table.

Nobody advanced. Most stepped back. Four or five girls, forgetting they were on a table, tumbled to the floor with screeches of surprise that in turn provoked ripples of nervous laughter. Some, like Bek, who didn't shuffle away were left like rocks revealed by a retreating tide.

'You, girl.' Kindness Undu beckoned in Bek's direction.

Bek looked behind her in the hope that someone else was advancing at her shoulder. The closest, a small, black-haired girl she'd heard called Brooth, was too far back for it to be her.

'You, the mousey girl with the nose.' The Kindness gestured impatiently.

Bek stepped forward with a sigh, making a mental note to keep to the rear of proceedings in future. She stopped shy of Lucia's glare, out of reach of her dead arms.

'Well, touch her, girl. We haven't got all day.' Undu's childish trill carried an uncomfortable weight of command.

Bek set a tentative hand to Lucia's forehead.

'Touch her! This isn't a first date!' Undu shook her head in disgust. 'You're rooting out the secrets of the dead here. If she had wounds I'd have your fingers under her skin. Touch her!'

Steeling herself, Bek moved her hands to Lucia's neck, finding the livid flesh unpleasantly cool and waxy.

'Listen. Try to hear the river. It's flowing all around us. Through us and her alike. Really listen.'

'I can't—'

'Listen!' Undu barked.

Something happened then, an explosion of violence, slow in the frozen heartbeat that trapped Bek, that kept her prisoner in an awful moment. Without a 'between' she found herself hitting the opposite table, the wood biting into the small of her back. She ended up on the floor, gasping for breath, clutching at her neck, desperate to breathe, suffocating despite the air pumping frantic from her lungs – in – out – in.

Two other acolytes hauled Bek to her feet at the Kindness's urging.

'Bring her here, quick as you like,' Undu shrilled.

The girls started frogmarching Bek down the aisle but as her strength returned she shook them off. Since Undu's 'quick' had not sounded as though it was optional Bek scooted under the table, scraping her head as she stepped over the divider.

'Here,' she announced self-consciously as she popped up on Kindness Undu's side.

Undu studied her with eyes so deep-set and glinting that Bek couldn't even guess their colour.

'Did you kill her?'

'What? No!'

Bek's shock seemed to convince the Kindness. 'Such a connection is highly unusual even between murderer and victim.' She held out her hands.

'I don't . . .' Bek patted her shirt as if expecting to find what Undu wanted.

'Hands!'

Bek reached out and let the woman take hold of her. It required a greater effort of will than touching the dead body had, and she failed to suppress her shudder, though Undu didn't seem to notice.

Undu was short, though still taller than most of the acolytes.

Her strength came as a surprise when those soft, clammy hands began to squeeze. Bek struggled not to cry out. She felt her bones grind together and a strange fire began to flow through her veins. When it reached her lungs the fire pooled there, filling both with that maddening scratchy itch that the dropsy had started to torment her with at night, only worse. She coughed, coughed again, wheezing as she drew in breath for another cough.

'Enough.' Undu let her go. She stepped back, addressing the class. 'The young struggle to connect to the dead. Life has you in its teeth and is shaking you too fiercely for you to hear the river's flow. Most of the lessons I teach you here will go to the river with you unused. But for the three who leave this place wearing the black as I did . . . those three at least have a chance – a small chance – of growing old. And the old dip their toes in the river every night. When you're old, with the right training and a bit of aptitude, any of you might do what little Bek did here in front of us.'

She knows my name, Bek thought. *She must know all our names.* And in an instant she was forced to reframe her view of the woman yet again.

Undu returned her gaze to Bek, staring at her as every other girl was. 'To find this power in a child means that we have had a true necromancer break her fast with us. That or she's close to her own death, dipping her toes in the river to test the temperature.'

Beneath the glitter of those small eyes, Bek's lungs burned again but she refused to cough and instead snarled at the Kindness who turned away with a small smile.

'Who else would like to touch your dead friend here?' Undu raised her voice.

Silence. At least nobody fell off a table this time.

'Anyone?' Undu humped her shoulders at the sides of her head in a shrug. 'All of you will do it then. Form a queue. Make sure it's a good feel – it's the last she'll ever get.' The Kindness watched as they shuffled, pushed, and finally began to take their turns. 'Get used to it, ladies. Death will be your companion here. You'll be carrying the dead out or you'll be carried out yourself.'

Eventually all of them had set hands upon the dead girl, some trembling, some sullen. Sharp grinned her wide grin, Mollandra crept by quiet as a mouse, Einsa stone-faced, Tmanga bored. Some girls sniffed and cried – for themselves, Bek thought, since Lucia had given nobody anything to miss her by. Little Brooth, almost as pale as Undu, spent longest, fascination in her dark eyes.

Undu shooed the last acolyte away. 'There's more . . .' She set two fingers to Lucia's throat and rolled her eyes up into her head till only the whites showed. Strangely, it was this, not the corpse and its stink, that caused a dark girl towards the back to lose custody of her breakfast.

Undu wrinkled her pale forehead in discomfort and reached for where her own throat was lost in folds of flesh and the black of her hard-won robe. She coughed, croaked, and spoke as if her voice had first to force its way through a straw:

'*Some little bitch came at me! Me! In the night. Tried to choke me . . .*'

A pause in which horrified glances were swapped back and forth. Bek stared only at her feet, trying to forget the awful constriction she'd endured as she shared Lucia's last moments.

'*No, I didn't see which one it was! That just means I'll have to punish them all! I'll grab—*'

Kindness Undu took her hand from Lucia's neck and blinked as her eyes resumed their normal positions. She coughed, swallowed, and coughed again. 'As you heard, Lucia is still quite angry about last night's events and not yet reconciled to the fact that she is dead. She remains on our side of the river, her discontent blinding her to its presence, leaving her deaf to the muted rush of time's passage, dark and liquid, ever flowing.'

Bek noticed that Einsa on her right and Mollandra on her left were both considerably closer to her now, pressed up for comfort. What part she'd played herself in closing those gaps she didn't know but she was glad of the press of warm bodies and hoped it would erase the memory of Lucia's cooling flesh.

Undu made to take up the sheet and cover Lucia again. An audible sigh hissed out of the audience, part of it Bek's own relief.

The Kindness paused. 'But wait,' she said, smiling as if at some old joke. 'There's more.' She made a pale fist and raised it above Lucia's chest. 'It would be a crime to let all that anger go to waste, would it not, children? Perhaps a greater crime than the murder itself, for we here at the Academy are agents of retribution, daughters of anger, forged to remind the world of its duties.'

And with that she struck down, hard, fist striking Lucia's breastbone. Once! Twice! Three meaty impacts, each jolting the corpse, until on the third, Lucia sat up sharply, turned her bloody eyes towards the rows of watching acolytes and, in the same voice that Undu had used when speaking for her, demanded, *'Which bitch killed me?'*

CHAPTER 8

Bek

Year One

Lucia Aqualas Divinanar had looked like being a bit of a nightmare while she was alive. Dead, she was *all* of a nightmare. Her corpse rampaged between the long benches, scattering stools as she lunged for any acolyte foolish enough to let her get close. She'd broken the arm of one girl, who managed to twist free and crawl away under the tables. But even as Bek turned from her own escape to watch, Lucia knocked down another acolyte and grabbed her ankles. She swung the girl – who had sat close to Bek at breakfast – overhead in an arc bringing her down to wrap around a stool. The cracking sounds as her spine made a U-shape in the wrong direction were not those of wood breaking.

Added to the violence was an incoherent roaring that seemed too loud to be issuing from her foam-filled mouth.

Kindness Undu had positioned herself at the main doors and announced that nobody had permission to leave the lesson until they dealt with Lucia, or the corpse ran out of steam.

'She doesn't look tired yet . . .!' Einsa had to shout for Bek to hear her, even though she, Mollandra, and a score of other acolytes were as far away from Lucia as they could get. They huddled together on the platform, where the Kindnesses and instructors had eaten, and pressed themselves against the wall.

'Do the dead get tired?' Bek asked. She'd only just regained her breath after running frantically from their last safe haven to this one.

'Get ready . . .' Mollandra hadn't said it loudly enough to be heard, but as Bek turned to see if she could press further into the crowd she read the words on the smaller girl's lips.

Glancing back, she saw Lucia throw down the smock she must have torn from someone and turn to glower at their end of the hall. Something in the weight of her deranged stare fastened a choking band around Bek's throat, reminding her once more of how the girl had died.

The acolytes started to shift to the left, anticipating Lucia's charge down the right-hand side of the hall. It hadn't yet occurred to Lucia's cooling brain that she could leap from table to table. If she started to copy what some of the girls had been doing to evade her she'd be nearly impossible to escape.

'We can't run forever!' Bek shouted. *She* certainly couldn't. Her diseased lungs already felt like nets trying to hold water. 'Undu could be lying about Lucia getting tired.'

'She never said she would.' Einsa hurried to the left after the bulk of the crowd.

'We should stop her while we're fresh then!' Bek grabbed at Einsa's thickly muscled arm. The girl was smaller than Lucia, but she was definitely one of the five biggest left.

'Stop her?'

'Kill her then.'

The retreat turned to a rout as panicked acolytes began to sprint.

'She's already dead!' Einsa shouted, not looking around.

Bek found herself at the rear of the group of girls fleeing along the side of the hall, Lucia's bellowing growing louder at her back with each of Bek's floundering strides. Her lungs just refused to provide her legs with the strength that terror demanded. Any trip or even stumble would put her in the monster's grasp and certain death.

Help. To her shame, she would have cried, 'Help!' But she hadn't the breath for it. The other acolytes were suddenly yards ahead of her. Bek saw Mollandra glance back from the rear of the group, surely thanking the stars that she was faster than the slowest person.

The hand that clamped down on Bek's shoulder felt more like an iron claw than flesh. Bek screamed despite the lack of air in her chest and began to fall.

She kept falling through a darkness that swallowed first the light and then all sound too. Bek had spent too much time imagining how she would die, how much it would hurt – not whether, because dying *always* hurt – and almost no time imagining what being dead would be like. She wouldn't have guessed there would be so much falling. So much of it that after a while she stopped trying to scream against it and found that it didn't really feel like falling any more.

'Where . . .' She sat up.

A bone sky offered no light, and yet somehow she could 'see' the black banks rising to her left, studded here and there with what might be thorn bushes or the antlers of monstrous deer buried too shallow. That these growths were also black didn't seem to prevent her sensing their outlines.

The sound of her own screaming, and the wheeze of her breath rattling into deficient lungs, had both been replaced by a low, constant rushing. She saw the lightless waters now, hurtling past, almost close enough to touch. A river of frightening speed, although she sensed no gradient.

Bek got to her feet. She hadn't recovered her breath so much as stopped needing it. She turned and stepped back in shock, one heel almost making contact with the turbulent shallows. Lucia stood just two yards away, angry eyes hunting the darkness, her back to the river.

'Hello?'

And in a swirl of noise and colour it was all gone and Einsa was hauling her across the dining-room floor.

'I . . . I'm—'

'Good, you're awake. Get up!' Einsa released her.

'Where's . . .'

'Lucia collapsed when she touched you. Both of you did.' Einsa frowned. 'This little idiot,' she indicated Mollandra, 'was already going back for you.'

Mollandra danced around Bek as she struggled to stand, her attempts to help more like bird pecks.

Not far away Lucia was also getting up.

'Shit. I thought it was too good to be true.' Einsa started to back away.

'W . . . what was?'

Mollandra pushed Bek. 'Go! Run!'

Flanked by Mollandra and Einsa, Bek began to run. Behind them Lucia's howling restarted.

Bek arrived gasping at the opposite end of the hall. The girls she'd been chasing were now clustered with dozens more around Undu at the doors. Some were even foolish enough to beg her to let them out. Several were weeping, close to hysteria.

Lucia had been distracted by another knot of acolytes and was rampaging after them while a score of other girls ran along the tabletops, jumping the gaps to maintain their distance.

Bek mastered her breath as best she could, not wanting to sound vulnerable. The weak are seldom listened to.

'Can you do that again?' Einsa asked.

'Do what?' Bek spread her hands. 'I don't know what happened.'

Einsa had more to say but for a moment Lucia's screams were added to by higher-pitched cries of almost the same volume. Back among the table rows Lucia had snagged someone else. The new screams ended suddenly and Lucia's howls fell silent almost at the same time. Bek could only see the dead thing's back as it bent over its victim. A moment later she couldn't see either of them and the hall fell silent save for weeping.

It didn't stay quiet for long.

'She's *eating* her!' The acolyte's scream sent everyone still out in the hall towards the main door, driven by a horror so great it might even overcome their fear of the Kindness.

'She's dead.' Bek swallowed against the urge to vomit as for a moment Lucia raised her bloody face. 'But if we put her eyes out she can't see, and if we tie her up she can't move. We should all attack her together.'

'But she's so strong!' An unknown girl behind her. It was true that Lucia's strength seemed to exceed even that promised by her height and powerful frame.

'She's not stronger than all of us put together.' Bek struggled not to pant. If they thought she was doing this to save her skin rather than out of bravery they would never follow her.

With a roar Lucia rose again, her mouth crimson, blood sheeting down her chin and neck, soaking her shift. She overturned the closest table with contemptuous ease. Without the tables they were doomed.

'She's drinking the blood!'

'She's getting stronger!'

Bek had expected Mollandra to join in with the panic, but instead the small girl lifted a fist from which a four-inch metal spike jutted. A second later she opened her hand to reveal the business end of the spoon she had clearly purloined from their breakfast.

'Meh.' Einsa, unimpressed, pulled out a seven-inch hunting knife with a serrated back by way of reply.

'What . . .' Bek didn't have time for more. Lucia was already barrelling towards them.

'Everyone together!' Einsa roared, brandishing her blade overhead. 'Together or we'll all die.'

Of the over eighty acolytes perhaps a dozen stayed. Bek couldn't really fault them. If she could have got someone else to do the work she would have.

'Grab stools!' She seized a nearby one and held it before her, legs aimed at the oncoming undead monstrosity.

A stool might not be much by way of armour but somehow the illusion of safety considerably boosted Bek's courage. Heartened by her example, most of the other dozen acolytes grabbed stools of their own and there were even others running back now to add their contribution to the thicket of wooden legs opposing Lucia's charge.

The bloodstained monster that had briefly been their fellow acolyte smashed headlong into the defensive wall. Several girls were thrown back, one of them falling, but the wall held. Grunting with effort, feet slipping on the flagstones, the girls refused to let Lucia through, and she hung on the forest of legs, howling, stretching for them. Gory hands clutched at the air just before Bek's face, but Lucia's reach proved not quite sufficient. Bek struggled for breath and struggled to hold her place.

'On my mark!' Einsa bellowed. 'Three! Two! One! Push!'

Strong as she was, heavy as she was, Lucia couldn't resist them. Yard by yard they forced her back. Halfway to the wall frustration penetrated Lucia's rage and she changed tactics. She yanked on a stool, and it came flying forward with Mollandra staggering behind it.

'Push!' The crazy red-head, Sharp, threw herself forward into the gap, angling the legs of her stool at Lucia's face and, by dint of knocking Mollandra to the ground, helped the girl to evade Lucia's grasping hand.

'Push!' Her cry wheezed out as more of a whisper, but Bek heaved her exhausted body after Sharp, and the rest of them followed.

Within a few more moments they had Lucia against the wall. A raging storm of strength but unable to break free or to properly lay hands upon her tormentors.

Bek had no idea what the next move should be. How long before the barely contained Lucia exhausted them all or reduced the stools to matchwood?

Before Bek had time to ponder further, Einsa matched Lucia's roar, bellowing, 'Let me at her!'

Bek could hardly see what was happening, but gradually the wall of acolytes started to part, opening a channel beside her.

'Keep her pinned!'

'Hold her!'

'Hold her!'

Einsa slipped through the gap, her knife to the fore, gleaming, the light catching on the wicked sharpness of the cutting edge. The blade should have given Lucia pause but she hurled herself into the chair-wall's breach without hesitation. Her reaching hands knocked Einsa's knife arm aside and a heartbeat later Lucia's bloody fingers locked around the girl's throat.

To her credit, Einsa refused to let the monster take her to the ground. The tight press of acolytes helped her keep her feet. Einsa staggered back, her face shading to crimson as she pulled silently at Lucia's wrists.

Bek saw that Einsa hadn't dropped the knife but instead had managed to stab Lucia in the stomach, leaving the weapon there, buried to the hilt. Frozen in the chaos and sheer horror of the moment not only could Bek not force her body to act, her mind could think of no plan to act upon.

Tmanga had no such problems. The girl dropped to hands and knees, slithered forward through the confusion of legs and shifting feet, and grabbed the knife, hauling it down to enlarge the wound.

Astonishingly, Lucia didn't even seem to notice the ongoing disembowelment. Einsa's hands, which had thus far stopped her attacker's undead strength from breaking her neck, fell away as the throttling choked off her consciousness.

Mollandra came out of nowhere, flying over the heads of the other girls. In retrospect Bek realized that she must have set up a stool and leapt from it, or perhaps made a running dive from the nearest upright table. She ended up wrapped around Lucia's head and shoulders, a small blonde fury anchored by both legs and one arm. With her free hand Mollandra repeatedly pounded her victim's face, an attack that only made sense when Bek finally spotted the spoon handle jutting from the girl's fist.

Lucia's disregard for Tmanga's sawing through her guts did not extend to the spoon attack. She discarded Einsa, who fell like a rag doll, and reached up for Mollandra, roaring.

The little girl dropped away down Lucia's back.

'Push! Get her over!' Bek found her voice.

Some of the acolytes had fled but enough remained to drive Lucia back with a surge, their high-pitched battle cries echoing Lucia's anger now.

Lucia tripped over Mollandra's hunched form and went down backwards. What followed was an exhausting fever dream where the acolytes took turns, reversing their stools to swing them by the legs and bring them overhead to crash the thick wooden seat into the struggling corpse.

By the time Lucia stopped twitching she no longer looked like Lucia, or like anything human. Almost every surviving acolyte had tired herself out pounding on her. It didn't seem possible that the blood spattering so many dozens had come from a single girl, even one as big as Lucia.

Mollandra stood panting, her rags all but torn away, clothed more in blood than in cloth, her hair standing out at odd angles.

'You—' Bek heaved in a breath. 'You were coming back for me. Why? Because I chose you yesterday?' She shook her head, unwilling to have the child attach herself so thoroughly to a sinking ship. 'If another girl had been sitting on that bed, I'd have chosen her instead. Understand?'

Mollandra straightened, wiped her face, just moving the blood spatter around, and gave Bek a complicated look. Finally, she shrugged and turned away. 'Sisters look out for each other.'

Bek reached for the girl's shoulder, angry both at her presumption and at how deeply the words had touched her, but before she made contact, the forgotten Kindness pushed her way between them, ploughing on through the acolytes' panting, gore-stained ranks, as serene as a barge passing through a cluster of little boats. She stopped beside Einsa, who Bek had shamefully forgotten about entirely, and who lay curled with her hands at her throat and her face to the floor.

Undu smiled around at them. 'Our first lesson is over. Instructor Mary is waiting in the corridor outside – she teaches fitness, so it's good you've had a warm-up. On Godsday you can go to the laundry where you'll be issued with your robes. Until then, try not to smear the fixtures.'

With a wheezing groan, Einsa lifted herself onto all fours and retched, spewing her breakfast, which looked exactly like the porridge had in the bowl. The splatter came within inches of Undu's feet.

Undu nodded as if this were expected.

'Welcome to the Academy of Kindness.'

CHAPTER 9

Rue

Rue had fallen beneath the mercenaries' blows. Instead of hardpacked earth what received her had felt like rotten sailcloth, barely holding her weight.

The thudding of kicks became a dull, distant thing, save for one bony heel pressing impossibly hard between her shoulders. The weak fabric that had held her up now tore beneath the increased pressure and without a scream she tipped into a second, far longer fall.

Silence and the darkness of her pain held her. Time passed without a heart to beat away the moments.

Slowly and against expectation, Rue heard a noise that she had spent years listening for. A smooth rushing sound that grew from nothing until, without ever seeming loud, it filled her mind.

Rue found herself standing before a black river whose waters ran between straight banks, swift as a horse with hardly a swirl or ripple. A black sun hung in the bone sky and while a few stunted thorn bushes studded the grey soil around her, the far banks lay desolate.

Rue knew the river and its name ached on her tongue, daring her to speak it. She knew what waited for her on the opposite shore. Judgement. Judgement and a balance in which her soul would be weighed. Rue spat into the iron-grey earth at her feet.

Cawwww!

'Gods eat me!' Rue spun around, angry at being made to flinch, even in a place like this.

Caw! The crow eyed her, somehow revealed by its blackness rather than hidden by it.

'Senna-fucking-Weaver?' Rue would have spat again but found herself too dry. 'Did you try to peck those bastards to death?'

The crow hopped self-consciously from one foot to the other. 'You pulled me down. Like I said: I've got to follow you.'

Rue made a quick advance on the bird, clapping her hands. They barely made a sound – here on the shores of death nothing did – but it proved enough to startle Senna into the air amid a dark explosion of feathers.

'You're not dead then.' Rue let disappointment colour her voice.

'Not properly. Should be after that arrow in the face . . .' She shook her head. 'But the dead can't fly.' She turned back to face the river, the grit of the shore coarse beneath her bare feet. 'Only one way across for the dead.'

Already she could make out the ferry as a faint dot on the roiling smoothness of the river. Unimpeded by the frightening speed of the current it made its way lazily towards them. Rue straightened herself, ignoring her nakedness – clothes were for the living: such comforts couldn't follow into the underworld.

'There's nothing for you over there,' Senna croaked. She'd flown only a yard or two, and that ponderously.

'Oh right, I'll cancel the whole being beaten to death thing then.' Rue tasted blood, faintly. Her own, since she couldn't remember biting any of them. She shrugged and scowled at the approaching ferry. She could have done better. Should have done better. A lot better. But at least she got their leader – Osick, was it? Asak? Failing to remember the man's name pleased her. He would have reached this shore before she did.

Senna hopped closer. 'You should—'

'Should what?' Rue snapped. 'Should have fought harder? Been better?' She waved the anger away with a quick flap of her hands. 'Besides, there's plenty for me over there. The great majority of the few friends I managed to make. A daughter. One and a half really. Have you buried a child, Senna? If you had you'd know what any mother who has knows – part of me has already crossed this river and is never coming back—' She bit off the words.

Senna had a son in Pye, grandchildren too. If not dead yet, then soon. 'I—'

The prow of the ferry ground into the gritty bank. Rue imagined that not everyone saw the same vessel or indeed the same ferryman. Hers resembled a rowing boat stretched to three times its length, with benches for perhaps a dozen. The sole occupant stood at the rear, tall and clothed in darkness from which only the coldness of his stare emerged, together with the pole with which he improbably propelled the ferry.

Rue shivered and ground her teeth. On the far side of the river Aello would be waiting. Perhaps her other daughters would be too. Ocy she had left with the nuns in Thellamid. The sisters had prayed around the girl as she lay on their altar beneath the diesis of the risen Christ, resurrected and crucified a second time. Her child had laid there cold and limp in the shadow of the order's double dagger – the symbol of their martyr's inverted cross superimposed on the first. The convent's reverend mother had said they could keep Ocypete's heart beating, but she would never rise from the death-sleep, the koma that held her.

And Cela, youngest of the triplets by half a day, the child who had given Rue the deepest of her scars, she could well be there too, across the river. Cela had burned too bright to endure. As warlike as the mother she so hated.

'You don't have to go,' Senna croaked. The crow fluttered heavily up the bank, landing by one of the bare thorn bushes. 'She gave you something – but you have to take it. She can't force it on you.'

'She?' Rue spat. 'Say her name.'

'She has many—'

Rue turned towards the ferry.

'The Morrigan.' Senna croaked it at her back. 'Maiden, Mother, Hag. Badb, Macha, and Nemain. Three who are one. The Norns. The Fates. Your precious Kindly O—'

'She forced you to be a crow,' Rue retorted, tearing her gaze away from the waiting psychopomp.

'No . . .'

Rue snorted a laugh. 'You *chose* that? And now you want me to make an idiot's choice too?'

The crow looked away, its beak pointing to a hitherto unnoticed fruit, hanging all alone amid bushes barren of everything but the cruelty of thorns. The lone berry managed to glisten in the deadlight, a single drop of midnight blood, pregnant with possibility.

'It's her gift,' Senna croaked. 'But you have to go and take it.'

Rue glanced towards the ferryman who had waited for her through all the long years of her life, ready to steer her way at a moment's notice. 'What kind of gift?'

'Power, of course. What other kind is there? You want ribbons for your hair?'

'Careful, Senna! I might suspect you have a backbone.' Rue looked out over the river and at the emptiness of the far shore. What lay there was beyond her imagination. All her dead. The ones she'd lost and the legions she'd sent ahead of herself. The many maybes that age had stacked up for her, and of a certainty, little Aello who she had washed in a mother's grief and buried in the heartbreak of a grave smaller than it should have been. How would such a reunion work, if there even were reunions?

Rue set her back to the ferryman and walked to consider the gift, easing her way among the thorns and cursing when clumsiness tore her skin.

'Will she give me back my youth, Senna?' Rue spread her arms, staring sourly at the ruin the years had left in their wake as they'd trampled across her. She had been strong once, tight, supple. Did she want youth back, truly? Would it be harder to lose a second time? Would she learn the lessons better for repetition? Hadn't she tried? Wasn't she tired? Due a rest? Then she remembered the looks on those faces as they'd closed in to stamp on her. That raw, animal hate. And even here, on the shore of the river, here beneath the ferryman's gaze . . . she felt a flicker of that same flame in her chest, that same shame. She hadn't finished with them yet. 'Will she give me back my strength, Senna?'

Cawwww! The bird fluttered closer. 'What do you think? Her gifts aren't kind.'

Rue pulled the berry free. The juice of it stained her fingers, darker than old blood. She thought of the heel pressing between her shoulder blades, bringing her back when she'd lain among the corpses before. There had been no river then, no gift dangling from a thorn bush.

'Hear me, old one!' Rue glanced around at the off-white sky, seeking a lone crow and finding none. 'Choose me as your weapon at your peril. I cut both ways.' She pressed the overripe berry into her mouth, trying not to gag on its foul sweetness. 'I cut always.'

A shock ran through her. Invisible lightning. It threw her arms wide, and the remnants of that strange fruit flew from her splayed fingers. She staggered back. One pace. Three. She fought for balance, fought to master the fire chasing through her veins. The crow that was Senna cawed a warning, but too late. Although Rue caught herself before she fell, when she looked down, the heel of her left foot had touched the river.

In the open grave Rue had had to shrug off the cold bodies, free herself of their intimacy, and fight to find her feet. Now it seemed as if she had been buried fathoms deep and needed to dig, to crawl, and to worm her way higher and higher, fighting the dead for every yard. And yet when she finally reached the surface, she opened her eyes to find herself alone.

She lay with her cheek to the hardpacked earth she had fallen on. She could see the dim interior of Debban's ale hut, his shitty tables and worse chairs, the backs of three mercenaries who had returned to their drinking.

Rue tried to flex the hand she could see before her, palm pressed to the dirt, fingers splayed. It curled and rose like a pale spider, bones grating. Whatever the Morrigan had given her it wasn't youth.

Slowly, and with a stealth born of curiosity rather than fear, Rue lifted herself, rising until all that kept her in contact with the ground were her fingers and toes. She had been stabbed. She had been broken. Worse: she had been old. And she was still all of those things but the anger flickering in the marrow of her bones didn't seem to care about that level of detail.

Anger. A friend had once said that anger was the easiest emotion to bring back from the deadlands. It wasn't hunger that made the undead fill their mouths with the flesh of the living, that friend had said: it was rage. To bite, that friend had told her, after that first lesson, was the instinct of true rage.

There was, Rue knew, another word for the curious mixture of hate and vitality that held the wreck of her body together and forced her heart to beat against its nature: necromancy.

Rue rose to her feet, unfolding in total silence save for the clicking of her joints. Her clothes, thick with blood and filth, felt strange around her after nakedness beneath a black sun.

The mercenaries at the table were the two large possible-brothers in the leather skullcaps, and the almost as broad Tabtha who the leader (Isik! his name came back to Rue as she stood) who Isik had titled 'shield-breaker' and 'heart-taker'. Rue had stabbed the woman in the thigh after breaking her finger and cutting her wrist, so at least she had a good excuse for not helping to drag out the bodies. What reason the brothers, who had flanked Isik so closely in life, had for not caring what happened to him in death, was less clear.

'Hello, dear.' Rue abandoned stealth. The woman was staring with the type of horror usually reserved for when you find yourself paralysed, with a head-sized spider steadily clicking its way up your leg. Rue licked her teeth: some were broken, some gone, others unsteady in their sockets. She had thought that age had robbed her entirely of what vanity had survived her childhood, but the fact that these louts, these blunt weapons, had maimed her so, proved enough to ignite the fire that she had kept tamped down for so long. Rue didn't like to fight angry. She had been taught to reserve rage for special occasions. Rage was holy. Not to be wasted on the unworthy.

'Oh shit . . .' Tabtha wasn't built for fear, but being wounded and vulnerable can suck the bully out of anyone.

The two brothers, tumbling their stools aside as they rose from them, grunted in surprise but apparently lacked the imagination to be scared. Rue was pleased. Hunting them down would be a chore.

As they approached, Rue forced herself to stillness. She wasn't unfamiliar with the intoxications of various drugs, and both necromancy and anger ranked among their number for overinflating the mind's assessment of the body's powers. Her miraculous return would be short-lived and rather stupid if she had come back believing herself a lion, only to unleash a mouse's squeak instead of a roar.

The slightly larger brother, with a touch of grey in his slightly bushier beard, took an ugly club from his belt. The other one unslung a hatchet, clearly of a mind to do enough chopping to ensure there would be no third coming. Both men towered over Rue. They looked like the competent butchers that formed the backbone of any mercenary company, creatures with stunted emotion and overgrown appetite.

If Rue had been ten years younger and held a suitable weapon she would have been confident. Thirty years ago she would have been contemptuous. Today, she backed away, slowly, patting her pockets for something, anything, that might help. In the old days she'd kept all manner of tricks in her pockets.

'Toss me a knife, Tabtha, and I might let you live.'

Tabtha barked a laugh, but there was no heart in it.

The brothers' lack of fear annoyed Rue. She had clawed her way back from the deadlands and stood before them clad in gore and dirt. Even now she could smell Isik's death as if it were smoke on the air. His blood, lying on the packed earth, called to her. How dare two beetle-browed illiterates just shrug that off and come at her with club and hatchet?

With patient focus the pair manoeuvred her into the nearest corner.

Rue's patting discovered only her pipe which by some miracle perhaps no less surprising than her own resurrection had survived her recent beating intact. She held the bowl in her hand with the stem extending, remembering as she did the small girl who put out the eyes of an undead monstrosity on her first day at the Academy. Rue would have swapped the pipe for a spoon in a heartbeat. Even so, she aimed her knuckles forward, the fragile clay stem extending.

'Why don't you boys—'

As she'd been speaking Rue had reached for the spilled blood that kept calling to her, robed as she still was in the invisible tatters of the underworld. Now, as they walked through it, Isik's blood, together with whatever dirt it had soaked into, grasped the brothers' feet. Not in an iron, unbreakable grip, but firmly enough to cause both to stumble and glance down in confusion.

One reason that Rue had survived so long was that she took her moment. She rushed in, slower than she would have liked, slower than in her prime, but much faster than she could have managed last week or last year. The pipe stem jutting between her knuckles she drove deep into the smaller man's eye and, twisting, left it there as she spun clear of his flailing arms.

She might have run then, between the tables, out of the back door, and into the wide world. Instead, she stopped. If running had been on her mind she wouldn't have marched here grim-faced from the open grave they'd tossed her into.

The larger brother had caught hold of his sibling as he staggered, twitching, his open mouth spilling drool and vowel-filled nonsense. With a grunt the uninjured brother released the other and he dropped with no attempt to break his fall. In the slow turn of the mercenary's head and the focused intensity of his stare, Rue found an echo of the anger whose ocean had always lapped around her.

Ten years of peace had quieted the storm, but it would take an eternity to evaporate the deep waters of her rage. What they had done to her, here, in the now, was just the tapping of the barrel. Rue understood that. She would like to say that the murdering of her friends, Jayne and Ambeth, lay behind this avenging. Or that she'd fashioned herself the saviour of young Soosa Smith and the rest of the innocent or not so innocent village children.

None of that was true. This ran deeper, and whether it had been put into her back when she was far younger than Soosa, or whether it had been born into her, deep as the marrow of her bones, Rue didn't know.

She rushed the mercenary, screaming, using her speed to get within the swing of his club and catching his wrist with one hand while attempting to jam the other thumb into his eye.

In turn, he tried to headbutt her, very nearly succeeding, and drove his knee into her, keeping her ferocity at bay. If he felt astonished that an old woman was holding back the thickness of his arm, he didn't show it, only huffed as he brought his full effort and weight to bear, pushing down.

Rue gave up on her attempt to blind her foe, and instead caught his other wrist, knowing that he might pull a knife on her at any moment. Slowly, the arm holding back the mercenary's club began to surrender before the man's brute strength. She braced herself, feet slipping.

'Twist her fucking head off, Brak!' Tabtha sounded relieved – the spell of the supernatural broken as the real world started to reassert itself. One old woman, no matter how angry, was never going to best a giant mercenary in a test of strength.

Even so, Rue gave ground only slowly. She changed her footing, tried to throw him, but again his knee slammed into her. By rights her thigh should have broken the first time and her hip the second.

'Crush her!' Tabtha warmed to her role as cheerleader.

Outside, a crow was cawing in alarm. Senna, no doubt, complaining about Rue's performance.

Brak dropped his club and pressed down with still greater force. Rue sank to her knees, grunting with the effort of keeping the man's hands from her throat. The bastard was going to beat her, again, by himself this time. She snarled and rose an inch or two before being thrust down further, blunt fingers clawing for purchase on her face.

Panic narrows your vision. That had been an early lesson. Panic shows you only one thing and you keep doing it until you die. And so, even as the mercenary forced her to the floor, seeking to wring her neck and tear off her head, Rue reached out for other ideas.

At the last, as the hands fastened around her throat, she saw the fire in Brak's eyes, the twist of a grin in the forest of his beard. The end had come.

A moment later he was gone, torn away to an accompaniment of Tabtha's screams, the arm of his freshly dead sibling braced against his throat.

Rue got to her hands and knees, spitting crimson drool. She scooped up the discarded hatchet as she rose above the brothers, one dead and one living, locked together in filial combat, one suddenly desperate, the other all rage and strength and the snapping of his jaw as he sought family flesh.

Rue ended Brak with a swing of the hatchet to the back of his neck. The other one she released, feeling his spirit tumble away down the long climb that had returned her to her body. Keeping him dancing to her tune was straining a muscle she'd not known she still owned, and she no longer needed him.

'Going somewhere?' Rue cricked her neck and looked over her shoulder to where Tabtha Heart-Taker was hobbling towards the back door.

'W-what are you?' The woman fumbled for her sword.

Rue turned and advanced on her slowly.

'Consider me a kindness.'

CHAPTER 10

Bek

Year One

The class hurried along the length of West Corridor, to the great iron door at the end, none of them wanting to be late for their first lesson with Kindness Marta. They stood before the door, still in the clothes in which they had arrived at the Academy. Still spattered with the days-old blood of Lucia, the general's daughter, who had been killed by one of their number on the first night, and then again, collectively, on the first morning after breakfast.

The lesson turned out to be far less traumatic than Kindness Undu's. Packed into Creed Hall the first years had been treated to a simple discourse on the world in which the Academy found itself – a world partly shaped by the deeds of the Academy's alumni over the many decades since its founding. To those possessed of even a basic education it was old news, and the main challenge was staying focused so as not to provoke the Kindness's ire.

Bek supposed that many of the class came from even deeper poverty than she had, and hadn't had the advantage of having a scribe – however poor – as a father. Even so, the depth of some of the girls' ignorance surprised her, and worse, she was shocked to find that Mollandra knew less than any of them, quickly attracting the Kindness's disapproval. Mollandra had seemed sharp enough back in the dormitory's gloom, but under the glare of Kindness Marta's questions it seemed that she knew almost nothing.

The Kindness eventually released them to the central courtyard. She watched them leave like a fox eyes hens when deciding on its next meal. The girls emerged blinking into the freshness of the day, the sky above them a hungry blue. The high walls were studded with patient crows drawn by the Academy's carrion stench and seemingly waiting for calamity to strike among the acolytes below.

The Year One girls had been told they would be permitted a short recreation period before Instructor Suni summoned them to her class again and continued to teach them how to break each other with fists and feet.

'We need to help her.' Bek kept at Einsa's side while Mollandra hurried out of the walls' shade.

'Or let nature take its course while we start thinking about a replacement.' Einsa said it without malice and with a certain resignation.

'Helping her can't hurt. Tutoring her will help us too, you know. My father says that teaching someone else something is the best way to understand it yourself . . .' Bek paused. Mentioning her father put a sour taste into her mouth. Maybe he *hadn't* had any good choices. But out of the bad options, he'd chosen the one that exchanged her for coins.

Einsa shrugged her broad shoulders. 'Shrimp!' She shouted after Mollandra, nodding to the side where a flight of steps up to the formal entrance hall made for good sitting. Mollandra arrived as Bek planted her backside on the cold stone.

'You don't know much, do you?' Einsa repeated Kindness Marta's point.

'I know lots of things,' Mollandra answered neutrally. 'They're just different things from the rest of you.'

'You know who rules the city then,' Einsa said.

'Baron Ha . . .' Mollandra furrowed her brow. There had been a *lot* of names in the lesson. 'No, Prince Co . . . Conner?'

'Prince Cormac and his lovely bride Princess Scalla – the man eater. Out of Regon. Princesses being the primary export of Regon on account of their "king", Handelf, only sowing girls in his wife's furrow, but lots of them. Prince Cormac is our king's younger brother.'

'Cormac . . . Scalla,' Mollandra repeated, committing them to memory.

'Don't forget the heir, Sunder, the pretty princeling,' Einsa added.

Bek twisted her mouth, studying Mollandra more closely. 'How far did your father bring you?' She could imagine Mollandra being raised in some broken-down farm on the outskirts of a peasant hamlet, but such people were unlikely to travel any great distance, even for the Academy's copper. She surely had to have come from within the borders of Abrona, and yet here she was struggling to remember the name of the king's own brother. 'What was the nearest town to yours?'

'I . . .' Mollandra looked more uncomfortable than when Instructor Suni had made her face up to Thurli, a solid girl nearly twice her weight, and told them to fight until one of them was bleeding. 'I come from the city.' Her hands closed into the same fists that had bloodied Thurli's nose.

Einsa stood up, towering over Mollandra. 'That city?' She pointed through the courtyard walls in the direction of Tandra-ah, just a few miles away. The city walls, along with the spires jutting over them and the low town sprawled beyond their limit, could all be seen from the Academy's bell towers. 'Is that the one you came from?'

Mollandra nodded, eyes narrow.

'What's it called?'

Bek snorted. Einsa had made a joke to break the tension, a question so laughably easy that Mollandra would grin, and they could start to fill in some of the gaps in her education.

'T . . .' The girl struggled, as if willing the name onto her tongue. 'Tandar.' She spat it out quickly, her voice muffled.

'Tandar?' Einsa asked.

Mollandra nodded.

'You think Tandra-ah, Abrona's second city, the place where you were born, is called Tandar?'

'That's what I said. Tandra-ah.'

Bek put her hand to Einsa's thick upper arm. 'It's what she said.'

'Huh.' Einsa folded her arms and sat back down. She shook her head. 'You, Bek, are too kind to be a Kindness.'

Bek opened her hands helplessly. 'I can't be what they want, so I may as well be what *I* want.'

Einsa growled, as if trying to manufacture the anger she needed in order to break with them and go her own way. 'She's not going to repay you, you know that? Even if we do help her. Even in the unlikely event that she does survive the year and become a half-decent acolyte. She won't save you when you need saving. None of us can look out for anyone else. Not if we want to survive.'

'It's true.' Mollandra's small voice broke into the silence that followed Einsa's challenge. 'I'm not a good person. I will let you down. Again.'

'Again?' Bek tried to ask, but Einsa surged to her feet, her growl louder than before.

'Teach her yourself, Saint Bek. The stray's just going to get you killed.' And with that, she stomped away.

CHAPTER 11
Bek

Year Two

Instructor Mary had barely survived her time as an acolyte, and before the Kindnesses offered her a rare reprieve and disfigured her by cutting off her nose, she had been maimed during her training. Three fingers from her right hand had been given to the cause, along with her left eye.

What the cause was, and why it was worthy of such sacrifice, Bek had yet to discover. Instructor Mary's acceptance of a life where day in and day out she helped drill the act of murder into children, in a process that would kill nearly all of them, enraged Bek. So far, the main lesson that a year at the Academy had taught her was to hate the institution and each of the components that made it function.

'We're falling behind again,' Einsa huffed.

The forest hemmed them in, sealing away all but a thin grey ribbon of sky where the path ran. Each bend removed the rest of the class from sight, and by Bek's count over fifty of the second year were ahead of them, with just Sallay, Mirina, and Thurli behind them. One sick, one hobbling on an infected foot, and the other slow but relentless. Thurli would overtake them soon enough if Bek couldn't pick up her pace. And when Thurli passed by it would leave just two girls between Bek and the instructor stalking them through the leaf-choked paths.

Technically it would leave Einsa and Mollandra there too, but Einsa could keep herself out of trouble, and Mollandra seemed able to run all day, perhaps because she was so light that the wind carried her along.

They called it the Hard Run and it had started in the second year, proving to be a monthly event. The girl who came last was killed, but only if she failed to complete the circuit within the time allotted by the water clock.

While a year at the Academy had hardened Bek's body, her lungs just got worse at their job, and she had only survived the previous two runs because she wasn't last. The final few drops had dripped from the clock as she'd staggered down the home straight. And each month, Instructor Mary reduced the time available.

'I heard that when Kindness Undu did her second year she left twelve corpses behind her and walked back,' Einsa panted. They'd all heard the story before, but it took Bek's mind off the pain.

'We could kill Thurli,' Mollandra suggested.

'No!' Bek gasped, wasting precious air. She glanced back and saw Instructor Mary rounding the bend in the road. The woman ran around at what she estimated to be the water-clock pace. If she overtook you she would be waiting at the clock with knife in hand. 'No killing.'

Einsa and Mollandra exchanged a look.

'No. Killing.' Bek wouldn't let Thurli die for her. If this run didn't make an end of her then the next one would, or the one after it. That was what they were for – culling the weak, finishing off anyone too injured in the course of their training to progress to the next year.

The instructor's slow, relentless pace ate away at the gap between them. They accelerated down the muddy, rock-studded slopes of the river valley, where roots coiled in a constant frozen effort to trip the unwary.

Bek splashed through the ford, jolting over the stony riverbed, gasping at the coldness of the water. As they climbed the wooded slopes on the far side, it began to rain, a grey deluge falling from grey skies.

Bek gasped and floundered in her exhaustion, losing coordination, glancing off a tree, the rough bark tearing at her. She'd told herself not to look back, but she did. Instructor Mary was hard on her heels, breath snorting through the ruinous hole left when the Kindnesses took her nose and spared her life.

How long, Bek wondered, before the woman failed to beat the clock herself? She claimed that on that day the Kindnesses would replace her too. And on she came, torturing them as she herself continued to be tortured, grim-faced, dedicated to the empty enterprise of manufacturing killers.

Einsa and Mollandra stayed with Bek as she fell further back, even after the instructor passed them, with Thurli just a yard behind, puffing like a smith's bellows.

Mollandra's loyalty Bek understood. Bek had picked her, one of the youngest and weakest, to join their trio. And Bek had helped teach her – not to read and write – which despite her peasant raggedness and her claims on entry day, she turned out to do surprisingly well. Instead, it was with the common things she needed instruction, the easy everyday stuff, how to eat, how to clean herself: begging the question of quite what frying pan she had been seared in before falling into the Academy's fire.

There was a surprising fierceness to the girl. Zero compromise. Which seemed to extend to their friendship too. Bek had tried to be worthy of that commitment.

Einsa was harder to work out. She'd walked away from them that first week, only to return the same evening, gruff, angry at herself, swearing . . . but there. And she'd stayed. The girl didn't need either of them. She was strong. Good at everything. Excellent at combat. Instructor Clakka had taught them the word 'pragmatism' which seemed to be a fancy way of saying flexible, but in terms of attitude. The word summed Einsa up in almost every aspect. She wasn't the kind to die on any given hill – everything could be surrendered if it became too much of a burden. So when Bek fell with a scream, snared around the ankle by a tree root, she couldn't say why Einsa hauled her to her feet.

Sallay puffed past them, crimson-faced, deep in the grip of a fever and still faster than Bek. It left only Mirina, and even now Bek could hear the cry of pain every time the girl set down her infected foot. A rhythmic chant of hurt but growing closer even so. And at last, as her senses closed in on themselves, from somewhere came the cawing of crows.

'Did we make it?' Bek lay in confusion, flat on her back, wheezing. Shadows flickered across the arched stone ceiling above her.

'No, this is the underworld and Lucia Aqualas Divinanar wants a word.' Einsa's face loomed into view.

Bek had a flash of memory. Einsa and Mollandra holding an arm each. They'd practically carried her towards the finish, towards Instructor Mary and that damned clock, no longer dripping. There had been screaming. Not her. But close behind. Poor Mirina, trying so hard.

'I hate them all,' Bek wheezed.

'Who?' Mollandra, sitting beside her, leaned into view, looking tired but victorious.

'The Kindnesses, the instructors, my family. All of them. I want to burn this place to the ground and bury the rubble.'

'Somebody's starting to sound like a Kindness.' Undu's bulk swayed vertiginously into Bek's vision.

'She didn't mean—'

'She meant every word.' Undu spoke over Mollandra's excuses and walked away.

Bek flopped her head exhaustedly to the side and watched the Kindness's retreat.

'Creed next.' Einsa leaned over Bek and offered her hand.

'Oh joy.' Bek took hold and let herself be pulled to her feet. Creed lessons made her angry too. Starting in Year Two, once a week, Kindness Marta taught the Creed – the theology that supposedly excused the torture, the killing, and every other horror that went into producing whatever it was that Kindnesses were. Assassins of a sort, though stealth was not their preferred route. Killers for a certainty. The triple-goddess, Marta told them, reading from scrolls cracking with age, wore many names and walked in many worlds.

She neither created nor ruled. She was, instead, a vital ingredient in any system. The snake in the orchard. The imperfection in perfection. The challenge – the test without which no meaning could be ascribed to victory. She was a form of justice. Not that of scribes and ledgers. Her laws were not written in ink, nor were they guidance for living. These were not the pillars of utopian justice. Rather they lay like snares, hidden in the grass, waiting for those who had already gone beyond justice and acted as laws unto themselves. The old lore that humanity keeps in its bones. These were the crimes that so often tripped the mighty in the moment of their triumph. These were the laws that gods were ill-advised to break.

Creed lessons happened in a dark chapel lit by flames licking from oil-lamps in sconces around the wall, and by a single round window high above the entrance, whose bloody light came through stained glass depicting a fortress in a sea of fire.

Mollandra sat scratching at her slate with furious concentration, tongue between her teeth. Einsa scowled as she made her own sparse notes. None of them would have paid attention save for the fact they knew the older girls were often called upon to argue points of the Creed when the continuation of their stay at the Academy hung in the balance. A poor performance would seal their fate.

The Academy's official motto was πίστη πάνω από τη συνείδηση, 'Creed above conscience'. Unofficially it was 'Leave the bodies'.

'Nothing,' said Kindness Marta at the front of the class, 'that we do to you here is as bad as the things that the world does to girls your age every day for no reason other than the gratification of those who hold power over them. We,' she looked around the class, her stare fixing every acolyte until they had met her gaze, 'take no pleasure in this work. We value the fast, the strong, the clever, all of those things, but what we are truly hunting amid all of the trials to which you are subjected is *endurance*. We are looking for those who can bend and yet not break. Those who can bear the worst of what the world already has waiting for them. What we teach is how to pay the world back for those cruelties.

'We are the furnace, you the iron that will become steel and take the required edge.'

The Kindness moved from instructing to questioning and it

turned out that she didn't need to hammer at them long to find a weak point.

'Your ignorance is an insult to this academy and an offence in the eyes of heaven.' Kindness Marta focused her stare on Mollandra who, Bek had to admit, still seemed to know astonishingly little about the world she lived in.

Mollandra returned the Kindness's glare with a narrow look that indicated her ignorance extended to not knowing how afraid she ought to be at this point.

'Let us hope that you are quicker-witted than the evidence suggests.' Kindness Marta, in fairness, did not look intimidating. Her fellow Kindnesses, Undu and Terra, were both immediately terrifying in very different ways. Which to Bek's mind meant that Marta might be the most dangerous of the three.

The Kindness aimed her next question at Einsa. 'Where does magic come from?'

'From the gods.' Einsa's frown said she knew more than that. Perhaps her mother had taught it to her after receiving her own education at the Academy.

'And which god does Kindness Undu pray to for necromancy?'

Einsa's frown deepened. The Kindnesses gave themselves over to the Kindly Ones, the Furies. And those three fearsome sisters were known for vengeance, for enforcing oaths, and for punishing the guilty. Animating the dead was not a power Bek had ever heard attributed to any of them. Einsa attempted an answer. Marta punished ignorance but tolerated or even encouraged free thought.

'Necromancy is different. It's about will. The belief that you can. You need an aptitude too – just like some of us are strong or fast. Some of us,' and here she glanced in Bek's direction, 'are good with the dead.'

'Einsa here is both right and wrong.' Marta's eyes searched the room. 'Necromancy is *not* different, and it *is* about belief and will. All magic is founded on these things. Religion is a lens that focuses belief, allowing miracles. Magic is both personal and collectively owned. It resides in the will of the one and in the dreams of the many. Though it can become bound into the physical world, into a sword, into the waters of a river, the flesh of a god, you would do well to remember that the source is always the same.' She tapped her finger to her forehead.

'And the gods?' Mollandra asked. She had been the first girl in the entire year to ask a question in Creed. Asking questions was both encouraged and dangerous.

Kindness Marta eyed the girl, still the smallest in the year. 'Will and belief bind themselves around ideas. Belief is the blood of the gods. This is why the king allows so many faiths to prosper on the streets of Tandra-ah and all across his realm. Almost every other monarch does. Allow any one faith to gain dominance and the power that will concentrate in the hands of its priests will not just be political. On the Road of Crowns that leads to King Orrin's gates there are temples to Zeus, to Shiva, and to Ghannum, there are churches of the Cross, Gardens of Enlightenment, Zoran chapels, cathedrals dedicated to the God of Swords, shrines to The Lady of Light, and to Hel herself. Many and divided, none of them a threat to the power of a throne.'

'What about our ladies?' Bek forced herself to speak. She had death inside her. Why should she fear where Mollandra had been so bold? 'Who would pray for punishment?'

Marta favoured her with a grim smile. 'Nobody prays for punishment, but everyone except those who are broken knows that they deserve it. Our sins cry out for justice. That is the belief that powers this place. Our crimes will seek us out however deep we hide. The guilty create the very magic that hunts them down.' The Kindness turned her smile on the class and suddenly, despite having few crimes weighing on her soul, Bek was afraid. 'And we, ladies, are the agents of that vengeance, the keepers of the oldest law. We ensure that even in the chaos of this world, there are lines that may not be crossed without reckoning.

'Where the Kindly Ones punish the gods, we punish those who are mortal. We survive because the powerful fear us. And they fear us because this' – she gestured at the walls, at the Academy all around them – 'this is how we are made.'

From Creed they trekked through the long Academy corridors, threading by older classes who they outnumbered, and passing the dining hall, where the first years, still numerous and wide-eyed with shock, took many of their lessons.

Technically there was a danger in passing the first year, since any of the girls could stab them without consequence – at least if they'd had Einsa's foresight and brought a knife with them. Bek had read the list of what she must bring with her to the Academy as a list of what she *could* bring with her. Einsa, with her mother being a Kindness, knew better.

In practice the first years were too busy surviving to make more trouble for themselves. And the shared horror of life in the second year, while it hadn't bound the acolytes together, had established an unspoken level of mutual respect that had thus far kept the murder rate to two in six months.

After what felt like a mile of corridors they arrived at the only lesson where Bek stood out among the others. Everyone called it 'knife' since that was the only weapon they'd handled so far.

Even in the Academy it would be considered wasteful simply to hand over blades and let the acolytes fight it out. The weapons were variously blunted or guarded, making it impossible to cut or stab too deeply, even with the sharpest of them. Of course, almost any cut can be fatal if it's delivered to the neck, and no stab to the eye can be considered shallow.

Bek's success stemmed primarily from the fact that she knew any prolonged fight would have her wheezing and gasping. The opponent would wear her down and the contest would end with Bek as the one being stitched up, the wound being one more burden to carry on her next run.

Since Bek's need to end any contest swiftly coincided with Kindness Terra's instructions – namely to overcome fear and move in fast – she came out as the winner more often than not.

Knife fights were between two, or sometimes several, acolytes with the rest of the class watching. The experience, even second-hand, was too valuable to be wasted. When the timetable allowed, other classes would be brought in to observe. Bek had recently seen the twelve acolytes of Year Eight do battle in the Wound Garden – as the circular training hall was melodramatically titled. The girls had moved with such practised grace, such speed and intensity, that they had seemed to be a different kind of creature entirely. Bek was convinced that she would never have such skill, and nor could she imagine any other of her classmates in such a performance.

Kindness Terra led the way out onto the stone-flagged floor of the Wound Garden. Bek couldn't guess the woman's age. She was tall, gaunt, seamed about with many scars. The light from high windows in the dome's roof painted the Kindness in sharp angles, and as she walked she reached out her arms, a long knife gripped in each, points aimed at the ground.

'This isn't good,' Einsa muttered.

'Nothing here ever is,' Bek growled.

'It's a death bout.' Tmanga rarely volunteered an opinion. Not out of shyness, Bek felt, but from a depth of confidence that didn't require she be heard.

'Oh!' Sharp pushed back her red curls and secured them with a tie, looking suddenly animated. 'That third year, Kessa, she told me we'd have these. Naked blades. No jackets.' She thumped her own padded chest and shook her arms as if eager to be free of the long, thick sleeves.

Kindness Terra turned to face the group trailing her, and tossed the two knives to the ground, the clatter and clang shocking the class to silence. In the shadows around the chamber's raised perimeter, scores of other acolytes had gathered, older girls expecting a show.

'I will select the combatants from among the volunteers.' Terra's near-white eyes scanned the class. 'Or from the cowards if there are no volunteers. The victor will be allowed to ask a favour – this will not include leaving the Academy.' A hand went up. 'Acolyte Wenda?'

'How will the victor be decided?'

If Bek had asked, a good portion of the class would have smirked at her foolishness. Wenda, being the best knife among them, and having never once smiled in the more than a year they had kept her company, was not to be laughed at. She had never made any threat of retribution – rather her whole person embodied the essence of such a threat.

'The victor will be the one who isn't dead.' Kindness Terra indicated the blades on the ground between them. 'Volunteers come forward.'

Wenda, who despite her grim demeanour had never shown any hostility to her fellow acolytes beyond repeatedly winning every knife fight, stepped forward.

Sharp swaggered after Wenda, bumping into Bek's shoulder on the way. 'You could ask to be excused from the Hard Run if you won,' she murmured.

Bek felt tempted. She might not be quite as good as Wenda or Sharp, but she was good. Luck plays its part in any fight. Perhaps . . .

'I'll do it.' Mollandra stepped forward meekly. Head down, face hidden in the sea of blonde curls that she refused to cut despite the dangers of such tresses.

'No!' Bek reached for the girl, but Einsa pushed her arm down. The Kindness would not approve. 'She'll die,' Bek hissed. Mollandra was at best average with a knife, far too defensive. She never got badly injured but that was perhaps because the others took pity on her – she was still small for her age and never stood up for herself. The best you could say for her was that she was lucky.

'She decided,' Einsa murmured, her face a mix of pride, astonishment, and horror.

'This isn't right.' Bek shook Einsa off, coughing. None of it was right. Not one piece of the Academy from deepest dungeon to tower top was in the least bit right.

'No one else?' Kindness Terra ran a cold eye over the trio of volunteers as if deeply underwhelmed. Nobody came forward. Bek stood, every muscle trembling with the need for action, torn by a dozen emotions. If she volunteered, the Kindness would pick her and Mollandra to fight each other. She knew it.

Kindness Terra looked around a final time. 'Then Acolyte Mollandra will fight Acolyte Wenda.'

As those not fighting spread out around the edge of the duelling circle Bek reached for the knife concealed at Einsa's hip. The big girl caught her wrist. 'What are you doing?'

'Something stupid.' The wheeze was in her voice all the time now.

'Well, I won't let you,' Einsa hissed, pushing Bek away. 'Especially not with my knife.'

Bek met Einsa's hard stare. '*I decided.*' If Mollandra could decide then so could she.

'So I get to lose both of you on the same day?' Einsa hadn't shown any real emotion in all the time Bek had known her. Scorn and irritation had been her limits. But it was there now, leaking past the impressively strong walls that protected her inner self. Fear colouring her voice. Fear and something more.

Bek banged a fist against her chest. 'You can't keep carrying me. And maybe I can be the one to make a change . . .' She paused as Kindness Terra's disapproval swept across them. In the ring Mollandra and Wenda had both taken up their knives. Bek reached again for Einsa's and this time the girl let her take it.

'Don't . . .'

'I will.' Bek locked eyes with Einsa once more then tore herself away, moving slowly around the circle as if hunting for a better view.

Kindness Terra stepped back from the combatants and the class made room for her at the edge. Bek still had no clear idea of what she was going to do, how long her nerve would hold, or how far it would take her. She should have volunteered for the fight – she knew that now. She had missed that chance and Mollandra had taken it. For a horrified moment Bek halted, mid-step, seized by the sudden conviction that it had been to stop her having to do the Hard Run that Mollandra had volunteered. She shook the notion off. Even Mollandra wasn't that dumb.

Bek came closer to the Kindness. In the ring Wenda and Mollandra had clashed once and surprisingly both had come away unscathed. All eyes were on the pair as they circled, looking for advantage.

Another flurry of activity and somehow it was Wenda who broke off, holding one arm to her chest, staining the light grey cloth with her blood.

Whispers started around the circle. This wasn't how Mollandra fought. The acolyte had been disguising her skill. Wenda would be more careful now. She would still win, they said. Bek suddenly wasn't so sure. It was hard to fight while carrying a wound, and the fear that the pain put into you was not your friend. Pain urged you to caution, but a knife fight required that you gamble with your skin.

Bek reached her destination, right behind Kindness Terra. Her decision shouldn't depend on who was winning the fight. This wasn't about who was friends with who, this was far bigger than that. The wrongness, the evil of the Academy extended endlessly, but if all the students, the remnants of a thousand, were to say no together, how could three Kindnesses stand against them?

Even so, with Kindness Terra's black-robed back within the reach of her arm, and Einsa's knife gripped tighter than tight in her fist, Bek paused and watched past the woman's shoulder to see Mollandra close with Wenda once more. Both girls' faces showed only focus, Mollandra's bright blue eyes locked to Wenda's dark ones.

Wenda lunged, snapping out her knife thrust. Almost too fast for the eye and with unnatural grace Mollandra twisted inside the attack and drove her own blade into Wenda's side. The collective gasp had only just started when Wenda somehow slashed Mollandra across the face, and as the girl staggered back, caught her with a spinning kick to the head just as Instructor Suni had taught them. The stab at her ribs seemed not to have harmed Wenda at all.

Mollandra fell like a tree taken by the axe.

'No!' Bek's cry lost itself in the onlookers' roar.

Stabbing the Kindness suddenly became the only logical thing to do. Bek swung, bringing Einsa's seven-inch hunting knife down in an overhead blow aimed squarely between the woman's shoulder blades.

In a rush of motion Bek found herself on the ground. She remembered the punch against her chest, and not much else. She tried to get up, but her body paid only vague attention to such commands. She lay within a forest of legs, with the Kindness's black robe sweeping the flagstones beside her.

Rather than look up at the woman towering above, Bek lolled her head to the side and found Mollandra, also curled on the floor, alone save for Wenda standing close by. Mollandra rose as Bek watched. Wenda, drawn by the drama around Bek, had her back to her defeated opponent. Any noise Mollandra might have made was drowned out by the commotion filling the hall. The girl rose as if pulled by an invisible thread, and although she held a glittering blade, and although her face hung open, blood spurting from her gaping cheek, Wenda didn't notice her at all, seeming unable to look away from the spectacle of Bek's disaster.

As Bek struggled to draw a breath into corrupted lungs she saw the hilt of Einsa's knife jutting from her own breast. She wanted to ask how Terra could have been so fast. How the woman had even known to move. But she let the questions go. She let everything go. And the last thing she saw before the darkness took her was Mollandra. Bek saw her sister then, recognizing her as the scales fell from her eyes. She smiled even as blood sputtered from her lips. *Sister.*

Mollandra stepped up behind Wenda while the darkness fell and drove her blade deep.

CHAPTER 12
Einsa

Year Two

Einsa carried the knife that Kindness Terra had wrested from Bek and used to kill her. It had been Einsa who brought the blade to the Academy – a gift of sorts from her mother, who had been a Kindness herself – and the blade had probably taken many lives in the woman's hands. It had always felt as if it still belonged to her mother, and that Einsa was merely its custodian. But now she could only think of it as Bek's knife. The weapon with which she had tried and failed to change their world.

The knife hadn't been all that Einsa's mother had given her. There was a reason behind forbidding Kindnesses children. A reason beyond issues of focus and purity and the plain meanness that seemed to underlie much of the Creed. There was in Einsa an anger and a fire that ran contrary to her nature. Her calm and her tolerance, her blunt good humour, all of these were gifts from her father. The man who would have fought to keep her from this place if her mother hadn't fled from him with Einsa the year before she died. He would have fought and he would have failed. Just as Bek had. Her mother, Einsa had since reflected, had by her abandonment, saved her husband's life.

Einsa had spoken to her mother about the rage – not the natural anger born of circumstance – but something other, something alien, flowing in her blood, coiled around her bones.

'They put it in me,' her mother had said, twisting her mouth. 'And through my blood I put it in you. It's good that you are your father's daughter. Never let that fire out. It will consume you and everything you love.'

And even as Bek lay dying and the fire had uncoiled within Einsa, smouldering on her skin, she had kept faith with her mother. The moment had passed and by the time she left the chamber with the others, only sorrow remained.

Mollandra now kept a knife at her hip too. The one with which she'd killed Wenda and that she had been allowed to keep. Instructor Jane, who taught, along with torture, the binding and stitching of one's own wounds, had sewn up the girl's cheek with precision but little care for aesthetics. She had hidden away the exposed teeth and gums once more, leaving Mollandra with a permanent half-smile that gave fairer warning of the child's hidden dangers.

With Wenda gone, her three became a two and Sharp parted ways with Tmanga to join Einsa and Mollandra. Einsa would rather have had Tmanga, but the girl didn't ask. Both of them were among the most competent in the class, but where Tmanga was level-headed and considered every action, Sharp would jump in with both feet, relying on her savagery to turn things her way.

Kindness Terra had not condemned Bek's attack. Rather she had afforded the corpse a modicum more respect than was usual at the Academy and said that initiative was a requirement in all Kindnesses, but that it should be tempered with realism.

Einsa, Tmanga, and Sharp had left their friends on the cold stone floor of the Wound Garden while Mollandra had been taken to have her face repaired. The next lesson had been the weekly instalment of the Creed, delivered by Kindness Marta, whose ordinariness Einsa was beginning to see for the superpower it was. Nobody would ever underestimate the threat Sharp posed. Put Sharp's spirit behind a dull face that would seem to have been plucked from the breadline in any poverty trap, and that threat simultaneously vanished and multiplied.

Even though in the Academy everything mattered and slacking off was as apt to get you killed as blind testing in the poisons laboratory, Einsa slumped across her desk and let the Kindness's words slide over her. It was good that Mollandra's wound had kept her from the lesson – she would still be raging. When she'd understood that Bek was dead she'd ignored her blood loss and the hopelessness of the act and had tried to throw herself at Kindness Terra. If Tmanga hadn't had the foresight to be ready to trip her, Mollandra too would be dead.

Einsa had seen over a score of her classmates killed since Lucia's mysterious demise on the first night, but somehow it hadn't prepared her for Bek's passing. Bek had had an air of permanence about her that made a lie of whatever cough was eating her from the inside. Bek could make you believe, even Einsa who had steeled herself against emotion, knowing it for the weakness it was: chains to hold you in place, chains to drag you down.

'I was sure she'd make it.' Einsa realized she'd muttered her thoughts out loud.

Sharp elbowed her to silence then returned her attention to scratching down the Kindness's words. Of all the deaths to date, perhaps the most shocking had been when Keeka, who aspired to being class clown, their light in dark places, had mistaken Kindness Marta's motherly looks and quiet ways for softness. She'd begun to talk in class, pass notes, feign sleeping. On Keeka's last day she had been rocking back in her chair humming some stupid tune to which she'd put words mocking all the instructors. Kindness Marta somehow made the trip from the front of the room to Keeka's side unseen. All she did was touch a finger to the girl's forehead. A gentle push put her past the point of no return and her chair fell over backwards. Ninety-nine times out of a hundred this would have ended in painful embarrassment. The way that the Kindness walked off without looking back and didn't so much as flinch at the crack of skull on stone, convinced the acolytes that Kindness Marta understood that this would be the hundredth time.

Returning to stand before the chalkboard, the Kindness had written in large white letters, When there is no need for speed, always wait for your moment.

Einsa, brought back to focus by Sharp's sharp elbow, forced herself to listen to the Kindness's words. For several long minutes the woman merely repeated elements of the Creed, making a virtue of the implacable nature of the Kindnesses, lauding their refusal of compromise, and extolling the way in which the roots of that harshness ran through the Academy.

'Today an acolyte attempted to kill Kindness Terra.'

Scores of faces looked up from their slates. Kindness Marta suddenly had the class's full attention just as she had had it the day she tipped Keeka into oblivion.

'The Academy of Kindness has taken in one hundred and seventy-three classes and not once in nearly two centuries—'

Einsa blinked. Surely someone else had tried to turn the tables on their tormentors in all those years?

'—has any class run its course from one hundred to three without such an attack.'

Einsa slumped. Not only had Bek failed, worse: she was nothing special, as expected as the sunrise.

'You might think that the record for the earliest attempt was on day one, and indeed there have been . . . five . . . such attacks. But the record was in fact set fifty years ago when one enterprising girl broke into the Academy a week before intake and attempted to murder all three resident Kindnesses with an explosive device. The longest any class has gone without an acolyte trying to kill a Kindness is Year Five.

'Although such acts of rebellion are in some ways reflections of the Creed in which I inculcate my pupils, they are also wasteful, and misguided. Such initiative is not rewarded with mercy. The system here is designed not to break and it will not break.

'It has been my habit to use a class's first attack as the sign that it is time to add a further level of explanation to what we do here. This is a talk that I withhold since the brutality, misfortune, and cruelty that the world throws at us does not come wrapped in justification, and acolytes under my care should experience the sharp edges of existence raw and without the comfort of any higher calling.

'A wiseman once said that anger is an energy. In the Wound Garden, Kindness Terra instructs you to put anger aside when you fight, for it clouds judgement and narrows choices. It is easier to teach you the technicalities of killing with a sharp edge when your emotion is controlled. Young Bek would have had a better chance of catching Kindness Terra unawares had she not worn her rage so openly. Still a vanishingly slim chance, but a better one.

'But those few of you that we release upon the world at the end of your harrowing are not sent as warriors or soldiers or assassins. They are sent as avatars of the Kindly Ones. It is not sufficient that you be deadly, you must be what they are, you must embody anger, your blood must smoulder, ready to burst into flame at a moment's notice.

'Have we upset you? Oh dear . . . Have we made you girls cross? Do you burn to get even? Does an ache for justice gnaw at your bones even now? It's almost as if it were planned that way, no?

'To survive this place, you must consume that anger before it consumes you. You must become it – wield it rather than be wielded by it.'

Marta slowly scanned the desks, meeting every gaze, her eyes flint in the almost motherly ordinariness of her face. 'Our anger is unceasing.'

Einsa returned that stare, saying nothing, hating the woman all the more.

'Our anger . . . is unceasing.' Marta, whose threat had always lain hidden, seemed suddenly lit by a different light, as if some unseen window had opened to a place of horror and in its harsh illumination every trace of softness, every touch of the ordinary had burned away. She seemed for those moments to be a different kind of creature, gaunt, lips drawn back from teeth more feral than should be possible, every tendon straining, every muscle bunched, and an awful, ancient hunger glittering in the pits of darkness that were her eyes.

'Our anger is unceasing,' she repeated, each word resonant with threat.

'Our anger is unceasing.' Einsa joined in with the class. She felt that anger today. Bek's death had lit a greater fire than the Kindness's words ever could. Einsa had been born with the rage of the Kindly Ones burning in her and only the love she had for her remaining friends had kept Bek's death from making an inferno of it.

'We are vengeance.' Marta stamped her foot, and dark tongues of flame shadowed her like an echo, finding an answer in Einsa.

'We are vengeance.' Fifty-eight feet stamped the reply.

'High or low, we carry justice.' Fist thumped to chest.

'High or low.' Einsa pounded just beneath her collarbone. 'Justice.' Would it have been justice if Bek's blow had landed? Einsa thought so, but truly she hadn't cared about rights or wrongs. She'd just wanted to see her friend win. 'I am vengeance. High or low.' She locked eyes with Kindness Marta, undaunted by her aspect and throwing the weight of her own rage behind that stare. She found no give in the woman, but perhaps, for a moment, she saw a measure of respect.

In the silence that followed, the Kindness dwindled once more to a middle-aged woman, but there was no doubting that any of the acolytes present would ever look at her again without also seeing the ghost of who she truly was.

Einsa left the lesson lost in her thoughts, easy prey for any acolyte who fancied reducing the odds or simply getting the practice. It seemed that Bek watched her from everywhere the shadows gathered, pale, silent, still with the knife in her breast. Bek with her patience and her resignation, both at odds with her vision and her kindness. It had been the compassion or the foresight that had somehow brought little Mollandra into their circle that first night and made the trio. Which of the two, vision or kindness, Einsa still didn't know.

She wiped away a hot, angry tear, then cursed. Einsa didn't cry. Crying was weakness – the dam breaking – the beginning of the end in a place like this, not that there were any other places like this.

A hand on her shoulder, brief then gone before she could reach for a weapon.

'Courage.' Tmanga passed her.

That night Mollandra had come to the dormitory with the ugly black stitches holding together the wound that Wenda had given her. She approached her bed and let her gaze settle on Sharp who sat with her usual nonchalance, cross-legged on Bek's cot. Mollandra's blue eyes sought out Tmanga, still in her own place halfway across the room, then returned to Sharp.

'What?' Sharp looked up, with her own slightly unhinged good humour challenging the smaller girl's newly acquired half-smile.

A fragile moment hung between them, and for the first time Einsa saw a hint of fear in Sharp, a nervous something that turned into her ever-dangerous laugh. It wasn't until that moment, viewing little Mollandra through another's eyes, that Einsa was able to revise the opinion she'd forged on the first day.

'What?' Sharp asked again, tensing as if ready to attack or be attacked.

Mollandra held up three fingers, sweeping them around to indicate herself, Einsa, and Sharp. Through gritted teeth and with evident pain she said, 'No more leaving.'

Sharp had the grace to show a fleeting instant of guilt at that, her glance flickering towards Tmanga. 'No more leaving.' She laughed. 'Kindnesses or corpses. It's us three. Nobody else.'

CHAPTER 13

Rue

Rue left the bodies behind her. The dead brother had killed the living one and both had fallen beyond her reach. Tabtha lay lifeless in a pool of her own blood and surprise. Rue had been leaving the bodies behind her all her life, a trail of murder, retribution, and sometimes, justice that punctuated her story all the way to this particular day and this particular moment.

She paused at the door, the cracks between the planking sun-bright. Her anger had been carrying her forward with its own momentum, and Rue never liked to feel steered, even by herself. The Morrigan had woken her within the grave they'd thrown her into. And now with her gift on the shores of the river, the goddess had pried Rue from a second tomb.

Gog and Magog stood alone in the ocean vastness, the only lands known. But the peoples who dwelt on these islands sprang from an ancestry that had more roots than any tree. A melting pot of faiths, languages, races, joined only by the fear of what had pursued them across the water. The Academy taught that it was the Furies, the Kindly Ones themselves, who chased humanity's remnants to this end. Among those chased, however, there were many names and aspects for the three-who-are-one, many beliefs, a whole library of stories, creeds, myth, and magics. The Morrigan some called her. Sometimes one, sometimes three sisters, three goddesses, sometimes maiden, mother, or hag. As the Morrigan, enigmatic embodiment of fate and of strife, she was wont to interfere in the affairs of mankind, but ever with her purpose shrouded.

The Morrigan had spoken – or so it seemed in Rue's death dreams – to Sunder, who Rue had first laid eyes on when he was merely a child considerably more than arm's length from the throne of one of Gog's seven nations. Half a century later, that same man held together an empire, seeking to bring the rest of Gog beneath his heel while the wounds of earlier conquest still wept.

Rue's association with Emperor Sunder was as complex as it was long, though she was sure he remembered her less well than she did him. He was one of those very few individuals remaining in the world who scared her. A fact she did not like to admit, even to herself.

Likely the emperor had forgotten her entirely, but she would never forget. She would oppose him, given the chance, simply for his role in the rise of the Cruelties and for his ties with her mother and her father. But she'd no interest in being the Morrigan's tool to test him as all those who seek power must be tested in order to determine whether they deserve the fate they're reaching for. The goddess could find another fool to play those games. Rue's service to any and all aspects of the triple-goddess had ended long ago. And if that sat poorly with the old bird, then she could take back her gift.

The door to the outside resisted her briefly as if something might be blocking it. But no, the street lay empty. Blood spattered the ground immediately in front of her. The young man . . . Rakkar? He'd fallen there but they must have dragged him off with Isik and the other.

Rue wiped Tabtha's blood from her knife and thrust it through the belt she'd stolen from her. The few remaining Kindnesses might say that the mere fact that a woman could have joined Isik's band of mercenaries based purely on her size and willingness to do violence was something she owed to two centuries of the Academy. Rue wouldn't argue with that any more than she would argue with the fact that a tornado can sometimes clear a forest from land a farmer had wanted to till. She would just point out that a tornado will often take the farmer's house at the same time along with the cows and the farmer himself.

Outside, the sun had decided to shine, gifting the village its first fine day since winter loosened its grip. Rue stumbled into the street, still not comfortable in her broken body or with the unholy energies that held it together. Necromancy kept her heart beating, her blood pumping, necromancy wrapped her veins, all the while reaching out for the corpses in her wake, questing forward in search of more.

The world had been a familiar place that morning, and now seemed a strange stage on which she was being asked to perform, though they had neglected to teach her any lines. First it had been the mercenaries in Stones Corner who had torn away one veil, revealing a different landscape, one she knew was there but had forgotten. Then had come the grave and the crow and the lifting of a second veil thrusting her back into a world made strange by her own strangeness.

Age had settled on her and made of her something she had never truly believed she would become, even in the unlikely event that the dangers of her calling spared her. She had understood that she would age. That an old woman's face would peer at her from the looking glass. But she hadn't known what expression that face would wear beneath its wrinkles. Astonishment? Shame? Pity? Revulsion? Resignation? She wouldn't have predicted the acceptance she had begun to see of late, and certainly never the patient almost-pride that in later years met her gaze.

She had thought that age was just a number, then seen it as a noose when it tightened around her, and then as something else, a type of surrender that she had never allowed herself. A letting go of sorts. But both those things had been trades that had two sides, something gained and something lost. Not equal trades but neither side without worth.

She had accepted that beneath a sufficient burden of years she would creak and she would ache and her speed would leave her. But she had not believed in her heart that she would be a different person. She had been sure that she would remain herself just the same as if she had chosen a different jacket to wear.

Rue did feel exactly that – she felt that her younger self still wrapped these old bones, imprisoned within the inadequate tomb of her ageing body. However, despite what she felt, what she *knew* was that the child she had been and the young woman she became were different, just as the young woman and the old one were different. One might reach back as the other reached forward and grasp the offered hand. Perhaps even embrace. But they were not the same person. If they were the same, then what purpose had those passing decades of experience served? If living life had not changed her, had she truly lived it? To claim the facts of her existence were simply that: a growing list of things that happened, rather than structural parts of her nature, was to cheapen them, to rob them of meaning.

She saw the village of Pye through new eyes. Neither those that had first beheld the hamlet as a place to spend the night, nor those that had slowly come to see it as home. Rue now saw something fragile, something easy to break, easy to burn. She saw the choke points, the opportunities for concealment, how to hold it, and how to take it. She saw the lives behind the walls and doors, saw the faint vibrations of their vitality, their fear, and most of all how temporary they all were.

The corpses the mercenaries had taken from her had left trails. Bloody ones to begin with but even when the dark smears had petered out and the scuff marks of dragging heels were lost in the rutted confusion of the road, something remained. A lingering difference traced by the passage of something that touched two worlds. Warm flesh that had schemed and hated and pulsed, and whose owners now stood beside the last river they would ever cross.

Rue followed the dead down Pye's main street. It was not the way of Kindnesses to skulk or hide, though they could do both when circumstances dictated. The Kindness wore her authority not with pride but with conviction. She carried the will of the triple-goddess and any who stood in the path of such retribution placed themselves beneath the same judgement.

A Kindness coming to reckon with the general of some mighty army would stride boldly through his troops, knowing that every soldier to raise a hand against her would, should they succeed in halting her progress, place themselves upon the list of another

Kindness. If the chosen target of her ire should prevail then the matter was settled, but a reckoning must be had.

'Come out! Come out! Wherever you are!' Rue aimed herself at the house of Tamaster Sams, the town's elder, neither elected nor born to the station but simply a man who people listened to and respected, and who in such a manner led the village when leading was required. His home, somewhat larger and somewhat grander than the rest, though still a hovel in the eyes of anyone not raised in the wilds, stood at the end of the main street, forcing the scant traffic to turn aside.

'You have something of mine!' Rue called. 'Do I need to huff and puff and blow your—'

The front door juddered open and one of the faces that had so recently surrounded her peered out. The man's jaw dropped.

'Give me Isik and the rest of you can leave.'

The man withdrew, slamming the door behind him, before pushing it open again for a second look then closing it once more.

Rue waited. If the goddess truly had pushed her back into the world it seemed discourteous not to lean into the role. She had considered bringing the heads from Debban's hut and tossing them before her when challenged, but the brothers had been balding beneath their caps, and heads without hair were awkward to carry.

The sound of approaching horses came from behind her, hooves thudding the ground. Rue turned her head slowly to see who was joining the scene. In carrying out the business of a Kindness one can never show fear. A Kindness is almost always outnumbered. Fear acknowledges that fact and makes it real. Even sensible caution undermines the cloak of legend that protects a Kindness where plate armour would surely fail.

Four mounted men had two dozen more horses trailing them. More than Rue had seen in Steffan's field earlier. The front door burst open and a woman in blackened chainmail stamped into view. The gawper followed – mouth now closed again – with others behind. If the woman was surprised to see Rue in her rags and wrinkles, blood in the white straggles of her hair, she hid it well.

'Isik,' Rue repeated. 'He's mine. The rest of you can go.'

'Bregar here, he says they killed you.' The woman wasn't tall like

Tabtha, or broad like Tabtha, but she looked more dangerous. Her hair hung in black ropes past skin burned almost as dark. 'Where's Brak and—'

'If I let you go, they won't be coming.' Rue shrugged. 'Are you in charge here, or was it Isik?'

'Enough of this.' The woman waved her followers on. 'Do it properly this time. I want her head when you're done.'

'I bring the oldest lore.' Rue's cracked voice still managed to summon the gravitas of her station. The words flowed as if it had been ten hours since she last delivered them rather than twenty years and more. 'I am she the gods fear. My sisters walk ever by my side.' She drew her knife, still bloody. 'Stand aside or be forever accursed.'

There had been a time when for lives of men the words she had just spoken would open a path to the object of a Kindness's wrath through all and any opposition.

The mercenaries hesitated, glanced around nervously at their numbers, and came forward.

Times change.

Cries from the house brought the mercenaries to a halt before they'd closed half the distance to her.

Necromancy involves the working of a muscle. Not of the body, and maybe not even of the mind, but a muscle even so. Perhaps it was the spirit that was exercised. Rue had never had such power but using what few necromancies she had left the Academy with had been similar to her current experience, albeit on a smaller scale. The muscle grew tired and needed rest. Pitting one brother against the other had stretched even her newfound might, and having any of the trio she'd killed back in Debban's ale hut march along with her would not have allowed her to recover that strength.

Now she brought Isik out among his former underlings, staggering like a drunk, his neck crimson below the wound that had killed him, his padded doublet thick with gore.

The men around him cried out in fear. They'd seen and carried out all manner of horrors, but even so, the breaking of a law so fundamental as that of death will unsettle the boldest. Rue still remembered the reaction of fourscore young girls when Lucia Aqualas Divinanar had unexpectedly sat up at Kindness Undu's request. The hardened mercenaries before her showed a similar response.

'Isik is all I need from you.' Rue met the woman's gaze since she alone had set her back to the dead man and returned her eyes to the true threat.

'I was wrong,' the woman said. 'Take her alive.'

CHAPTER 14

Einsa

Year Three

Everyone understood that Sharp was crazy. None of them had understood quite *how* crazy until Kindness Terra put a sword in her hand in Year Three.

Einsa took to the sword well, just as she had taken to the knife. Her mother had shown her the rudiments not long after Einsa had started to walk. She had learned in a single day lessons that most children acquire over years. Her mother hadn't told her not to run with scissors, she had told her not to fall over.

Einsa had few equals in the class when it came to swinging a sword. Tmanga, Brooth, Mollandra, and Thurli were all good, but Sharp was in a league of her own, as if she had found a lover rather than a blade.

In the winter while the east winds howled around the Academy's fortress walls, leaching heat from already cold stone and trying to tear loose every shutter, the third year came once more to the Wound Garden. Sharp, with Mollandra to her left and Einsa to her right, bustled in through the doors, already equipped with a training blade from the stores.

'It's a carnage kind of day.' Sharp swung the blunted sword

left and right, almost catching the robes of the acolytes ahead of her.

'Watch it.' Tmanga glanced back, getting out of Sharp's way.

Three fifth-year girls strode towards the exit, among the last of their class to leave the chamber. Each carried an earned blade, long, thin, bearing a slight curve to aid the slice.

'Scram!' The foremost of the trio was a hard-faced girl with short black hair and a slice across her cheek weeping blood that oozed down over old scars.

Einsa stepped aside with the rest. Big as she was, two of these three matched her height and all of them could teach her a short, fatal lesson on the combat floor.

'I said scram.'

'Don't want to.' Sharp stood her ground.

Einsa reached for her shoulder to pull her aside. 'They'll kill you.' But Sharp slipped away with a shrug.

The trio were far from the best swords in their year but even to be drawing breath after five years in the Academy meant you were a survivor. Some called it luck, but Einsa knew differently. Some people were just harder to kill than others, and it wasn't down to any particular skill. They were the weeds, there among the crop the whole time, but when the blight came, or a tyrant salted the ground, they remained, as others fell.

In addition, each of these girls had seven times the sword training that Sharp had, seven seasons to her single season. It was nonsense.

'There are three of them,' Mollandra said.

Her warning implied misplaced trust in Sharp's ability to defeat even a single fifth year, along with underlining their friend's sudden and inexplicable inability to count.

'Give it up.' Tmanga sounded bored. 'Take the beating.' Despite Sharp abandoning her after Wenda's death, Tmanga had shown no signs of bearing a grudge. She was right too – unless Sharp attacked them the acolytes couldn't kill her. They could and would use her insolence as justification for a beating, though.

'Your sword doesn't even have an—'

'Surprise!' Sharp hurled herself into her attack even before Einsa could get the word 'edge' out, throwing her sword towards the roof, underarm, point first. It was a trick she'd tried dozens of times in the dorm room with Einsa's knife, pulling it off maybe one time in five. She'd nearly lost a finger earlier in the year.

At the same time, she hurled herself forward, dropping to the floor beneath the dark-haired girl's swinging blade. Sharp's momentum, built in two quick steps, carried her feet-first into the ankles of her rearmost opponent, taking the girl's legs out from beneath her. The big girl hit the floor as Sharp rolled into a crouch. Somewhere during that roll she contrived to catch the sword she had earlier thrown into the air. She snatched its hilt a yard above the ground and brought the blunt blade down on her fallen opponent in a beheading swing.

Swords, being steel bars, don't need to carry an edge in order to severely fuck you up if they hit you in any part of the neck. The throat is particularly vulnerable.

If the two standing fifth years had acted quickly, Sharp would have ended up impaled on one or both of their blades. But Sharp had given them the promised surprise and, despite all that they must have seen across the course of five nightmare years, both let a beat pass. Sharp used that moment to snatch up the choking girl's sword, discarding her own.

'You should take turns.' Sharp pushed red curls out of her face, grinning fiercely, the point of her new weapon levelled at the black-haired girl.

In the heartbeat in which the two fifth years exchanged a glance, considering the option, she attacked, targeting the second of the larger girls who parried too late, taking a bloody slice across her ribs.

'You can go.' Sharp danced back out of range.

The wounded acolyte cursed and spat, then despite the accusing glare of her friend, and the judgement of the three additional fifth years who'd come to join the audience, she limped off, clutching her side with crimson fingers.

'Just you and me,' Sharp said. She frowned. 'Is it "you and I"? I never can tell. I hope they teach us . . .'

The dark-haired girl came at her with controlled fury, stepping over the friend who still lay on the floor clutching at her crushed throat and making horrible wet noises.

Sharp stood her ground, and they crossed swords. 'Ha!' She danced away once more. 'You nearly got me.'

But for Sharp's outrageous reactions, and her instinct for the fight that seemed to have been in her from the moment she landed wet and bloody on the birthing mat, she would have lost her sword hand or at the least been sliced from the heel of her palm to her inner elbow. The fifth year might not be good for a fifth year, but she wasn't terrible either, and compared to the third years, new to the art, she might as well be a hero stepping from legend.

Sharp let out an unearthly scream and threw herself at the girl. In the next fraction of a heartbeat both of them were on the ground, Sharp on top, her blade through the acolyte's shoulder, one foot pinning the girl's sword hand to the floor by the wrist. The screams as Sharp moved her sword as if churning butter echoed through the Wound Garden, ceasing only when the dark-haired girl fainted from the pain.

Sharp left the sword standing, recovered her practice blade, and went on out into the hall. Her attack shouldn't have worked. But it did. Behind her, the third-year acolytes swarmed the two wounded fifth years, stealing everything of worth. Einsa couldn't bring herself to join them.

'What even was that?' Gholla asked, looking close to vomiting.

'That,' Mollandra said, following in the victor's footsteps, 'was Sharp.'

Einsa swapped a look with Tmanga, finding the girl's dark eyes unreadable, shrugged in the hope it would free her of the horrified amazement weighing on her shoulders, and finding that it did not, followed Mollandra.

In all her time at the Academy Einsa had carried with her the unshakeable conviction that she would be one of the three survivors. The testing, the killing, all the horror was merely the process of deciding which pair of her fellow acolytes would be graduating with her. She had thought that one of them would be Bek, based partly on the girl's calm confidence but mainly on her gut feeling. She had believed that Mollandra would fall early on, and only recently had truly begun to understand that the girl had a different kind of steel at her core. Looking around herself of late Einsa had started to wonder for the first time where her own place among the final three was. And if there even was one.

A short while later the class was in pairs scattered across the fight floor. Sharp's victims had been dragged away to die somewhere less inconvenient. In the surprising event that either survived then they'd be unlikely to last to the end of the week. Being injured or ill did not grant an acolyte any respite from the Academy's constant training, challenges, and threats.

'What's up?' Mollandra swung a side cut, the blow they were to practise.

'I'm fine.' Einsa parried the blow. 'I'm always fine.'

'You lie well with your mouth.' Mollandra swung again, hard, fast, accurate.

'Well thank you, Molly. I think that's the nicest thing anyo—' Einsa swung back, Mollandra deflecting the blow without effort '—anyone's ever said to me.'

'But your body gives you away. You hunch up when you're sad. You did it after Bek. For a long time.'

'You did too,' Einsa muttered. Mollandra had been inconsolable. Full of wrath and sorrow. 'We both did.'

Mollandra nodded. 'You're doing it now.'

'I'm not sad,' Einsa lied. All of them were sad of course, apart from a few crazies like Sharp. And, strangely, Einsa had never really been able to read Mollandra. She'd thought her a friend – she had to be a friend, after Bek there was no one left – she had thought her friend was an open book, only to realize that she'd been reading what she was given and had never even turned the true cover.

'Well, cheer up. We've got dungeon practice next.' Another cut, this one almost too fast for Einsa to turn away.

Einsa struck back, unable to keep a smile from twisting her face. Dungeon practice with Instructor Akki was the worst of the lot.

CHAPTER 15

Einsa

Year Three

The acolytes called Instructor Akki's sessions 'Dungeon Class' but the correct title was something far less interesting that Einsa struggled to remember and occasionally to pronounce. 'Extrication.'

Sometimes the object of the exercise was to get into a place in order to extract someone else. Sometimes it was themselves the acolytes were required to remove from a situation, be it a set of chains, a locked room, or a tedious conversation. The ability to navigate a social setting was, Instructor Akki maintained, as important as being able to open a locked door.

A Kindness frequently used intimidation to reach her target, but there were times when it was better to use a more subtle approach. Justice might be enacted on the spot – after which the individual's protectors often had far less interest in interfering – or the person in question might need to be removed from the setting and be dealt their reckoning elsewhere. Kindness Marta said that in some cases justice must not merely be done, it must be seen to be done, and moreover it must be seen to be done by the right audience.

King Ardna of the Ottoths, who raped the daughters of Queen Amandanas, was taken from the pleasure gardens at the heart of his capital. But he was not scourged before his court. That message was delivered by the trail of bodies later discovered along the route from the river passages through the bowels of the palace, and by the shrivelled remains of his severed manhood, left on the royal throne. Ardna's appointment with the wire whips, salt, and fire, waited for him back amid the ruins of the city he had razed, and he was offered up before what scant crowds the survivors could muster.

The Kindnesses were not, of course, given to policing wars, but the oldest laws, including those pertaining to hospitality, oaths, and blood loyalty, could not be broken without consequence. Quite how the Kindnesses discovered the crimes they punished, and who decided when the moral lines that they patrolled had been crossed, Einsa's mother had never revealed. It was, she said, part of the mysteries into which acolytes were introduced should they survive long enough. And becoming an acolyte was something that Einsa should avoid at all costs. Einsa hadn't ignored the warning, but when her mother died, she hadn't run far enough or fast enough. She had wasted whole hours grieving. She should have run immediately and kept going until she reached the furthest shore. And if even that hadn't proved sufficient then she should have started swimming.

Although the Academy did have subterranean cells that might be called dungeons, the description extended to a whole range of chambers on several levels, reaching down to the Bone Garden, the place where the bodies eventually accumulated and where Kindness Undu was said to unveil the deepest mysteries of necromancy to a favoured few.

The dungeons proper were rarely occupied. For any acolytes put there it might be considered a reward rather than a punishment, removing them as it would from the nightmare of their daily lives. Infrequently, Kindnesses from the field would bring in prisoners to be kept in the cells. The future for these captives was generally bleak, even by Academy standards.

Today's lesson concerned extricating oneself rather than others. Why the Academy owned ten hinged iron coffins that were lockable both from the inside and from the outside Einsa had no idea. But at some point Instructor Akki had commandeered them and had the lot transported to the sump chamber where any overspill from the Academy's stream-fed laundry would accumulate in times of unusually high rainfall.

The chamber lay empty now, save for the coffins, and a quarter-inch layer of dark, stinking mud that required constant vigilance to avoid slipping in. Akki, the youngest of the instructors, aimed her lantern, the only source of light for the class, at the rusting coffins. Save for her absent nose she could pass for one of the older acolytes and Einsa had often wondered where this would place her on the sympathy scale. She felt that those closest to the experience should have the most concern for the suffering of the girls still enduring it. She had, however, yet to see a glimmer of compassion from any of the instructors. Akki, if anything, seemed to be deliberately cruel, which most of the others weren't. They didn't need to be since the system was cruel enough to satisfy most sadists without requiring additional torments.

'First ten.' The instructor waved them forward.

There was a logic to waiting and learning from other acolytes' experience. Some, like Mollandra, liked to get things over with. Einsa watched as her friend and nine others, including Tmanga, went to lie down in the coffins. They hadn't been told to but acting dumb with Instructor Akki had been proven on multiple occasions to be a bad idea.

Sharp remained with Einsa, apparently having used up her quota of crazy for the day.

The instructor went around closing and locking each coffin. 'I hope you've all remembered to bring your lock picks, or you'll be here indefinitely.' After turning the key in the final lock Akki straightened up and clapped her hands, 'Go!'

Einsa knew she'd brought her picks but rummaged through her robe to check anyway. The Academy did not provide picks. Acolytes learned that they were expected to acquire their own tools, or they didn't learn and ceased to need them. Most girls had spent many hours in the dormitory after lights out working to shape random bits of scavenged iron into new additions to their pick set. They were also among the most prized items to be claimed from corpses.

'I should have taken those bitches' picks,' Sharp muttered.

Einsa nodded. She should have. But they wouldn't have helped here. Each new pick needed to be understood and practised with before it could be of much help.

They watched, and in due course the coffins began to clang open as first one acolyte and then another managed to spring the locks. Mollandra was the second one to emerge, rust-streaked and sweaty but looking relieved.

Each empty coffin was swiftly refilled. Some of them had had three occupants by the time the last of the first ten, Tremanay, managed to get out. After a long period of failure there had been several minutes of hysteria before the girl calmed again at the urging of her friends and managed to free herself. She hurried over to join the successful acolytes by the stairs where Instructor Akki watched on, unimpressed.

Sharp and Einsa were among the last to take the challenge, with only half a dozen girls still hugging the wall. Many of the acolytes, as they emerged, would flash the pick or picks they'd had success with towards their friends. A risky act. But Instructor Maggery had taught them a bit of stealth.

At last Einsa stepped forward and lay down in the most recently vacated coffin. She would have waited longer, but sometimes there were unpleasant surprises for the tailenders. Sharp headed for the leftmost of a pair of coffins where the acolytes had escaped within moments of each other. They elbowed past the two girls now heading for the freedom of the stairs.

Her temporary tomb clanged shut and the instructor's key turned in the lock.

Escape, Instructor Akki had taught them, was always at least as much about waiting as it was about action, and very often waiting was by far the most important ingredient. Einsa had listened to the lessons and certainly, if she were to be thrown into a gaol cell with guard rotas and a complex to navigate before she could reach freedom, she would wait and observe before making her move. In the dank darkness of the coffin, though, she felt that her waiting had been done on the outside and already she was hunting for the keyhole.

Panic built distressingly fast as her fingers slid back and forth, failing to locate what she needed. The inner surface was a mess of corroded pits, flaking rust, and rivet heads. Finally, her fingertips returned to a dent they had rejected, and her nails revealed what had to be the keyhole. The girl before her – Treecie, the daughter of a wealthy politician – must have crammed it full of mud and rust. Not enough to stop it being locked but sufficient to disguise the hole. The bitch hadn't even glanced Einsa's way as they passed.

'I'll put a new hole in her when I get out.' The loudness of Einsa's voice surprised her in the enclosed space.

She set to digging the muck out of the mechanism. The lid was just an inch or two above her nose, not allowing her to roll on her side, so the pick-work had to be done at an awkward angle. Her left arm had to reach over her body, squeezed on every side. Her right arm needed to be painfully crooked so that her hand could be level with the lock. Little Mollandra probably could have rolled around, slid up and down . . . she'd had it easy . . .

'Last girl.' The instructor's voice boomed. It was probably Meery. Meery had to be ordered into every trial and yet somehow survived them all. Not only that, she emerged more swiftly and in better shape than many who had gone before her.

Einsa jammed what she felt was her most suitable pick into the lock, gritting her teeth and imagining she was driving it into Treecie's eye. She began to wriggle it around. The scream from nearby fitted so neatly with her vision of revenge that for a moment Einsa accepted it as Treecie's agonized cry.

'Shit!' The voice was Sharp's but the fear had to belong to someone else, surely?

'What is it?' Einsa wasn't the only prisoner calling out to know.

She caught the word 'water' among the confusion of answers and distress. Then she heard it, the splash of falling water. They were flooding the chamber! It would have been easy, likely the instructor just had to turn a wheel to divert the stream's water into the room.

Einsa continued to wrestle the locking mechanism against a background of splashing and screams. Her pick ground uselessly among the mud and rust flakes, finding no purchase. She had studied the pins and tumblers of sophisticated locks, along with the ratchets and cylinders of older, more basic models. She'd practised until her fingers bled and calluses formed. Everyone had secret fears, or at least if they were sensible they were secret. Hand that advantage to your enemies — and in here the instructors were the enemy — and they would torture you with it.

Einsa had several hidden fears, but her terror of confined spaces was the biggest secret. Meeting a better sword on the floor of the Wound Garden would never be a pleasant ending but she had steeled herself against that eventuality. Until today she'd yet to imagine a worse ending than being trapped in some small enclosure and left to rot. But drowning in one now topped her list of awful ways to die.

Panic can make a nightmare of even the simplest tasks. When your life hangs in the balance on the outcome of buttoning up a shirt, the act of doing up a button can seem like juggling five balls at once.

Einsa couldn't feel the water. Her coffin had been damp and muddy to start with and it seemed to be keeping out the rising tide for now, but she could hear the splashing intensify, and the quality of sound in the chamber had changed in some ineffable manner that spoke of flooding. The robustness of her coffin would be moot, however, when the water level reached the row of airholes about two thirds of the way up.

Einsa fumbled through her picks for an alternative. She heard a coffin lid nearby clang open and she cursed, jealousy and fear drawing obscenities off her tongue. She wanted to beg the girl for help, though it would do her no good.

Einsa began to poke about in the mechanism with her narrowest and simplest pick, hoping to form some kind of picture in her mind of what opposed her and where she needed to apply the forces that would turn the lock.

It was the coldness rather than the wetness that she noticed first. Cold water leaked from the keyhole over her trembling fingers.

Another lid clanged open.

'This isn't your coffin, Einsa.' Sharp rapped briefly on the iron before splashing away.

Time passed. Einsa cursed and wept and struggled with her picks.

Two more coffin lids opened with great splashes and the acolytes couldn't keep from cheering as their friends emerged, though they would pay for the celebration later.

'Gods . . . no.' Einsa had two picks in the lock when her attempt to twist the larger one resulted in a release of tension. If she'd had less experience living in her hands she might have thought that the mechanism had rotated. But Einsa had broken enough picks to know the difference between a lock surrendering and the pick giving up. 'Please no . . .' With a piece of broken metal jammed in the workings a lock could seize up permanently.

Slowly, water began to spill down on both sides of her, dribbling through the airholes the flood had just reached.

Einsa choked on a scream. She couldn't leave like this. Not like this. Not howling until the waters filled her mouth while the class watched on.

With what felt like infinite trembling patience, she rotated the pick back and withdrew it, the waters still dribbling through the lock that must now be inches below the waterline. The relief of finding the pick head distorted and ready to break but still attached to the stem made a brief dent in the high tide of her own terror.

Einsa hadn't jammed the lock but, cradled by the icy water which now touched her ears, she rapidly returned to the panic that had been tightening its vice around her. She replaced the pick with an alternative and began to work both the new and the old around the grime-choked mechanism in what the small still-rational corner of her brain told her was hopeless stirring.

Above the splashing and the cries of other trapped acolytes being consumed by their fears, Mollandra's voice somehow reached through Einsa's frenzy. 'Einsa! Stop! Wait!'

'Fuck you!' Stop? The little bitch was shouting for her to stop from the safety of the stairs? She probably hadn't even got her toes wet.

An image of Einsa's mother jolted through her mind, unasked for, unbidden, silent but filling her blind eyes. The stony countenance, that had broken only in rare and precious moments of affection, was one Einsa had come to understand over her years in the Academy. It showed nothing now save faint disappointment. Perhaps without Mollandra's 'Stop' Einsa would never have thought of her mother, at least not until the drowning's end when the pain left her waterlogged lungs, and she sank into the endless depths.

'Stop. Wait.' Einsa took a deep breath and withdrew both her picks.

With the keyhole vacated, and with Einsa's guiding hand not squashed against it, the leak became its own little cataract, water jetting out since the pressure at the lock was greater than at the surface.

'Stop. Wait.' Einsa let the breath out and inhaled slowly. The water filled her ears now, deadening sound. It reached the corners of her eyes, and she raised her head so that her nose pressed against the heavy coffin lid. She tried to picture the workings of the lock, tried to put what her picks had revealed together with what she had learned. Distantly she was aware of the wild shrieks and thrashing din of a neighbour who had also forgotten the lesson. Maybe that would be her soon, but beneath the cold memory of her mother's stare she vowed to keep herself together for as long as humanly possible.

Slowly, she returned one pick to the lock. Miraculously everything felt clearer and more certain. She had waited and the water jetting through the lock under pressure had undone Treecie's sabotage, cleaning out the mud and rust. Einsa advanced the metal tooth, seeking the pressure point she needed to turn the mechanism.

Often, doing all the right things could still deliver the wrong result. This was one of life's harsher lessons. When you did the right thing belatedly it was even less reasonable to expect a good outcome.

Einsa calmly worked the picks even as the water reached her lips. She closed her mouth, pressed her nose hard against the unyielding iron, and worked on, reaching, testing, applying measured force. And when the water reached her nostrils she stopped breathing and kept working.

CHAPTER 16
Rue

Although mercenaries are paid to fight, they spend only a tiny fraction of their time actually fighting. The average life expectancy of a mercenary is lower than in most professions, but if they were to go into battle every day few would be expected to last more than a week or two.

The great majority of a mercenary's time is spent waiting. Travelling comes a distant second. Fighting a very distant third. And all that waiting needs filling with distraction. Which in part accounts for how good mercenaries are at taking prisoners. A prisoner who can be ransomed provides money, and money is the reason most mercenaries claim to do what they do. A prisoner who can't be ransomed provides entertainment, filling those empty days when there would otherwise be nothing else to do but sharpen blades and think about the battles to come.

All of this explained the ready availability of nets among the sell-swords swarming towards Rue, and the well-practised encirclement manoeuvre they employed. In the old days nobody would ever think of charging at a Kindness, especially not if they were just hired blades hoping to get paid. But these were new days, and times – as Sharp had always liked to say – are a-changing. Plus, while there were no Kindnesses who might be called young, there were perhaps only two older than Rue, and neither of those by more than a year or two.

With the corpse of one of their commanders advancing jerkily from the rear, charging the old woman ahead of them turned out to be the much-preferred option.

Rue had seen cultures where the old were respected, but the larger the groups into which humanity clumped itself, the smaller the circle of old men still afforded that respect became. Most of the elderly were seen merely as useless eaters. The wisdom of age, it turned out, had an increasingly short period in which it held value. In the modern era, experience was viewed more like fruit, quick to soften and rot.

'Shit.' Rue let Isik's corpse collapse. Maintaining it was occupying too much of her attention. She sized up the young man heading the pack, his long legs devouring the distance between them.

A crow swooped low between Rue and the enemy, unleashing a mournful caw. And in the closing moments Rue admitted that the wisdom of age, at least the wisdom of *her* age, had been severely lacking in this instance. She had allowed herself to be wrapped up in the strangeness of the Morrigan's blessing, and had swiftly bought back into the myth of her order, and now she was heartbeats away from being embarrassingly trampled into the dirt of the one-horse town where she should have ended her days staring toothlessly into the embers of her cottage fire.

The youth tried a sliding tackle, which Rue sidestepped with minimal effort. The next man, a hefty, bearded fellow, slapped at her knife hand with the flat of his blade. Rue, understanding that they intended to capture rather than kill her, took advantage of her predicament and spun inside his reach, stabbing the man twice in the neck and using his body to shield her from the flood of mercenaries passing on both sides.

For a few frantic moments Rue slashed and moved, cutting away reaching fingers, ducking beneath attempted grapples. She made sure that the wounds she dealt were deep and well placed. Even as they bled, the mercenaries had sufficient discipline to remember their orders. A shield slammed into her back, staggering her, a kick to her thigh almost put her on the ground, the hilt of a sword grazed her skull.

The necromancy that had stood Isik back on his feet, even though

Rue had stopped his heart perhaps an hour earlier, now turned inwards, shoring up what the ageing body it inhabited could not. Where she should have shattered and fallen, Rue endured.

'Whoresons.' Rue spat her blood into the dust as the mercenaries backed beyond the reach of her knife.

Half a dozen kept backing off, through the ranks of their comrades, clutching wounds that might kill them and that certainly would keep them from this fight or any other for weeks to come. Two men, the bearded brute and a narrow, corn-haired youth, lay in the dirt, the younger one still convulsing.

The first net hit Rue from behind, folding over her.

'Should have opened with that.' She threw it off as she'd been taught, but it had hooks that snagged her left arm even as two further nets came at her from the front.

It didn't take long before she lay beside the two men that the mercenaries' pride had killed. The nets held her while strong hands bound her more effectively with lengths of rope. After that they took her shoulder-high in an ignominious procession back to the doorway where their leader, the woman, Gressa, stood frowning.

They hung Rue on a hook that had once supported the antlered skull of a plains elk that Tamaster Sams had pretended to have hunted down in his youth. From her uncomfortable perspective, heels half a yard above the ground, Rue had a good view of the old mayor's 'dining hall', which was just the largest room of his modest house. Gressa paid Rue scant attention, instead turning her back and returning her focus to a set of maps spread across an oak table. Three other commanders joined her, all of them dwarfing the woman but showing by their body language that hers was the opinion that mattered most. The men, one Rue recognized from Isik's crew, glanced uneasily in Rue's direction from time to time while Gressa jabbed at various objectives on the maps.

From her position on the wall Rue could feel the dead around her. Isik and the others had been brought into the house and left in the root cellar. Gressa had ordered the corpses be bound hand and foot, and a guard set on the cellar door. She'd raged at her underlings' fear when some hesitated to touch the bodies. If necromancy was more than a parlour trick, she had shouted, then necromancers would rule the continent. If death magic triumphed over swords and spears, the warlord would have populated his court with practitioners of the art or mastered the unclean sorceries himself. But no, Lord Sunder had placed half the world beneath his heel with military might, and unless the cockless cowards currently questioning her orders wanted to feel Gressa's own military might, they would do as they were told, and quickly.

Rue hung in place and said nothing. Long ago she had been taught the value of waiting. *Stop. Wait.* The fact that they'd stuck her on the wall like a trophy spoke of their contempt. Gressa had seemed an able commander, but here she was revealing plans as if she were the villain from some shadow play, spilling her secrets before the hero who would inevitably escape with them.

Rue watched the room with sour eyes. She had only herself to blame. She'd been drunk on power, too filled with her own return from death to recognize the truth of Gressa's words. Necromancy had its place, but it didn't win wars. She'd stridden out into Pye's only street thinking she was walking the same path of fifty years ago. Mercenaries wouldn't have stood before a Kindness back then. No man would – not for mere coin at least.

Ignoring the tightness of her bonds, Rue reached out with the necromancy wrapped around her core and, closing her eyes, sought for options. Immediately she became aware of a source of power close at hand, perhaps in the same room as her. The thing had a necromantic reek to it. Not a corpse, but something pure and contained. Save for the artefacts that could, very rarely and at great peril, be discovered where the Academy catacombs thread among the outer fringes of the deadlands, Rue had never sensed its like. The thing was of no use to her, though, locked away from her influence within the intimidating shell of its own power.

Rue broadened her search. Apart from the bodies in the cellar there were others, further off, dumped behind the mayor's privy hut at the back of his now chickenless yard. Tamaster Sams himself was there, along with his wife and two sons. Three others had been added to the heap. Old women these, strange champions of the village to have fallen in its defence. Perhaps they put themselves between the mercenaries and what they wanted. Their grandchildren most likely. Rue knew their names, though she couldn't say how any more than she could explain how she knew the number and disposition of the dead.

Seven bodies, neither bound nor broken. Gressa was right, though. Unless the mercenaries were so filled with horror that they chose to run, seven corpses would not defeat them. The peasants were neither armed nor armoured, and even if Rue could put weapons in their hands she doubted her ability to coordinate their use. Currently the limit of her power seemed to be to return the dead's anger to their fleshy remains and set them loose in the desired direction.

'Who sent you?' Gressa's sudden approach shook Rue from her exploration. The woman had turned from her maps and planning, to confront her prisoner. 'You look like a peasant but you talk like one of those witches that got outlawed way back. They called them . . .' She snapped her fingers, as if seeking to surprise the name out of herself.

'Kindnesses,' supplied the oldest of her three subordinates at the table.

'Kindnesses,' Gressa repeated. 'That's a stupid name.'

'Justices rather than witches.' Rue could hear a whistle in her voice. From her missing front tooth, no doubt. She was sure she looked a state. She'd never been vain but even so . . . She probably looked like a witch to them. A hag. Justices . . . it had been a poor sort of justice to let slide so very many crimes and excuse others for wergild, but it had perhaps curbed the excesses of a savage world. It had perhaps given a taste of justice to the many who then craved more. 'Avengers rather than justices . . .'

'You made a corpse walk,' Gressa said.

Rue shrugged. It hurt. 'Witches then. If it pleases you.' Her body ached but somehow it was being forgotten that hurt more. Rue would have happily ground the Academy to dust beneath her heel. But that would have been vengeance on the avengers. To have those two centuries of suffering – the deaths of all those little girls – erased so completely in a few scant decades that this woman had to stretch for the name that had once inspired terror across the lands . . . that hurt.

Gressa reached up to slap Rue across the face. 'Who sent you?'

'I live here.'

It was true. Kindnesses were not schooled to resist interrogation save through the general hardship of their forging. A Kindness's motivations were not intended to be secret. The deaths brought by Kindnesses always came with a message and with the intent that it be easy to read.

'Lie to me again and we'll skip the warm-up. The irons are hot enough already.'

'I live here. There are many ways to verify this fact, child.' Rue saw no point in appeasing her captors. Hot irons were never allowed to cool without being used. It was in the nature of the species – power existed to be exercised.

'Why would an old witch live . . . here?'

'Where should I live? A cave?'

'A witch should not be suffered to live,' growled the young man who had taken Isik's place at the table. Rue remembered his angular face looking down at her before being hidden behind a descending boot.

'Why did you attack us?' Gressa frowned as if genuinely puzzled.

'What you should be asking, and will eventually end up asking, is what I wanted with Isik.' Rue's patience had always been her weakest point. That was why the lesson about waiting was one she had needed so badly.

Gressa sank a fist into Rue's belly. She had a good punch for a relatively small woman. Rue sucked up the pain and let her necromancy crackle around it.

'Why,' snarled Gressa, 'did you want Isik?'

'I would have settled for his head,' Rue said. 'I was going to ask him who told him to come here and who directed the sacking of Stones Corner. And when he'd given me your name I would have asked who told you to do it, and so on and so forth until I came to a person worth killing. Someone who wasn't just earning their living. That person owes me their life. Or the wergild of seven ounces of gold.'

Gressa huffed in amusement. 'I can tell you that for nothing, much good it will do you—'

'You really shouldn't,' Rue said. 'Information is power. Don't just go giving it away.'

'Baron Mancer's agent was the one who hired the Iron League.'

'The Iron League?' A wry smile twisted the corner of Rue's mouth. 'That's what you call yourselves?'

Gressa narrowed her eyes. 'You seem less scared of hot irons than you should be, old woman.'

Rue met Gressa's gaze. 'Seen worse. Had worse. Done worse.'

Gressa's anger faltered, more likely at something cold in Rue's stare than at the bravado in her words. The commander turned her back on Rue. 'You'd kill Baron Mancer of the Regon Heights over a handful of dead peasants?'

'Over *two* dead peasants. Ambeth Potter and Jayne Clay.' Rue cricked her neck. 'And Mancer doesn't have to die. You people don't seem to know how to listen. He could pay the seven ounces.' Wergild was a strange thing. A very old thing. The recognition that money was life. That gold could sustain a family, a whole clan, allowing many of the victim's kin to survive when otherwise they may well have died. Blood money. The tariffs the Kindnesses used were far older than the Academy. They valued rich above poor, young above old. They put the price of a murder beyond reach of the commoner, made it a costly mistake for the landed class, and a minor indiscretion for nobility.

Rue had offered the option of wergild out of habit, as if in returning to her former role as an agent of retribution she should adopt all the trappings, all the rules. But she *had* said it and she would stick to it. It was what it was. The goddess's power ran through her, and while she hoped to use it she would walk within the bitch's rules. After all, without the Morrigan's strength in her veins Rue would die within moments, killed by the wounds she had already sustained in this self-imposed quest.

'You could always shoulder responsibility,' Rue told the mercenary. 'Pay the gold over. You must have way more than that between you. Sacking all these villages. Pay up and put all this to bed. I'm too old to go marching off after Baron Mancer.'

Gressa's lips thinned, her eyes narrowed. She looked like a woman who understood herself to be the butt of some kind of joke without yet knowing what that joke was. She shook her head, a small, sharp shake. 'No. You didn't do all this for fourteen ounces—'

'Seven.'

'This is a lie. You're playing a bigger game and I'm going to know what it is. I'm going to break you, witch, and you're going to tell me the truth.'

Gressa placed her hands to either side of her on the tabletop, leaning over the maps. For a long moment she held the room's attention with her silence. She sucked air in over her teeth, favouring Rue with a slow, speculative look. 'Everybody out.'

Nobody moved.

'*Now!*'

The mercenaries made for the door to the hall, exchanging glances, some puzzled, some annoyed.

'Berric!'

The ageing mercenary who'd hung Rue on the hook paused at the door.

'Bring me a head.'

'Sorry . . . what?'

'A fucking head. A fresh one. Quickly!' Gressa sounded nervous. As the door closed behind the last of her men she glanced up at Rue. 'You drove me to this.'

'To what?'

Gressa ignored the question and went to rummage in the saddle bags tossed against the far wall. 'Pray he leaves you to me and the hot irons.'

She removed a small leather-wrapped bundle from one of the bags, bringing it to the table gingerly, in both hands, as if worried it might burst into flame. Slowly, she unwound the bindings, to reveal what looked like a bone, one of the longer ones from within a hand, but jet black. Rue recognized it instantly as the source of the power she'd sensed earlier. Trying to intimidate this woman with necromancy had been a mistake.

Shouts and screams rang out in the middle distance, along with the raucous cawing of a crow.

Berric returned carrying a head, holding it by one ear since its thinning hair looked insufficient. Blood still dripped from the severed neck. 'It was the killing that was to be fresh?' the mercenary asked. 'Not the person. There's still children out there if—'

'Yes, the killing.' Gressa took the head off him by the other ear and waved Berric away.

She set her trophy on the table and turned it to face Rue, who found herself looking into the vacant eyes of Sebrin Weaver, father of five, and son to the late Senna. Unlike his mother, Sebrin had been friendly if rather dull. His children had loved him, though.

'Right . . .' Gressa picked up the black bone at one extreme, between finger and thumb. With trepidation she used the bone to strike Sebrin's forehead, one sharp tap, two, a third.

'What! What is it?' Sebrin's lips moved, and frown lines ploughed across the dead forehead as the eyes cast about, left and right. 'Where is this?' The eyes fixed on Gressa. 'And who are you?'

The voice echoed painfully in Rue's skull although the head, lacking both lungs and quite likely vocal cords too, could force no actual sound past its bloody teeth.

'Well now, *you* ain't Sebrin.' Rue knew that for a certainty. The live Sebrin would have been incoherent with fear, and the dead one raging. Whatever had installed itself in the farmer's skull was merely annoyed.

'And who's she?' the head demanded.

Gressa, her stare jumping between the head and the finger bone, which seemed to be vibrating in her grasp, appeared to be sharing the head's struggle to make a noise, but finally swallowed and found her voice. 'I-I'm Gressa Saramant, third captain of the Iron League, Baron.'

'Never heard of you, where's that Ossot fellow?'

'First Captain Ossot died in the frosts, Baron. Died of his wounds.'

'Wounds? They're peasants for gods' sake!'

'Saddle sores. An infection. Blood soured. I . . . uh . . . I took charge of his effects until a new first captain—'

'Why am I here?' The baron wrinkled Sebrin's nose. 'Wherever "here" is. It looks like a shabby, oversized privy. Who's the old hag?'

'The prisoner is a Kindness who has killed seven of my command—'

'Eight,' Rue corrected.

'—and wounded several others. She has also ... uh ... raised the dead. She claims to be seeking a wergild of fourteen ounces—'

'It's seven,' Rue interrupted again.

'Seven ounces of gold for the villagers we killed.'

'Just two of them. Jayne Clay and Ambeth Po—'

'This elderly peasant killed seven Iron League mercenaries?' The baron – presumably the same Baron Mancer that Rue had been told about earlier – studied Rue with eyes he didn't own.

'Ten if you count the two in Stones Corner. And she's ashamed it was so few,' Rue said.

The head's eyes widened. 'She can hear me?'

Rue had been waiting her moment and took it. Surprise, even if caused by something wholly unrelated, has a paralysing effect. She reached out with all the necromantic muscle remaining to her, attempting to get beneath the skin of the severed head, past its watery eyes, and into the brain where the baron nested like a macabre cuckoo.

'Fuck ...' The pain splitting her forehead surely had to be worse than Gressa's promised irons. She had no chance of evicting the baron, and still less of exercising any sort of control over him. Wherever the bone came from, its enchantment was far stronger than hers, certainly in this narrow function.

'Ouch!' The dead face twisted up in pain. 'The old bitch hurt me! Tell her if she— If you do that again I'll have the captain cut your teats off. Hurt her a bit right now, Captain.'

Gressa dropped the finger bone as if it were a piece of fox dung, and came towards Rue, smacking knuckles into palm.

Since it seemed that it might be touching the bone that let Gressa hear the baron, Rue lied. 'He's saying he changed his mind.' She had always been of the opinion that you should enrage torturers. They were going to do their best to hurt you anyway. And they'd probably do the job less well when angry. Plus, you might as well have one last laugh.

Gressa looked doubtful but turned around and went back to the table, unable to hear the baron's heated denials until she once again picked up the bone. She made to set it back down, but the baron stopped her, his anger growing with every word.

'Nobody would come at the Iron League over a shithole village. She's pathfinding for some resurgence of the Kindnesses, any fool can see that! Nobody would do this for ten ounces of gold, not for a hundred.'

'It's sev—'

'Shall I get the irons, Lord Mancer?' Gressa sounded almost obsequious.

If Sebrin Weaver had ever once revealed in life the narrow snarl that Baron Mancer now fashioned for him then it was a secret face kept for the privacy of his ramshackle home to terrify his family. 'Keep the irons hot. But since she's so partial to the locals, let's start this way.' He raised his silent voice, blood and spittle falling from his lips. 'Kill everyone! Burn everything.'

Rue hadn't come as the village's saviour, but to be the one to initiate their massacre was too much. If she couldn't stop it then at least she would no longer endure it. Perhaps it was cowardice to run away – it felt like cowardice – but to give Gressa and the baron anything back would only encourage their cruelties.

Rue let her chin fall to her chest. She rolled her eyes into her head in the manner Kindness Undu had taught them in front of the gates to the Bone Garden, leaving only the whites to watch the world.

Her vision changed. The low rush of water became the only sound. And she stood once more by the banks of that river which divides worlds. Her gaze found the far shore where the mysteries of death would be unravelled and where so many that she had known now dwelt.

'Hello, sister.' A breathless wheeze from her right.

'Sister.' A bubbling voice to her left.

'My sisters.' Rue's vision blurred as unbidden tears crowded her eyes. She found herself unable to turn, unable to breathe, paralysed by deep-sunk claws of emotion that she had believed the years to have pried free.

A dry hand took hers on the right. A wet one on the left.

'Ghosts . . .' Rue struggled to speak.

'Ghosts,' wheezed the first speaker.

'Still here . . . after all these years?'

'Always.' From the second speaker.

'Always?'

'For as long as we're remembered.'

Rue let them go and stepped back from the black flood so she could see them both. Still children. Shocking in their youth. Bek, pale and bloodless, still carrying the wound that Kindness Terra had made with her own knife. Einsa drenched, water running from dark hair plastered across her face.

'Oh, my sisters . . .' Rue fell to her knees.

'Little Molly.' Einsa knelt beside her.

'Mollandra.' Bek knelt too. 'You haven't changed a bit.'

CHAPTER 17
Eldest

There was a garden and Eldest had not been the one to find it. A night garden where light never found its way. It had been Milk-Eye who discovered the secret corner, and when, with soft and infinite patience Eldest's fingers had mapped out three firm stalks, three smooth caps, three undersides delicate with gills, she had understood the gift her sister had given her.

Eldest had never seen the door by which Father came and went, but when it opened, something changed in the house. The air shifted. Sometimes new scents filtered into the parlour. Several times she had heard the deep challenge of some kind of animal, and once: distant laughter.

The click of a lock reached her through the wood of the parlour door. 'He's gone.'

She moved her head back, breaking contact between her ear and the greying oak panel. With the outer door closed again the silence and the suffocation returned. But at least Father would be gone from the house for a while.

'Gone for sure?' Lip-Scar asked.

A slight hunching shrug showed him how sure she was.

'He'll be back.' Lame gathered to her narrow chest the rag bundle that she said was her baby.

'You'll stay here, Lame, so we know when.' Eldest walked away, not looking back to see if her order was obeyed. To do that was to admit the possibility of rebellion, which was practically to invite it.

Eldest thought of the street door as her hope, for she had long ago lost any other kind. She looked back across her brothers and sisters, pressed together in a tattered clump. Even the youngest of her siblings knew there was an outside, though opinions on what it contained varied. On two things they were all agreed: none of them knew how they knew the outside existed, and none of them could remember ever having left the mansion.

'Ready?' Milk-Eye grinned. Though she had been in the mansion nearly as long as Eldest she had more spirit left to her than any of the rest. She loved building traps, and though Father had yet to show any wounds, Milk-Eye always claimed on the next morning that she saw him favouring one side, or wincing when he reached to discipline someone. One day, she swore, they would find him impaled on one of her carefully sharpened stakes.

For a short time they would have free run of the upper floors. Eldest would direct her siblings, children who had no names but for the ones she had placed upon them in her loneliness. They were many and though she had been taught her numbers, the figure that Eldest reached when counting them never seemed to stay the same. And when it shrank by one or two, she could never say who was missing.

The parlour was the best place for listening, but also the most dangerous. Every other part of the house lay in darkness save for whatever whispers of daylight might creep down the chimneys. In the parlour, however, a great wooden chandelier held a dozen candles far beyond reach, making the children's eyes sting and weep. Here the mansion's decay revealed itself to more than just touch. Torn and faded curtains failed to conceal bricked-up windows. Furniture lay in tumbled disarray. There were books too, strewn in careless profusion.

Day-Father was the one who would fill the trough with the gruel that he brought in from the outside and leave buckets of water in the Dining Hall. It was he who had, with the threat of hand and rod, taught them to read below the light and drip of high candles. Day-Father was stern, and cold, but seldom cruel.

Night-Father, who wore the same skin, hunted them all, seemingly with no purpose other than to torture those he caught. Eldest tried to organize her siblings into the business of barricading entrances and constructing traps. She tried to find new and better places to hide, and to teach them all she had learned about erasing herself.

They went from the parlour to the dining room, where on the great table's pitted surface the trough lay with its contents steaming. None of them rushed for it, though other stomachs growled just as loudly as Eldest's. It was in the food. Whatever was being done to them was in the food. All of them knew it, even the youngest. There was, in the gruel that Father slopped out for them each morning, something the opposite of edible. It had been hidden in the mess, beyond the ability of any of them to pick out.

Hunger is the most relentless of foes. There's no weakness more fundamental. Any mind that can resist hunger's attack carries within it the option for self-destruction, and in so cruel an existence such an option is often a death sentence.

Famine changes the way people look at the world. Things that would never have been considered foodstuffs become worth chewing on in the hope that they might be. Old leather might carry the savour of the cow. Perhaps what could be scraped from the bottom of barrels in the pantry still remembered the grain or pulses that were stored there. Even the obviously inedible: wood for example, might be nibbled upon. The small holes in the chair legs record the fact that *something* found sustenance there. But there are other substances that remain the opposite of food – things that even a starving man would not place in his mouth. Copper coins, cleaning salts, metal polish.

Whatever Father hid in the gruel was worse than any of that, though it carried no taste other than a wrongness that dried the mouth and set teeth on edge.

They ate. Forcing themselves to endure these moments in order that their bellies would pain them less during the long night ahead. None of them spoke. No noise save the slop and drip of the gruel, and the swallowing. Occasionally there was chewing, on rare bits of substance – gristle in the main, or blobs of fat. Someone retched and for a moment Eldest struggled to hold what she had put into her belly.

Forgetting came next. Forgetting always followed after eating. One moment Eldest was scooping the gruel into her mouth. The next she was blinking in the quarter-light, disoriented, with her siblings standing around her, motionless until she shook them back into the now.

On the previous night Eldest had hidden for several hours in one of the attic rooms that had once housed servants. When Dancer woke her for her time on guard, Eldest had sat with her head to one of the rafters, searching with her fingertips for the names she and others had carved into the wood. She found the expected mix of familiar legends set there by her siblings, and older unknown names, perhaps of the servants themselves.

Time had crawled by and Eldest's exploration of the rafters occupied her hands while her ears strained for the telltale creak of Night-Father's approach. She found her own name and remembered the blister that setting it there with an iron nail had earned her. That had been months before, no hint of the callus remained.

One fingertip traced the letters, until . . . a new name, the curl of its first letter just crossing over the final letter of hers. Definitely over, rather than under. An 'S' trespassing over the 't' ending 'Eldest'. The new name led off, nearly at right angles to hers. 'Strong'. That was it, just 'Strong'. It seemed like the sort of name that she would hand out to a sibling once they had shown enough of themselves to earn one. Strong.

But she didn't know any Strong. She had no brother or sister with that name.

That morning she had asked all her siblings. None of them remembered Strong. None of them had carved the name on the rafters. And yet there it was. A message? A cruel trick of Night-Father's? Or had they had a brother named Strong . . . it felt like a brother . . . Eldest could summon no image of him, no memory, but her fingers remembered closing around a thick upper arm. *Strong.*

Sometimes the poison in their food would steal a day. Sometimes a week. And perhaps sometimes it stole a lifetime, so completely that not even those who hadn't lived it could remember the person who had.

Now as she waited for the others to emerge from the trance that the mind-poison dragged them into, Eldest repeated the name of her lost brother. *Strong*. She felt, for a moment, an arm around her shoulders. With a snarl she began to carve the name into her flesh, scoring the letters with her fingernail, setting them on the inner side of her forearm above the tendons and veins. With the 's' she gained a shadow of this missing sibling, an outline caused by his absence. The 't' brought a sharp intake of breath above the hiss of her pain. They had called him 'Eldest' before her. 'Strong' was the name yet another 'Eldest' had given him before that one vanished and ceded the title to Strong.

More letters, more torn skin, more blood leaking, black in the faint light reaching into the dining room from the parlour. Eldest couldn't see her brother's face or hear his words, but she remembered the smell of him, the warmth of his strong body. He had been brave. She knew that. Too brave. Perhaps that was what had doomed him.

Strong had been a promise. A promise that even with Night-Father hunting them and the unspeakable horrors of the cellar, he would somehow protect them from the worst of it.

Strong was gone now, leaving nothing but another hole cut into her memory and a name cut into a rafter. He was a lesson. A broken promise. His strength had been an illusion, a fragile lie, his protection forgotten. She was the Eldest now. Before she'd been Eldest she'd worn other names, handed down by her predecessors. For a time, she had been Lucky. Not that any of them were lucky, but somehow she always came out near the top of any scramble while stronger, faster, cleverer siblings fell foul of the constant dangers. For a time she had been Hard, though whether she'd earned the name for her endurance or because her brothers and sisters found little comfort in her, she didn't know.

The last letter hurt the most and bled the least. She finished the 'g', teeth gritted against the pain. With her brother's name burning on her arm, she looked up and shook herself into the now.

'Are we all here?' She looked around at the vacant faces. 'Are we here?' Had Strong vanished into nothingness, or had they simply forgotten him as he forgot himself? Had his strong body lain at their feet on the dirty floor, misplaced, unremembered? Had they stepped over and around him as they left? Was he there now, reduced to unnoticed bones by the rats?

'Lip-Scar!' She shook the boy's shoulders. 'Say my name!'

When she had made each of them say her name and then their own, she stood back to address them all. 'Follow me. We'll block the west door to the Music Room first.' She led off into the gloom at a brisk pace, aware of every obstacle, stepping over or around the delicate piles that might warn of Night-Father's approach should he brush against them.

Behind her, broken crockery slipped to the floor, fragments clacking against each other. 'Idiot! Who was that? Was it Tune?' She called that sister Tune because she would sing a faint and trembling little song when terrified. At least she had until Eldest beat the habit out of her. Better a beating than Night-Father's tortures.

'N . . . no.' Tune's voice. Eldest could still see the girl silhouetted against the parlour's glow, standing beside the warning pile she'd toppled.

If Eldest were the eldest of them, and she thought she was, then Tune might be the youngest. Perhaps not even six, capable of holding a tune but little else be it a lesson or a silence.

'I should . . .' Eldest stopped, seeing the child flinch. She should beat her again. Sometimes she thought that while Day-Father taught them many lessons, how to read, how to reason, even how to fight, that Night-Father had only one lesson to teach. He wanted Eldest to beat Tune. He wanted both of them to learn to hate. 'Build it back, then come to the Music Room to help us.'

They crossed the Dining Hall, took the East Corridor, ascended a flight of stairs and entered the Music Room.

'Get chairs. The least broken ones. Interlock them like I showed you. Scab and Finger, you wedge the door first. All the way up, especially where the hinges were.'

A voice rose, sounding dissent. 'It's stupid to block this door. There's more routes out of the Library. The ceiling hole's too slow. The North Stairs are rotted through on this level so—'

Eldest silenced Grumble with a swift sharp slap, finding his face in the blind dark.

'When he tries the doors, and they're blocked, he'll spend time forcing one of them. Time he could have been hunting us.'

'But . . .' Grumble must have decided to bite his lip, remembering the slap's lesson, at least while it still stung on his cheek.

'We won't be in there. We'll already have climbed up into the Clove Room, taking as much time as we need.'

'He won't bother with the door if there's nobody in there.' This from Round, from the back of the group, safely out of slapping distance. He had been around once. Now he was as skinny as the rest of them.

'I'll be in there while you're all erasing yourselves. I'll stay in the Music Room and let enough show to waste his time.'

'But you'll get caught,' Milk-Eye gasped.

'I won't.'

'Where will we hide?' Lip-Scar asked.

'I don't care, but in the West Wing, he'll come from the east. Best I don't know where you are. Then he can't make me tell.'

At first the fear of Night-Father's cruelty had been crippling. Fear had drowned Eldest's mind and like the rest of them she had been nothing but a victim, as surely as if she were chained to the wall. She had bent herself into whatever shape she imagined might save her, done whatever she thought might placate him, however much it shamed her. But nothing had made the slightest difference.

'Why do you do it?' Milk-Eye asked as she rummaged through the broken chairs, hunting splinters large enough to make good wedges. 'You could just run. You're the best at hiding.'

'Because I'm the oldest.' Eldest couldn't see her sister's face in the dark, couldn't know if she would see suspicion there, or admiration, or perhaps that tight satisfaction the parlour's light sometimes showed in the twist of Lip-Scar's mouth when he thought she wasn't watching, the look that said he was happy to use her, to profit from her foolishness.

'That's no reason,' Runner said, passing by with a burden.

'We can't all run,' Eldest said. 'And besides, there doesn't have to be a reason for everything. Why does Father change at night? Why does he hunt us?'

'If we lost you . . . I wouldn't be able to do what you do,' Milk-Eye whispered. She was probably the closest to Eldest in age, though it was hard to tell. Of all of them the girl seemed to be the one who most shared Eldest's burden of care. 'I couldn't . . .'

'Because I'm the oldest,' Eldest repeated. But a truer answer might be, 'Because I am me.' Perhaps there was a reason for the horror that was their lives. Day-Father taught them to read, to fight, to think. Night-Father taught different lessons. Where Day-Father used words, examples, slaps, and diagrams to make his points, Night-Father simply applied pressure, squeezing them into what he required, forcing them to quiet their souls, erase themselves, become nothing so that as he prowled they might remain unnoticed while he passed by.

With his howling and his cruel nails, with his sniffing in the dark, wild laughter, and whispered threats Night-Father sought to make them bury themselves in the void. He forced them to dig so deep that they erased not only their presence but their present, deleting who they were so that they could be further moulded to suit his purpose.

Eldest had always known that while her body screamed that escaping the agony was the most important part of her fight, this more subtle struggle was the real one. Father, Day or Night, did not want her to save her brothers and sisters. And while the fear of being caught in their place ran so deep it could spill the contents of her bladder down her legs, she still clung to that deeper fear that who she was might run from her just as easily and more completely.

Night came, too soon as it always did, and Father became the thing that hunted them. The mansion had many places to hide – twenty-six rooms, and that was only the above-ground ones. In the cellars there were dozens of small chambers. Eldest would almost rather let herself get caught than risk the cellars, though. Mother lived there.

The detritus of a former, brighter life crowded every room. More furniture than Eldest could imagine a use for: rugs, pots, pans, chandeliers, iron suits, screens, rotting tapestries, even paintings that when carried into the light of the parlour revealed the stern faces of grand lords and ladies, all of them spotted with mildew as if it might be the disease that had carried them away.

Thousands of places to hide. Even so, with Father unsleeping, ceaselessly searching, the nights were a torment and sleep a prize that mixed danger with release. Eldest often felt that her days were the fever dream, and that Day-Father's cane, keeping her awake during the constant lessons, was worse torture than any at Night-Father's disposal.

'Take her.' Eldest, standing on the flower table, hefted Tune towards the ceiling hole where waiting arms would reach past the sharp and splintered edges to haul her through.

'I can't . . .' Tune sobbed as they took her.

'You can.' Milk-Eye's voice in the darkness. Milk-Eye would be a good leader. She still made mistakes, but she would try. She would try to save them. Not like Lip-Scar. He would have them work for his benefit then abandon them all, scattering them as offerings to delay Father. Even without the benefit, Lip-Scar would want to rule them. He saw it as his due. You could see that in his eyes.

'You can. You will. You must.' Eldest pushed Tune's feet, losing contact as the others lifted. 'Find the blackness.'

It was an old mantra. *Find the blackness.* That was the poison that Father put into them, that was the dark forgetting that coiled around their bones. The art to releasing it was to release yourself, to let go of any holds that might offer safety and to drown in the oblivion, knowing that it didn't want to ever let you go again. To do that was like deliberately burning yourself or pushing a needle into your own eye. The body doesn't want to do it. The mind doesn't want to do it. But in that oblivion sanctuary lay. Erase yourself and Father could no longer find you. All his sniffing, all his poking his sharp stick into corners, throwing back covers, tipping over tables, all of it would avail him nothing. Embrace that blackness and you would be gone.

CHAPTER 18

Mollandra

Year Three

Even as the water level in the sump room reached the airholes set into the sides of the ten coffins, Mollandra still knew that Einsa would defeat the lock. She and Meery were the only two still trapped but Meery's uncanny luck and Einsa's endless competence would see them free before . . . before . . .

'They're drowning!' The words burst from Mollandra unbidden. 'Get them out of there!'

Tmanga and Sharp were on her before she could move, each anchoring an arm while some few among her classmates tore their fascinated, horrified gazes from the coffins to glance her way in puzzlement. This was what the Academy did. This was how a hundred became three.

'She could still do it,' Tmanga grunted with the effort of holding Mollandra back.

Time passed with an impossible combination of agonizing sloth and the speed of a racing heart. The relentlessly rising water reached the top of the nearest coffin and flooded over the rusted metal plate.

Any noise from within the occupied coffins remained inaudible beneath the rush of water and the sound of acolytes whose survival depended on their fellows' deaths urging Einsa and Meery even now to break free. Gholla had been tight with Meery since the first year, and her screams were already the heartbroken heartbreaking kind. Brooth, whose necromancy made Mollandra expect her to be as cold and strange as Undu, called Einsa's name through streaming tears.

Mollandra fought her friends, on the very brink of violence. 'I have to—'

An unexpected light lit within Einsa's coffin, red rage shining out through every airhole, bleeding into the water.

'What . . .?' Mollandra's comprehension failed.

Steam began to break from the surface of the troubled waters around Einsa's coffin, bubbling fiercely. And into the acolytes' astonished silence a muffled detonation thrust its way a mere heartbeat before a white explosion of frothing water and flame felled them all.

Darkness and confusion reigned until, after the passage of some unknown time, Instructor Akki returned bearing a lantern from the next chamber to replace the light that the wall of water had extinguished.

Free of Tmanga and Sharp now, and with her bearing restored, Mollandra rushed towards the coffins, splashing noisily through the knee-deep flood. The lid of Einsa's was gone, blown off and sunk. And for one glorious moment Mollandra believed she would find her friend sitting up amid the steaming waters.

Tmanga splashed up to her side, Sharp on her heels.

'Give them nothing.' Tmanga put her hand on Mollandra's shoulder.

'Akki's looking for you to break,' Sharp hissed.

Einsa's face was peaceful, and Mollandra envied her that, but the rest of her body gave the lie to that impression. Impossibly, livid burns marked her skin and sections of her robe lay torn or charred or both. Missing fingernails, and rust flakes jammed beneath those that remained, told the story of her final panic and hopeless struggle.

Mollandra turned and looked at Treecie, the acolyte who had occupied the coffin immediately before Einsa. There could be many interpretations for the girl's look of sick fascination as she stared at the floating body. Many would be imagining that it could have so easily been them lying there, or would be still wrestling with the source and nature of that final explosion.

Two places along, Instructor Akki opened the last coffin that remained locked. Meery's uncanny luck had finally deserted her. She wore a vacant expression, perhaps with a hint of mild surprise, long fair hair floating around her in the water that had ceased to rise.

Mollandra looked back at Treecie on the steps before returning her gaze to her friend. 'Something . . .' Mollandra reached a hand towards Einsa's coffin, her fingers questing as if they could pluck answers from amid the wisps of steam. She felt a strange quality in the air, as if veins of heat ran through it, like quartz through rock. The steam held a scent too – one unlike any that Mollandra had smelled before. A scent that infected her lungs and trembled in her blood, as if rage had been made accessible to all the senses. 'There's something there . . .'

'You look sick.' Sharp grinned, as if this were a good thing, as if their friend wasn't lying drowned just yards before them. 'Your lips are blue.'

'She was so angry . . .' Mollandra recognized the trembling of her own weak necromancy. Kindness Undu had despaired of her, but the Kindness had always said the connection with loved ones was the strongest of all: *Those we would most wish a peaceful sleep to are the very ones we're most able to disturb.*

Mollandra snapped around to face Treecie. 'You did something. Something to the lock. That's why she couldn't get out!'

'No! I didn't.' Treecie shook her head violently, face shading crimson while her neck went white as alabaster. 'I would never. I liked—'

'Liar!' The roar that burst from Mollandra was far louder than any noise she'd made before and surprised her as much as the rest of them. Nearly everyone took a step back. 'Death challenge. You choose the battle.' Mollandra rubbed her neck.

'Get out.' Instructor Akki waved them away as if she had no time for their foolishness.

Mollandra turned towards the woman, who now had her back

to them once more as she reached to heave Meery from her coffin. The water soaking Mollandra's robes had begun to cool, already losing the heat of Einsa's last fury. She took a step towards the instructor, and again Tmanga caught her arm while Sharp only broadened her grin. Mollandra shook her head. Bek's madness had infected her but she wouldn't go down like Bek. The Academy had more to teach her before she could teach it a lesson of her own.

The acolytes hurried away, muttering among themselves. It was a bad month if they lost a single member of the class. To have lost two in a day with a third promised was high drama.

Mollandra kept her eye on Treecie. She was the type to try to end the death challenge before it even started. They all were, to be fair. But killing a classmate was a surefire way to get the rest of the class to band against you. If Sharp, for example, was to start working her way through Year Three with sword in hand on the floor of the Wound Garden, one death challenge after the next, then the whole class would rise against her. It was the only sensible course of action. Thus, Mollandra had given Treecie warning and the choice of both weapons and ground. She couldn't afford to be seen as a general threat. This was a personal matter and Treecie's end would be the end of it. This was also the reason that Mollandra had murdered Lucia in secret on the first night and had never admitted it to anyone, not even to Bek or Einsa.

The walk from the dungeons to the dorm was a long one, despite what some said about the gap between sleep and death being so slender. Mollandra lagged at the rear of the group. The fact of Einsa's death was a large, sharp-cornered thing that wouldn't sit comfortably in her chest, and every time she tried to wrestle it into a better place it made her hurt. The pain leaked from her eyes just as it had with Bek, though there she had managed to reach the privacy of her covers before allowing the agony to have its way with her.

'You're with us now.' Tmanga fell back to walk with her.

Sharp joined them, pressing her habitual smile into a flat line. 'Einsa was all right. That's all I'm going to say.'

Mollandra kept her head down, refusing to comment on the implied new dynamic. Tmanga shared what Einsa had had, a belief in herself that ran too deep to need to be stated or shown. But belief alone wouldn't carry anyone to the end of the Academy's cruel games.

'You shouldn't have let Treecie choose,' Tmanga said. 'She's strongest where you're weakest.'

'It doesn't matter.' Mollandra kept her stinging eyes on the floor, safe with Sharp and Tmanga at her side. 'It doesn't matter.'

'Ha!' Sharp's laugh sounded hollow in the vaults. 'It really doesn't. Nothing does.'

Einsa had mattered to Mollandra, though she had never said so. She didn't say so now either. Sharp skipped along the surfaces of the world. Perhaps it was just a defence to keep from hurting, or it might be that was all she was. All of them were broken in some way or other. If they hadn't been when they arrived, after three years they were more fracture than flesh. That seemed to be the Academy's recipe: grind them down and build something new from the pieces.

'Are we going to talk about what happened?' Sharp leaned in, still kneeling on her own neighbouring bed.

'She drowned.' Mollandra didn't have any more to say about it.

'She exploded!' Sharp mimed the eruption of water with both hands. 'What in all the hells was that?'

'Magic that her mother taught her,' Tmanga said. 'Something the Kindnesses know.'

'She should have used it earlier.' Sharp shook her head. 'I'd be using it all the time.'

'It didn't look like very safe magic,' Tmanga said.

'So?' Sharp gave her a puzzled look, turning to Mollandra for support.

'She loved us.' Mollandra shrugged helplessly. 'She would never let that loose with friends around her.'

'She—' And for once Sharp had the grace to hold her tongue.

She would never have made it to the last three. Mollandra knew what Sharp had been about to say, and was grateful that she had not said it.

'I'll take first watch tonight.' Tmanga settled on Einsa's bed.

Mollandra shook her head. 'It's not like I'll be sleeping.'

Tmanga shrugged, running her fingers down the pink scar that jagged across her brown cheek. Mollandra had thought them all fractured but, wherever her fault lines ran, Tmanga alone kept them totally hidden, as if her scar stood in for all of them, a visible representation of what must run through her soul. 'Asleep or awake, I know you won't be watching.'

And so Mollandra surrendered to her pillow and lay in the stillness and the quiet. Later there would be screams. No night went by without the nightmares calling on at least one girl. After the coffins it would surely be more than one.

Einsa filled the blindness of Mollandra's closed eyes. Einsa floating. Einsa scowling. Einsa frowning at Mollandra's weakness. Einsa's rough smile. This last one fastened Mollandra's jaw, so tight that her teeth hurt, and the muscles sang, but at least it kept the larger pain at bay, stopped it bursting from her throat. Finally Bek came, standing by Einsa's side as Einsa wrung the wetness from her hair. Her presence made Mollandra feel both better and worse. Happy for the comfort Bek offered their friend. Sad for the full scope of her loss being on display.

Until that first night under the Academy's roof Mollandra had believed her life to be a worthless one. She hadn't expected any recognition from Bek, nor that the girl would offer her sanctuary. But despite all that Mollandra had done, Bek had seen her and called her to her side. Einsa she had not trusted at all. Mollandra had expected cruel tricks from the others, ploys to lower her guard, as a prelude to murder in the dark. But somehow Bek's open smile and Einsa's gruff disapproval had made her hope.

It had been the fear that she was right, and that this miracle, this thrill of feeling, was real, that had been the spur that set her to the murder of Lucia. Mollandra had murdered her to put Bek's mind at rest, to keep her safe, even if only for a short time.

Mollandra hadn't even considered killing an instructor until Bek died. Whether she would have added Akki to her list after today's events if Treecie hadn't worked her act of sabotage, she couldn't say, but for now Treecie was the one who would have to pay. Mollandra didn't know if it would stop the hurting that she still so poorly understood, but if it did, even a little, then the killing wouldn't stop with Treecie.

Mollandra sat up suddenly, causing the girls in the nearest half dozen beds to reach reflexively for their knives. 'I'm going to have to kill them all . . .'

Sharp snorted from the bed behind her. 'Welcome to my world.'

Treecie's chosen ground was the Bone Garden. Her weapons: whatever could be improvised on the spot. Her reasoning was clear. Mollandra would destroy her with sword or knife. Barehanded, Treecie's height and reach should give her an advantage, but nobody expected Mollandra to lose that fight either. The reason for the choice was not, however, that Treecie would feel much more confident clubbing Mollandra with a thighbone. It was that the Bone Garden was such dangerous ground that it evened many odds, and that while Mollandra had shown little talent for necromancy, Treecie was second only to Bek and to pale little Brooth when it came to interacting with the dead.

For Treecie's plan to have any chance she would need Kindness Undu's permission. Undu held the key to the Bone Garden and neither acolyte had ever been through those iron gates. The third years had been given necromancy sessions in the hand-hewn cavern before the gates on several occasions. Here, Undu said, they were close enough to gain some benefits while avoiding the many risks of entering the catacombs beyond, though why Undu would talk of risks in an academy that regularly tried to kill its pupils, Mollandra didn't know. Perhaps she just liked to have more control in the nature and timing of their deaths.

Mollandra had both hoped and expected that Kindness Undu would refuse their request out of hand. Killing Treecie more easily and more publicly would please Mollandra better. But against the odds the Kindness had favoured both girls with a measured stare from the black and deep-set stones of her eyes, then smiled one of her rare, unnerving smiles. 'If that's your choice, dears.'

And so, instead of eating the midday meal, the majority of the third year followed Kindness Undu and the clinking of her keys down through the dank corridors and slippery steps that wound into the Academy's depths.

Mollandra came wearing three crow's feathers in her hair. She had found them that morning on the courtyard steps where she and Bek and Einsa had sat so often, watching their classmates – their competitors – enjoying the truce that held beneath the open sky. There had been good moments amongst all the fear and death and dying. Sunny days when Einsa had made them laugh. Mollandra wore two of the black feathers for the deaths of her friends. And one for her own death which, whether it came soon or late, she would meet with a snarl and a fight to the bitterest end.

The stink of the Garden built slowly, then rapidly, until it became a choking attack on the nose, throat, and lungs. Trips to the Bone Garden were never taken on a full stomach. While the vast majority of the over ten thousand girls to have been carried down to the catacombs were now, as the name implied, mere bones and grinning skulls, there was inevitably a constant flow of 'fresh meat' that rotted there. Any girl whose family had not requested that their remains be repatriated through the lichgate was taken to the catacombs.

No effort was made to disguise the stench. Mollandra had smelled it on her first day and lived with it for years. Only when she came to the corridor leading to the final chamber did it start to bother her. Otherwise, it was simply a constant element of her life. She breathed death in every day.

'She'll be in there already,' Sharp said, elaborating as if the idea wouldn't have haunted Mollandra all night. 'Einsa. Unless Undu's kept her for one of her experiments. She's always after the right ingred—'

'She knows.' Tmanga put her hand on Sharp's shoulder, silencing her. Anyone else would have lost fingers. One day Tmanga might too.

'I've heard things,' said Thurli, keeping her voice low. Mollandra had time for Thurli's opinions. The girl was solid in her thinking, matching her solid body and iron resolve. She'd had a bad leg that had almost killed her, but she'd survived despite the instructors' indifference.

'Have you now?' Sharp laughed, her eyes challenging the broad-shouldered acolyte.

The tow-headed girl ran a hand through the short crop of her hair, eyes hardening as she met Sharp's gaze before returning her attention to Mollandra. 'From that sixth year who's sweet on me.'

Sharp snorted. Sharp was sweet on Thurli too, and other girls besides, though it never stopped her picking fights.

'She says the Garden gets closer and closer to the shadow lands as you go further back. Might even find your way there, she says. At least, that's what the sixth years think: it must touch or else how do the monsters get in? But,' she raised a hand to forestall Sharp's interjection, 'what kills you before you ever see a monster is the fear. It'll cripple most before they reach the third chamber. It's only the true necromancers who can abide it. They say it's ghosts. Touching you and such . . .' She trailed off, looking earnest, embarrassed, and worried all at the same time. 'Good luck, Mollandra. If she did screw Einsa over, you rip her heart out. Einsa was . . .'

'She was good,' Tmanga said, surprising Mollandra. 'Too good for this place, but she never understood it.'

As they wound down yet more steps, Brooth caught up with Mollandra to offer her own advice. Mollandra liked the girl. She seemed too compassionate to have lasted this long in the Academy, but she had hard edges too and was good at most things, dealing with the dead especially. She was also the prettiest of all the year according to Sharp who would usually intercept her if she approached Mollandra, which rather limited their conversations.

'I made this for you.' Brooth pressed something into Mollandra's palm.

'Thanks . . .' Mollandra glanced down. 'A . . . tooth?' A large human tooth with a long root, all of it a strange, almost metallic, grey.

'For the fear,' Brooth whispered and let Mollandra walk on.

They reached the cavern and Undu walked to the gates with Treecie and Mollandra at her heels. Treecie had the twitchy look she got when she was scared, but there was a fluid anger beneath it, the same anger that had kept her alive where so many others, seemingly better suited to survival, had fallen. She was, Mollandra sensed, a fellow weed, harder to kill than she should be. After all, her family were rich. What were nine bronze marks to her father? They'd sold her because they'd understood the wrongness in her. Wanted it out of their lives.

On the gates, wrought into the iron, were the words 'Stop, this is the empire of the dead'. Something about them fascinated the eye, imprinting that command upon the mind.

Undu produced the largest key from her ring, something heavy and black like the iron of the gates, an object of suitable gravitas for what the acolytes said was a path to any hell you chose.

'Ready?' Undu squinted her doubt at them.

Mollandra eyed the keyhole and imagined Einsa's last drowning struggle with a different lock, one that Treecie must have sabotaged. 'I'm ready.'

'I didn't do anything,' Treecie said. 'It's not my fault she drowned. I didn't lock her in the box.'

Part of Mollandra believed the girl. Part of her didn't care. If Sharp and Tmanga were going to wear the robes of a Kindness at Mollandra's side then Treecie had to die. All the rest of them did. Even so, she would have left it to the Academy to make an end of them if doing so weren't to say that Einsa failed on her own. 'You jammed the mechanism and you're going to pay for it.'

Treecie's look of fearful apology turned into a snarl in an instant. 'You'll die in there.' She nodded to the darkness beyond the gates that Undu was even now drawing open. 'You haven't got a drop of necromancy in you. The terror will eat you alive. You'll die screaming.'

Mollandra shrugged. 'I'll tell you a secret, Treecie. There's something that makes me different from you. From all of them.' She nodded back to the rest of the class, watching with pale faces and wide eyes.

Treecie pretended to ignore Mollandra but she flinched as the gates clanged back against the walls.

Mollandra spoke softly, just for the two of them. 'All of the others were sold here, like you were. I wasn't.' She drew in a long, slow breath. 'I asked to come.'

CHAPTER 19
Mollandra

Year Three

The first chamber beyond the gates had been hand-hewn from the bedrock like the one before it, but towards the rear the mouths of natural tunnels yawned, carved by the stream in times when it must have been a river and run a different course.

Undu had given them each an oil lantern and had let Treecie go ahead. The girl had hurried off into the leftmost tunnel, the lantern light painting a glowing ring on the rock around her until she disappeared past the bend.

'Off you go.' Undu nodded to Mollandra. As the challenged party Treecie got to choose her ground, so Undu had let her run off to find it.

Mollandra eyed the options, glanced back at the watching acolytes, then set off after her quarry at an unhurried pace. She held her lantern ahead of her and the smoke helped with the rotting stench of the place.

The first thrill of fear ran through her as she entered the tunnel. Mollandra knew it as something external, like cold. Some of the girls had noted early on how Mollandra never seemed scared by the horrors that the Kindnesses heaped on the class. All of them had calluses on their souls now, those who had survived nearly three years of the Academy. But Mollandra had arrived pre-numbed to violence and abuse. It wasn't that she was immune to terror, just that for her it tended to spring from different sources than those of her fellow acolytes.

To be wholly without fear was to lack imagination, and imagination – though a two-edged sword – was important for survival. Mollandra had plenty of imagination. Right now she wished she had considerably less. The fear that wafted over her set her shortest hairs on end and tightened her stomach into a knot. It was sourceless and primal. As if the raw emotion had been bottled like one of Instructor Jane's poisons, creating the need to flee without any attending reason. Mollandra clenched her teeth and walked on, trying to focus on what lay directly ahead in case of ambush, and also to prevent her mind racing off to invent its own stories to justify her pounding heart and cold sweat.

The tunnel twisted in its descent, often so narrow that Mollandra could almost have touched both walls at once, the ceiling low enough that in places someone tall would have to stoop. Mollandra trod the hardpacked dirt and navigated the water-smoothed rocks jutting through the grime. Smoke had darkened the walls and roof. Generations of instructors had carried the Academy's waste product along this route, an almost daily pilgrimage.

When the tunnel finally opened onto the next chamber, Mollandra stopped in her tracks. Without knowing how, she was sure that the dark ahead of her concealed some vast space that the meagre light of her lantern couldn't touch. The walls to either side lay thick with flowstone, stone teeth descending like the wax dribbles below the candles in the altar shrine. Shelves had been carved into the rock, arcing away into the blackness, and scores of skulls watched her, their empty eye sockets angled towards the entrance.

Mollandra descended the steep slope to the floor of the cavern and found herself walking on bones, a field of them stretching beyond the circle of her vision. They clacked and shifted beneath her boots, soiled by the passage of many feet. She saw arm bones, leg bones, ribs. Whether the carpet was inches deep or yards she couldn't tell, but it lay even and undisturbed by rocky protrusions.

She paused, unsure of the way. Treecie would no doubt find her eventually, but Mollandra didn't want to give the girl any more time to prepare than she had to. With eyes closed, she turned slowly. Completing her revolution, she took the direction she least wanted to go in, letting her fear guide her. If something terrible was lurking out there, better to face it head on than to let it stalk her.

Treecie had said that the catacombs would do the work for her. This place, she'd said, would kill Mollandra. So, it made sense that she would have gone as far in as she dared, challenging Mollandra to follow.

It took a hundred yards before a wall loomed out of the darkness to intercept Mollandra's light. Bones had shifted beneath her feet all that way. Acres wide and of unknown depth, a garden of misery grown from the suffering of those who lived above it.

Mollandra followed the wall and came quickly to the mouth of another tunnel, this one even narrower than the first. She patted for the hilt of her knife out of habit, finding it gone. Neither of them had brought any weapon save themselves. Mollandra shivered as she entered the tunnel, hugging one arm across her chest. Another waft of external fear encompassed her, filling her with the need to run but still supplying no reason.

Undu and the older acolytes worked necromancy in these halls, but without their presence to part the veils to the netherworld the dead would lie still. Mollandra had already seen corpses walk. It wasn't the worst thing she'd seen. She sniffed, spat the foulness from her mouth, and followed the passage.

The next chamber was smaller, but shelves had been carved everywhere, and skulls lined every inch. To fight off the tendrils of fear seeking to find a way under her skin Mollandra began to talk to herself.

'Yes, I feel watched. All right.' She eyed the skulls critically, challenging their hollow stares. 'Truthfully, I expected more from the catacombs . . . but I guess this sort of thing is the only option really. Someone got told to store a million old bones down here, not to create art . . .'

Her defiance sounded thin in the cave's cold void, but it made her feel better even so. Here and there, lines of the Creed had been carved into the shelves beneath the skulls. Much of it was the boring formal lore, the detailed accounting of revenge and the scales of the wergild in which some measure of it might be balanced by blood gold. But there were also more apocalyptic lines that echoed the fury of the Kindly Ones and of their avatars who walked in the robes of the Kindnesses.

'*The world must turn its gaze from this, for my vengeance is not for mortal eyes.*' Mollandra's fingers read the legends. '*Justice must be crueller than the crime.*' She moved on, passing by one exit only to return to it when the next felt less threatening. The passage led steeply down, perilously slippery at points. Mollandra tried to imagine making the trip carrying a fresh corpse. The grime underfoot suggested that was exactly what the Kindnesses and their helpers did.

'Perhaps Undu stands the dead up and makes them walk ahead of her . . .'

Mollandra had heard that in the distant chambers, the places where it was hard to say whether you were still in the living world, and where monsters from the outer dark wandered, there were treasures to be found. Not gold and gems or books or ancient lore, but the kind of treasures necromancers crave: a drop of blood from a dead god, small enough to fit a hand but heavier than a man, a tooth from the maw of a hellhound, still too hot to hold, or perhaps an angel's feather, razor edged and white as bone or blacker than death.

In the third chamber the terror hit her in the chest as soon as she stepped from the passage. The breath left her lungs along with the strength from her legs. She found her traitor body turning to run without instruction and stopped it by gripping the wall.

With her back to the chamber now, the certainty that something worse than she could imagine stood behind her was overwhelming. She thrust a hand into the pocket where she'd put Brooth's gift. She gripped the tooth so hard that it bit into her palm. Together with her anger it was enough to allow her to turn around. Nothing but the darkness greeted her. What she could see of the cavern floor was paved and even, and empty save for a sparse scattering of bones, a shoulder blade here, the small bones of a hand or foot there. As she advanced, pushing back the shadows and letting them close in behind her, a lone skull revealed itself, lying on its side, missing teeth.

Somehow the emptiness of the chamber felt more threatening than the hundreds of skulls of the previous cave. Mollandra pressed on, feeling that her small circle of illumination was constricting a finger's breadth with every step.

The paved floor gave way to raw rock at the rear of the chamber and a sinkhole close to the wall appeared to be the only exit. This time Mollandra might have chosen a less frightening alternative had there been one. Her hands had gone white and tingled with pins and needles. Her breath came in short, panting gasps no matter how she tried to slow it, and her heart beat out a rapid tempo that her feet longed to match in a sprint to freedom.

Flowstone coated the sinkhole's slick gullet and Mollandra was far from confident that she could climb back out if she went down. Doubts started to assail her. A weasel like Treecie wouldn't have had the guts to go this way. Maybe the sinkhole just led to some drowning pool. She hadn't come this far to drown like Einsa did only with much less excuse.

'Blood and shit.' Mollandra scratched her nails slowly from cheekbone to throat, using the pain to focus her. She returned to the skull, snagged it through an eye socket, then took it to the hole. She dropped it and the darkness gobbled it up. The rapid clattering of bone on rock terminated without a splash. Mollandra got to her knees and backed in, feet searching for support as her hands tried to grip the stony floor.

More natural caves followed, strewn haphazardly with bones, skulls perched wherever the processes that carved the chambers left any opportunity. The sense of dread built steadily but without any sudden shocks to the system.

Two hundred yards on and maybe fifty deeper, the biggest chamber yet waited, lit by a pale glow that revealed a cathedral-like architecture wrought by water and time, flowstone teeth meeting in columns, vaguely organic and coloured by faint sheens like the wings of ghostly butterflies.

A band across the centre had been levelled and paved, dividing the chamber like a boundary that Mollandra would have to cross in order to reach the passages leading from the far side. She approached slowly, burdened by the doom that haunted the space all around her, unseen but certain. She could see no source for the light, and it made her eyes ache.

Drawing closer, she could see that vast numbers of small bones had been used to mark out complex patterns, including several large circles surrounded by symbols spelled out in the frail white bones of children's fingers.

Although the skulls were beyond sight now, Mollandra could feel their gaze upon her, the weight of their judgement suddenly a physical thing. She had broken the old lore on the very doorstep of the Academy on the day that she joined it. To kill one's parents — there was no higher crime upon the Kindnesses' lists. And she had taken their coins while her father's corpse cooled by the roadside. She had been marked for failure since that day. And now the reckoning was here. She would never leave this place.

As she set foot on the boundary Mollandra fell to her hands and knees. Everything that had come before was as nothing to this. She gripped the tooth in her pocket, and it burned fiercely cold. Drool hung from her panting lips as she fought to resist. Before, she'd battled the urge to run, but here the chance to run felt long gone. Here if she failed to eject this consuming nightmare from her mind, it would kill her. Her heart would beat itself into oblivion.

'It's . . . just . . .' she spat and crawled one pace forward then another '. . . monsters . . .'

Tooth and claw, blade and skull, rot and horror — she had seen these things before. Death and the threat of death were no strangers to her or any acolyte. Whatever terrors stalked these caverns, be they of this world or any other, the instructors had worse waiting for her upstairs.

Another forward yard, about to pass between two of the bone circles. Without warning, the oldest and foulest of Mollandra's memories invaded her, knocking aside the walls that cracked only in the depths of her worst nightmares. She fell on her side, curling in on herself to make a smaller target, but finding no respite. This torture employed all the fears that were integral to the foundations of who she was.

At last, among all the many challenges of the Academy, Mollandra had met her match. She lay paralysed, unable to defeat herself, rigid with emotions that had surpassed fear and were driving her body beyond its limits. Memory strangled her. She was, once more, the tiny child hiding despite the inevitability of being found, the little girl pressing back into cupboards in rigid, unbreathing, desperate silence wanting only to be saved and never once believing salvation existed.

In this place of ghosts Bek and Einsa came not as spirits but as simple memory. A glimpse of their faces, their rare smiles breaking through the choking clouds of past and ever-present horror.

Mollandra sucked in a convulsive breath. Neither Bek nor Einsa had ever known that they had saved her, albeit far too late. Neither knew that what they offered, what they didn't even consider kindness, let alone love, had been to her the key to the locked box of her life, a glimpse at another kind of world she hadn't known existed.

A clenched hand opened. Sore eyes unscrewed and regarded the darkness. Mollandra thought of what had been taken from her, and by whom, and slowly, agonizingly slowly, converted the fear that had infected her back into the anger it had been.

She finished the crossing of the boundary on two feet, kicking aside the patterned bones without caring what harm might come.

The next cave marked the limit of Treecie's bravery. The constant foulness of the air reached a new level in the tunnel leading down to the chamber. Breathing became difficult and Mollandra decorated the stones with the part-digested remains of her breakfast. The atmosphere felt physically thicker.

At first Mollandra saw only Treecie, standing on the slime-slick rocks at the edge of a sickly green lake that stretched beyond the light of their lanterns. The girl watched her with pale resolve, hands empty. Mollandra, realizing that she should have picked up a weapon, even if only a loose rock or sharpened bone, began circling away to the left, following the wall.

She saw first one body, and while fighting the urge to retch again, saw another, then another, and understood that an unbroken mass of decomposing corpses lay on the cold stone, one overlapping the next. Each had been stripped of their acolytes' robes, and Mollandra stifled a hysterical laugh at the realization this must have been done in the name of economy. Heaven forfend the Academy should waste anything other than young lives . . .

Bodies lay in every stage of the journey from flesh and bone to just bone. Mollandra lowered her lantern before she had a chance to see whether or not one of them was Einsa, but not before she discerned that the slope of the rock shelf was sufficient to deliver the products of putrefaction into the water. It was even possible that the water wasn't water at all.

A faint splash turned Mollandra's head. Treecie had set her lantern down and stepped backwards into the lake. She stood almost to her knees in the foul brew, her robes floating around her.

'Look at what they've done to us . . .' Mollandra said. 'Look at what they make us do.'

The same hysterical laugh that Mollandra had kept in broke free from Treecie, half of it wild terror.

In that moment Mollandra would have turned and left, swearing never to kill again save in self-defence. She would have let the Academy deliver any justice Treecie deserved, and that only if it could manage to do so before Mollandra managed to burn it down.

But Treecie retreated another step, the cold slime reaching her waist, and as she raised her hands the dead girls at the edges of the heap began to stir. Mollandra could see the shadows heaving at the periphery of the lanterns' illumination. Soft, wet sounds accompanied the motion.

She could have run and let Treecie hunt her. Perhaps the girl's control would weaken as she left the chamber. But Mollandra hadn't given chase only to run away. Empty-handed she followed Treecie into the pool.

Beneath the watery foulness and its floating fats the rocks descended in uneven steps, causing Mollandra to throw out her arms to keep herself from stumbling. Treecie, going backwards, had a tougher time of it and fell away with a strangled cry.

By the time she rose from her floundering panic the girl was shoulder-deep, her hair plastered across her forehead, gobbets of rot rolling down her cheeks.

Behind Mollandra, splashes announced the arrival of the first corpse. Rather than face the horrors animated by the rage that Treecie had returned to sour flesh, Mollandra threw herself at the focus of her own anger. She fastened both hands around Treecie's scrawny neck.

As Mollandra dug her thumbs into the softness of the girl's throat Treecie's fingernails sought her eyes. Mollandra ducked her head and as Treecie tried to pull away, both of them went under.

Refusing panic, Mollandra clung on, knowing she had the advantage even if neither of them could breathe now. She tightened her grip and kept her mouth and eyes screwed shut.

When Treecie went limp Mollandra knew it was too early and held fast, imagining that desperation had driven the girl to try such weak deception.

Only when the hands closed on her arms and fingers tangled in her hair did Mollandra understand where Treecie's concentration had been aimed.

The inexorable strength of the dead pulled Mollandra's arms free. Sheer blind luck allowed her to surface, though the dead might not have reached them so easily if the fight had taken them out of their depth. Mollandra snatched a lungful of the foul air, blinking away slime. Two rotting husks held her, with others crowding in behind. All of them must have been acolytes she'd shared her life with. Even if they were from other years she would have passed them in the corridors, broken bread beneath the same roof at mealtimes. They were too far gone for recognition though, turned into nightmares by soft decay.

Mollandra fought, but the dead wrapped her in their rotting arms and, slippery as she was, she found herself trapped. Where with a living foe she might break a finger, gouge an eye, or stamp on feet and let the pain create an opening, the dead had no concern for any hurt she might do them. She expected to feel their teeth at any moment, but unlike Lucia, who had woken from death's sleep with an appetite, these acolytes seemed less eager to devour her. The stray thought that she might already have seen Lucia's skull rolled across the furious storm of Mollandra's thinking. The girl's bones might have spelled out one of the symbols she'd kicked apart.

'Bitch!' Treecie surfaced, choking and spitting.

Mollandra startled despite herself.

Treecie turned this way and that for a moment, caught in distress and disgust, swinging at the air then wiping at her eyes. As she calmed, a smile found its way onto the girl's dripping face. 'Going to kill me, were you?' The words emerged in a hoarse croaking mockery of her usual voice.

Mollandra stopped struggling, hoping her captors might relax, allowing her to jerk free. 'I gave it a try.'

Treecie stumbled into shallower waters, her shoulders emerging from the filth. The smile stayed in place but the anger in her eyes made a lie of it. 'Me! You were going to kill—'

'Get it over with.' One way or another Mollandra wanted to finish this fast.

'If you begged a little, I might let you go.' Treecie advanced another step, smoothing the stinking liquid from her hair.

'Begging wouldn't have saved you.' Mollandra flexed slightly but the many hands on her maintained their painfully tight grip.

'I did it, you know?' Treecie said. 'You were right. I jammed the lock full of dirt. Why not? It's not like we have rules.' She showed her teeth in a white line as if *she* were the one most likely to want a mouthful of Mollandra's flesh. 'I could have them hold you under so you could know how it was for her at the end. But I want to see you die. And besides . . .' she rubbed at her throat, wincing '. . . the old lore says an eye for an eye.'

Dead fingers clamped around Mollandra's neck, sealing away her air.

Mollandra fought, knowing that to conserve her resources would only draw out the inevitable, and if she could unbalance her captors some chance might present itself.

It did not.

Her vision began to vanish behind a crowding blackness. She stopped being able to feel her limbs, let alone fight.

Undu had often said that the connection to the shadow realms was strongest the closer a necromancer was to it. And this could be by physically approaching death's outer regions through such places as the Bone Garden, but more simply by being personally closer to death, be that through disease, injury, or merely age. Right now, Mollandra knew herself closer to death than she had ever been before.

She stretched her will towards the corpse with its hands about her throat, hoping to break Treecie's control. Undu's lessons in these arts had never meant much to her, rather like Thurli could never master the division of one number by another no matter how Instructor Clakka explained it.

Mollandra experienced something different this time. She felt the dead around her and sensed Treecie's power wrapping them like dark, pulsing vines. Against the black flame of Treecie's necromancy her own felt feeble. A child's strength against an adult's.

Even so, with the dying flutters of her heart she was ready to try when visions of Einsa returned, pushing out all sight of the unequal battle she had been about to dive into.

Mollandra, for the only time in her life that she could remember, gave up the fight. Why not spend her last moments in the company of one of the tiny number of people who had shown her any warmth, any true kindness, or charity? She reached instead for her friend.

Something opened Mollandra's eyes and lifted her head on the half-dead muscles of her tortured neck.

Treecie stood, deep in concentration, her face twisted with violent pleasure. A dark shape broke the mottled surface behind her, it loomed above her spilling filthy water. Corruption had not yet laid its hand upon Einsa. She stood as she had in life, though deadly pale.

She wrapped an arm around Treecie's neck, the girl understanding her peril only at the last moment . . . and snapped it with a sharp twist, gifting her the unearned mercy of a swift ending.

Mollandra's sight failed her at that point, and she fell into her own darkness where the lanterns' light could never follow.

CHAPTER 20

Rue

Kindness Undu had stressed that both geographical closeness to the deadlands and physiological closeness to death were important aids to any necromancer, allowing them to perform feats they would not normally be capable of.

She had often spoken about the importance of physical proximity to the corpse or corpses when seeking to work the black arts upon them. Her remarks on the help that emotional ties to the dead individual might provide were brief. Rue had come to believe that this was through lack of personal experience. The Academy had never encouraged having many friends. They were discouraged in the early years for obvious reasons. And Undu in particular was perhaps still, of all the people Rue had encountered in a long life, the individual she had the hardest time imagining having warm feelings for another.

The fight with Treecie long ago when they had both been children, one of them fated to never be anything else, had opened Rue's eyes to this unsung power. Einsa's corpse had risen in response to Rue's unconscious will, and full of far more than just her friend's anger, it had made an end of Treecie, saving Rue. The control exercised had, even with Rue's weak necromancy, far exceeded that of her more talented opponent.

This one fact presented any necromancer with a horrible paradox. The bodies that they least wanted to desecrate were in fact the ones they could most easily make dance to their tune. The same held true with ghosts, though in a less gruesome manner. Anyone, even those without necromantic training, might see a phantom under the right circumstances, but the spirit that haunts them is much more likely to be that of a loved one than a stranger.

Rue's own ghosts had haunted her down the years, wandering into many empty moments, painting themselves into the shadows, stealing whole dreams. But they rarely spoke, and then never more than two or three words.

Here by the bank of the last river anyone ever crosses, Bek and Einsa were no longer spectres struggling to be seen. She could speak to them, even touch them, though that was still unsettling, as if their flesh – though no longer the wispy suggestion of a phantom – was still a matter of opinion, warm when the good times were remembered, cold when she recalled their deaths, and edging towards something worse if she lingered on thoughts of how long they had lain in the catacombs.

For the longest time Rue could only weep before them. Crying for her failures and her failure to grieve them. Weeping both for letting them go, and for what she had become, how she had betrayed their memories while still in acolyte's robes, and for what the years had wrought of her thereafter. Though neither saw anything but the girl she had been, Rue still wore the years she'd wrapped herself within, and the shame of uncountable deeds that lay beneath her friends' opinion of her.

As she tried to gather herself, tried to think what words she might possibly say that could cross the gulf of decades between them, the world seemed to jolt. Although the river kept flowing within its banks and the starkly dead bushes didn't so much as shiver, Rue was thrown to the ground. She felt it again, a lurch within her.

'They're trying to wake you up,' Bek said.

'Get you back.' Einsa nodded. 'So they can hurt you and find out what you know. Mostly it's for the hurting though.'

'W-what should I do?' Suddenly, instead of one of the oldest Kindnesses in existence, Rue felt as if she were that little girl on her first day at the Academy again, not worried by her surroundings so much as by the opinions of those around her. She had wanted to find something better then, and still that hope was in her. Despite all she knew about the shadow lands, some small part of her still clung to the idea that on the far shore, out beyond sight and every other sense, something good might wait for everyone.

'You're a Kindness, Molly.' Einsa fixed her with dark eyes, water still trickling down from soaked hair.

'You saw that?' Rue felt almost shy. Within the circle of her friends she was a child again.

'We saw.' Bek nodded. She raised a hand as Rue opened her mouth. 'You did what you had to do.'

'I didn't have to—'

'We follow our fate,' Bek said. 'You can't have sought us out, here by the river, expecting to be judged.' She put her arm around Rue's still-trembling shoulders. 'We're not here for that.'

Another jolt nearly returned her to the ground and shook the question from her again. 'What should I do?'

'You're a shadow cast by the three who punish the hubris of the gods themselves. What do you think you should do?'

'Go back.'

'Hells yes!' Einsa smacked fist into palm.

'Or stay,' Bek said. 'If you go back, make it be for you, not them.'

'But wait for your moment,' Einsa said.

'You waited in that coffin, when we told you to.' Rue could hardly get the words out as guilt wrapped its hands around her throat. 'And it killed you. We killed you.'

'It wasn't until I took the picks out and pushed the panic away that the water could flow through the lock and clean it out.' Einsa smiled a smile that seemed impossible given her memories. 'I almost made it. Because I waited my moment.'

'Almost . . .'

Rue opened her eyes. The man who had slapped her wasn't paying any attention, but she still hung from a hook on the wall by bound arms she could no longer feel. Gressa and one of her lieutenants were still studying the maps on the table. Sebrin Weaver's head lay on its side away from the charts, eyes vacant. The rest of the mercenaries were out of sight. The smell of smoke hung in the air, though the hearth lay cold.

The parts of Rue that she could still feel mostly hurt. Her mouth especially, where she'd lost teeth earlier in the day. Returning from oblivion immediately seemed even more stupid than it had before she left the black river and the comfort of her friends' company. It had been Bek and Einsa who returned her to her body. Not what they said, simply the desire to be seen as good in their eyes. And if not good, then at least strong.

It should perhaps have been a desire for vengeance or for justice. Rue had known Jayne and Ambeth who died in Stones Corner on the previous evening far longer than she had known Bek or Einsa. But they had met as old women and, though it seemed sad to say, the first friendships of young girls burned so much brighter than the companionship between those who had seen the decades flow by. The latter was a comfortable thing, a slow delight. The former something painful, thrilling, wonderful, and imperative, all at once.

Rue's instinct was to speak, to accuse the man of hitting like a child, to dare them to do their worst. But long before Gressa or any of her mercenaries were born Rue had been instructed by a maimed young woman called Akki to wait her moment. And so, although it pained her to act as if she feared her enemy, Rue lowered her head and feigned the unconsciousness she had recently thrown off.

Where that moment would come from, Rue had no idea. Logic said there would be no such opportunity, and that bound, injured, and ancient as she was, only an agonizing death awaited her. One she had been stupid to come back for.

The mercenary, an unreasonably tall man who stood level with Rue though her feet were half a yard off the floor, remembered his task and swung again. His hard hand jerked Rue's face around to the right and through the slits of her eyes she saw something.

'Wait!'

Many captives must have begged Rue's looming tormentor to wait. What stayed his hand was that it wasn't a plea: it was an order from someone who expected to be obeyed.

Rue opened her eyes fully, then squinted, doubting what she saw.

Einsa's ghost frowned back at her, standing close by Gressa and her lieutenant at the map table.

'What are you doing here?' Rue worked her jaw, wincing, then spat out a bloody mess.

'Hey!' The man with the bald head, pale eyes, and hard hand, reached for his anger, trying to reassert himself.

Gressa and her subordinate had both turned to watch, surprise vying with amusement.

'What are *you* doing? That's the real question,' Einsa said.

'Me? I was waiting my chance. Just like Instructor Akki—' Rue snapped her face towards the bald man who had started to raise his hand. 'I. Said. Wait.' She looked back at Einsa. 'Just like Instructor Akki taught us.'

'I taught you a better lesson than that,' Einsa said.

'Did you scramble the old bitch's brain?' Gressa asked the bald man.

'What's she looking at?' The lieutenant was staring at Einsa as if he could see *something*, but not enough to be sure. A fault line in the air perhaps, twisting the light.

'You taught me to check the lock first.' Anger coloured Rue's words. She didn't understand why she was angry with Einsa, but she was.

'I taught you that this' – the ghost moved her hands rapidly in front of her chest, the motion towards Rue indicating some connection – 'works so much better when you love the person.'

'Necromancy?' Rue blinked. 'I didn't—' She bit off the habitual denial. Of course she had loved her friends, and if that was weakness then yes, she Mollandra Plight had been weak.

'Necromancy!' Gressa's amusement dropped away. 'Stop her doing that.'

'I didn't love Tamaster Sams! Wha—'

The hard-handed mercenary's hard hand closed over Rue's mouth.

Einsa's dripping ghost rolled her eyes, looking for a moment like the young girl she was rather than the stern giant Rue remembered. 'You love this place. All the people. Maybe not individually. But as a whole.'

Rue wouldn't have got all of her denial out even if she had been able to speak. It was true, though she'd never admitted it to herself. If she'd admitted it she would have seen it as weakness and felt compelled to do something about it. But she had liked her life. Something she had for many years never imagined was possible. She had enjoyed pottering in her vegetable rows, walking too slowly down the street, passing houses beneath whose roofs little happened that wasn't shared as gossip, watching the village folk craft and weave the necessities of their existence. She had cared for some people more than others. She wondered even now if Soosa Smith had made it to the woods, and how the foolish girl would live in the wilds all by herself. She had liked being someone they knew was solid, whose word they knew was hard-given and hard-kept. She had liked that they knew she had an edge but had no inkling of how many it had cut. She had liked that mothers left their babies in her care, and that they were nervous asking to do so. They knew that she might make them sweat but if the wolf came it'd likely tuck tail and run when Molly Plight turned her scowl its way.

'What was she looking at?' The lieutenant, a beefy man with a sizeable gut and a black beard, was still staring at Einsa, entranced.

Rue felt the dead as if they were candles flickering to life one after the other in some cathedral vault, each a faint star in the consuming void. She would have breathed the words 'so many' had she been able to speak. She would have moved swiftly to anger at their stupidity. How could they be such ignorant peasants? They had so little, was it that hard to leave it behind? Why ... why hadn't they just run away?

The anger would turn towards herself later – she knew that too, though it made no difference now. She understood what had tied them to their homes, their animals, their plots of land, their families.

As she tried to spit and bite at the hand across her mouth, Rue drew the candle flames closer. Their heat burned across her skin. They were flames because the corpses of the villagers were burning in their burning homes.

On the table the eyes in Sebrin Weaver's discarded head suddenly swivelled and found Rue where she hung on the wall.

Rue sought and found Soosa, not ablaze but just as dead, discarded in a ditch after cruelties no less than that of the fire. Rue rejected the girl's fate, cursing behind unclean fingers, watching both the one corpse, and the many. Gressa was approaching now, a gutting blade glimmering in her hand. Rue reached out to the dead, to the ruin of the life she had loved. And as she did so Soosa Smith rejected at least part of what had been imposed upon her too.

Rue sensed them all, those whose names she hardly used, and those whose company she might seek, pretending it to be an accidental wandering. As Soosa stood up, bloodless in the gutter running by Shymon's field, every other corpse in the village stood too, many thick with flames, some shouldering aside burning timbers or shaking off hot embers.

'Stop her!' Baron Mancer shouted silently with Sebrin's cold lips. 'Kill the bitch!'

'What in fuck's name is that?' Gressa turned towards the shuttered windows.

Those among the dead that could howl roared their anger. The others mouthed it, some lipless with blackened teeth between which smoke issued as if the fire had given them kinship with dragonkind.

The first corpse to come crashing through the shutters was on fire. In the main street beyond, Rue could now see what she had only sensed before: in the village's single street a score of mercenaries found themselves assaulted by the peasants they had recently slaughtered. The people of Pye might have been terrified in the moments of their death, but they returned filled with such anger that their flesh could hardly hold their bones. The strength in their smouldering hands tore heads from shoulders and launched men into the blazes they had started. The remains of a young woman staggered beneath an axe blow: then, with the blade buried deep in her chest, she seized the near giant of a mercenary who had swung the weapon. Together with a blackened child she took him to the ground.

'Kill her!' Gressa yelled, now echoing the unheard baron. The hoarseness of pain infected her voice as she wrestled with the burning peasant who'd been first through the window. Her yells rapidly became howls.

The bald man, whose hand had slipped from Rue's mouth as his attention strayed to the screaming corpses breaking through the remaining shutters, had the presence of mind to draw his knife and stab Rue in the chest.

'Gods dammit!' Rue shouted as two peasant women dragged the man down, pulling the blade free. 'That hurt!'

She hung, throbbing with the pain of her wounded lung, as the dead increased their number. Gressa died screaming in the end, her toughness seared away by the flames of the man who burned like a melting candle as he wrapped his arms around her while others sought to tear her flesh from her bones with their teeth.

Rue didn't direct the actions of her servants: there were too many for that. She simply aimed them towards their targets, and even that was probably unnecessary. At last, with the great majority of the mercenaries slain and the rest having run off, the dead's anger abated and they fell to aimless wandering.

The room had filled with smoke and heat, tearing at Rue's eyes, filling her good lung with knife blades of its own.

'Get me to the street.' She coughed a breath out, wheezed another in, instantly regretted it and coughed again.

She had Artur Tanner's corpse lift her from the wall hook and carry her outside before setting her on her feet. She staggered and almost fell, her legs uncertain of their task. Under her direction, Artur, a tall, greying man killed by a single sword thrust through the heart, strode back into the smoke-filled hall, eventually emerging once more with the knife that had been used to stab her.

Rue directed the remainder of the still-smouldering dead to leave the house and focused her attention on other individuals, setting one to beating out the flames that had taken hold among the shattered ruins of the shutters.

Rather than rely on the dead man's jerky knife-work to free her hands, Rue would have preferred to have him hold the blade steady and to have sawed herself free. But her arms hung like pieces of rope, paying no heed to her commands, which she found strange since they were the deadest part of her. With a sigh, she focused on Artur, who was not the tanner that his surname suggested. It was his father and grandfather who had tanned hides, though some claimed the stink still clung to the man decades after his sire and grandsire had quit the business owing to being dead. Right now, however, all anyone in Pye, living or dead, smelled of was smoke. Many other corpses, especially the burned ones, dropped to the ground as Rue shifted the bulk of her attention onto Artur. Although her various wounds hadn't killed her or even slowed her down, each felt deeply wrong, like an unanswered insult or a spider on the skin. She had no wish to have her wrists opened in the act of setting them free.

When her hands came loose, Rue released the dead. Some remained for a few moments, gazing about them as if they might stay of their own volition. Soosa Smith was the last to fall, confused in her mud-smeared beauty, too young to let go of that which she had owned so briefly. She hit the ground like a grain sack and lay vacant in the street. A pain flowered in Rue's chest as if the body hitting the earth had been a punch she had herself sustained. With a snarl she pushed away the image of her own daughters that had intruded into her thoughts, cursed and spat and told herself that the peasants had been nothing to her, just cover. As if the decade she'd passed among them was merely a prolonged mission in which they served as camouflage, and she an actor, simply playing the role of an old woman.

She set her back to Soosa and the others. Her lies offered no comfort. There had been a time when she could fool herself. That time had passed. She wiped at the tears that the smoke had wrung from her – the smoke and nothing else – and stalked back towards the burning house she'd just escaped.

'Gods damn . . .' Her arms were strangers to her, lifting only fractionally when commanded. The thatch smoked and flames had climbed the table where Gressa unfolded her maps. Rue found Isik in the root cellar where they'd left him.

'You were the one I wanted all along.' Rue shuffled to stand beside his head, feeling old once more. She raised her voice. 'I would have let them go.' She doubted Gressa would have heard her above the crackle of flames in Tamaster Sams's 'hall' even if she weren't dead and on fire herself. But it was true. Mass slaughter was never the Kindness's chosen path. It was the Kindness's creed to find the person responsible for the crime's existence, not those following the order to carry it out.

In this case, Rue wasn't sure any grand crime had been commissioned. Wars, for example, were not forbidden. But she was no longer a Kindness, and this was personal. Despite this, she would follow her old methods. Even with the Morrigan's gift, Rue was never going to be able to knife to death every mercenary in the Southfold Margins, and doing so would offer no justice. Baron Mancer had paid this company to slaughter their way across the lowlands. Rue wanted to know more. The 'why' was of interest but the 'where' was paramount.

She decided to take a page from Gressa's playbook. It took five blows to decapitate Isik, but Rue's arms had largely woken up by the time his head rolled free. She carried the head away from the heat of the burning house and set it on the Round Stone by the gate to Sarah's Field. The locals said giants had left the round stones scattered across the 'fold. The giant children had tossed them like Pye's children tossed bobstones. At the Academy Rue had been told a great sheet of ice had smoothed them as it flowed across the land and left them stranded when it finally melted. Both stories were hard to believe.

She positioned Isik's head on the rock, and dark rivulets of blood oozed sluggishly over the curving stone. He looked to be asleep. One of his braver comrades must have closed his eyes a second time before they threw him in the cellar.

'Isik.' Rue flicked the man's forehead, no enchanted bone required, but then she wasn't planning to talk to people far away. 'Wake up, Isik!'

His eyes opened and his lips curled in a voiceless snarl.

'Answer my questions and I'll let you go.' She made it seem like a choice. The answers would be less slippery if she didn't have to squeeze too hard to get them out of him. The dead couldn't refuse to reply, and she would be able to get the truth from most, but a strong will might defy her or twist out a half-lie.

Dead eyes fixed on her, a growing spark of recognition amid the hate that filled them.

First a question she knew the answer to. 'Who hired the Iron League?'

'Mancer's woman.' Isik didn't need lungs to reply, and she didn't need ears to hear him.

'Woman?' She supposed the baron would have had his agents make the deal rather than lower himself to such negotiations. 'Why does the baron want villages burned?'

'What's it to you, you old bitch?' Isik had more bite to him than most dead men. The dead didn't tend to ask questions.

Rue squeezed and Isik howled in silent pain. Starlings in Mako's field took flight, hundreds of them rising from the furrowed ground.

'They're his.' Isik narrowed his eyes. 'He can have them burned if he has the notion.'

'His?' This was new. 'Ain't it some duke that's got dominion over the Westfold?' Rue reached for the man's name. She doubted he or any of his forebears had been out as far as Pye in generations. 'Cataract?'

'Duke Cataras.' Rue could almost hear the sniff of contempt Isik would have made had his lungs not been left thirty yards away. 'You peasants don't—'

'So it's Mancer now . . .' Rue nodded. It wasn't as if anyone in Pye had cared much what happened in Chaim City. 'Why would he do this?' She glanced around at the burning homes, the corpses, the drifting smoke. Pye, Stones Corner, more beside most likely. They were his villages, held in the emperor's name. Goods and taxes flowed his way. Slowly of course from so poor a region, but many villages paying taxes for many years might buy the man a new hat or two. 'Why burn them?'

'I don't know.'

But Rue knew enough about speaking to the dead to press the point. 'You might not know but you would have had suspicions. You weren't an idiot, Isik. Well not completely . . . You did let me cut your throat though.' She lifted his head by the salt and pepper grease of his hair. 'Why do you think he wanted them burned?'

'To start a war.'

CHAPTER 21
Mollandra

Year Four

It was said by the people of Tandra-ah, the city whose spires could be seen from the heights of the Academy, and whose walls had once encircled Mollandra's life just as completely as those of her new home, that the three towers of the Academy each housed a single Kindness. In truth, Kindnesses Marta, Terra, and Undu slept in rooms within the main body of the fort. Wealth was not a promise that the Academy made to its pupils or teachers, nor was power really, for although the Kindnesses had the ability to accomplish many things and to wield great influence, this was not their purpose. Instead, they were agents of chaos or fate or revenge, depending on what angle you chose to view their activity from.

The greatest promise made to the acolytes was that were they to survive their education, they would be free, free to interpret the will of the triple-goddess, free to be judge, jury, and executioner. The only restraints upon them would be those of their fellow Kindnesses – a conclave of equals.

The Kindnesses claimed a kind of divine guidance from their patrons, or perhaps patron, for the Furies took many forms and sometimes the three were one. Sometimes they were Alecto,

Tisiphone, and Megaera, but in other shrines they were the arbiters of fate, waiting by the foot of Yggdrasil weaving the fates of mankind, Urd holding the threads of the past, Verdandi clutching those of the present, and Skuld, holding tight to many futures. In the north they spoke of the Grey Sisters, a trio sharing a single eye, a single tooth, and many secrets. The travelling folk carried the sign of the Morrigan and their heroes held her as both bane and benevolence. She of the crow and the wolf and the three who are one, Macha, Badb, and Nemain whose scream could make armies flee the field.

The Furies bore many other names, other guises, and among them all lay a common core of belief from which power might be drawn. This many, this multiplicity, sprang from the ancients who had fled across the sea in their great armada. Those who had beached themselves on the great islands of Gog and Magog were not a single people. They had hailed from more cultures and creeds than there were ships in their fleet. A multitude united by fear and divided by every other measure. But they all knew about guilt and carried with them belief in some or other avatar. Even the followers of the cross had angels and demons who between them judged and punished sin.

The Kindnesses, they said, could see guilt, smell it, follow its trail across trackless paths and even the storm-tossed sea. Whether that was true or not, and what guilt Kindness Marta might see in the children who suffered beneath her tutelage, Mollandra couldn't say. Perhaps, if she lived long enough, she would learn the truth of it.

The eastmost tower where Mollandra, Sharp, and Tmanga came for their war meetings in the fourth year housed only a single bronze bell, far taller than the tallest acolyte and streaked with the green of verdigris and the white of bird shit. The confection of perforated stone that veiled the bell from the city's eyes did little to stop the rain and even a full-grown crow could, and did, find its way through in places when it had a mind to join a murder.

Ravens, Sharp had said, would not be welcome, for a gathering of ravens was an unkindness and that could hardly be tolerated at the Academy of Kindness. Mollandra, who had never before heard Sharp attempt any humour that was not aimed, blade-like, at someone, was so surprised that after preventing herself from falling down the narrow spiral of stairs that had brought them to the belfry, she said so.

'Was that your first joke?'

'Fuck you,' Sharp said, comfortably, continuing to hone the blade of her knife.

'Bek told it to her,' Tmanga said without looking up from the scroll in her lap.

'When did Sharp ever talk to Bek?' Mollandra asked, genuinely surprised.

'All you ever see is a part of someone's life, even when we live in each other's pockets like we do here.' At this point Tmanga did lift her black eyes from the writing that had fascinated them. 'Don't confuse your handful for the whole.'

'Why are we here again?' Sharp reached out with her foot and used the strength of her leg to impart the slightest motion to the great bell. It would take a lot more than that to set it tolling. A sound they had all heard at least three times. The bell was rung at high summer when the three newest Kindnesses left the Academy's gates, never to return, unless as a replacement for one of the resident trio.

'We always meet when the class shrinks.' Tmanga returned her attention to the list of ingredients. Poisons tests were never anything less than harrowing, and failure to brew either the right toxin or an effective cure was often fatal.

'We're here to plan our attack,' Mollandra said with feeling. 'This place needs to burn.'

Sharp twisted her mouth. 'It's not exactly flammable.'

'The rocks we can push over after everything else is ash.' Mollandra's anger burned hot enough to consume stone in any case. The fire had started with Bek's death and flared when Einsa passed. She had thought that killing Treecie might help, but it hadn't given her even slight respite. The solution, she had decided, was to kill not only the Kindnesses, instructors, and servants, but to burn the Creed, break the shrines, and raze the place so low as to wipe it from human memory.

'We're a little outnumbered.' Sharp didn't dismiss the idea out of hand.

'We'll succeed because we have the element of surprise on our side.'

'Child, we do not.' Tmanga traced a finger down the list in her lap.

Mollandra hated it when Tmanga called her 'child'. 'Don't call—'

'Almost every acolyte goes through this phase, usually in Year Four or Five. And the ones who don't tend not to last to Year Six. You're not even early. If this place ever wasn't full of Year Fours plotting, the Kindnesses would know they were doing something wrong.'

'That's a lie!' Mollandra jumped to her feet. Tmanga didn't sound as if she was lying but Mollandra wanted it to be a lie. 'How would you even know that?'

'Einsa told me. She started reading histories of the Academy after Bek died.' Tmanga put the scroll aside. 'Sit down, you're making Sharp nervous.'

Sharp smirked.

Mollandra shook her head. 'Einsa wouldn't . . . She hated this place too!'

'You can hate a place and still know that you're expected to hate it.' Tmanga shrugged. 'Einsa's mother was the same. Einsa found a record saying when her mother was here she even killed an instructor. She didn't tell you? Probably didn't want you copying Bek. Did you know that if you kill an instructor and fail to reach the last three in a way that's not immediately fatal, they make you a servant here? Or – if you got to Year Nine or Ten, they might put an instructor's staff in your hand.'

Mollandra waved all that away. 'How does this . . . I mean . . . Why's it all still here?' She paused. 'Years Four and Five? And what then? They just stop trying?'

'This place turns you.' Tmanga tapped her scroll. 'The Academy is a poison and we're part of the ingredients, stuck between mortar and pestle.'

'That doesn't mean anythi—'

'When a thing holds you captive long enough you start to love it. That's how this poison works. When we walk out of the gates we'll sing the Creed with our whole hearts and think that we were stupid children to ever doubt it.' Tmanga held Mollandra's gaze, inviting the challenge.

Mollandra slumped, but slowly, fighting the inexorable realization. The Academy had stood the test of time. It hadn't been waiting nearly two hundred years for someone as extraordinary as her to turn up and fix things. She was ordinary, expected, part of the system before she had even known that there *was* a system. The truth that Tmanga had already accepted and that Sharp didn't care about was that the place would twist them, crush them, only to reshape them and put them out into the world, or – more likely – into the catacombs with all the other failures.

'I don't believe it.' Mollandra growled it out as a challenge, but truly the challenge was for herself, the deep core of her that did believe it and perhaps had known it from the start. She spat into the yawning space beneath the bell. 'It wasn't right what happened to Thurli.'

Thurli had been solid in almost every regard, a doughty fighter, clever fingers, able to climb and delve far better than her stocky figure had implied. More importantly she had known how to endure.

'Everyone but us has to go in the end.' Sharp stretched luxuriously.

'You and her . . .' Mollandra shook her head. Sharp had visited a lot of beds but Thurli's more than any other. 'How can you—'

'You'd rather I chose Thurli and let you fall?' Sharp put an edge on her reply.

'Vault Studies, though? They killed her over dates! She was tough, dependable—' Likeable, Mollandra wanted to say. Loveable. '—She could have been something. She was . . . useful . . . dammit.'

'They think she's *more* useful this way. Spurring us on to try harder. Keeping the legend of the Kindnesses alive.' Tmanga stood to go.

'But Vault Studies?' Mollandra herself was no great shakes when it came to the academic stuff that Instructor Clakka insisted they absorb from the dusty tomes in the library vault.

'You don't think it would help to know how to find the people we're sent after?' Sharp got up lazily. 'Tandra-ah's not the only city, you know. It's not even the capital. I don't know why you act like it's the whole world. A little geography is never going to hurt.

Except when it does. But the point is that we're going to be chasing our targets all over the place. It'll help to know where they can and can't run.'

Mollandra ground her teeth against a hot reply and followed the other two down the stairs towards the window they'd entered by. Sharp wasn't wrong. The Kindnesses didn't sniff out every crime in person. Often the misdeeds of the powerful reached the Academy on the currents of trade and gossip that flow through every civilization. If a queen murdered her son, if a king abused his daughter, if a prince offered the shelter of his hall then slew his guests, these and other crimes would aim a Kindness across whatever distance might need to be crossed.

An involuntary snarl escaped Mollandra's lips. She didn't want Sharp and Tmanga to be right – she wanted them to agree with her. To share her anger over what had happened to Thurli. The girl had failed to list the realms and monarchs of Magog. Instructor Clakka, her anger flaring, had dragged Thurli screaming from the room. It had been all Mollandra could do to keep herself from trying to stab the woman between the shoulder blades. If she'd known the punishment Clakka would choose there was no doubt in Mollandra's mind that she would have attacked – and died.

Thurli had been put in a cage hanging from one of the five gibbets above the main gates. The cages were shaped for a person standing and the iron bands from which they had been fashioned allowed little movement as their prisoners starved while exposed to the elements. The crow-pecked bodies were eventually moved to the catacombs but stayed long enough to horrify the outside world. The joke that circulated in the blackest currents of the Academy's dark humour was that if there was ever a day when at least one of the cages wasn't occupied, the walls of the Academy would come tumbling down.

Sharp hadn't been wrong about Mollandra's ignorance when it came to the wider world. She had arrived at the Academy having never before left the city. Her education had ignored the world outside. It had come as a great surprise to Mollandra that the miles beyond Tandra-ah's walls, which she had imagined to be an endless carpet of mountain, forest, and field, were in fact almost entirely water, with the great islands of Magog and Gog huddling together for company in the midst of an ocean that dwarfed them both.

Instructor Clakka had also taught them something that could hardly have shocked Mollandra more than if she had told them the world was not the centre and that the stars wheeling overhead weren't bound on their course around it along with the sun and moon.

She had said that hundreds of miles away, on Gog's Coast of Bones that runs the length of Carrowland, there were, along with the spines and ribs of great whales and of still greater leviathans, the ribs and spines of vast ships. Whatever wood composed these skeletons had withstood many centuries of wave and wind. So many that the subjects of the carvings graven into their ornamentation had escaped humanity's memory. Creatures and runes beyond knowledge.

There were, the instructor said, stories written between those landings and the present, in languages that modern tongues had twisted away from. Scholars reported that these tales spoke of demons pursuing the ship-makers across the ocean. The Kindnesses knew that rather than demons it was the Furies that had chased humanity over the waves, their rage greater than any storm. The remnants of mankind had fled a calamity of their own making, and while they had been able to outrun the fires in their wake, their guilt could not be so easily outdistanced, not by the crossing of mere distance and time.

Mollandra had first broadened her horizons from the house where she had been born, to the city that contained it, and the change had amazed her. The Academy had pushed those horizons further. First, to the coastline of the two great islands that composed the known world. Then to the vast ocean in which they huddled alone. And then to some unknown and unreachable foreign shore from which her ancestors had fled in ships that none now could fashion. She wondered where this process might end. Where she might find a final boundary within which she was wholly contained and could take stock of her surroundings. The idea that there might be no such limit unsettled her in ways she could find no words to frame.

All of this pondering was, of course, simply Mollandra's attempt to push from her mind the fact that Thurli, who had never been anything but decent to her, was now suffering in a cramped cage that would keep her until she died, and then some. The wonders of the wider world were Mollandra's allies in not thinking about the horrors of the smaller one which she could reach out and touch. And greater than the horror of the cruelty that Thurli was enduring was the understanding that Mollandra, Tmanga, and Sharp had just said goodbye to her, each stating clearly to herself and the others that she wouldn't lift a finger to save the girl.

'I am not, and never have been, a good person.' Mollandra muttered it to herself as she followed Sharp into the dining hall. 'Am not. Never have been.'

CHAPTER 22

Mollandra

Year Four

A full day passed before the next Vault Studies lesson. In the break before the class Mollandra didn't follow her fellow acolytes to the courtyard. Instead, risking punishment, she climbed the stairs to the roof and picked the lock that almost every girl in the Academy had picked. Now, beneath bright and open skies, she went to the western tower. From the outside it was a twin to the one she had visited with Sharp and Tmanga. Inside, instead of a great bell and a shaft in which its voice could resonate and its rope could hang, this perforated dome was solid floored.

The Academy housed the messenger crows here. Birds of a larger, more cunning breed than the carrion crows who haunted the rooftops, drawn by the stench of death. These dark messengers sometimes accompanied Kindnesses on their duties. The Academy also maintained towers for them in a score of cities so that far-ranging alumni could send back word of their progress or requests for reinforcements.

Not only could the birds find their way back to the Academy and the city towers, but they could also be imprinted on individual Kindnesses and by some instinct of their breed could seek them out across hundreds of miles.

Drawn by some poorly understood instinct of her own, Mollandra entered through the wrought-iron gate, having to pick a lock considerably more complex than every other in the building. The crows watched her, wise-eyed, patient. One in particular, its eyes a ghostly grey haze unlike the black beads out of which the others watched her, studied her with peculiar intensity, its beak parting from time to time as if on the point of passing comment.

Ignoring the scrutiny from nesting box and perch, from the birds still in the perforations of the tower's outer skin, and from crows that had paused their strutting outside to peer in, Mollandra sat cross-legged, careless of the dirt and droppings.

'I can't do this.'

A scatter of gentle caws answered her. Not the harsh cries of crows on the wing, but the crooning that such birds use between themselves at close quarters. Half curiosity, half commiseration.

'I need...'

She didn't know what she needed. A void echoed within her, the empty space she had thought that killing Treecie might fill. The grey-eyed crow dropped from its perch, feathers and wings and flapping. It landed before her, meeting her stare with a luminous regard that had to be a trick of the light. And it seemed that the day was dimming around them.

The tower's interior grew darker as more and more crows arrived, filling every one of the many irregular entryways piercing the stonework. Dozens, scores, hundreds perhaps, extending their wings to create a false night in which the eyes of the crow before her became twin pearls that promised a view into a different world and time if she could only look beyond to what lay hidden.

The crow croaked, cawed, and croaked again, and somehow it sounded like words. 'What would you say to her? To Mollandra back then. Back in the crow tower?'

In the grey depths of the bird's eyes, through the obscuring mists, Mollandra could make out two old women, both of them strangers to her but also curiously familiar.

The closer one was seamed with age, older even than Kindness Terra. Tough, though. She looked as if she had been hard-bitten by life and had bitten back just as hard. She answered after a long pause, her voice also the croaking of crows. 'If it couldn't change things, why say anything at all?' She paused as if expecting a reply, then sighed. 'I'd tell her what she knows already. To fight. To never give in. To protect her friends because she won't have many, and to avenge them when they're gone. I'd tell her that she'll never be rid of the anger they put in her. So, she might as well use it. I'd...'

And in the next moment the scores of crows that had been blocking the light took wing with raucous cries. Half-blinded by the sunshine streaming in, Mollandra took a moment to clear her vision, and by the time she had, the grey-eyed crow had gone too.

Instructor Clakka had survived at the Academy for longer than any of her five fellow instructors, all of them serving beneath the three Kindnesses. The woman was all bone and gristle. Her skin, wrapped too tight to wrinkle, had the appearance of paper that has been crumpled then smoothed out many times. The pages of the older tomes in the library were often foxed, marked by the brownish mottling that age brings, and Clakka appeared to have caught that same contagion.

Mollandra imagined that the instructor had had a patrician nose. The ugly hole she had been left with when the Kindnesses of her time mutilated her was there to shame her for her failure, to remind every class that sat before her that this woman had fallen short. The lesson here was that this was as close to mercy as the Academy came and that here, even mercy was not a pretty sight.

The woman favoured her class with a wintry stare, her mouth a tight pucker, as if their youth was sour to her. She rapped on Mollandra's desk with the short metal ruler she habitually carried. 'Attend to your books.'

Outside, on the Academy wall, Thurli still suffered in her cage. She had fallen silent in the night but would still be waiting on death's mercy. Beside Mollandra, Tmanga bent over her open text. Mollandra, still bound by the strangeness of her vision within the crow tower continued to stare at Clakka's back as the woman walked away.

World Studies had once been Mollandra's favourite subject, widening her narrow window on the world with each lesson.

Mollandra had felt constant astonishment as Clakka pushed the horizon ever outwards. World Studies had later become Vault Studies when the acolytes moved past the woman's verbal accounts to the source material in the library vaults.

'Acolyte Sallay will summarize the structure and importance, both political and economic, of the Callornian Spice Guild.' Clakka indicated Sallay with her ruler. The girl, who threaded sharp twists of wire into her braids to stop others from grabbing them, stood with a look of panic in her eyes. Thurli's punishment still held the foreground in everyone's thoughts.

Clakka's talk of trade and of nations was a far cry from the stories told in Creed where the Furies, having chased humanity's remnants across the ocean, finally relented and let their earthly bodies fall, sprawling across the landscape, sinking deep into the ground as if it were a mire rather than forest and bedrock. The three's true essences then returned to the celestial for long-overdue reckonings with miscreant gods.

While Sallay stammered through her account of the guild in distant Callorn, Mollandra's thoughts slid towards her first lesson with Clakka. The instructor had produced maps depicting the two islands, Magog and Gog, named for a pair of legendary giants. The many borders dividing these two great land masses made both islands resemble plates that had been dropped and then glued back together. Scores of cities and the banners of more than a dozen royal houses were picked out in bright illumination.

No map, Clakka had told them, remains useful for long. The ocean's work may take eons to change the coastline through eroding storms, but the love of power ensured that the borders within those coasts swept back and forth with such speed that the old could hardly recognize the world they had grown into.

Even so, it had struck Mollandra as a bright and colourful world, overflowing with mystery and possibility, so much bigger and more complex than she had ever imagined it might be. A second map provided a very different perspective, rendering the pair of islands tiny despite Magog being nearly five hundred miles in length. On this second chart the twins huddled together like lost children, surrounded by the endless and unbroken blue of the ocean. It was,

Instructor Clakka had told them, all the world. The seas had risen and drowned the rest. Perhaps some day the gods would tire of the twins and drown them too.

The city of Tandra-ah, that had once seemed endless to Mollandra, wasn't even the capital of the kingdom in which it lay. And the kingdom of Abrona was far from the largest or most powerful of the seven realms into which Gog had at some point fractured. Abrona survived not by strength but by alliances, trade, threats, and subterfuge. History, Clakka had shown them, was a great churn in which kings, queens, countries, and castles were in continuous chaotic motion, swelling their borders, swallowing their neighbours, dying of indigestion. A struggle hardly less vicious than the one in which the acolytes had engaged every day of their short lives.

In rare quiet moments Mollandra liked to place her finger randomly upon the map of Gog and imagine the life she might have had if she had been born in the spot where her fingertip landed. On her last attempt, fate had delivered her to a place she'd never even heard of. The Westfold barrens on the westmost border of the kingdom of Regon, Abrona's western neighbour. Beyond the Westfold lay the serrations of a great mountain range, sloping down into Tavoland, a wild place that claimed a long stretch of coastland – the sea was likely the only thing that made life possible there, for it's hard to grow crops among snowcapped peaks.

A sharp slap brought Mollandra's attention back to the classroom. Not a blow against her but the flat clap of the instructor's ruler against Sallay's cheek, leaving a white imprint surrounded by scarlet flesh.

Mollandra was half out of her chair before Tmanga caught her arm and Sharp leaned out from the next row to stop her desk from falling. Instructor Clakka didn't even look around. She finished addressing Sallay. 'Do better next time, acolyte. Your analysis was shallow. The work of a lazy mind.'

Only then did the woman turn slowly to face Mollandra. And Mollandra, who didn't even particularly like Sallay, was left wondering how it was that she had snapped now. Not for Thurli who she had both liked and admired, not for Einsa who had been her friend, not even for Bek who had felt like she had always imagined family should.

To fight. To never give in. To protect her friends.

Sallay probably *had* done a poor job. And she'd got off lightly – the edges on the ruler's lower half were razor sharp. Several girls bore crudely stitched wounds from its touch.

'Sit down!' Tmanga's hiss held an unfamiliar edge of desperation as she hung onto Mollandra.

'Going somewhere?' The instructor advanced on Mollandra with a measured pace. 'Some desperate need of the privy?'

Mollandra should have leapt at the unexpected offer of escape. Instead, she took it for weakness. Sharp sensed it too. Both of them had a killer's instincts.

Do or die.

Mollandra shook off Tmanga, moved clear of the desk, and brushed Sharp's arm aside. She stepped to meet the instructor. Acolytes snapped all the time at the Academy. Bek had. There didn't have to be a reason.

Thurli was beyond saving. But she could still be avenged. Wasn't that the Academy's lesson, after all? Vengeance above all.

She still had her book in one hand, gripped around the spine. Elwin Madory's *Crowned Heads of North Magog*. The volume trembled in her grip. Not from fear but fury. She should be shouting Thurli's name, or Einsa's, or Bek's, or even claiming some defence of Sallay, but her mouth couldn't frame a single word. The snarl that broke from her had little in it that was recognizably human. Mollandra would have scared herself had she not been so very angry.

Clakka swung, understanding that the shield of her authority had broken. She was fast. Much faster than Mollandra had imagined possible. It wasn't conscious thought that placed the *Crowned Heads of North Magog* in the ruler's path and captured its razored edge among the dullness of its many pages. It wasn't Mollandra's strength that so easily twisted the weapon free of the instructor's grasp. Rather it was something the rage loaned her – drawn from unsuspected wells.

Years of training lived in Mollandra's muscles now and she relied on it as she threw herself at Clakka. Her fury left no room for conscious control. Mollandra felt Clakka's strength as she bore the woman to the floor. She beat at the instructor's ruined face with both hands, howling, each blow bearing with it all her hate and rage and need for justice, revenge, and above all that, an end to the pain inside her.

The instructor fought back, but Mollandra's fists seemed like a storm, as if she were a dozen girls and not just a single acolyte. And, seemingly in the next moment, she was falling back panting, deserted by her strength, being pulled away from the unrecognizable mess that had been their instructor. Mollandra sat on the floor, supported by Tmanga. She held her bloody hands before her, heaving in great lungfuls of air, sobbing and laughing, both at once.

Others among the class were still kicking the corpse when the door opened, for in the end it truly had been all of them. Sharp was in the act of stamping on Clakka's head as Kindness Terra pushed through into the room. She completed the action and met the Kindness's gaze, an undeniable challenge in her eyes though Terra was a battle-seamed veteran of the chase and not a broken-down teacher.

Terra cast a flinty glance around the classroom. 'You'll be needing a new instructor. The rest of this lesson will be courtyard time.' She sniffed. 'And get Acolyte Mollandra to Instructor Jane. She's been stabbed. Best not to mention Clakka until the wounds are seen to.' The Kindness paused, her gaze lingering on the instructor. 'Clakka was her aunt.'

CHAPTER 23

Eldest

Tune found the petals in the cold and dusty clutch of the parlour grate. Two white and one pale blue, shaken from a bird's tail, Eldest said. The blue, though faint, was as vivid a colour as had ever entered the mansion. To repay Tune's gift Eldest shared the secret of the garden with her, though the child was too clumsy to be allowed to touch.

They added a petal to each of the fungi and called them flowers, though none save Eldest, Tune, and Milk-Eye would ever know that they had bloomed.

'There were three sisters. Three terrible sisters. They were made to chide the gods, to chase them across the heavens should they transgress. Fashioned not by any being but by necessity. Necessity was their mother, and they are her invention.' Day-Father had the children gathered in the parlour. He sat in the scarred, high-backed chair, his own back straighter than that of his seat, his black hair as ragged and unkempt as the children's. He had their gaunt and hungry look too, though who kept him from eating his fill they couldn't say.

He held a heavy book open on his knees but did not read from it. Instead, he watched them all with night-black eyes and spoke his words from memory. 'Humanity lay beneath their notice and stayed there for thousands of years. There are, however, creatures older than the gods, perhaps even older than the sisters and their mother. The titans were born of the sky and the earth, conceived where one touches the other, from the sunset or the sunrise according to their nature. They are many and various in their ways. Much of our world is fashioned from their corpses.'

Eldest longed to ask her questions, but the answer would be a slap. Had the mansion been built from the bones of titans? What killed them? Were any still alive?

'Theus,' Day-Father continued, 'was clever and stupid at the same time. He liked to walk among men, as if he were a father to them all.' Day-Father glanced around at his children, seeking challenge. All of them looked away, save Eldest who watched him but kept her lips pressed tight together. 'Theus gave fire to humanity, and with that spark they burned the world. The sisters noticed our kind then. Alecto – she of unceasing fury; Tisiphone – mother of revenge; Megaera – greatest among equals, she who has bathed in the rivers of memory and forgetting, she who swims in the currents of time, she who will never forget.

'They chased the wrongdoers, across continents, across oceans. No vault was so deep that they could not find the guilty, no door too thick for them to breach. They pursued those who woke the fire of the sun on our green earth, sought them across endless seas, even to the shores of Gog and Magog. The sisters are immortal, eternal, but the bodies they fashioned themselves to bring justice into the mortal world were not. And here, at last, on our shores, after centuries of war, those bodies fell.'

Eldest tried to imagine it. The three sisters running across the limitless ocean, the last scraps of humanity scattered ahead of them in a final armada, lashed by whips of flame. Had the sisters been vast as titans wading the deeps? Did they burn with the fire of their wrath? And when at last they reached new land, had they sunk to their knees and fallen apart like the armour in the great hall?

'Their spirits returned to the heavens to hound whatever gods still dwelt there, and their flesh, all but incorruptible, lay untouched by wolf or raven until the land itself drew a veil across the remains. But what was lost can be found, and—'

Eldest blinked. She had been sitting with her brothers and sisters, listening to Day-Father's story. But now she stood by the long table with the tongue-shrivelling taste of the trough in her mouth and her vacant siblings on every side. The meal always stole time from her but today it had stolen part of the lesson they'd just had. And she was the first to waken from it. Would the rest of them even remember that there had been a story?

Memory. That was what was being taken from them. Without shaking the others back into the moment, Eldest stepped away from them, away from the table and the trough. The understanding didn't come in an instant, like the flint's spark, kindling a greater light. Instead, it seeped into her, a liquid knowledge soaking into parched ignorance.

Eat of my body. Drink of my blood. That was what the priests told the followers of the cross. She had read it in one of the books strewn so carelessly across the parlour floor. Of the various faiths Day-Father had said vied for power, the followers of the cross were not alone in consuming their deity, or at least believing that they were. But here, now, in this mansion, Eldest and her siblings truly were being fed the remains of the divine, or of something that divinity had reason to fear.

And where did their power lie? Surely the heart for Alecto's burning fury and Tisiphone's icy revenge. But Megaera's eternal memory would haunt the labyrinths of her brain.

Eldest returned to the table. She touched her fingers to the cold slop still lying an inch-deep in the trough. The urge to choke it all down seized her, to drink it as if it were the River Lethe itself, and drown in the oblivion, as unremembered as the brothers and sisters whose names scarred the attic rafters but left untouched the minds of those who remained. *Strong*, there had been a Strong. A brother. Eldest before her.

'... Eldest?' Tune's voice broke the spell.

'Wake the others.' Eldest turned sharply and walked away into the gloom, carrying her own darkness with her, and another that had been put into her by the man who called himself their father.

Later, in the scant privacy of a corner, she forced fingers down her throat until the meal returned in a retching spew, emptying her stomach. The resulting hollowness soon turned into a hunger which gnawed at her all day.

She repeated the process after the next meal, imagining what pumped from her mouth in such a hurry wasn't so very different from what she had so reluctantly swallowed shortly before. With only water from the rain butt to fill her, hunger became starvation more quickly than she had imagined it might. By the seventh day she had raided wardrobes in the grandest bedrooms to add three scarves and a mouldering shirt to her ragged clothes, all to disguise her emaciation. She could see the bones beneath the skin now, but she couldn't let Day-Father see them too.

Her weakness began to draw notice. Lip-Scar cut her in the knife lesson and rejoiced in his triumph. Shrill began to watch her closely, the sly-eyed girl at least two years younger but always precocious in her ambitions.

The nights became harder, though she could still hide herself from Night-Father better than the rest of them could. The eighth night of her fast was one of those rare occasions when unknown duties kept Night-Father from the hunt. As ever, the children gravitated to Eldest, asking to hear stories. This time she told them fantasies of a world outside the mansion's walls and of lives where Mother and Father were not their parents but had been replaced by others. For each child she imagined a new father and a new mother, ones who fed them food that made the mouth water and the stomach sing. Eldest struggled to name specific meals though her mouth could almost taste the wonders she conjured.

'Potatoes, and salt, and grain, wheat, butter, milk. Tune's father would be a big man with a beard, and he would pick her up in his arms' – Tune whimpered in fright – 'not to hurt her but to . . . cuddle . . . that's the word, soft holding.'

Perhaps it was starvation that had infected her imagination, but Eldest's mind bubbled with ideas, half-seen images, half-felt emotions. She carried on, spinning tales for her entranced audience, stories so full of colour and kindness that even Lip-Scar and Grumble made no murmur of dissent.

In the depth of her hunger she found a story about Strong falling from her tongue, each line a mystery to her until she spoke it aloud and turned it into revelation. She understood, as she held the other children captive with her tale, that this was memory, not invention.

'We had a brother called Strong. And a sister before him called Pierce who set that name upon him.' She told it like the storybook in the parlour told its stories, the book without a cover, now divided into a dozen cherished pieces, hidden from Day-Father. She changed the type of language she used, even her voice. It was easier to tell it as a story. To keep it at arm's length where it might hurt her less.

'Strength, children, is often misunderstood because it is found in so many kinds. Every strong thing, if you turn it this way and that, will look like weakness from the right angle. And some things that are weak will show their strength in surprising circumstances. You might think that I am becoming weak, but there's a different kind of strength growing inside me.'

Lip-Scar made the gentlest of snorts at that but said nothing. Eldest pressed on, needing to speak this story in order to drag it from the depths of her forgetting.

'On the day that we all forgot there had ever been a Pierce, Strong promised to lead us and to protect us. If we swore to obey him, he would swear to be our king. A king in times of war had hard decisions to make, there would be sacrifices, the enemy had many advantages, but in the end we would triumph. Strong would take Day-Father's chair and rule the night without terror.

'We all agreed to it. Strong had many kinds of strength, not least the swiftness and power in his arms, but where none could equal him was how he talked, how he made you see a great future, however impossible that might seem, a future where everything had changed and one that had a place for you within it. When he spoke, it seemed that anything was possible. He lit a fire inside all of us and called it hope.'

'I don't remember any of this,' Milk-Eye whispered, her need for it to be true clear in her voice and warring with the facts as she knew them.

'Father poisons us. He found something – the Ingredient – years ago. In a mine, I think. I can't remember properly. But I'm sure I was told or I overheard or I spied on them, him and Mother. He was digging somewhere very, very deep. Somewhere he was put.

The Ingredient gave both him and Mother power, enough for him to leave that place and claim this one. But it changed them both. Too much to live among other people – I don't believe them about the outside, this place is not all there is. It changed them because they couldn't grow around it and instead the Ingredient twisted them around itself.

'Mother was the one to understand first. It was her idea to feed it to children. They've been experimenting on us. Finding out just how much we can take. They gave Pierce too much and the world forgot her. Maybe there were others before Pierce too, erased from everyone's thinking. Each time they tried a lower dose, but though Strong was strong and had promised to keep us safe, he couldn't keep himself safe.

'I almost remember his face. I remember the feeling of his arms when I was hurt. Like a brother. Like a father should be. But they took him from us. He fell out of memory. Out of mine at least, out of ours. And he's gone. Just his name scratched on an attic rafter to say he was ever here – and now on me, etched with his memory, lost in the blackness but returned by the hunger.

'They gave me less than they gave Strong, and if I had failed, they would have chosen another of you and reduced the amount again. They're breeding us, changing us, trying to make us into a weapon, but I don't know who they want to use us against. I think it's whoever put Father in that mine in the first place. Whoever chained him in the dark. Only he's changed now and whatever his vengeance was back then, now it's worse, darker, more cruel, and all of us are caught up in it.'

Tune's wavering voice spoke into the pause. Eldest would think her the last to speak up, but when a tale has its teeth in us it can draw out questions past all of our inhibitions. 'You won't ever leave us though? Not like Strong did?'

Guilt tightened the already tight knot of Eldest's stomach. 'Would you forget me?'

'No!' Tune gasped at the idea. Her 'No' found echoes in others among the gathered siblings.

'If you remember me then I will always be here.' Eldest hated herself for her dissembling, but she offered more. 'If you are ever able to escape though, sister, run.' And with that she set them to various tasks to stall any further questions.

On the tenth day something in Eldest's foundations began to shift. Whether it was the collapse of her body announcing itself or something becoming unhinged in her mind she couldn't tell.

Another meal, another regurgitation. But this time, holding there on all fours, trembling, too weak to attempt to stand, she saw flashes of something more colourful than her life. There at the back of her mind, a tiny garden, glimpsed through shutters. Sunlight burning on flowers too vivid to be believed.

With a gasp she fell to her side, hands clutching at her heart, mind grasping for the warmth of that fading memory.

'Memory . . .' When she hid from Night-Father she erased herself, not from her own mind but from *his* while she clung to the memory that she existed. The poison's gift, if you survived it, wasn't forgetting but *remembering*.

Even with the poison precipitating into the back of each child's mind the process of erasing themselves was still nearly impossible. It was as if the hiding place lay beyond a doorway too small to pass through, and like Alice in that ancient story, they were reaching an arm through towards salvation, unable to squeeze any smaller. And perhaps, Eldest thought, that was why Night-Father put such effort into breaking them all. Only in pieces could a person fit through the portal and reach that place forbidden to mortals. He broke them with pain and fear, and in the darkness of forgetting they were intended to reconstruct themselves into something new.

Gathering all her strength, Eldest stood and returned to the others on faltering feet. Only the power of her voice compelled obedience now. Her siblings were a pack that would soon turn. With harsh words and dark threats she set them to their labours. In the blindness of the mansion she couldn't see the rebellion on their faces, but she knew it was there. When the others left, Lip-Scar lingered. She could smell him. Shrill was there too, the slight rasp each time she inhaled giving her away.

'Scar! Shrill! Come on.' Milk-Eye had returned. 'Now. Or I'll be doing the cutting next time he gives us knives.'

They went with her, their reluctance silent but heard.

In the hours that followed, while the others laboured on the traps and barricades that they hoped would keep them safe, Eldest sat by the great hearth in the main hall, holding out her trembling hands to catch the faintest strains of the day's light in the place where fire once danced.

There had been a before. She had experienced years that were now lost to her. She wanted them back. There had been a before and she sought to sift it from the nothing just as the spread of her fingers sought to catch each particle of the light that dared its way down the chimney. And as the soft light slowly and faintly began to trace the width of her palms, hard-angled somethings started to rise from the blackness of her misplaced past.

Slowly, slowly she began to piece together the outlines of her life. There was a puzzle in the mansion's parlour, a faded picture of a tree and a house and a stream, cut into hundreds of interlocking pieces. Some toy of the wealthy children who had once lived very different lives under the same roof as Eldest. To put the puzzle together you started at the edges. Eldest had learned that lesson well. She started at the edges.

Later, when Night-Father began his hunt, Eldest and the older children concealed themselves in the kitchen having left clues that led away from the younger ones in the West Lounge. Tune she kept with her. The girl was too likely to give herself away and, by extension, all the younger siblings.

Eldest slept in one of the tall cupboards, beneath collapsed shelving and an arrangement of pans. Or rather she lay there, drunk on lack of dreaming, plagued by a bladed hunger, turning bright new memories over and over in her mind. The kitchen didn't seem to have been used in decades, and yet its association with food somehow lingered. It was here that Eldest's self-imposed famine gnawed hardest at her bones.

'I had a family.' She whispered it into the mansion's night, quiet so that her siblings wouldn't hear, but loud enough for the darkness to challenge. Some truths must be spoken or else they are not properly true. 'Father is not my father. That thing in the basement is not my mother.'

'Eldest?' A voice from the next cupboard. Milk-Eye – the sister who was not her sister. 'I think he's coming.'

'Quiet then. Make yourself nothing. All of you.' Eldest wasn't sure why she still cared. They weren't her family. She could run and Father would waste the night hurting them while she found sanctuary. But she did care. Something, some annoying band around her heart, wouldn't let her desert them. 'Look into the blackness. The dark inside. Let it unwrap and cover you.' She felt their struggles, and the slow release of a fraction of the power that had been put into them. 'Tune!' She woke the girl with a careful kick, displacing none of her own cover. 'Tune, you should run. The barrels by the trapdoor to the West Wing cellars. That's the best place. He looked there last night.' Tune had often tried to erase herself too, but she'd got nowhere. Night-Father would find her in a heartbeat if he came close.

Eldest sank into her own void, deeper and faster than she had before. 'A family. I had a family.' This time nobody heard her though she spoke without whispering. The words entered the ears of her false siblings, only to erase themselves before comprehension settled across them. Eldest could almost see their faces, her true mother, her true father, and . . . one other . . . a true sister, older than her. She must have been stolen from them. Taken by force. The details of that, she could still not remember. Was her older sister one of the names on the rafters? Had she been overwhelmed by Megaera's dark gifts and scrubbed from history like a stain washed from a smock?

The morning bell's discordant clangs jolted Eldest into the waking world, gummy-eyed and with a hollow belly. The children scrambled from their hiding places, hastening to the parlour, where after another broken night the day's lessons would proceed in the semi-delirium that prolonged sleep deprivation brings.

It had never made sense to Eldest, but now she remembered something Day-Father had said: if you wish to reshape something, break it first. She found herself remembering many things on her journey down the flights of creaking steps. She had a family. She remembered that. Their faces still refused her summons. She saw them only as if they were pressed to a curtain, the taut cloth revealing the planes of their faces but hiding all detail.

The children lined up beneath the flicker of the parlour's chandelier, eyes slitted against the light. Eldest stood at the back today rather than taking her place at the front. Yesterday's discovery had driven a splinter of hope into her heart. She had managed to separate herself from the awfulness of her existence, to sever the unwanted bonds of kinship with Father and Mother. She had felt a momentary sense of worth and belonging. The ghost of actual love had warmed her, not at the hearth of memory but a reflected heat that promised more if only she could sweep aside the remaining veils.

Today new worries stalked her, as if there had been room for them in the queue all along. Had her family given her up? Had they placed her here, unwanted, a reject from their perfect lives? Starving and sick now with a thin cough trying to burrow into her lungs, Eldest sat silently and let the waves of Father's lesson wash over her. Today he wanted them to know about pain. As if he were describing nothing more than a recipe for a cake, Day-Father laid out the theory behind the practice that Night-Father demonstrated to the unlucky during sleeping hours.

When at last they were released from their lessons Eldest once more resisted the gruel, though the reek of the loathsome stuff had become a fragrance and her sunken belly cried out to be filled. The others watched her, aware now of her abstinence as they were aware of her weakness. She knew it wouldn't be long before she lost her place as their leader. She shouldn't care, they were an anchor on her, not the prize that Lip-Scar and others with ambition might think. Without her the youngest would suffer, but . . . She walked away from the table.

'I'm not a good person.' Perhaps that was why her family had given her up. Had they let her be cast into this hell because they saw the evil in her, or was it her weakness? 'I'm not a good person.' A good person would fight to lead because she knew it might save the others. A good person would care more, do more.

None of her siblings asked what she was doing when she hauled the mirror from the grand bedroom down the stairs, one loud, jolting bump at a time. There were shards littering many of the rooms, but this mirror, cracked as it was, was the only one still entire in its frame. Brother Small had killed Sister Quick with one of the shards from the Music Room. He'd driven it up through her chin during an argument over something ... Eldest couldn't remember what, something ... small. Brother Small had died weeks later. The injuries Night-Father inflicted on him were no worse than the rest had suffered, but something inside him broke. Eldest thought maybe Small had died from fear. Perhaps it was fear that led him to kill his sister. Fear was the author of many crimes.

The scrape of her dragging the mirror through the dining room into the parlour felt loud enough to fill the whole house like one of Night-Father's maniacal screams. At last, weeping at her weakness, Eldest brought it beneath the candlelight.

She had wanted to see herself whole, not her eyes staring through a wedge of fractured mirror. She had wanted to see all of herself at once, and now she could. She stared at herself, skeletal in the bundle of her scarfs and the stained satin of a dress repurposed as a cloak. Sunken eyes returned her study.

She hadn't performed this labour to admire her features. Rather, as she approached the silvered surface, setting her fingertips to the razored webs of cracks, she hunted for whatever it might have been that had made her parents reject her. For surely, she couldn't have endured years in this place if they had truly wanted her. They would have come for her by now if she were worthy of them. Was the imperfection visible among the hollows of her face? Could the guilt that had condemned her be seen at a glance? She thought she saw it there, in her eyes, a shadowed hurt that invited the blows that had changed her life.

Satisfied, she toppled the frame, letting the last mirror burst into bright fragments. It was easier this way. The hope had been too painful. If Father had planned this, if he had seen her waste away and known her purpose, then he had excelled himself and found a new cruelty that outdid all those that came before.

CHAPTER 24
Rue

'I was wondering where you'd got to.' Rue rolled Isik's head into the ditch and turned back to the bloodstained round stone where Senna now perched, having landed in an inelegant thrashing of wings. In truth Rue had forgotten all about the bird and the attendant strangeness of it also being Senna. But exposing weakness wasn't something she'd ever been inclined to do.

'It's not just here. Trens Town is burning. Smoke in the east. Probably Ginta, and that little place on the Ripple,' the crow said.

'What about survivors? From here?' Rue asked. 'Someone must have got away.'

She wanted to sit down, needed to: age had never weighed on her so heavy. Yet she stood with the crackle and spit of fire all around her and the sting of smoke wafting over every time the wind shifted, pausing the upwards gyre. She stood like a spike driven into the hard soil, and though she wanted to sob and to rail against a world that allowed such horror, she did neither.

Bek watched Rue from the fire, Einsa looming at her side, though both seemed small now, reduced to little girls who should have been at play, chasing through forests, running through alleys, doing the thousand and one soft things that the girls of Pye had done despite that many would have called their lives hard. Two little girls who should have been doing literally anything except learning to murder each other. Though Rue thought of thirty-year-olds as girls now.

The shades of her friends, standing now as shadows among the flames, didn't see Rue, didn't see the creature that the years had fashioned. Their eyes saw through time. It was Mollandra they watched, bent and twisted even then, but not yet broken.

I'm not her – I carry around the imprint of that child. Her hurts and truths are my foundations, but I am not her. I was the castle built upon that hill, and now the ruin. I am haunted by the ghost of myself. By the ghosts of myself. By the little girl, the young woman, the mother, wife, by the widow fresh in her grief. Even yesterday watches with a stranger's caution as it stands at my shoulder.

Rue returned her gaze to the crow who seemed hardly to have moved at all. 'What about survivors, damn you?'

Senna cocked her head. Whether the bright beads of her eyes held sorrow or a hunger for the carrion her fellow villagers had become, Rue couldn't tell. 'Didn't see any.'

'Dammit Senna, these are your people, not mine. Your son—' Rue bit the words off, aware that she was being cruel, trying to force out of Senna the emotions she couldn't find in herself.

'My son . . .' Senna cawed, something closer to a low moan than any bird's cry. 'I'm a crow, Mollandra Plight. I can't cry. I can't smile. I already died once. And so did you from what I can tell. Don't ask me how to feel. This is an evil dream that bitch goddess of yours has trapped us in. And if it's all the same to you I'm just going to follow it along until I'm allowed to leave and try not to think about it too hard.'

Rue eyed the crow. She'd not expected Senna to be able to frame such thoughts when she was a gossipy mean-spirited old woman. To have them spoken through a beak had her wonder what contribution the bird had made. Crows were uncommon clever after all.

'Scout the roads—'

'I've already looked.'

'Do it again,' Rue barked. 'Everything coming and going from this spot. If there's a lone donkey heading our way, I want to know about it.'

'I've alread—'

Rue took a quick, threatening step towards the crow, sending it cawing into the smoke-scarred sky. Rue nodded at the bird's dwindling dot. Bitch or not, Senna shouldn't be here for what had to follow.

With Senna gone, Rue returned to Tamaster's hall, the only house not yet fully ablaze. She held her breath against the wafting smoke and narrowed her eyes against the sting. It took longer than she wanted to locate the finger bone. She picked it up still in its smouldering leather wrap, not ready to touch it. Sebrin's soot-stained head she found in a corner where it must have rolled after being kicked. She carried it out into the day's grey light, checking first that Senna had not returned.

'You're still in there. Don't hide.'

Sebrin's eyes angled sharply towards her. 'Enjoy your last hours, old woman. Someone is already coming for you.'

'You should have paid with gold when you had a chance, Baron. Now you pay the hard price.'

Baron Mancer's sneer appeared once more on Sebrin's lips.

'Why are you trying to start a war?' Rue asked. 'It seems a big thing for a little baron to want.'

Mancer just stared at her. Rue shrugged and drove a thumb into one glaring eye. Sebrin's face spasmed.

'Perhaps it wasn't your idea?' Rue said. 'Is there someone else I need to talk to?'

'You won't last till dawn.' The baron's voice sounded strained. He'd felt the eye, but not as much as Rue had hoped. 'There's only one more person you'll ever talk—'

Rue pitched the head into the burning ruin of Carter James's shack. Senna's dark form was arrowing towards her from on high, not yet close enough to have recognized her son.

The crow landed on a nearby wall.

'So, what else did you see up there?' Rue's gaze flickered to the heavens. 'How many mercenaries?'

'I'd already looked.' Senna cawed bad-temperedly. 'Hundreds. A dozen bands. Spread out over twenty miles and more to the Wiseman's Wood.' She leaned to scrape some scrap of carrion from her beak. 'But just now—'

'Just now what?'

'Why should I help you?' The crow fluttered to a fencepost out of Rue's reach. 'You're part of this. The reason for it. You did this to me. To them.' She flapped a wing towards the burning village – the roof of Debban's ale hut chose that moment to collapse, sending a tornado of swirling embers climbing towards the vault of heaven.

'You said you had to follow me,' Rue pointed out.

'Maybe she just wanted me to watch you die. I ain't forced to help you.'

'I killed the people who killed everyone, you know.' Rue gestured to the bodies smoking in the main street.

'I know what you are!' Senna cawed. 'I know what you are!'

'And what am I?'

'You told them. *I am she the gods fear. My sisters walk ever by my side.* Well, I don't see any sisters but I'm old enough to know that the Kindnesses didn't just walk through stories. They were real. The nightmares were real. You started this! You started it! I knew you were trouble the day you came. I told them. I told them all, but would they listen? I said you weren't right—'

'I'm not right.' Rue nodded. 'Never was. Not once. Broken from the beginning. But Kindnesses don't start things. They end them.'

Senna watched the fires, another roof collapsing, the blaze reflected in her eyes.

'I had daughters, not sons.' Rue surprised herself by speaking. 'Three of them. Triplets. Came closer to killing me than the Academy did.'

Senna's caw sounded more like an old woman's than a crow's.

'One died young, so I know a mother's loss.'

'Ain't the same. Kids die young. Babies die like flies. Can't love them till they're—'

'Don't spoil it, Senna. We're having a moment here. And you know that ain't true. We love the babies just as much. More maybe, because they've never had a chance to disappoint.'

The crow shrugged, like crows don't. 'Still got two then.'

'One's as good as dead. Left her with the convent. I doubt they've managed to keep her alive this long. The other, Cela, hates me. She's probably dead too. Never could back down from a fight . . .'

Senna wiped her beak on the fencepost. 'Sebrin was an arse. Got that from his father. But he loved his mother and his children. I will miss—' She cawed low and long. 'It's done. Burned. Tomorrow it will be ashes.'

'So, what did you see?' Rue still didn't trust the bird but she felt she understood the woman now.

'A man in black. I think it was a man. Walking alone on the Trevvan Road, coming this way.' Senna shook as if trying to rid her feathers of dirt.

'What was special about this one man?' A chill of premonition ran the length of Rue's spine. 'Did he have a bigger axe than the rest?'

'Couldn't see a weapon. But he looked like he knew exactly where he was going, and he's heading our way.' The crow glanced to the north. 'And . . . when I looked at him . . .'

'Yes?'

'I felt like I was falling. And not just because my wings failed me or something. More like I didn't have wings. Like I'd never had them, and I was back in that market, falling backwards, not understanding what had hit me or even where.'

'Shit.' Rue turned south and began to walk off swiftly.

'Wait!' Senna took to the air, cawing. 'Where are we going?'

'I don't know where *we're* going, but me, I'm running away.'

CHAPTER 25
Mollandra

Year Five

In Year Five when the class had shrunk to three dozen, Kindness Undu introduced the survivors to the elixir.

Mollandra had been expecting another session with the mouldering bones of former acolytes. Some of the girls could work wonders, though none were as good as Treecie had been. Sallay could tell you whose bone she held, and maybe something about them. Brooth could make a little homunculus from the smallest bones of fingers and feet, and set it walking the perimeter of the table. The things had something of the insect about them and made Mollandra want to scream.

Instead, Undu took them down a spiral stair they had never seen before, unlocking heavy iron gates at four different places, and waiting in a small alcove for all the girls to pass so she could lock all the gates after the last acolyte.

The girls expected some new atrocity to be waiting for them in the depths. Some method to thin the herd still further, born from the sickness of a diseased mind. A strange stink entered the air as they circled downwards. Not the pervading rot of the catacombs but something almost spicy – such flavours being known to

Mollandra only from Instructor Jane's poisons, some of which needed to be hidden behind a strong taste.

'So, did Einsa tell you about this one?' Mollandra posed the question to the back of Tmanga and Sharp's heads, still not entirely reconciled to the idea that Einsa had shared things with either of them that she had not spoken about to her.

'Not me,' Sharp said.

The scent grew stronger the deeper they went, setting Mollandra's teeth on edge and filling her with restless energy. And suddenly she knew what strange perfume filled her nostrils. She had mentioned Einsa and perhaps it had been the scent – ever the path to memory – that put the girl's name on her tongue. This had been what she'd smelled in the steam above Einsa's watery grave. This had been what lingered in the aftermath of her final fury.

Farther back, infected by the second-hand anger in the air, Sallay began bickering with Gane, which was always a stupid thing to do in Undu's classes even if she was at the other end of a spiral.

The stairs terminated against the side of a vault with a high roof and circular floor. An extensive mosaic covered the ground, its design unfurling and colours deepening as Undu walked the perimeter lighting candle after candle in niches around the walls. Decoration was almost unheard of in the Academy.

The Academy, via the Kindnesses, claimed whatever took their fancy from the corpses of the guilty, as well as one tenth of any wergild paid under their supervision. Those riches were not spent on the fort, at least not where the acolytes could see it. Whether that wealth flowed back out into the world to fund secret projects, or lay heaped in neglected piles in the Academy vaults, Mollandra had yet to learn.

On the wall opposite the stairs was a large circular iron door with a wheel-driven locking mechanism set at its centre. Undu returned to this door after lighting the candles.

'Sit. Make a circle. Make sure there's nobody closer than two yards to you.'

The Kindness set her bloated white hands to the spokes of the wheel and applied her strength – which Mollandra knew to be remarkable – to turning it. Metal ground against metal and the wheel rotated. After several revolutions Undu heaved back, leaning into the action.

The woman weighed as much as any three of the acolytes arrayed around the chamber, but even so the door responded with almost imperceptible slowness, stealing into motion over the course of five measured breaths.

Mollandra would have remarked on its thickness had either of her neighbours been close enough to whisper to. At least eight inches of black iron sealed the entrance.

The Kindness disappeared into the shadows beyond the door, her strange, gliding walk carrying her from sight. Time passed, and the acolytes watched each other in the dance of candlelight. Sharp amused herself making faces at the girls she liked and at the ones she didn't. Of late more of the acolytes found comfort in each other, but Sharp had never approached Mollandra or, to her knowledge, Tmanga. Probably she sensed that neither sought that kind of company. In her first years Mollandra had ached for the simpler kind of love shared between sisters, between a mother and her daughter. She knew it existed despite what her short life had taught her, and without even understanding what she was doing she had reached for it as any green thing will reach out for water even in the parching heat. Bek and Einsa had cured her of the need for such affection. By dying. Love, even the rough affection Einsa had shown her, was a wonderful thing. But the price lay beyond what Mollandra could afford to pay.

Tmanga closed her eyes and rested her hands on her knees, legs crossed. Mollandra watched the vault entrance, wondering what might need such protection here in the depths of the Academy's substructure. She felt unaccountably annoyed, her usual gnawing anger at their lives now supplemented by something more febrile, flickering like the flame. The scream that lived in her chest wanted out. The shifting light made strangers of her fellow acolytes, girls she had known for years now, casting their faces into new relief. She saw their hunger, the violence lying just beneath their skin, the sharp questions in their eyes as they glanced this way and that.

'Still alive, I hope?'

Everyone turned as Kindness Undu re-emerged, holding before

her a pair of iron tongs that in turn gripped a long-necked flask. Although the fluid in the flask's round belly had not glowed in the darkness of the vault, the candles' light found a deep crimson answer in the swirl within.

'Did I remember to say to "study the floor"? I hope so. It *will* be important.'

Thirty-six pairs of eyes immediately began to hunt the designs tiled around them. Geometric patterns, scrolling waves, chasms, fire, the spirits of the wind cracking their cheeks. All omens of disaster. There, one of the Kindly Ones riding a lightning-wheeled chariot through boiling clouds, hair aflame. Mollandra almost didn't see the goblet. At the centre of the circle the acolytes had made, following the symmetries of the design, lay a black almost-circle, a gyre of darkness, picked out in nail-sized tiles of ceramic, an area nearly a yard across. The black goblet stood at the centre of the gyre, camouflaged.

Undu set the flask on the mosaic, keeping her distance as if it had just been drawn from the furnace mouth. 'There are stories of occasions when our kindness becomes something . . . less kind.' She spoke in her strange, lilting child's voice. 'There are stories of times when a sister becomes a thing of legend, touching the very skirts of the Furies themselves.'

Around the circle sharp breaths were drawn. That name was seldom spoken.

Undu smiled, a rare act that showed her years, counted in the lines where the crow set its foot to the corner of her eyes. 'In this vault it would be a sin not to speak of the three, of the Furies, they who punish gods. We must name them. Alecto, our patron, unceasing in anger. Tisiphone, the avenger. Megaera, the keeper.'

When Alecto's name passed Undu's lips the crimson flame within the flask broke free and for a heartbeat burned across the glass. As the fire drew back Mollandra found herself rising to her feet, fists clenched as tight as her belly, teeth bared, challenging the others, all of whom seemed on the point of racing across the circle to rend their opposite number.

'Sit,' Undu commanded.

Tmanga was the first to obey. She sat heavily, unclenching her hands, the deep furrows of a frown spreading across the customary smoothness of her brow.

'There are stories of our kindness becoming something else,' Undu repeated. 'Even before the founding of this academy, when our cult ran wild, springing up here and there like fire in the drylands, the records show occasions when divinity laid its hand upon a sister.

'Seven hundred years ago it is said that the princes of Themda denied Kindness Heera at their gates, and on high walls a thousand archers strained their bows. So great was her fury that it lifted her feet from the ground, blew the great bronze gates of Themda from their hinges, and sent lightning flying faster than any arrow to strike down those who raised their hands against her.

'Kindness Kretr, in the time of the northern fall, sought out the coin-lord in his high tower only to find the True Guard arrayed to block her path. The ruin she smote among those paladins that day brought an end to the order. Bones and smoke and blackened armour – nothing else remained.

'Twelve years ago, on the islet of Yoth, Kindness Terra's true sister, Kindness Ome, went to bring judgement against Agga Manda, the pirate lord, rapist, eater of children, salter of fields, murderer of guests. Kindness Ome did not return, but no ship has flown the black claw since, and grass has yet to grow again on Yoth.'

Mollandra had heard the names Heera, Kretr, Ome, among many others in the shrine services that were held with the cycles of the moon. She had accepted the legends of the broken years as just that, the kind of tales people spin up into something more each time they are told. That Ome's deed was supposedly done within her own lifetime was definitely new information. Also, suspicious information. No amount of training with the sword and knife would explain an island, even a dot in the ocean like Yoth, being burned to the bedrock. Necromancy could wither the crops, kill trees, and set the dead against the living – but the song of Ome made no mention of the necromantic arts.

'This.' Undu extended the pale, puffy hand of a drowned woman towards the flask and its fading glow. 'This is the key to fury. The poison that opens doors to power. A story that your tongues will burn to tell. But believe me when I say that the suffering that waits for any who speak of today outside this room is beyond your imagining.

'I have waited because you were too young, and too many. Too young because the elixir requires a toughened vessel to contain it. Too many because the elixir is precious beyond gold or anything that might be purchased with it.

'Why then, would we not wait until the three had chosen themselves and risen from the boneyard of their fellow acolytes? Because, ladies, this is an ungentle brew and many of you will be carried back up those stairs that acolytes Sallay and Gane gossiped their way down. Probably the survivors will have to gather the pieces first.' She gestured to a pile of grey sacks that had gone unnoticed by the wall.

Sharp snorted as if this were amusing rather than a chance to lose most or all of her friends in the space of an hour.

'If we waited until the Kindnesses had been chosen then shared the elixir and its secrets with them it might be that we found ourselves with only two or one . . . or no Kindnesses at all to release into the world that year. It is, as with all things, a balance between risk, and waste, a matter of timing and, ladies, your time has come.'

As if summoned, Kindnesses Terra and Marta entered the chamber from the stairs. Marta first, followed by Terra, encumbered by a large, heavy, and complicated object that turned out to be a particularly big crossbow with a stand to steady it. The Kindness used a two-handled winding mechanism to put an extraordinary amount of draw on the firing cable and loaded an iron quarrel as thick as both Mollandra's thumbs together.

'Rather than investigate your varying levels of bravado and cowardice, I will merely go around the circle in the order you have chosen. We'll begin with Sister Sharp and see if we have finally found something that exceeds her limits. The rest of you are to keep your places. Anyone standing without being told to stand will not be standing up again.'

Even for girls who had faced the distinct possibility of death every day for nearly half a decade, the prospect of a mass slaughter without even any resource to the skills they'd been trained in was a daunting one. All around the circle glances were exchanged, friends held each other's gaze. If the spacing had been smaller, hands would have been grasped.

Mollandra had, for the longest time, been hardening her heart against such loss. If the Academy's mythology were literal truth, she welcomed her draught of their poison. Anything that put the fire of the Furies in her belly she would drink without hesitation. Death's axe swung at her every day and offered little save the whittling away of her competition. This time something was being offered in exchange. Something unexpected.

Undu took up the tongs and the flask again, arms trembling with a strain that suggested a much heavier burden. She stepped toward Sharp but stopped short, angling the flask towards Sallay who sat beside Sharp's neighbour, Gane.

'Actually, I think we'll start here.'

Sallay, a slender girl with milk-white hair that fell past her ears, looked startled.

'Let's see if you've been paying attention.'

The girl swallowed. Undu's displeasure seldom failed to leave a mark wherever it landed.

'Fetch the goblet.'

Sallay looked wildly around. Several girls in the circle pointed to the black heart and at last Sallay spotted what lay there.

'No!' Mollandra threw her knife as the girl started to stand. The blade, a small one she'd fashioned herself, hit Sallay in her calf before she reached her feet and set her rolling, clutching at her leg with a muffled scream.

Undu shrugged, speaking into the pause as Sallay drew breath, sitting now, and staring daggers of her own at Mollandra. 'The acolyte saved your life, child. You may not have heard my instruction, but Kindness Terra did, and she would have put a much larger hole through you had you reached your feet.'

With the small knife still jutting from her leg, Sallay crawled over to recover the goblet. She returned without meeting Mollandra's eyes.

'Hold it out, then. Steady. If you spill any your corpse will be my new project down in the catacombs.'

Undu removed the flask's stopper with uncharacteristic haste.

Mollandra had never seen the Kindness scared before. Despite that hint of fright, Undu's hands, when she poured, remained steady. The dark red fluid flowed like hot water, steaming as it fell in a thin stream. The scent of spice and of wrongness intensified, along with the stink of a dead fire, blackened timbers in the rain ... and most of all, anger, as if anger had a smell and just by breathing in they were being filled with it.

With effort, Mollandra resisted. It wasn't that anger was a stranger to her, more that she didn't appreciate it being imposed from the outside. She didn't want the snarls she saw around the circle to be mirrored on her own face. The Academy already pulled too many of her strings.

'Well, drink then!' Undu urged. 'It's not for putting behind your ears.' She stoppered the flask.

Sallay hesitated. Years of being locked into coffins, thrown off walls, dropped into pitch-dark wells armed only with a hammer ... all of it toughened the survivors but there was only so far most could go. Humanity and its associated concerns were tenacious. 'I don't wa—'

Undu gestured to Kindness Terra who lowered her aim, adjusting the monstrous crossbow on its stand.

'No!' Sallay gulped down the measure of elixir. A mouthful at most.

Mollandra had been trained in several broad classes of poisons. The ones you hoped a victim would ingest of their own free will had either to be without taste or to mimic the flavour of something appealing. Many of the deadliest poisons were sweet. She'd experienced torture poisons too. Some slow, taking hold hours after they were swallowed, some instant, acid on the tongue. The elixir seemed to be one of the latter, not immediately as bad as the worst in Instructor Jane's arsenal, but Sallay's pain had twisted her face, and her nails left furrows where she clawed her throat. She lowered her head, trembling, threads of drool hanging below the thin veil of her hair.

Sallay had been on the edge for more than a year, her skills just enough to get her to Year Five but seeming unlikely to carry her further. Her swordplay, knife-work, and unarmed combat all placed her in the lower quarter of the remaining acolytes, and while she scored higher in other areas – poisoning ironically being her best – in none of them was she outstanding. She had a mild, unmemorable face, her faint prettiness the sort destined to evaporate with the first flush of youth. Never once had she looked intimidating: her anger a lightweight thing.

Now, as Sallay slowly lifted her face, the veins in her neck stood in sharp relief over rigid muscle, and the rage that possessed once familiar features smote like a fist. Even though Gane and Sharp sat between Mollandra and this stranger in Sallay's place, some primal instinct made Mollandra shuffle away on her rear.

The scream that burst from Sallay as she threw her head back and aimed her gaze at the vaulted roof seemed to contain within it every piece of Mollandra's own anger, harvested from a lifetime of grievance and released in one soul-tearing sound.

Sallay tore Mollandra's blade from her leg and the blood that poured from the wound *smoked*. With another shattering howl she shot to her feet and her neck disappeared into a mess of crimson chunks and spraying gore. For a moment Mollandra believed it to have been the force of the scream. But as the corpse fell, she understood that Kindness Terra had followed Undu's threat with action and that the great bow had spoken, less loudly than Sallay but with greater effect.

Einsa's mother had drunk this devil's brew. Mollandra knew it now. And some measure of its potency had passed to the baby in her womb, released only in the moments of her death, perhaps by Einsa's fury at Treecie's treachery rather than by fear of her own demise.

'Gane.' Undu nodded to the goblet that had bounced but not broken. It would be Sharp next, then Mollandra.

Gane, smaller than Mollandra these days, was a dark-haired ferret of a girl, quick on her feet and quick to betray. Sallay had been an unlikely friend and her only one. She shuffled across the spattered, steaming floor to gather up the goblet and held it out, staring hate at the Kindness.

Unperturbed, Undu poured Gane's measure. 'Quickly now, no sipping.'

Gane looked around the circle as if fixing the faces of her enemies in mind so she might find them in the afterlife. 'Slanthe.' She knocked the brew back with an eastern drinking salute.

For the space of three or four heartbeats Gane merely looked surprised, smacking her lips as if she had expected more flavour. In the next moment, as if held in the palm of some invisible giant that had suddenly made a fist, she curled up into a ball of sharp-angled pain. Every exposed patch of skin turned scarlet, and her growls sounded like those of a trapped animal. Fumes rose from her hair. The air was filled by the acrid scent of burning. The acolytes stared in horrified fascination, flinching away as a single flame lit on the back of the girl's neck.

One flame became a gout of fire, the inferno erupting through Gane's robes with the ferocity seen in the chemical flares Mollandra had been taught to make. The girl burned with such violence that chunks of her spat across the floor, prompting Sharp to roll clear. The cremation caused almost no smoke, as if it were too fierce to allow anything to escape. Limbs fell away, became bones, and finally a smouldering skull detached from the carcass and rolled a surprising distance, stopping just shy of Tmanga's feet.

The acolytes watched silently, the stinging air making all of them weep, though any real tears were for themselves and the ordeal that lay ahead.

Undu's eyes streamed too, though her tears looked more like tears of joy than any form of grief.

'Sharp!' The Kindness held the flask ready.

To her credit, or to the credit of her madness, Sharp showed no hesitation. She used her knife to break away the smoking finger bones still encircling the goblet's stem, and picked it up, pursing her lips as if she had expected it to be hot.

She drank as soon as the draught was poured. Sharp wasn't one for delay.

'The subject must show control,' Undu declared while Sharp sat back, stunned, eyes wide. 'They must be able to contain the divinity they have been gifted. They must be able to direct the holy rage that comes with it. Failure to do the former . . .' she paused as Sharp keeled over clutching her throat and shuddering '. . . will result in immolation. The rage must be your servant, not your mistress. We need Kindnesses who can direct their anger at the guilty.'

Sharp rolled onto her front, clawing at the floor, her skin starting to smoke. Mollandra had never really considered the possibility that the Academy would get the better of Sharp. If any girl was born to be a Kindness, it was surely Sharp. Watching her struggle, Mollandra understood that she was not prepared to lose another third.

'Sharp! Sharp! Fight it!' Mollandra had to shout to be audible above Sharp's growling.

Tmanga joined her deep, resonant voice to the effort. 'Calm! Be calm. Find your centre.'

Sharp's roar sent her upwards, as if she'd been punched from below. She rose with the air rippling in front of her lips and pale flame engulfing her hands.

Two things happened at once. One was that Mollandra launched herself at Sharp, and the other was that Tmanga scooped up Gane's still-smoking skull and threw it at Kindness Terra.

Mollandra hit Sharp's narrow chest and felled her, wrapping her arms and legs about the girl as they dropped. The bolt that would have taken off Sharp's head before Mollandra carried her to the ground hissed past her ear and hammered into the wall. The skull that had hit the crossbow, fractionally shifting its aim, fell to the ground in a shower of blackened pieces.

Mollandra found herself on the mosaic floor, wrapped around Sharp, who might at any moment burst into flames. Even if she didn't burn, Sharp might stab her to death in the grip of holy fury. Or, given that it was Sharp, just because Mollandra had knocked her down.

'Hold her still!' Undu leaned over them, a long stiletto in her hand that seemed, impossibly, to have been hidden about her person. She raised the blade aloft. 'Hold her head!'

'Try it and I'll gut you!' Sharp shrieked. 'I don't care who you are!'

Mollandra released her friend as if she was hot, which a few moments ago she had been. Sharp sounded furious, but that was how she always sounded if you riled her. 'Don't kill her! She's back. She's under control.' At least as much as Sharp ever was.

Undu paused, her face bulging with something beyond surprise. Shock maybe.

Mollandra, glancing around, quickly saw that not one but three Kindnesses loomed over them, Terra with her great sword drawn from the scabbard on her back.

'Acolyte Sharp?' Kindness Marta enquired, her forgettable face far more sinister than Mollandra could ever recall it looking. 'Are you calm?'

Sharp, who looked anything but, gritted her teeth against the cutting answer that anyone else would get and spoke through them. 'I. Am. Calm.'

'Remarkable.' The Kindnesses exchanged glances, a moment of unheard-of uncertainty. 'You were told not to stand. We will discuss your punishment later.'

'And Tmanga's,' Terra added.

'And Mollandra's,' Undu hissed.

'I didn't stand!' Mollandra discovered she had not finished gambling with her life. Besides, she still had her own draught to take. She was damned if she was going to cower and *then* burn.

Undu's smooth brow tightened, rippled by small lines of disapproval. 'We will reverse the order.'

And so Mollandra sat and watched as one by one the remaining thirty-plus acolytes ahead of her swallowed their fate. The start with Sallay, Gane, and Sharp proved to have been unrepresentative of the casualty rate. Even so, by the time the goblet reached Tmanga nine more acolytes had died, five shot when their rage drove them to their feet, ready to kill anyone within reach; four immolated. Of the casualties, the one Mollandra liked best, Chancy, became a hot coal, her carbonized skin cracking to reveal fierce orange lines that spread and consumed her, searing her shape into the mosaic. Denetra, a silent girl from the Rangi, the high desert of the far isle, stayed silent to the end then literally exploded, sheeting deep red fire across the floor. Her neighbours, Anamaci and Loom, both needed to be extinguished and received superficial burns. Bocc was the last to catch fire, and the only one around whom streamers of lightning danced, shattering erratic paths through the mosaic tiles as the girl shook in the grip of unseen forces.

After Tmanga it would be Mollandra, and the initiation would be at an end. Tmanga took the inky goblet in a hand nearly as dark and swilled the liquid contemplatively before knocking it back. She spared no last glance for her friends but sat cross-legged, hands gripping her shins, head down beneath its mass of curls. For several long minutes she sat with no motion save a trembling in every muscle, hands making claws about her legs. The anger seemed to bleed from her skin, curling Mollandra's lips into a snarl. And finally, Tmanga's head shot back and a single huge cry of rage tore from her throat. With that it seemed the fury had left her and after panting to regain her breath she passed the goblet to Mollandra then turned her black eyes towards Undu.

'Acolyte Mollandra.' Undu swung the flask forward.

The liquid hit the goblet with the weight of molten lead, making Mollandra fight to keep her arm steady. She looked left at Sharp, then right to Tmanga. It felt for a moment as if Bek and Einsa were standing at her side. She glanced at the two Kindnesses by the stairs, then up at Undu, wondering whether if she burned she might be able to wrap her arms around the woman and carry her to the floor.

Close up, the elixir's scent set her heart racing, the blood fluttered through her veins, and her teeth chattered in her head as if she were freezing rather than drenched in her own sweat. Einsa's fire – that's what it was. With a growl of defiance she knocked the stuff back, letting the liquid sear her tongue then burn its way down her throat.

In that moment a sensation that Mollandra had not felt in many years rose within her: a void opening deep in her core, swallowing the world.

She blinked back the blackness. Wiped her mouth. Looked up at Undu. And, without meaning to, said exactly what was on her mind.

'Fuck you.'

CHAPTER 26
Eldest

Eldest's fingers found the ruin of the garden: that shared and sacred secret held only between her, Tune, and Milk-Eye. Her fingertips explored the vandalism, discovering the fragmented stumps of three stalks and of the fourth and newest, growing between them. For a moment she thought that she herself, in the delirium of her starvation, might have dared their flesh, and somehow forgotten the act, though a life sustained by such destruction held no value to her.

Whether rats, or Father's rage, or mere accident, her fingertips couldn't read the story. But the tears that had remained uncried through terror upon terror, grief upon grief, made their message clear in their coursing. She could stay no longer.

All the children had attempted at one time or other to escape the mansion. The books they had access to spoke of a better, bigger world, even if Father assured them it had been swallowed in a lake of fire. Even Tune saw the fallacy in that. If the mansion lay surrounded by fire, why did it get so cold for months on end?

None of them had come close to freedom, though. Their efforts had to focus on avoiding being caught at night. Any slow progress towards the outside would be uncovered, undone, and punished. How these labours were detected or attributed to the correct child Eldest didn't know, and not knowing was, to her, even more frightening than the immediate consequences, terrible as they were.

Eldest had set the others to their tasks. Lip-Scar had argued, called her plan stupid. Eldest had been prepared for this. She knew Lip-Scar's complaints would escalate by stages to violence. Her weakness meant she could not allow him to strike first, and so, bypassing all the usual stages of confrontation, she attacked. She slashed him across the face with a crescent of glass fractured from the bedroom mirror. In the dark she couldn't see the damage she had wrought. She could hear the patter of blood though, in the shocked silence that followed his shriek. 'Challenge me again and it will be your throat.'

Now she stood alone in the kitchen's tiled hall, a place of echoes, somehow still haunted by the smells of actual food that called to her belly far more strongly than the gruel she had refused for nearly two weeks. The room had not, in all of Eldest's time in the mansion, been used for its intended purpose, and in the earliest days that she could recall she had established through diligent searches that it held nothing she could eat.

The kitchen boasted, amid its treasury of pans, pots, platters, and pitchers, the largest fireplace in the whole mansion, save for the hearth in the great hall.

Like all the other fireplaces, a set of iron bars sealed it just a couple of feet up the flue, preventing its use as a place to hide or, potentially, as an escape route. Bending the bars had proved far beyond the combined strength of the children, even with chair legs used as levers.

In the hearth a faint glow showed the fire-blackened bricks, a whisper of the day's light reaching down from above. Eldest crouched and let the daylight's echo play over her dirty hand, showing her the many small cuts that had felt much larger and deeper in the darkness. She was about to move away when she saw something, a white line against the sooty bricks below her fingers. She picked the something up, and found it to be a feather, white-quilled, the rest a devouring black in which, at certain angles, the light found shades of deepest blue. She took it for an omen. The promise of flight.

She had to escape now while some semblance of strength remained to her. Whether the others would pull her down before Father discovered her starvation, she didn't know, but either Father or her siblings would bring an end to her ambitions soon enough. Probably a permanent one.

As Eldest felt her way around the kitchen, seeking the pieces of her freedom, the famine that she had imposed on herself carved another piece of truth from the obsidian that imprisoned her memories.

For the first time she saw her brother Strong. He had been golden, brave, tall. If they hadn't called him Strong they would have called him Brave. And then he had been Eldest and the burden of their future sat upon his broad shoulders and for a short time she had felt almost safe.

She had fallen in the chase once and somehow Strong had known and thrown himself at Night-Father. He had lost that contest of course, and his screams had echoed through the house until dawn. The next day though, despite his bruising, his bloody eye, and his limp, he had smiled at her across the parlour in Day-Father's lesson. A small, lopsided grin, but a grin even so.

That same morning, they had fed him the meal that had erased him. Father had called him from the trough to eat from a porcelain bowl. Eldest remembered now how blue that bowl had been, inseparable from the summer sky.

Eldest ran her hands across the kitchen worksurface, heavily scarred by absent cooks. These were memories that predated her own and might well outlast them too. As her fingertips tried to decipher the alphabet of scars, another image surfaced from her past, one that sucked in her breath in a faint exclamation of pain.

She saw Strong, glimpsed him from eyes that weren't aimed his way. He looked younger than she remembered him, yet it was the day of his erasure, the day after he had sacrificed himself to free her from Father's claws. He had been crawling. Inching his way blindly across the parlour floor, grey with pain. The others had moved around him, seeing him only with the part of their mind that steered their feet. He crawled beneath Father's gaze without those dark and wicked eyes so much as flickering his way.

Eldest hadn't seen him then. This was more than memory. The images were written into the Ingredient itself. She was reading her mind's own scars. The last she had seen – or rather, not seen – of

Strong were his heels as his faltering progress took him from her line of sight. He had been struggling towards the door.

She hadn't seen Strong, none of them had, but he had seen her. His gaze had found her and for a moment held her, and for a moment, there in the kitchen, trapped by the memory, she felt the protection of his arms again, the most bitter and the most sweet moment of safety. And then he had looked away, hung his head, and crawled from view.

Feeling utterly alone, Eldest hugged herself tight, shocked at her thinness. She reached the kitchen fireplace, the stones still coated with hints of the grease from a thousand roasts.

She reached out with both hands, searching blindly. Cold iron links met the fingers of her right hand. Eldest took the chain that had once been used to suspend a cauldron above the flames. She wrapped it around two bars, securing it with a bent nail, and trailed the remainder across the kitchen floor. She added to its length the chain that had once turned a rotating spit from which all trace of meat fat had long ago been licked by rats or children. She added to that the thinner but still sturdy chain that had once drawn heaped loads of silverware up the service shaft to the higher floors. She doubled this one for strength. Another length of the chain she used had been found in one of the bedrooms, purpose unknown. Finally, won at the highest of costs, were three yards of heavy chain retrieved from the cellars during the previous year.

This last section allowed her to reach the basement door. It had never been locked, to her knowledge, but it felt capable of withstanding any assault if it ever were. The thing was riveted iron, thick plates of the stuff sandwiching two inches of wood. She could feel the rust beneath her fingertips. What the previous owners might have kept in their basement that required such security she didn't know, but pressing her forehead to the gritty surface, she wondered how long it might resist Mother.

The door opened inwards and on both sides had an iron handle with which to heave it back and forth. Eldest pulled the chain taut and carefully adjusted its length. Before laying her clanking burden on the ground, she looped it around one half of the double hook that had once allowed the cauldron in the kitchen to be dangled over the fire.

No physical restraints kept Mother below ground but only in her fiercest rages had she emerged to prowl the corridor and venture into the nearest storage rooms. It seemed almost that she was a creature of the earth, constrained to dwell within it. All of which meant that Eldest would have to enrage her.

Carefully, Eldest oiled the rusty hinges using the inedible grease she had long ago found in a tub within the kitchen cupboards.

Easing the door open brought with it that familiar stink of damp soil, mould, and decay. Eldest could see the waiting stairway only in her mind's eye. She had never seen it with her actual eyes. Save the parlour, the mansion lay in darkness, but it seemed to pool in the basement, so thick she could feel it all around her like a mist.

The lower levels had a hunger to them. Night-Father would not pursue the children down here, but some of Eldest's siblings had chosen to let themselves be captured rather than seek sanctuary below. Mother's attentions were such that even the certainty of torture might be preferable to a chance of being captured by her. Eldest had felt her loathsome touch only once, and still the skin on her arm wanted to shrivel at the memory of those fingers against her flesh.

Night-Father worked with pain, but Mother touched the mind, her unclean fingers staining thoughts and emotions, leaving deeper and longer-lasting wounds. Mother made you feel that this was your fault, and that what was happening . . . that it was almost love. At least it seemed more that way the longer she had you.

The pair of them appeared to have divided the mansion between them, and Mother had no obvious role in what happened in the main house. Even so, Eldest had always felt that the power lay down there in the darkness, and that Father, in both his skins, day and night, was Mother's agent, up here in the world where she fit so poorly. Quite how they had hatched their plan together, and what that plan was, Eldest didn't know. But she was sure that there was a plan, and she wanted no part of it.

Recovering the memory of her family, or at least the outline of that memory, the fact that the monster in the cellar and the one who haunted the mansion were not her blood – that had been a moment of unutterable relief. It had been a diamond filched with blind fingers from the murk and grime of her past. Something hard and clear and pure. Something to hold onto. A purpose in and of itself.

The cellars had three entrances but fortunately Mother wasn't given to lurking near them, preferring the deepest places until something drew her attention and set her prowling. Even so, Eldest trembled so badly going down the first flight of steps that had she still been carrying chains they would have rattled.

A lightless corridor brought her to the wine cellar. She had explored this place by touch on her previous visit. Beneath the brick arches of the largest of these vaults lay scores of barrels. Fewer than half of them were intact and all of them were empty, at least of wine. Amid the scattered stays and shed hoops of corroding metal were barrels large enough for three children to hide within, and barrels too small for even Tune to squeeze herself into.

If she went any further into the underground complex Eldest would enter a region where Mother might come at her from any one of multiple directions. But here at the far end of the wine cellar she could be ambushed only if Mother knew she was coming and had concealed herself along the way. Since nobody ever came down into the basement during the day, Eldest felt relatively safe. Or rather she felt totally unsafe and terrified, but her intelligence told her she was as safe as anyone could be in such a place.

She found an empty barrel with its base still in one piece and inverted it, shocked by her own weakness. Next, she began the slow process of arranging the remaining barrels across the cellar floor, creating an obstacle field complete with two walls of barrels, all of it seen only in her mind.

Every misstep, every scrape, rang terrifyingly loudly in her ears, seeming to echo back and forth beneath the curved ceiling. Totally blind, she kicked a barrel hoop and sent it skittering. She worked on, cursing silently, heart hammering, sure that Mother would arrive at any moment. It seemed impossible that the noise Eldest had made wouldn't have woken her.

By the time Eldest found her way back to the inverted barrel, placed closest to the archway she'd entered by, her limbs were trembling with exhaustion as much as with the fear of what was to come. Eldest took three deep breaths then hunted for a loose stave and struck the base of the barrel with it. She hit her makeshift drum again, the boom both startlingly loud in that silence and yet not so loud as she had imagined.

'Show yourself...' Her voice came out small, a croaking apology. She coughed and filled her lungs. 'Show yourself, monster!'

Mother's weapon of choice wasn't pain but fear itself. Father used pain to instil fear, but Mother jumped that stage entirely. There was something so awful in the dry strength of her embrace, and the wrongness of her whispered affection. Eldest's hands shook. Her legs felt weak.

Boom! 'Show yourself!' Boom!

That Mother would genuinely show herself was another part of the horror. Somehow, although the cellars held not even a whisper of light, when Mother came she could be seen, her outlines drawn in pale white strokes that illuminated nothing.

Being able to see Mother's approach helped the children escape her if they ever ended up in this awful place, but she knew how to hide and although she moved like a broken thing, she moved fast. When she had caught Eldest it had been in a chamber on the second level of the basements, a cold box of a room strewn with old bones. Eldest had knocked against something and sent it tumbling from a decaying shelf. She'd made a blind grab for the object as it rolled noisily across the stone floor, and somehow, she'd got a hand to it.

Mother had risen from a far corner, shedding her sackcloth covering in the same moment that Eldest's exploring fingers had revealed the object to be a skull. Mother had lifted from the ground as if drawn on invisible wires, her arms and legs bone-thin, each joint swollen, her hair a wild tangle aglow with its own lightless light.

The clicks her body made with each of its unnatural motions set Eldest's teeth on edge and made her think the creature had escaped from some awful dungeon where they'd twisted every limb, drawing each joint from its socket.

Eldest had run but Mother caught her in a trice, bringing her face up close, her eyes, wide, staring, and hardly human. '*I have spiders under my skin.*'

Boom! 'You're not my mother!' Boom! Eldest's voice shook with memories of the horror she'd endured nestled in Mother's arms. The loathsome whispering. The terrible true lies that had unwrapped her mind to the woman's touch.

And there she was, suddenly, sliding into the archway opposite. '*Daughter.*'

Eldest shook off the paralysis she knew would come beneath the creature's incurious predatory stare. Even so, Mother had covered a third of the distance before Eldest could turn her back on the pale horror and start to run. The barrels Eldest had arranged hardly seemed to slow her. She flowed over them with broken grace, not so much as rattling a loose stay.

Darkness, thick as blankets, wrapped itself around Eldest. She wanted to sprint, but starvation and fear mired her in the moment. It felt as if she was wading back towards the door, all the while with Mother's scream clenched around her heart. The steps were a mountain for Eldest to labour up beneath the weight of all her terror. Dry fingers clutched at the back of her neck at every step, fading to phantoms until the next heartbeat manufactured another anticipation of the inevitable.

Shrieking her panic, Eldest crashed through the gap where she'd left the basement door ajar, skinning her shoulder. She grabbed the hook and for a chain-rattling moment it seemed she'd miscalculated, giving herself an inch too little's reach. But with a gasp and a grunt, she had hook through handle and was running again, following the chain.

Mother gained the door before Eldest got to the kitchen. The chain sprang and bounced as Eldest ran beside it. Another jerk, and then with a roar, Mother applied her true strength. At the other end of the chain the bars across the chimney tore free. One of them caught Eldest a glancing blow above her hip. Deep in her fear she staggered forward, ignoring the pain.

Had she been well-fed she would never have squeezed through the gap the bars had left. She was six feet up by the time Mother reached the fireplace.

'*Child . . .*' The word slithered from the monster's lips. '*Come back to your mother, child. I've more treats to feed you.*'

Eldest climbed, showering ancient soot behind her.

'*Child!*' Mother tore another bar loose.

Damp stone and weakness betrayed Eldest, her toes slid, fingers lost their grip, she fell, screaming.

Her heart stopped. *She* stopped.

Eldest hung, wedged in the widening chimney, every muscle straining, feet pressed furiously against the brickwork on one side, shoulders against the other. Not far below her Mother hissed and spluttered, showered by the debris dislodged by Eldest's fall. High above them both, impossibly far away, a circle of daylight burned.

'*Come to your mother.*' Another bar tore free. An arm reached through, clawing at the air just beneath Eldest's heels.

Straining every muscle, Eldest shifted herself by degrees, patting for holds in the brickwork, trying to move from horizontal to vertical without being snared.

'*Sweetling, there's no need to be shy . . .*' Mother snatched at a dangling ankle, but her reach into the chimney breast was tentative, as if the old fires still burned there with furious heat.

The light! The light might save her. Eldest found the smallest of ledges, wedged her toes, shifted herself, and began to climb.

'*Come down, sweet child,*' the creature crooned. '*Don't go. We love you so.*'

A yard, another yard, Eldest kept climbing for the light.

'*Come down, bitch! I'll skin you. Keep you in the oven till you're ready to eat! Burn you with—*'

A brick, dislodged by Eldest's questing toes, cut off the tirade.

'*Father! Father! I'm getting your father!*' Mother's voice faded.

Eldest climbed blind. Even though the light was growing in intensity with every yard she rose, it rapidly changed from too dark to see to too bright to see. As she gained height she felt the air change, growing colder, and with a hint of motion to it. She could see the circle of daylight through her eyelids now, growing closer. Every limb trembled with fatigue, her filthy fingers bled from torn and split nails, her hip ached, she hung by the thread of her own desire, just a heartbeat from a ruinous fall . . . but she was so very close.

She was going to make it. She could almost touch the day. They couldn't stop her now. Not far, just a little—

The fist punched through plaster and paint and sent another brick tumbling. The hand, glimpsed through eyes screwed tight, groped empty air just inches from her stomach. She pressed her back to the chimney wall to put more space between Father's clutching fingers and her belly.

While Father hissed at the sudden influx of light, Eldest scrambled upwards, loaned strength by this fresh terror. His hand scraped her foot but failed to find purchase. Howling at his miss, Father began to pound the wall, enlarging the hole he'd made.

The burst of panic brought Eldest up to the blinding circle of light. It had grown as she approached it, but now in the final few yards it had shrunk alarmingly. The square cross-section of the chimney, barely wide enough for a child, now became a circle defined by a cylinder of blackened clay. The chimney pot was longer than her arm and hardly wider than her head.

Falling bricks punctuated Father's unintelligible roaring, her name the only thing she could pick out amid the froth of his rage.

Eldest's strength, braced only by her feet against the flue's walls, found no give in the chimney pot. Even at her prime she doubted she could have shifted it without tools and a secure perch.

'*Eldest* . . .' Mother's voice insinuated through a gap in Father's howls, reaching the length of the flue.

Desperation drove Eldest. With her hands together as if in prayer, she snaked up into the narrow tube, supported only by toenails clutching the gaps where mortar had fallen from between bricks. Serpentlike, she advanced up the earthenware cylinder, a feat that would have been impossible without her recent starvation.

With her shoulders practically driven into her eyes Eldest wedged herself so tight that she could release her footholds. She drove herself further up. The end of her escape, trapped in the chimney pot, seemed inevitable.

She breathed soot into a constricted chest, saw nothing save her own tight-pressed limbs, and despaired, but somehow, she wormed her way up by fractions. When her fingertips found the chimney pot's edge she advanced a swift hand's length before running out of room to bend her elbows. She caught the breeze in her palms now, comically and tragically trapped but close enough to freedom to touch it.

Father's demolition work below was muffled but constant. Eldest saw his twisted features in her mind's eye and redoubled her efforts. Probably he'd send up one of her sisters to rope her ankles so he could pull her back down.

Her eyes passed the confining upper edge, having reached it so slowly that the light no longer burned away her vision. Even with her shoulders out it proved all but impossible to use her arms to help her, bent double as they needed to be to reach the rim beneath her armpits. The chimney pot chose this moment to start to wobble, beginning to work itself loose from the main shaft below.

Birds further along the rooftop, perched on the chimneys rising from other rooms, took flight on black wings with raucous cries. Eldest wriggled furiously. Her imagination painted the very real scenario in which the chimney pot toppled with her inside it and rolled down the roof to dash itself on the ground three storeys below. Her struggles slowly ejected her as the wobbling grew more substantial, the cracking sounds louder.

'Traitor! Come back!' The voice of one of her sisters not far beneath her, too tight with effort for recognition. 'Stop!'

Eldest redoubled her efforts, imagination closing fingers around her heel at every moment.

'No! Don't!' Somehow, she found the breath to shriek her fear.

Her final escape was swift, passing some tipping point where she could wriggle free, albeit at the cost of more skin. She dropped and would have fallen but for the neighbouring chimney pot which she grabbed hold of. With her other hand she steadied the chimney pot she'd emerged from and heaved herself up to stand beside the smokestacks, five of them in a row. Glancing down the flue she'd escaped, she saw light reflecting in the upturned eyes of whichever sibling had been sent to retrieve her. Brighter in one than the other. Milk-Eye! Would the girl choose to escape too or, bound by fear, do their parents' bidding?

Save for the wind's cold moan and Milk-Eye's grunting ascent it was suddenly quiet. The absence of Father's roaring was worrying. She knew in that instant that he was heading for the street door to gain the roof from the outside.

Eldest tried to ignore the wide-open panorama of rooftops so that it wouldn't overwhelm her with its half-remembered strangeness. Other buildings stood all around, closer than she had ever imagined. People on every side living normal lives almost within touching distance of the private hell she shared with her brothers and sisters. Close, but none close enough for there to be even a remote chance of jumping the gap.

The grounds surrounding the mansion were thick with overgrown bushes, pierced by a handful of trees. Decisions had to be made swiftly. Escape or die. Capture was not an option.

Eldest peered once more down the chimney pot. Milk-Eye's face looked up at her from the flue, almost within reach now. The girl looked desperate, though whether from fear of falling, fear of failing, or desire to escape, Eldest couldn't say. Despite sharing extremes with her sister – her false sister – for years, Eldest didn't know which way she'd break under such stress and faced with such choices. Eldest *did* know that she was too weak to fight off her younger sibling though.

'Help me . . .' Milk-Eye's filthy arm reached up, hand grasping.

Eldest stared with frozen horror. If she took that hand the girl could drag her back down, hold her there at the very least.

She found herself reaching for Milk-Eye, the gap between those stretching fingers and her own already reduced to less than a foot. In that moment the memory of Strong, broken and crawling for the street door, speared through her again, a physical pain that contracted her muscles, pulling back her hand.

'. . . sorry . . .' A gasp. A soft cry of agony. 'Sorry,' she muttered again as she withdrew, telling herself again that the girl was not her sister. Not her blood. A wipe of her hand sent a cloud of soot down to blind the one good eye staring up at her. A shove sent the loose chimney pot falling, aimed in the opposite direction to the one she planned to take, and in the faint hope it would roll and crash on Father as he emerged. When the pot broke away it revealed Milk-Eye's blackened, spluttering face in the flue, now just inches from the open air.

If she'd had the strength, Eldest could have pulled the girl free, out into the world and new possibilities, but fear and weakness stayed her hand.

Eldest ran. Along the ridge towards the East Wing, then veering down across the slates in an unstoppable curving run towards the guttering. She aimed herself at the tree that grew nearest to the mansion on the far side from the street door. Fear of the fall didn't factor at all. Terror of Father's revenge drove her on.

The roof's slope gave her speed that her tired legs could not have manufactured. At the last moment she leapt for the branches and shot through the air, arms pinwheeling as the thick foliage devoured her.

The drop didn't end until the ground hammered the air from her lungs. Eldest remembered only the sense of falling, the sound of splintering, and the branches' repeated blows to her body. She rolled onto her front, drawing air into her wheezing chest, and began to crawl, moving slowly through a thick green jungle that was cold, wet, and sharp. She hoped that Father would be climbing the mansion's outer wall to gain the roof, too distracted by the falling chimney to hear her distant encounter with the tree.

As Eldest crawled she tried to erase herself. She didn't stop moving though. Trusting only in what Father had taught her felt . . . too trusting. What had been the point of all those nights of pain and fear? To teach the children to hide themselves. To terrify them into feats of concentration that might be beyond any less motivated mind. But would Father truly teach them to hide from *him*, or could he see through such tricks?

Eldest trusted the cover of the bushes, thorned or not. On hands and knees, she advanced through brambles, tearing her clothes and her skin. And when she came to the garden wall, she peered through the leaves to see the black figure of Father prowling the roof ridge, hunting around the chimney stacks. A thick tree provided the cover she needed to climb the wall unseen. An oak, she thought, though how she knew that she had no idea. She dropped down into the street beyond, barefoot, filthy, bloody, and more tired than she had ever been. But she stood in daylight and though the sky was leaden, promising only rain, she had never felt more free.

CHAPTER 27

Rue

'Why are you running away?'

Rue ignored the crow and continued what could at best be called limping briskly away.

'Stay and fight!' Senna cawed. 'I thought you were all set on justice!'

'Anything that won't bend can break us. It's convictions that make monsters.' Rue shook her head. 'I set my convictions aside early on. It's part of what made me so hard to kill.'

'That sounds like a very long way to say you're scared.'

'I'm scared,' Rue growled.

'I thought you Kindnesses were the big bad.'

'The important word in that sentence is "were". The news is five years out of date this far from civilization, not thirty. Didn't your memory fit inside that bird skull?'

Rue stamped onward. Her body felt one part dead and three parts alive, and all of the parts were too old for any of this shit. Her injuries hurt less than they should and impeded her less than they should, but they still hurt and still got in the way.

The road out of Pye led west towards the border. Pye, the Vale, and the rest of the region that had once belonged to a copper-crowned king named Handelf, had been swallowed by the empire ten years before Rue's arrival. Villages had burned, and fields had been watered with the blood of Handelf's axemen. He'd been a warrior who had carved his way to his throne and wasn't ready to surrender it whatever the opposition. There had been battles, but in Pye they'd seen only distant smoke and the gathering of ravens.

Those fields now belonged to Emperor Sunder, though he might ride three swift horses to death in as many days and still not reach them from his golden capital. He'd given their administration over to one of his barons, Baron Mancer, and whether the man had considered it a gift or a reprimand, Rue didn't know.

The emperor's newest neighbour to the west was now King Armand, third of his name and ruler of Tavoland whose mountains rose in sharp defence before falling away in a long descent to the sea. Or it would have been had Armand not himself fallen . . . from his horse mere yards from the gates of his palace and succumbed by degrees to an infection that sank its teeth into a fractured hip. The two years that had passed since had seen the title settle on his widow, the 'Battle Queen', having crushed opportunistic invasions from the north and south, giving the lord of the rock-strewn kingdom of Hard Hill a very bloody nose and wreaking worse ruin upon the Marsh King.

To judge from Senna's report the mercenaries were burning settlements on both sides of the empire's border with Tavoland. Rue knew for certain that the emperor didn't give a bent copper for the lives of the peasants out in these supposedly unfarmable hills. She doubted that this Battle Queen out of Tavoland would give one either but pile enough corpses on the margins of a country and eventually the ruler's pride would be hurt sufficiently to do something about it. It had to be said though, that the Battle Queen forged her name fighting alongside peasants. Shortly after the invasion of Regon, twenty years earlier, she'd supported Regonian rebels up in the Red Hills on their side of that same border. They still sang songs about the battle of Caden's Pass. So Armand's widow might respond this time. If Tavoland stayed silent though, Sunder would have to pretend to care about his farmers and use his own antagonism as a pretext for expanding to the western sea. Similar tactics had initiated wars with Svellard to the north and Kintcha to the south. Both countries now mere provinces of Sunder's empire.

Rue's friends, home, and village had all been destroyed as part of the pretence staged so that Emperor Sunder could claim the moral high ground in a war of his own making.

Senna swooped low, cawing. 'Your lot got a taste of your own medicine.' The bird's thoughts were still on Rue and the Kindnesses that had raised her. 'A bitter enough taste! I remember that.'

'They stopped being "my lot" long before Sunder's purge.' Rue struck out over a ploughed field, the ruts swerving here and there to avoid stones too large to move. In her mind's eye Rue could still see Martha Craven cursing her ox, Low Bo, as she coaxed him around the turns. 'Sunder saved me the effort.' A lie but it soothed her. 'Sunder and the Cruelties that served him.'

'Burned that big castle, didn't they?'

'Academy,' Rue muttered. Try as she might to distract herself, the crow's cawing scraped along her spine. Rue might have taken flight and eventually lost herself in the backwaters of empire, but Senna was right, whether she knew it or not. The Kindnesses *had* been 'Rue's lot'. And when their end had come in fire and chaos, despite the wrathful vows of her youth, it hadn't been her doing. 'Not castle. Academy.'

Senna flew ahead and fluttered to a halt on the gatepost at the field's exit. Beyond the dry-stone wall the ground became progressively rockier and sloped up to a wooded ridge where the trees leaned sharply with the prevailing wind.

'Running from one man . . . Wasn't one man tore down your castle, was it?'

'I wasn't there.' It had been a mob. Not one man. Senna was right about that. Thousands had flooded out of the city once the resident Kindnesses were gone. With that many there together, driven by the surging collective will, they hadn't known if they were there to save the children, to kill the monsters, to wipe the slate clean to remove the stain on their conscience, or just to loot and burn, hunting for the fabled wealth that surely must lie behind the next locked door.

'Why are you running?' Senna cawed. 'They told us the Kindly Ones brought the fire. Said they could crack the earth itself. Raise storms. Call the waves.'

'You're remembering a lot all of a sudden.' Rue made a lazy swipe as she passed the gatepost. Senna took to the air, squawking, a stray feather whirling in her wake. 'And I did bring the fire.' She glanced back at the black smoke rising. The sun had poked out between cloud wracks and the flames below the smoke were hardly visible in the light of day.

Senna swooped by. 'You didn't bring that fire. Those bastards set it alight. They burned the place and killed everyone. And you let them do it.'

Rue didn't answer. She had never managed to unleash the full might of the elixir. The talent was rare and few among the Kindnesses had burned as brightly as legends like Heera and the handful of others once remembered in the lesser creed. And now days nobody did. That fire had gone out of the world. Rue considered this to be a good thing since small as the number who could touch divinity were, the number who could survive the experience were smaller still. Heera herself was said to have endured two grand rages before being carried off at the height of her third and final unleashing at the gates of Themda.

The propensity for holy rage increased with each draught of the elixir consumed but having found candidates for a trio at the expense of a sizeable portion of the class, the Kindnesses were loath to kill off their promising acolytes with a second drink of the poison. It wasn't an act of compassion. All but three of any year were doomed. But the process over the five years of the second half of their training was designed to select those best suited to the role. Simply dosing the class with the fabulously valuable elixir until all but three of them had exploded, burned to a crisp, or just keeled over dead, would not allow the rest of the training to achieve the brutality required when honing a Kindness.

The fact that Kindness Undu had poured Rue a second draught following her insubordination had, however, still not gifted her the power to unleash the full rage of the Kindly Ones. Nor had it served the punitive function the Kindness intended. Rue had gulped the liquid down, felt that same distressingly familiar blackness flutter in her chest, and then . . . nothing. She had found the Kindness's eyes again, but this time had refrained from voicing her thoughts, instead releasing a belch that Sharp later gleefully recounted as being far too loud and long to have come out of such a slight child.

On a very small number of occasions, Rue had been a door for some fraction of the Furies' fire. But to open that door required the incandescent fury that only true calamity can provoke. She prayed never to visit such extremes again.

Rue stumbled over a rock and cursed. She shook off the memories that had stolen her attention. 'I wish—' But Rue wasn't quite self-absorbed enough to complain to Senna about the things she wished she'd had time to recover from her hut. She might have had useful possessions burned up, but Senna had lost family. Senna's husband had left with a visiting tinker woman years before Rue arrived, tired, no doubt, of her sharpening her tongue on him. But her son, his wife, their children . . . Rue clamped her lips together.

She would miss the village and many of the people in it, but she hadn't been born there. It wasn't the totality of her experience: she had suffered loss before. Even so, she really did wish she'd brought her heavy coat, a skin to hang over bushes for when it rained, a flint and kindling, some salt, the coins she'd kept under her hearthstone . . . so many things. A cartload really. She was too old for tramping across the wilds. She'd been too old for it ten years earlier when she'd tramped her way to the Vale. Now the great outdoors resembled a do-it-yourself torture kit. A decade of straw mattresses and woollen blankets, albeit thin grey ones that harboured a variety of wildlife, had made her soft. The years themselves had made her soft, comforts aside – the soft decay of age had found its way past her hardness and the barriers forged at such cost.

Among the trees the gloom already anticipated evening. Senna fluttered overhead, cawing irritably when she lost track of Rue. Though Rue reasoned that if the crow was compelled to follow her then surely that must come with some sense of direction . . . or how was it a compulsion?

'He's closer. Gaining on you.' Senna landed in the clearing Rue had just entered, by a spring that bubbled up near the middle of the glade, carpeting the ground in moss before running off among the thirsty roots. 'He's reached the trees.'

'He's better at following me than you are,' Rue commented, patting her skirts for the twentieth time in search of a heel of bread or any other vaguely edible thing. She hitched the folds of cloth up and sank to her knees with a groan, cushioning them on the green carpet as she bent to drink, scooping water to her lips. In peril's grip she had fought, demanding obedience from her body, ignoring its complaints. In the relative safety of the forest every action even slightly out of the ordinary seemed to require that she herald it with a grunt, groan, or the puffing of breath, as if her limbs needed each service to be individually acknowledged.

Rue stayed on her knees. It wasn't exactly comfortable. The moss was soaking and cold. But she really didn't feel ready to stand again. She wondered what it would be like to lie down and refuse to move until he found her.

'Get up!' Senna cawed.

'I thought you wanted me to face him down, burn him to a crisp!'

'*Can* you burn him to a crisp?'

'No.'

'Get up then!'

'I'm tired. I can't outrun him. And Kindnesses don't hide. It's not in our nature.'

'You've been hiding for years! Pretending to be a normal person!'

'Normal?' Rue forced the bitterness from her voice, spitting it out as a laugh that made the crow startle. She had learned early on to consider herself something different – as if as a baby the true Molly, sweet and pink in her innocence, had been offered up on an altar and replaced by a changeling, stained in her sin. It was easier to imagine all that had been taken from her removed in one bright stroke of a blade than torn away a scrap at a time. Easier to stop herself believing it could return to her. And yet despite the iron of her resolve, age and ten quiet years had let those feelings seep past her barriers. She had been steeped in peace and normality. 'I have been hiding. That's true. I wasn't a Kindness any more. I had set that aside.'

'I saw a Kindness walk out of that inferno.' The crow's unnerving stare skewered her.

'They should never have come.' Rue saw the single mercenary again, back in the alehouse in Stones Corner. A harbinger of doom, like the first hunger-bug dropping from a clear blue sky, of little consequence by itself, but herald to a million more.

The icy wetness of the moss received her, softer than any bed. The sky showed the cold grey heart that beats behind the blue, the bare fingers of a dead tree reaching in from the corner of her vision.

'You hated me because you were never happy there, Senna. Pye gave you everything you had, and you resented it for choking you, keeping you, hemming in your horizons. You hated me because I'd seen what the world had to offer – the sharpest edge of that in any case – and I'd chosen to come to the Vale. Worse, I chose to stay!

'Yes, I was angry and short-tempered, and I didn't have the spoons to be nice – but old women don't divide into grandmothers and witches based on whether they smile and nod and bake oatcakes or . . . don't.

'But some of them saw past that when they looked my way. Some of them saw someone whose opinion they cared about, and I appreciated that. Jayne could see I had scars and they called to her – she had her own. And Ambeth, gods bless her, she couldn't pass by a hopeless case if her life depended on it. She thought I was all bark and no bite, and thankfully I never disappointed her, even though I'm mostly bite with a little bark showing above the waterline.

'The goddess put you in that crow because, of all of them, you're the one who most badly needs to learn something, however old you are. And she put me in this . . . half-corpse . . . because I'd made a trio. And she might be an evil, crazy bitch . . . but she was right.'

Rue sat up and pulled the knife from her belt.

'I made a trio. And they took it from me. And someone has to pay.'

CHAPTER 28
Mollandra

Year Five

Mollandra could taste the elixir all day. The stuff burned on her tongue through one class after the next, through dinner, and through the cleansing of her teeth. Whatever had been in the liquid had found a home in her, tingling along her bones, colouring her sight with invisible shades. Something, some single ingredient, had changed them all. Mollandra's certainty brooked no argument. This wasn't the work of an alchemist, a cunning mix of rare substances, open to anyone with enough gold, time, and cauldrons to reproduce. But what it was, and why it should have immolated one girl, made another spark with holy fury, and had almost no effect at all on her, she couldn't say.

Later, in the darkness of the dormitory, more empty after the day's losses, Mollandra lay in her narrow cot, staring up at nothing. Quiet sounds reached her: the soft conversation of survivors seeking to make sense of the day's slaughter, the gentle noises of those girls who could find comfort and distraction in each other's bodies. Sharp would be one of them: danger always gave her that particular need, and she had never been in more danger than today. Though whose bed she might be sharing, Mollandra didn't know. Some, like Jemna and Takki were sweethearts, lovers, always in each other's company. Mollandra envied them their closeness though she would never give the world such a weapon to hurt her with if she could help it. Others, like Sharp, were careless with each other's hearts. Perhaps like Mollandra, they feared the wounds that true affection could open. It worried Mollandra though. Would Sharp one day discard their friendship as easily as she shrugged off the girls with whom she shared her passion?

Tmanga came to sit at the foot of Mollandra's bed, startling her from her thoughts. She vowed to be more alert. Her next visitor might not be a friend.

'Something happened with you today. You saved Sharp and you saved yourself. Sharp won't remember, but the Kindnesses will.'

'*We* saved Sharp.'

'The elixir was going to burn her up whether she got to her feet or not. *You* stopped her burning.'

Mollandra hadn't tried to do anything, except foolishly hold a girl who was about to burst into flame. The flames hadn't come. No doubt the Academy would give both of them many opportunities to wish that they had.

'I . . . don't know what happened.'

Anyone else would have pressed harder. Tmanga's weight left the bed and she retreated to her own blankets.

Mollandra lay on her back, eyes open, seeing nothing. The darkness that had spoken lived at her core, in the marrow of her bones. It was something she had brought with her to the Academy – the only thing she'd owned, save her scars and the thin smock she'd been wearing. She didn't think it had been born into her. Not all of it at least. It had been done to her, like the fury in the vault today. And now it ran through her veins, battling this new invader. She wouldn't sleep before dawn – she knew that much. Maybe she wouldn't sleep again.

The visitors came two days and no sleep later.

'Visitors!' Sharp careened into the practice hall, casually side-kicking a punch-dummy on the way through.

Constant terror had squeezed such frivolities as play, enthusiasm, and curiosity out of most of the acolytes, but Sharp behaved much as Mollandra imagined a 'real girl' would. Except for all the killing. It sometimes felt as if she saw an entirely different world to the rest of them, and Mollandra envied her that.

'Visitors!' Sharp briefly took the edges of Mollandra's robe in both fists and shook her before discarding her and slinging an arm around Tmanga's shoulders, steering her away from Freeda, careless of both acolytes' swords.

'We don't get visitors,' Tmanga said.

Several of the girls were looking up from their various exercises now. Mollandra imagined that behind their narrowed eyes thoughts of the parents who had sold them into this place were twitching, hope – ever cruel – springing from the salted earth of their regret.

'We do now.' Sharp folded her arms, triumphant.

'The Kindnesses get visitors,' Mollandra said. 'Couriers come with the black scrolls.'

'Deliveries aren't visits. And these aren't couriers. I saw them. They look like a king and a queen, and they've got a prince with them. A handsome one. I expect he's come to marry me. We'll have lots of babies and I'll get fat and eat cake all day.'

'You want to marry a prince?' Tmanga shot Sharp a sideways glance.

'Did you not hear the part about cake?'

Tmanga picked up her whetstone again and returned to honing her blade.

'That's it?' Sharp looked around.

'We'll know if they want us to know,' Tmanga said. 'Handsome, was he? Might be Prince Sunder, one of the king's nephews. They say he's breaking highborn hearts in the city.'

'How would you know?' Mollandra stamped her foot. 'And if you say "Einsa told me", goddess help me, I'll make you eat that sword!'

'I heard Twendri talking about it. You should practise your espionage more.'

Mollandra grunted. Twendri was one of the six Year Nines and got to go out into the world on practice missions. It was plausible that Tmanga had got it from her. Though Mollandra still suspected her friend of having secret channels. Certainly, with the exception of the elixir, there didn't ever seem to have been anything she hadn't known about in advance.

The call came less than an hour later. Year Ones, being most plentiful, were dispatched to summon every acolyte to the courtyard. A red-faced child, nearly drowning in her robes, hammered on the door of the practice hall.

'Parade! Parade!' And she was off.

'Were we ever that small?' Sharp frowned.

Tmanga flicked a bit of fluff from Sharp's sleeve. 'Mollandra was.'

'Parade' simply meant lining up by year in the courtyard. There were no flags or special uniforms or ceremonials. Mollandra had heard that in the city in high season there were dancers in the streets, priests of many faiths decked in silver chains, carrying jewelled staffs, foodstuffs sold from stalls, and colour everywhere. The Academy eschewed colour. The only way to see more than grey was to bleed.

The acolytes lined up beneath a dark-bellied sky, the blanketing cloud pregnant with rain. All six instructors strode around imposing order with sharp looks, loud commands, and the occasional slap. The full complement of servants stood in a grey wall by the entrance gate as if ready to block any bids for freedom.

When the three royals came through the main gate led by Kindnesses Marta and Terra, and trailed by Undu, the vivid hues of their costumes – Mollandra could only think of them as costumes donned to play a role – were an assault on the senses. Plush blues deeper than any sky, green velvet no leaf could match, the sparkle of gems. The people too looked more than real, as if their current bleak surroundings might be scenery in some play, Mollandra and the rest of the acolytes merely a supporting cast in drab.

'Who are they?' Sharp had ended up standing in the front rank of the Year Fives even though they were supposed to be arrayed by height. Her whisper reached over her shoulder, carried on the chill breeze to Mollandra in the second rank with Tmanga at her side. Receiving no answer, she continued with her potentially suicidal indiscipline. 'Treecie would have known. She was rich. But no, Mollandra had to go and kill—' Even Sharp had the sense to shut up when Kindness Terra's gaze swept the courtyard from beneath a frown.

The royals moved with infuriating sloth. Much as Mollandra didn't want to get back to the business of frequently fatal training, she also didn't want to stand in silence in the courtyard for hours, alone with her thoughts. She imagined there would have to be more lessons in being silent and alone as the class shrank further and the survivors came closer to being sent out into the world. She doubted Kindnesses were welcome guests . . . anywhere.

It seemed unlikely that the older pair were in fact the king and queen of the nation. Surely someone would have recognized them and sent the whisper around. But clearly, they were important enough to command the attention of three Kindnesses, not to mention the entire academic body. Whoever they were they seemed to have a million stupid questions and to enjoy staring at acolytes.

Quite a few of the aforementioned acolytes, Sharp among them, were staring back when they felt they could do so unobserved. Not at the older couple doing all the talking but at the young man slouching in his finery behind them. His colours were less garish, primarily black and silver, his hair a dark gold, falling between his shoulder blades to a length few of the acolytes dared to match for fear of handing classmates – or their tutors – a weapon to use against them.

Mollandra had seldom had the time to reflect on qualities such as 'handsome' or 'pretty', and couldn't say with confidence whether the prince's even features were one or the other or neither. But she had no trouble describing him to herself as 'striking'. Even from a distance. Sharp was fond of saying that she wasn't sure if she wanted to fight someone or fuck them, concluding with 'first one then the other', and Mollandra was pretty sure from the intensity of her stare that the girl was thinking it now. Especially as boys were in rather short supply in the Academy and Sharp always liked to try new things.

But as Mollandra's gaze lingered on this tall, broad-shouldered young prince, something refused to let her look away. There was something about him. Something . . . something she recognized?

'Sunder,' someone, maybe Lurgan, whispered behind her. So, it *was* the king's nephew, and the man must be the king's youngest brother, since two of the others were dead, and one married overseas to the daughter of the Warlord of Darrak far away on Gog. At least this was the case according to the late Instructor Clakka's 'World' lessons, the only window that Mollandra had to offer views other than the distant city walls and the surrounding patchwork of woodland and field. The instructor's replacement, Quendri, knew far less than Clakka had. Until recently Quendri had been a tenth year, saved from the catacombs only by Mollandra's act of murder. She stumped around at the front of Vault Studies on her broken leg, her freshly mutilated nose still weeping, and frequently repeated that Mollandra had only herself to blame for reducing the quality of her own education.

Mollandra caught another look at this Prince Sunder. Again that sense of familiarity lanced through her. She shook her head and held back a snort of amusement at her own foolishness. The king's nephew. She had felt for a moment that she had seen him before. Foolishness in itself for she knew no one outside these walls and never left them. Why would she think she had a bond with someone who might, if a handful or two of nobles died, inherit the throne? She snorted then, unable to hold it back, and dragged her gaze away to the boy's father. What was the king's little brother doing here beneath a rain-dark sky?

She guessed it must be an inspection. A statement, however hollow, of authority over this vicious hive of women that sat so close to their city.

Although the Kindnesses considered themselves to be far above worldly considerations, delivering justice to the high and mighty without fear or favour, the Academy did have to sit somewhere, and that somewhere inevitably lay within a kingdom. History had chosen the undistinguished kingdom of Abrona for the holy site.

Abrona had seemed for generations to be a country destined to be consumed by its larger neighbours. The luck of its rulers would surely run out, but time and again, fortune favoured them.

The presence of the Academy had led to a certain tension between the kings of Abrona and the new cult seeking to put down roots in that soil. Inevitably, large and uncharacteristic doses of pragmatism had been required by the Kindnesses. They'd aimed themselves at miscreants beyond the kingdom's borders, whilst all the while building their strength so that when their gaze turned inwards, they were too dangerous to be evicted. This presented an obvious problem for the present incumbent King Orrin Devin.

Mollandra's eyes had returned to Prince Sunder when she sensed it. A sick dread thrilled through her, a once-familiar feeling that she had long ago managed to crush down into the darkest and least visited corner of her mind. Glancing frantically around the grounds, she saw it. The shape moved between Years Two and Three on the far side of the courtyard, refusing definition, denying its presence. None of the young acolytes so much as twitched as the thing prowled around them. If not for the unnatural way it moved, the alien, almost insectoid motion, fluctuating from frenzy to statue in the space of a heartbeat, Mollandra might also have let the enchantment seduce her into believing that it wasn't there.

Even as she looked, a terrible understanding washed away illusion and the man stood revealed in the act of lifting a small girl's hair, sniffing her neck, staring into her eyes, taking care only not to block her line of sight to the alluring prince.

The first heavy drops of rain started to fall. The man, clad in black, black-haired, black-eyed, skin pale as if his blood had been drained, glanced this way then that. He moved past three more girls in that ungainly flurry of motion, stopping to examine the fourth. Instructor Mary, standing to attention near the back of the group, frowned, and glanced his way. Her gaze flittered across to the Year Threes then returned to the visitors.

Mollandra stood with a stillness she had never called upon since stepping through the Academy's gate, an immobility that would challenge a statue, stilling her breath to the faintest whisper, even quieting her heart despite every instinct trying to make it race, trying to set it pounding against her ribs.

Again, the man sniffed at an acolyte, as if inspecting a carcass at a poultry stall. The rain started to fall in earnest.

Leave, damn you! Mollandra couldn't see the royals but she knew they were still there, subjecting their finery to a soaking. What kind of aristocrat endures a downpour to discuss future dead girls? *Leave and we can leave too!* She wouldn't feel safe with half a dozen locked doors behind her, but she'd feel a whole lot safer than standing out here in the open, on display.

As if sensing her eyes upon him, the man spun, reversing himself as quick as a finger snap. Mollandra kept her gaze nailed to the royals who, now darkened with rain, had sedately interposed themselves between her and the intruder.

Cold rain ran down Mollandra's back and chest. The downpour reached epic proportions, thundering earthwards with a ferocity rarely seen in the east. Mollandra blinked it from her eyes, puffed it from her lips. Desperately focused on the king's sister, all the while tracking the man in her periphery as he crossed the courtyard.

She had forgotten how to feel this terrified.

When he moved he was at his most alien, fixed where he should flex, supple where humans weren't meant to bend. His head and shoulders seemed peculiarly connected, as if both arms looped over an invisible broom handle that ran behind his neck. He moved in loping triples, eating up the distance, stopping, devouring more.

He circled the dripping royals and the Kindnesses, his clothes as black as their robes. Kindness Undu sniffed the air as the man came close, causing him to veer off. Kindness Terra half-drew her knife, out of the royals' sight, and glanced around in suspicion, her gaze briefly attaching to the man before sliding away. Marta, in conversation with the older man, Prince Sunder's father, seemed to sense nothing. Only the king's nephew saw the man for certain, looking away, not in fear but as if he might be an accomplice in the deception of eyes and minds.

The intruder kept his distance from the Kindnesses, moving clear of them. He became a ghost in the rain until he loomed suddenly from the deluge at the front of the Year Five group, so close that Mollandra could almost reach out and touch him.

She kept her eyes locked on the Kindnesses and their guests, teeth clenched, painfully aware of the man at the edge of her vision, running his hands across an oblivious Sharp, a scant inch from making contact.

The intruder abandoned Sharp and circled to the end of Mollandra's rank. Somehow when he insinuated himself between the sodden rows of acolytes they accepted it as the buffeting of a non-existent wind. He paused at Tmanga's side, and she turned, rubbing at her scar, mouth twisting as if tasting something foul. An acolyte in the front row staggered forward as the man gave Tmanga space and moved towards Mollandra, reaching for her with a hand at once both human and monstrous, the fingers limp and dangling as rainwater trickled from the tips.

Mollandra caught his wrist, though she was almost too slow.

A black pulse beat through her. Sick-making, nearly powerful enough to carry the world away.

She would have sliced through every vein and tendon in his arm, but by the time her blade made it from her belt he'd wrenched free.

The spell broke, its fragments washed away with the rain in the space of an eyeblink. The acolytes saw him first, some screaming in fear – a difficult reaction to provoke after five years of the Academy – others crying out in alarm or anger. All of them, through some unnamed instinct bedded in their shared humanity, recognized the man as something alien, something unclean and dangerous. Even acolytes who might in two or three years be fully fledged Kindnesses, drew back as if fearing that Father might sink his teeth into their flesh.

Instructor Maggery, whose lessons in concealment had never even scratched the surface of the intruder's skillset, got to him first. Or would have if he hadn't danced out of reach. His laughter, high and wild, sent shudders through Mollandra and her strength almost deserted her.

Kindness Terra closed on him, her great sword bared and held before her in both hands. On all sides the instructors came forward, knives at the ready.

'Ladies! Ladies!' The man motioned with downward palms for the lowering of blades, his grin so wide that one might expect it to bleed. 'I'm not here to fight.'

Kindnesses Marta and Undu arrived to flank Terra, a pace or two back. 'You may not have come here to fight.' Marta spoke into the weakening rain. 'But you seem to have come here to die. State your business with the Academy.'

'Oh, that's simple enough.' He levelled a bloodless finger at Mollandra. 'I came to take my daughter home.'

CHAPTER 29
Eldest

In a dark corner of a dark room, soot-black hands found the ruin of a garden and understood the shape of a betrayal that had been too large to comprehend.

Eldest ran, and stopped only when her legs and lungs refused her. She stood propped against the wall of a house, gasping. She had expected to reach a city wall or fields before exhaustion trumped her fear, and yet the metropolis had kept on going, street after street, block after block.

She'd passed people and houses, men and women, children from rich to poor, though none quite as ragged as her. Several women had called at her to stop. One fat man had tried to block her path, grinning broadly. Another had shouted, 'Thief!' But she had left them all behind.

She'd ended up in an area dominated by warehouses whose gaping mouths seemed ready to swallow her. None of the workers appeared much bothered by her presence, save to wave her away from the stacked crates, lines of barrels, and heaps of mysterious bundles.

A light rain had started to fall and although the cold numbed her aches and pains, it had also begun to sink through her tired flesh towards her bones.

New sights, sounds, smells all threatened to overwhelm her. But overwriting even her astonishment were the faces of those she'd left behind. Father's manic, twisted rage, and the look Milk-Eye had given her at the last.

Milk-Eye had called her 'traitor' and told her to stop. But what if that had been for Father's benefit while he could still reach into the chimney and catch a trailing foot? What if she'd trusted Eldest to see past the words? What if—

Eldest doubled over, leaning against a wall, and vomited the acid emptiness of her stomach.

She pushed away thoughts of what she'd left behind and looked around. As she'd run she had let chance decide her path, or rather, she had surrendered those choices to the deepest part of her mind, beneath the layers where words and images swim, the place where the most basic, instinctual foundations of thought hold sway. Eldest might swear that she had never seen this place, never walked this street or viewed those distant towers. But even so, there was something familiar here. Nothing specific, but something general and pervasive.

She turned from one path to the next, aiming herself at one alley, a tower top, a road, a gap between two buildings hardly wide enough for a man to walk. If she tried to argue a case for any one of them she would drown in maybes. Instead, she chose without thought, pushing away 'what if's and setting off on sore feet.

Constantly she looked behind her, expecting to see Father's tall figure looming. Time and again there was nothing, or just more suspicious strangers whose stares told her to keep moving. She kept moving.

Her chest hurt, bright needles of pain jabbing inwards with any deeper breath, her hip ached, she had cuts in places she didn't remember getting hit, and every other spot was tender to the touch. She picked up the pace, struggling to keep hope at bay, fighting to keep the smile from her lips so as not to tempt the gods' malice. Had she escaped? Had she truly won free?

The sun, hidden by clouds, slipped across the sky. Eldest's feet walked unaccustomed miles, sometimes circling the same area two or three times. Trying a path, losing the feeling, retracing her steps. And at last, with the light failing and lamps starting to flicker to life behind the shutters, she began to grow sure.

This she had seen before. This she had touched before.

This was the reason that the outside had not left her shocked at every turn, undone by each simple problem of navigation. She had seen it before. Somewhere beneath the memories that would come when called, all this was wrapped around the bones of who she was.

She turned left at the square where the old man's statue stood glaring at encroaching bushes. She turned right down a small alley rank with used ale. She hurried along a street where tall houses huddled shoulder to shoulder in a long terrace. Somehow, she knew that a different family inhabited each floor. Another right took her into a narrower terrace where shorter houses scowled across a street more mud than cobbles. She remembered washing strung between opposing windows. The lines lay bare now save for a lone off-white shirt flapping in the damp wind.

The sun burned red at the end of the street as she turned to face the door whose image had floated into her dreaming when starvation thinned the veils. The door had come first, the family behind it later. It would be the same now. In her mind she had already walked to the steps, gone up, and knocked. But here she was, still shivering in the street.

What if they were gone? Worse, what if they were still here but didn't recognize her? What if they didn't want her?

Eldest heard coughing. A shutter shuddered open, the dim glow of a candlelit room beyond. A girl stood there, her head and shoulders silhouetted in the window frame. '. . . Mol?'

Someone moved in the space behind her. 'Godsakes, close that window, Rebekka!'

'But she looks like Mol . . .'

'Who does?' The larger figure came to the window. A thin woman with grey in her hair and tired eyes leaned out, staring. 'Little Mol?'

'I . . .' Eldest found it hard to speak. 'I . . . don't know.' But she knew her mother's face, and her sister's. The fantasy that had crystalized into memory as starvation bit now stood before her, reality, flesh, blood, and all the more delicate for it.

'Mol!' The woman vanished. 'Cocran, it's Mol!' Her voice muffled in the house. A moment later bolts clacked back, the door opened, and in a swirl of skirts and scarves this new Mother, or this old one, had swept Eldest up into a hug.

The hard, sharp-angled shape within Eldest, the one that had been built to brace her against the waking nightmare of her existence, melted. Even the scar tissue from the basement where the monster dwelt couldn't armour her against this moment her heart had forgotten.

Eldest breathed in the smell of home, of cooking, of security, the scent of it all unlocking more memories than she could process, flooding her with belonging. She had crawled in this place before she could walk. She had gathered language to her within these walls. Tasted life.

She broke then. Eldest who had been so strong, so relentless, implacable in her desire. She fractured in the softness of her mother's arms, crying so hard she could scarcely breathe. She felt herself carried, glimpsed their small room, felt the crackling heat of their fire as Rebekka threw sticks into the hearth, and saw her father's lean form follow them in, lifting his round, wireframed spectacles to run a hand down his careworn face.

Time passed in a whirl of questions and hugs and laughing and worried talk of how thin she was, concerned glances passing between her parents. The night thickened outside behind shutters Eldest would have rather had been left open. She'd never felt so warm as she did beside the red embers of that fire. Rebekka sat with her, braiding her hair, having spent an age combing loose whatever mats didn't need to be cut out.

They fed her too. A bowl of beans seasoned with salt and accompanied by a heel of hard black bread. Eldest devoured it, her attempts to pace herself abandoned when she discovered it to be the most delicious meal she could remember.

Later, Mother sat in her chair with Eldest at her feet. Eldest rested her head on the cradle of her arms, supported by her mother's knees. Weariness weighed on her, making any movement an effort.

'One morning you were gone from your bed,' Mother said, beginning as if she were retelling one of the old hearth stories. 'Your sister didn't wake up, and she was sleeping under the same covers.

But you were gone . . .' She trailed off, her voice constricted by emotion.

Eldest sat up sharply. 'They came here?' Her heart, which had been slowed by the warmth, lurched back into racing pace. Night-Father could be approaching down the street even as they talked.

'No.' Her true father, a thin man with kind eyes and ink-stained hands, shook his head. He exchanged a glance with her mother. Eldest remembered him as given to wearing waistcoats, and jackets with patched elbows. 'You used to sleepwalk a lot. So, I put bolts on all the doors. That morning we found the bolts on the front door undone, but you were too small to reach the top one. We didn't think you could do it. Not at six years old. Not while asleep. But you must have got a chair . . .' He hung his head.

'Whoever took you must have snatched you from the street.' Mother kept very still, eyes down, hands knotted in her apron.

'They won't know where you live.' Father nodded.

Rebekka, frowning, went to the window, trying to see through the cracks in the shutters. 'I always keep a knife under my pillow. If they come back, I'll . . .'

'The only one coming back is little Mol,' Father said. 'Time for sleep. It's dark outside and we don't have money to burn.'

Eldest followed Rebekka up the creaking stairs to the tiny room dominated by their bed. Across the hall, her parents retired to the other small bedroom. After the mansion it all seemed very cramped, which felt better in that there were fewer angles of attack, and worse because there were fewer angles of escape. The unfolding within Eldest's chest, which had started when her mother's arms wrapped her, continued slowly with each small step towards this once and future normal.

'This will be strange.' Rebekka huddled under the thin covers. With just the fire glow from the main room downstairs for light, everything was shadows and suggestion. 'Five years . . . I've missed you. Every day.'

Eldest couldn't find anything to say. She got under the blankets, still in her rags, and curled up, facing her older sister. It seemed strange to still carry the name 'Eldest' when she wasn't, but she had worn it so long she found it hard to set aside, although she did remember being little Mol.

The two girls spoke in whispers for a while, sharing memories of the doll, Woodweana, of climbing the wall into the garden where apple trees grew, of chasing through the alleys. The recollections were less important in their specifics than they were in establishing the truth of their shared lives and ensuring that neither was sleeping with an enemy.

Rebekka grew tired, the whispering slowed, and she slept.

It seemed unlikely that sleep would find Eldest that night. For a long time, she pretended to sleep in case her parents should look in and be disappointed in her. Father had said she was safe. Waiting there, curled in the dark with a razor-edged crescent of mirror glass in her hand, was tantamount to Eldest calling him a liar.

For a while, there in the dark that lay so much thinner than that of the mansion, she thought of Strong. Had his broken crawl taken him to the street door? Had some miracle left it unlocked for him? Had he slipped beneath the notice of the rest of the city too, and starved in some cold corner? Had he . . .

She woke, startling into a sitting position. Beside her Rebekka lay coughing, loud enough to wake the dead. Eldest had to grab the wrist of her own right hand to stop herself from covering her sister's mouth and hissing for silence. If Night-Father found her here it would not be because of a girl's coughing.

'Are you . . . all right?' Eldest asked when a gap in the painful hacking presented itself.

'I'll . . .' Rebekka wheezed in a painful breath '. . . be fine. It's . . . just a cough.'

When near-silence returned, Eldest lay listening to the rattling of her sister's breath and the sharper rattle of the shutters in the wind. The enormity of her changed circumstances kept her eyes wide, staring at the darkness. This was the life that had been stolen from her. Question circled question. How had it happened? How could she stop it happening again?

In time she closed her eyes, only to see in the new darkness the image of Milk-Eye's desperate face, framed by the broken base of the chimney pot. She'd left them. She'd been the eldest, the one who worked to keep them safe . . . and she'd left them. For the longest time she lay, unable to rid herself of Milk-Eye's accusing stare. At last, she let the blackness unwrap from the marrow of her bones, and rather than have it hide her, she turned it inwards, drawing night's curtain over her sister's betrayed face, over the memory of her siblings, quieting their voices until she found a measure of peace.

The last thing she remembered when she woke the next morning was the soft sound of crying from her parents' room.

Her first thought on waking was that she had never walked in her sleep within the mansion. That must have been because she never had the chance to dream deeply enough, she reasoned. She lay in the grey dawn wondering if she should tie her ankle to the bedframe in case it happened again now she was back.

The following day was a day for remembering. Every touch, every smell, every sound came freighted with reawakening memory, all of it blurred by the lens of the small child Eldest had been when those days had imprinted themselves on her mind.

They ate breakfast, more plain fare, simple porridge but wonderfully free of taint. Eldest's mouth and belly rejoiced. Her father watched her, encouraging her to eat, saying how happy he was that she had returned to them. And Eldest, unable to remember a single kind word in any of the preceding years, had to blink rapidly to keep back the tears.

Her father worked in a little attic room above the bedrooms, hunched over a desk where his quill scratched its way across endless pages. Copy work in the main, scribing documents for various concerns who hired him by the day or by the week.

When the light failed, he would cap his ink and put down his papers. The job seemed skilled but didn't pay enough for the candles needed to pursue it into the night. Rebekka whispered that the medicine Father took for his nerves slowed him down and that sometimes he had to throw away whole pages because of mistakes.

During the day Rebekka had chores, though only light work because she'd taken ill recently. Eldest helped with the cleaning of the house. There were also ingredients to grind for the various inks their father would use, and parchment to be cut and trimmed and sorted. Father bought cheaply and made do.

Rebekka explained that she had been learning the skills she'd need to be a scribe. In their grandfather's time a woman would never have been accepted in the role, and even though it was still a hard path for a girl to tread, Rebekka had been ready to try. For some months though, Father had been too busy to teach her, and she had had to practise by herself.

The second meal, the one in the evening, took Eldest by surprise, even though she remembered it as soon as the word 'dinner' was mentioned. Her mother gave her the biggest portion, and again it proved delicious beyond imagining.

They had sat in the main room, all of them together, with a tiny fire in the hearth and the skittering of mice in the rafters. Rebekka had darned a sock, their mother knitted, and Father sharpened his quill with exquisite care. The comfort of it was as if Eldest had been sunk in warm water, floating in perfect tranquillity, the pain and sorrow lifting from her limp body leaving only scars and bruises in their wake.

In bed Eldest had still lain with her sliver of glass, listening intently for any approach. The sense of security and remembered normality were both a wonder and a torment. Somehow even if the possibility that Night-Father might find her here felt far more remote than in the mansion, it also felt far worse. The idea of his sick grin and the glimmer of his eyes in this place, this sacred place of sanctuary and warmth, felt so wrong it made a knot of Eldest's stomach, so tight that it threatened to return her meal.

The day of her escape had been the only time she had actually *seen* Night-Father. She had glimpsed him through the broken chimney in the filtered daylight. And while they had always known Night-Father and Day-Father were the same man, Eldest had believed that he must adopt some monstrous skin in the darkness that ruled beyond the parlour. He had looked just the same though, and that was somehow more terrible than if he'd grown horns and fangs.

Eldest drifted in and out of sleep, weaving a pattern through the night. She was awake, blade in hand, when Rebekka woke herself with that dry, hacking cough of hers.

'Sorry,' Rebekka whispered when her lungs allowed a pause. 'I get like this for a few nights, and then it's better. For a while.'

Eldest didn't ask why her sister was whispering. She'd been loud enough to wake the neighbours on both sides. Eldest could hear them stirring. 'Don't worry about me. I don't sleep much.'

'You used to.' Rebekka stifled a cough. 'I practically had to drag you out of bed. You'd come down the stairs half asleep.'

'Not any more.'

Rebekka had asked Eldest about where she'd been. Her parents hadn't spoken of it yet. Eldest preferred silence on the subject. To speak about the mansion, the monster beneath it and the cruelty that stalked its halls, would be like throwing up across the dinner table or fouling the bed. It would introduce something obscene into the precious thing that she had found. To her sister's questions she had answered only that she had fallen into a terrible dream and been unable to break free.

'I would have come for you, if I'd known where you were,' Rebekka had said. 'After all, I'm the eldest. It's my job to protec—'

The violence of Eldest's sobs, driven by the acid guilt that ate her, shocked her sister into silence and stopped her questions. Rebekka put her arms around Eldest, who flinched away. 'I'm sorry.' Her sister squeezed her tight and they had hugged for the longest time.

Morning came. More light, more food. And already it started to seem as if the universe was fulfilling some promise to her, returning to her the life that had been snatched from her hands. The weight that was slowly lifting from Eldest felt almost physical and it was one she hadn't properly understood had burdened her. Each new day she felt lighter, stronger, more whole.

When she had first remembered that she had another family, a true one, it had seemed an awful, wondrous, dangerous thing, carrying as it did the possible salvation of having once had worth, and having been loved, but also the riddle of why she had been rejected which in turn served only to make her think that maybe she deserved what had happened to her. Now the thought that she was tainted, that the mansion might be where she belonged, was fading.

Eldest was shedding layers of protection with each passing day along with the dirt and rags that had accompanied her on her escape. The nagging guilt of having left the others behind still stalked her, and though it pained her like a knife to the skin, she didn't reapply her skills of forgetting to it. That would be too easy on herself. And in this soft new life that she didn't deserve, she couldn't absolve herself of all pain.

On the third day Father invited Eldest to his office. She stood with her arms held close to her sides, worried she would knock scrolls off shelves or ink off the desk in the cramped and crowded space.

'Let's see if we can't teach you your letters, Mol.' Father beckoned her closer. 'I could do with some help around here.'

'Wouldn't Rebekka be better? She knows so much—'

'Bek's going to the Academy soon. She'll be busy there.'

Eldest knew that people studied hard at academies. Maybe this copy work would be beneath her sister. 'I can try. I know a little bit.'

Father rubbed his kind, tired eyes, put his glasses on, and drew the first letter. 'Give this one a go.' He turned the scrap of stained parchment around and laid the quill beside it.

Eldest copied the alpha, doing her very best to be true to the lines Night-Father had drilled into them. She wanted her real father to be proud of her.

'Hmmm.' Father studied the letter. 'Very good.'

'Here.' He wrote five more letters, dipped the quill and wrote a word in cursive.

Eldest copied those too.

Father turned the page, his eyebrows lifting. He brought the candle closer, his frown deepening.

'Did I do something wrong?' Eldest knew she must be making mistakes that only a scribe could see. Of all the children at the mansion though, she had been by far the best writer. It was a skill she shared with Day-Father, much as she disliked the idea that they had anything in common. But she did have a sure hand, both with the quill and the knife.

'Try this.' Father bent over the parchment and with furious concentration filled the remaining space with several lines of the classic poem, 'Hegda on the Bridge'. He wrote with speed, spotting ink only in one place, trembling some of the loops but in all a clean piece. 'Fast as you can.' He turned the parchment over to expose a new face and thrust it at her along with the quill.

'Quick as I can . . .' It would slow her to turn the parchment to check the words every so often, and Father couldn't have wanted that. But luckily it was a piece she knew. Day-Father had made them memorize many poems and tested them regularly. Children who performed badly missed a meal.

Eldest bent to her task and wrote out the stanza in a clear flowing line. She finished faster than her father had and sat back smiling with the ink still glistening on the parchment. She'd thought her smile would be echoed but her father looked almost angry.

'That's enough. Go down and help Myra.' He crushed the parchment in his fist as she left.

On the fourth day after breakfast, Mother took both sisters to the Sun Market, the best one for fruit and vegetables, named for the square it was held in. They went from stall to stall, watched over by a weathered statue of Apollo. Mother seemed snappy and impatient with them, but compared to the monster in the basement and to torture in the dark it was a small thing, concerning only because it signalled some unhappiness Eldest didn't understand and couldn't mend. It was a new kind of hurt, small but deep.

Eldest wore one of Rebekka's old smocks, grey and fraying but a big improvement on the stinking rags that Mother had burned the first morning. She had no shoes, as they had sold Rebekka's when she grew out of them, but her feet were well wrapped in strips of parchment, offcuts from her father's work.

Eldest kept her head down, meeting no one's gaze for fear of finding herself face to face with Day-Father. The numbers though were such that any worries seemed far-fetched, and this was just one of the city's many markets, Mother said, and a smaller one at that.

Eldest watched as her mother, who looked thinner, greyer, and more drawn than the mothers of other children at the market, counted out her coins with a miser's care, buying only small amounts of the least interesting staples: potatoes, carrots, barley for thickening the meatless stews she served. Eldest compared the concern creasing

Mother's face to the joy bubbling beneath her own tensions. She worried now that rather than her return answering her parents' prayers as it had her own, it might have added to their burdens.

'Mother looks sad,' Eldest whispered to her sister.

'She was sad before you came back.' Rebekka took Eldest's hand and squeezed it. 'Father doesn't make much money . . . And they worry that I'm sick.' Rebekka looked sad now too and Eldest felt her own joy wilting, as if sorrow were a disease that had spread between them.

They followed Mother home, passing a statue of an older sun god, Helios – deity of the dark sun, whose fire is time, the blaze in which humanity burns. His legend tells that the day-sun is his mouth and one day it will open to consume all the planets. Eldest kept her head down, carrying the rope bag containing the vegetables. She spoke to Rebekka in a low voice as they trailed their mother. 'Father said you're going to go to the Academy. I don't want you to leave.'

Rebekka coughed and looked grim. 'I'm not pleased about it either. It's a bad place.' She tried a smile. Eldest recognized it for the strained sort of grimace she herself had manufactured for the smallest children many times before. 'At least Mother and Father will still have you.'

'I want to come too.' Eldest wasn't sure that she did, but she didn't want Rebekka to be alone.

'You really, really don't. It's worse than you can imagine,' Rebekka said, deadly serious. 'Don't say it again. Certainly, don't let Father hear you!'

Later Rebekka went out with a basket of scrolls and papers to deliver to the various concerns that employed their father.

'That's why he calls me Bek,' she said to Eldest at the door. 'I'm at his beck and call.'

'Bek suits you better,' Eldest said. 'It's to the point. Like you are.'

Mother said Eldest should stay home because the city was a big place that she was no longer used to, and they had lost her in it once before.

The afternoon passed in chores while shadows lengthened outside.

Eldest helped her mother in the kitchen, all the while looking to the front door for Rebekka's return. When the stew was ready, Mother took a bowl up to the attic where Father worked through the day. Eldest told herself it was something in the slow climbing of those stairs that made her follow, to find out what sadness it was that weighed her mother down. Surely it wasn't something as small as the iron pennies in her purse? Eldest could eat less, do more chores . . .

She told herself it was concern for her mother that made her climb so stealthily behind her and listen at the foot of the attic ladder. But she knew there was another side to that coin. Mistrust had been scored into her, deep as the darkness had. It was something she'd brought with her out of the mansion, and hate it though she might, it had its hooks in her.

'. . . don't need to send Rebekka . . . the Academy . . .' Mother's voice.

'Nine marks, nine *hundred* pennies!' Father.

'Cocran!'

'We can't afford to have the healer round again—'

'But . . . when *he* comes – that one . . . he'll give us something, won't he? He'll want the girl back.' A pleading in her mother's tone. Eldest's whole body clenched like a fist. It was the taint of mistrust, the dirt inside her, that was making this happen. If she hadn't listened, they would still love her.

'Maybe he will, maybe he won't, there's no contract.' The sound of shuffling papers. 'Are you going to argue with him?'

'No . . . but . . .'

'And if he does throw a few pennies at us . . . it's not like the healer can stop it, just slow things—'

'He can *try*. There are medicines . . .'

'Medicines we can't afford. Even nine marks would get eaten up by what they charge!'

'But—'

'If she gets any sicker they won't take her. And if the Academy spends that much on her they'll pay for medicines too. And when she leaves there, she can have anything she wants, take anything she wants!'

'She won't leave though. You know what they do—'

'Enough. It's already done. I sent the letters yesterday.'

Eldest had until this moment been paralysed with shock. The words *'He'll want the girl back'* ran through her mind like a bramble tearing at everything, filling her skull with blood. They couldn't have done it to her, not her mother whose arms were a haven, not her father with his kind eyes and hard work. They couldn't have given her away back then. They couldn't be doing it again. Not for mere money.

At last, she found the strength to release her death grip on the ladder. Rebekka chose that moment to return, racing up the stairs at a run as Eldest turned to go down them.

'There's a man . . .' Rebekka's eyes were wild in the white of her face. 'He's coming.'

'Did you— What does he look like?'

'His smile . . . that grin. He saw me and smiled. I just ran.'

It was enough of a description to remove all doubt. Day-Father, Night-Father, it didn't matter. He was here. Her family *had* given her up. *Again!* Eldest sank to her knees. An expert in pain had hurt her many times, but this . . . this came from inside, there was no escaping it, no surrendering to it, a kind of suffering she had formed no calluses against.

The darkness that flooded from her came like a dam breaching. With vicious force of will she tried to erase herself, not from the attention of those around her or from the approaching Day-Father, but from the world itself, completely. She was done with everything, better to be gone entirely, as if she had never been. Gone from true parents who didn't want her, and from false ones who wanted her for terrible reasons. Gone from hurting herself and hurting others. The pulsing darkness faded, leaving the walls around her grey and brittle. She had hollowed herself. A long-banked potential expended in a few broken-hearted beats.

She rose slowly, feeling too fragile for the scream she wanted to unleash.

'Who are you?' Rebekka blinked. 'Mother! Mother! There's a girl in our house!' She reached to grab Eldest.

Stunned to be seen, and empty as if all of her strength had been tipped out of her, Eldest swayed aside, evading Rebekka's grasp and running down the stairs.

'Cocran! We're being robbed!'

Eldest turned at the base of the stair to see her mother on the ladder, staring at her, no recognition in her face.

She ran out of the back door, through the shared yard with its single box of withered blooms, past the outhouses, over a wall, alleys, another wall, a short street, a long road, lost in the grinding bustle of the city again. She ran without fear. Even her sorrow and her bitterness were whispers. The emotions that had brought the darkness roaring from her had themselves been flattened by its power. She had hollowed herself such that her thoughts echoed within her, and when she finally stopped her running she stood alone among the crowding city, a husk that a wind of any strength might carry off in whatever direction it blew.

Eldest returned a day later to haunt the family, drawn by the faint strings of what few memories remained to her. She had, after all, no other place to go. She watched them using the skills Day-Father had cut into her. Not the explosive flood of power that had stolen all trace of her from their minds, but the constant refrain that removed her from their notice as she shivered on the steps of a tenement opposite.

Day-Father did not return. His kind wouldn't fathom her attachment, twice betrayed and still lurking like an abandoned dog. They had sold her to him when she was barely old enough to know it and called him to collect her when she'd escaped and found her way back. A small but persistent voice that she didn't recognize urged her to enter the house during the night and slice her parents' throats. She cut two lines on her forearm instead, staining her mirror shard crimson. That quieted the voice for a while. Or throttle them, the voice returned, and she realized it had been her own all along. Take a shirt from the chest and throttle him first, then her. That would be quieter. Cleaner. Slower.

It was a relief when Rebekka emerged with her father as the light was failing. Their mother's weeping followed as Father led one sister away by the hand and the other by a very different bond. Eldest tried to imagine that the tears were for her. That someone, anyone, had once cared enough to cry for her.

Father and Rebekka headed off in the direction of the West Gate. Rebekka walked as if she were being led to her own funeral, but she didn't fight. Some battles are lost before you start them. She coughed once, twice, three times, and then no more.

Eldest followed them. She followed through the poor quarter known as The Lean, through the warehouse district, through streets of finer homes, and out with the dwindling evening traffic into the farmland that haloed Tandra-ah. Followed three miles along the Padlow Road, until the city shrank behind them and a squat fortress loomed ahead.

Eldest watched as Father and Rebekka lined up with hundreds of others, parents and girls, outside the grim lump of stone that must be the Academy. The stink of death hung about the place, unapologetic. It stood within sight of the city walls, but not too close. Like an outhouse, needing to be close enough to serve, but at sufficient distance that the unpleasantness there could be forgotten until it was required again.

Although Father arrived early, the sun was falling toward the horizon by the time Eldest saw her sister sold. Rebekka never broke, never wiped her eyes, even as girls on every side wailed, begged, pleaded, and fought.

Eldest watched her father return with a lighter step, his hand going constantly to his pocket, never once looking back. She killed him amid the lengthening shadows, feeling nothing as she slit his throat from behind, only empty. She left the mirror shard beside him and scattered the money across his body for whoever found him first.

The queue was short when she returned to the Academy. Several families were turned away – their daughters found wanting for some unspecified fault. Eldest steeled herself against the same rejection. She expected no less. And it seemed as the numbers dwindled, more and more were being sent away.

She didn't have to wait long. The woman with kind eyes and a long robe seemed surprised to see her unaccompanied. Her father had had kind eyes too. Eldest no longer trusted them.

'What are you doing here, child?'

'I'm coming to the Academy.' She didn't make it a challenge, but her tone brooked no argument.

'We do have a few places left. Some girls are unsuited, and there are always others who manage to change their parents' minds at the gates. It's the smell. It makes things real.' She fixed Eldest with eyes that no longer seemed kind. 'Do you know what that smell is, child? Do you know what we do here?'

'Death.' Eldest sniffed. 'Death and rotting. You do bad things here.'

'We pay nine marks.' The woman scoured the night as if still expecting a father or a mother to step forward.

'You can pay me.'

'And your name is?' The woman waved and a taller, younger woman, also in robes with a noseless horror of a face, stepped forward, slate in hand to add her to the tally.

'Mol,' Eldest said. 'Mollandra.' She frowned, remembering the name on her father's certificate, hanging even now on the wall of his office. A voice urged her to return and burn the place down. 'Mollandra Plight.'

CHAPTER 30
Rue

Rue stood in the clearing, hemmed in by trees on all sides. Spring had trailed its fingers through the forest, touching every bud, waking the green. But still the day was dying, and Rue felt the cold of a reaching winter. Every part of her ached, the muscles with misuse, the joints with too many years, the bones with old sorrow.

She held the knife at her side. No point setting off to find trouble: it would find her soon enough. At her age you let others do the walking where possible. There had been years when she strode the world as if she could walk forever. She had tracked the Bone Shaper across the width of Magog. She'd even taken ship to Gog and hunted the northern mountains for the Earl of Huunakka when he fled his crimes.

The wind flexed and leaves filtered down into the glade. Rue shivered as if she were a branch herself. But if she had been a branch, it would have been her very last leaf she was clinging to now.

The ghosts of her past watched her from the gloom that gathered among the tree trunks, Bek and Einsa clearly seen, others mistier, standing at their shoulders, rank upon rank, back beyond sight and memory. Even so, it was to Jayne and Ambeth her mind returned as Senna cawed her warning from on high.

The bird landed close by, crashing onto the bough of a tree that looked to have wandered into the clearing then stopped when it realized it was alone.

'I'd never spent much time with people.' Rue hadn't meant to speak but here at the end of the road she found herself in a reflective mood, and even if her only audience was Senna Weaver dressed in feathers Rue's mouth seemed set on talking. 'I wasn't much for company. Not until I came to your shitty little collection of houses.'

'You don't say?' Transformation hadn't blunted Senna's sarcasm any.

'I'd never spent much time with people,' Rue repeated. 'Not "real" people.' She turned her knife, catching the light. She watched the shadows where the bird's attention was aimed. 'They call you peasants simple folk. But actually, you're a lot more complicated than everyone I grew up with.'

Before Jayne, and then Ambeth, Rue hadn't ever had a 'real person' as a friend before. Not once formed a bond with someone who was not themselves a product of nightmare.

'You never stopped thinking you were better than us.' Somehow seeing Rue's fear of what was coming had removed Senna's fear of Rue.

'I never stopped knowing I was different. That's true.' In the Vale lives had been hard but lived much as they were in other places. Maybe the spectre of hunger had waited rather closer to the front door but the violence that had ended the peasants' lives was as alien to them as the luxuries in distant cities known only by their names. People there grew as people are meant to. Rue's childhood had taken a very different path.

'You brought this on us!' Senna cried.

'I did not. They were surprised to find me here. If they'd known who I was, what I was, then the man following us would have been the first one I saw – and probably the last.'

The bird's cry expressed her disbelief better than any words.

'They call you the small folk. Simple souls. But it's untrue. I was taught to be simple. A hammer.'

Rue had observed that real lives were complicated and therefore delicate. Tendrils of obligation, interest, and concern expanded into a wider community. Wants and cares and love were distributed across the limbs of a slender tree. When one person came up against another they must negotiate, orient themselves, edge closer, so that the vulnerabilities of one could mesh with those of another without damage.

Life in a hamlet educated her in new truths. She saw how hearts could hang upon fragile things she had held as no more important than spiderwebs strung across her path. How the more connections a person made the more precious small things became. Marriages, meals, even moments.

Young love, especially, seemed both a monumental indulgence and at the same time a vital pulse in life's veins, the foundation of so many things, both as trivial and as fundamental as competing views would claim.

Rue took a step towards the darkness between the trees. He was coming. She felt it.

'You're endlessly complicated, Senna. Even the reason you hate me has a million pieces. But us Kindnesses, we've been pared down to the bone. We are simple, direct. The stakes are life or death: little else matters. We are not part of society, or family; we are not subject to others' opinions or governed by them. We lack the capacity for the many minor joys and hurts that real people dance around. We are blunt weapons. All or nothing.'

Rue thought of the friends she had shared the recent years with. Real people might be thickets of emotions, cares and wants coiling like brambles, ready to snag on every interaction. But age starts to prune those branches, to strip a person down, to shape them for the simplicity of death. The old had less time, and thus the clever ones had less time for nonsense. And so, as life in Pye had finally given her a chance to grow just when others of her age start to draw in, she had found her match in two old peasant women: Jayne's gently pointed wit, Ambeth's unashamed bawdy humour, both had given her something she had never hoped to own, though in her time her hands had brimmed with gold and jewels.

She saw the hunter's eyes first though they were deep among the shadow and black. Judgement had arrived after a long and misspent life. Surely few deserved it more than she did. She had dispensed a Kindness's justice, all the while with the blood of patricide staining her hands. Hypocrisy might not be a crime on the Kindly Ones' list, but Rue ranked it high on hers and had spent most of her life bent beneath its burden.

She glanced at the crow. 'Fly away.'

Senna exploded into the air in a thrashing of wings as the Cruelty stepped into the open.

The man hunched within the black shroud of his cape. Dark eyes watched the crow's retreat, black hair plastered his forehead as if heavy rain had fallen.

'I should have taken a sword,' Rue said.

'It wouldn't have made a difference.' A crooked smile revealed crooked teeth.

Two scars divided the man's pale face. One ran from cheekbone to jaw, almost a twin to the wound that Wenda had given Rue back in the Academy when she had sliced her cheek open. Wenda had been very skilled. Rue had killed her from behind, much like she had killed Cocran Plight. Without the distraction Bek had provided, Rue would have died fighting Wenda that day.

Rue understood now how the man had found her, and how she had felt his approach. They had a bond, forged long ago in a dark place.

The second, smaller, older scar, scored its way across the man's mouth, notching both lips. Rue had given him the larger wound and had named him for the smaller one.

'Lip-Scar,' she said. 'You're looking . . . young.'

It was true. As Eldest she had been at most two years his senior. Now it seemed two decades would be needed to span the gap. The Cruelties, it was said, could forget years as easily as anything else, but that if they shrugged off a year then every memory of those months went with it. Rue had wondered if it was worth living a year you had no recollection of. Now she wondered if her sibling from the dark mansion had, as part of his payment for youth, shed their childhood and the horrors they'd shared.

'And you look old. But not too old to pay for this.' His fingers traced the scar she'd cut into him long ago with a sliver of broken mirror.

'You didn't forget me then.' Oddly it pleased Rue that he hadn't. She wasn't sure how it would feel to be the only one to remember. As if she were holding half of something that should be whole.

'Those years taught me too much to let slide,' Lip-Scar said.

'I should have taken a sword,' she repeated, meeting his gaze.

'All that iron. A heavy load for an old woman.'

'It's true.' She'd left them all behind for exactly that reason. 'Always did prefer a knife in any case.' She readied herself. Lip-Scar looked to be in his mid-forties, and though grey hadn't yet found its way into his hair, years of summer sun and winter winds had crinkled him like an apple on the turn.

'It would be undignified to fight you.' The Cruelty pressed his lips into a flat line.

'You and I were made to fight each other, little brother.' She didn't feel it, though. Not now he stood in front of her. When they had been young, she'd felt his ambition rub against her authority, a rough and splintered thing. She'd known his greed and selfishness as weapons that he might turn against the others had she not stood in his way. Now all that seemed far away. They had been *children*. He was a child. In an awful, awful place. And she . . . she had run away. Left them all in Father's care. 'We were *made* to fight each other.' She had said 'made' one way at first: 'created to fight each other'. Now she said it the other way. They had been forced into it. 'But we don't have to fight . . .'

Rue knew now what she had only suspected when she had lived beneath the mansion's roof. They were being fashioned, all the children, moulded into creatures like the one that stood before her. They were being poisoned, tainted, changed. Ten centuries ago, the Kindly Ones had walked the world, summoned perhaps by an excess on Earth of the wickedness they had traditionally punished in the heavens. Three sisters, Tisiphone, Alecto, and Megaera. And somehow, when those bodies had been relinquished, having hounded the last of mankind across the endless ocean to beach itself on Gog's shore . . . those celestial corpses had lain imperishable, shunned, then forgotten, then covered by time. Lost until they were found.

Night-Father and Mother had fed their children the Ingredient. Some distillation of midnight. The mind of Megaera. The black matter of her brain. The Kindnesses had made their charges drink the elixir. The essence of fire. Alecto's blood.

It had taken Rue decades to unravel and there was still much she didn't understand, but the desire to know had left her. She had hidden in her pretend life and pretended that such things no longer concerned her. But the past had come to find her. Lip-Scar had become the Cruelty that the monsters had always intended him to become.

'We don't *have* to fight . . .' She muttered it again, knowing as she looked into her one-time brother's eyes that they did.

A shrug deepened Lip-Scar's hunch. He lifted a narrow hand towards her, showing his palm. Megaera's darkness pulsed between them, bringing down leaves on all sides in one great fall, as if they'd forgotten the season. Megaera, keeper of grudges. She would never let this go.

'What was the point of—' Pain cut off Rue's question. Blood flooded from her chest wound, pouring hot from the hole Isik's knife had put in her. She sank to her knees, unable to sustain her own weight. '. . . Oh . . .' and fell face forward into the cold embrace of the forest floor.

'Shit . . .'

Rue stood once more on the banks of the river whose dark and rushing waters have to be crossed before a soul can be judged. On the far side whatever rewards or punishments her life merited would be levelled. There would be only punishment – she had never been good.

'Damnation!' She lifted her hands, finding them empty, the knife gone. She hadn't expected to win the fight, but she thought she would at least get to try. She'd been going to mock the Cruelty for trying to nullify her rage. She would have shown him the empty vial she kept close to her heart, long since drained of elixir. But his pulse of negation, whatever it might have been aimed at, had found the goddess's magic, the enchantment that had sustained her past human limits, and had emptied her of it.

Rue understood the Cruelties' power far better now than she had when she first faced them. Alecto's rage seemed a simple thing. Fire and rage. Her gift was destruction. Megaera kept grudges. Memory, Kindness Marta had taught them in Creed, was misunderstood by the masses, and by many of those who called themselves wise.

Memory, they claimed, was the record of time. Megaera's flesh taught a different story. Memory *is* time. The mind remembers but so do rocks. Iron remembers. Worlds remember. Where the most powerful Kindnesses could destroy armies and level castles, the most powerful Cruelties could, on the scale of an individual or single object, work a great range of far more subtle magics affecting memory, the mind, and the state of matter.

'Was that it?' Senna descended angrily from an iron sky, breaking into Rue's reverie, all feathers and flapping wings. 'All that talk just to fall over dead the moment you saw him?'

'It wasn't the plan.'

Rue turned away from the terrifying flood that reached to within inches of her toes. The banks shelved up, the tiers studded with dead thorn bushes. One had borne the fruit that had been the Morrigan's gift and had returned her to her body after Isik's mercenaries had stamped the life out of her. The dry limbs lay bare of all but thorns now.

She had been expecting to see Bek and Einsa, sitting among the briars, frowning their disapproval at her, but found herself alone save for the feathered annoyance describing great circles through the still air.

Rue felt the approach behind her much as she had felt the Cruelty tracking her from the Vale. A pressure on the back of her neck as if the touch of a stranger's gaze had become two cold fingertips pressed to her skin. Inevitability turned her to face the river more than any movement of her feet. Her body, after all, her true body, lay face down in a forest she'd never learned the name of, waiting for the worms to gather their courage.

'That's not good.'

The skiff had already covered half of the distance from the opposite bank, propelled by sure strokes of a long pole in the hands of its cloaked boatman. The river's current should have swept the craft away, and its depth should have made the pole all but useless. Even so, the boatman and his boat grew swiftly closer.

The boatman's identity was hardly a mystery. The lands had many faiths but certain truths ran beneath them all. Whatever songs the clerics sang, they all spoke of a guide who led souls along the last mile of their journey, or of a gatekeeper, and while these psychopomps might wear many forms, they all sprang from the same source. And for Rue it was the river and the ferry, and the ferryman.

She stood and watched. Some things could not be run from. She should have stood her ground and faced the Cruelty in the warmth of the inferno that had been her home rather than fleeing to the cold forest. She could hardly have announced herself as a Kindness without having to face one of her family sooner or later. Though it did seem strange that one of her brothers had been so close.

As the skiff grounded itself on a bank that would offer no purchase to any other boat, Senna descended, landing on Rue's shoulder.

'Get off me, you filthy animal.' Rue growled it out of the corner of her mouth.

'I can't . . .' Senna croaked.

'If you shit on me, I'm going to pluck you.'

The boatman's pole thumped against the skiff and the tall figure crossed half the length of his craft, the cowl of his robe obscuring his face. He held out a bony hand, palm up.

'He wants you to pay,' Senna croaked softly.

'I know what he fucking wants,' Rue hissed back, patting the pouch of her bloodstained smock where she typically kept split pegs for the line, bits of twine, a cloth to wipe the snotty nose of little Kera from next door when she wandered over to chase the chickens—

Something chinked beneath her fingers. Too heavy to be a bent copper or an Ibral penny that she might sometimes carry for trading. She reached in and drew out a handful of bronze marks, each heavy coin stamped with the head of King Amtal, or of his son Orrin who was king after him and whose sister once visited the Academy at Tandra-ah.

'This,' she closed her fingers around the nine coins. 'This is what they paid me . . .'

Half a century ago Kindness Marta had paid the fathers of nearly a hundred girls nine marks each. Little Molly however, too young for the Academy but willing to lie, had sold *herself* and taken the coins in her own small fists.

Rue lifted the handful closer to her face, habit only, for in this place the tricks that age had played upon her eyes were undone. On every coin the three whips of the Academy had been neatly incised like three nested 'S's. The whips of the Furies. Placed to mark the coins as payment for a life. It had been done not to shame those who took the money – though it did that too – but so that when they entered circulation and pulsed through the veins of first the city and then the nation, they would remind every person whose hands they passed through both of the existence of the Kindnesses and of the existence of another market for girl-flesh. It was, to put it bluntly, a form of advertising.

The boatman's hand stayed where it was, palm out.

The river rushed by, hissing at the delay.

Rue clenched the coins until her hand hurt. This was what they had bought her for. Less than you'd pay for a sturdy mule, as Kindness Marta had so unflatteringly put it.

'Pay him!' Senna squawked, unable to endure the tension.

Rue glanced back to the riverside and the thorn bushes where Bek and Einsa had spoken to her before. She looked along the banks, left and right, wondering what strange sea the river might reach and from what mountains it had sprung.

'Pay.' The boatman's voice grated like one vast stone across another.

Rue put her hand back into her pocket, and stared at him, daring him to raise his head and meet her eyes.

'Fuck you.'

CHAPTER 31
Mollandra

Year Five

In the cold light of a rainy afternoon, stripped of the magic that he had hidden himself within, Father looked far more human than Mollandra remembered ever having seen him. Even so, the wickedness in his black eyes carried the same awful promises that had made the Academy seem a place of refuge.

Perhaps if the royal visitors had not been present to witness the deed, the Kindnesses would have killed the intruder and let the older acolytes practise their necromancy on his corpse. Under the curious eyes of the king's brother, Kindness Marta chose to reply to Father's claim on Mollandra with words rather than a blade.

'Acolytes cannot be taken from the Academy. Their families no longer have any claim on them. It is for this indemnity that a fee is paid.'

'Of course. Of course.' Father executed a mocking bow, one arm extended, one cradled to his chest, the fingers on both hands raking the air as if playing the strings of some oversized, invisible instrument. 'But in the case of this particular girl, no fee was paid to her family, to wit, myself or her beloved mother. And as such she is not an acolyte and can be returned to her rightful home.'

'A fee is *always* paid.' Somehow Kindness Marta managed to make 'always' sound like a threat.

'If some abductor of children took your coin and fled into the night with it, that's hardly my concern, Kindness.' Father turned to the nobles. 'Highnesses, I'm sure you could not countenance such theft within sight of the walls of the kingdom's second city.'

Prince Cormac, looking rather like a drowned rat stuffed into imperial finery, coughed into his hand, and glanced from the dangerously calm face of one Kindness to the next. At last, his gaze settled on Father's barely contained insanity. 'Well . . .' The elder prince hemmed and he hawed and he looked almost grateful when his wife elbowed him impatiently out of the way.

'Of course, the Academy can't steal children. The child's parent must be paid! . . . Or their official guardian.'

'Or owner!' Prince Cormac interjected, pleased with himself for the contribution and puffing up within the wet confines of his embroidered jacket.

'Whoever sold my daughter into this establishment was neither parent, guardian, nor owner.' Father dusted off his damp hands and stepped towards Mollandra, reaching for her with fingers so very like claws.

Kindness Terra's great sword blocked his path, placed between them so swiftly that if not for the hiss of the air it cut, Mollandra might have thought it had simply appeared there. 'We will examine the records.'

Mollandra's throat, constricted by old fear, had been unable to give voice to a single word until Terra's blade, as long as she was tall, lay between her father and herself.

'I sold myself. I have the marks here.' She held out her hand, showing the coins she had been working free from the hem of her robe as they talked.

Father's terrible eyes narrowed. She remembered when he was the beast, chasing the children through the mansion's corridors, crawling through the attic space, stalking the blindness of the bedrooms. The Academy had killed far more of its charges, but the place had seldom come close to evoking the same fear she had experienced even on the least bad of the days she remembered in the mansion's darkness.

'The girl can't sell herself. She doesn't stop being my daughter just because she has crossed over the threshold of my home and gone out into the world.'

Mollandra locked eyes with Kindness Marta. 'I've never seen this man before.' She closed her fist around the money they had given her at the gate five years earlier. 'But this is mine.' She raised the hand. 'And children sell themselves on the streets of Tandra-ah every day. How is that allowed if not this?'

'The father's claim outranks the child's.' Princess Scalla kept her face a mask, eyes hard.

Why such a high-placed noble should care about an acolyte's fate, or the demands of a trespassing parent, Mollandra had no idea, but the timing was far too convenient to be taken as coincidence.

'A parent owns a child. The girl—'

Her husband coughed over her before hemming loudly, determined to stop his wife's pronouncement without actually making one of his own.

Undaunted, the princess pressed on. 'The girl should be given over to him.'

With his bare hand, Father pushed Kindness Terra's sword aside and came forward unopposed. Mollandra released her coins into a pocket. Within the cover of her robe she drew her knife. The first row of acolytes parted before the man. All save Sharp whom he shoved from his path as if she were nothing.

Careless of any threat Mollandra might offer, Father took hold of her, overlong fingers with swollen joints wrapping like cables around the muscles of her lower arm. Agony shot from that contact, spreading through her veins, running through the marrow of the bones beneath. The familiar pain almost felled Mollandra, but she kept her feet and managed to drive the fear from her voice as she spoke.

'What are Kindnesses if not oath keepers? I took your payment. We made a bond. Until death.'

Kindness Terra scowled and shifted her grip upon the hilt of her sword. Undu's eyes glittered dangerously, black stones in the white deadness of her face.

Marta frowned. 'Has anyone seen this child in your care? Does she have siblings? Were we to visit your house would she be known to them and to your neighbours?'

'We . . .' Father's eyes flashed angrily in Mollandra's direction, almost blasting away her resolve in that brief contact. 'We are a very private family.'

The younger prince, the handsome, unaccountably familiar, Sunder, seemed on the point of saying something, but Kindness Marta cut across him. 'You should have come to us with these claims years ago. The acolyte's training has progressed too far for her to be released. She will leave here as a Kindness, or she will never leave. This is our way.'

Mollandra tried to shake herself free, but her father's grip was an iron band. In her core the dark thing stirred – the blackness that they had put into her. He and Mother had fed it into her, and now it was her only defence against them.

'Let her go.' Terra raised close on two yards of cold steel and cruel edge.

Amazingly, despite the threat of three Kindnesses, Mollandra sensed the tension coiling ever tighter in Father's body as if he were on the point of springing upon them. The thunder on his face seemed to promise that he would make a fight of it.

A cry of pain escaped Mollandra despite her determination. She felt bones grating in her arm. The knife she had planned to drive into the side of her father's head suddenly seemed too feeble a weapon to harm such a man.

'I must insist,' blustered the elder prince.

His wife, shading to crimson beneath her rain-washed paints and powders, opened her mouth to utter some more forceful decree.

'How is it that you are here now, in this moment?' Undu's child-like trill flowed into the dangerous stillness before the princess could speak. 'Why today? How is it that you come here, passing our gates without invitation, on the coattails of the king's own family, and so many years after this supposed loss?' She advanced on Father, her small flowing steps making it seem that the great bulk of her simply floated towards him. 'What information led you to suspect that a daughter of yours might be in our care? I find it passing strange.' She halted so close to Father that her breath might be felt on his mouth, and smiled her curious smile, wide yet thin-lipped, the one Mollandra knew she must share with the dead down in the catacombs' fetor.

Father, more than a king within his own walls, had no reply other than a baring of teeth.

Mollandra jerked her arm and this time won free of his faltering grip. She stepped back several paces. Trembling fingers traced the line of an old scar on the wrist of her knife hand, now exposed. Fingertips followed a white arc of indentations that traced the shape of Father's bite: however bad his bark, the man's bite was definitely crueller.

'You haven't heard the last of this.' Father began to retreat towards the closed gates. And then, as if realizing how weak that sounded, how like the words of some costumed villain treading the creaking boards of a small-town stage, he strode forward once more towards Terra's great sword and Undu's smile.

'Enough!' Princess Scalla barked. 'Enough.' More softly, acknowledging the limits of her authority. 'Kindness Marta, I would count it a personal favour if we could avoid violence in front of my son.'

Prince Sunder gave a lopsided smile at this, meeting Father's eyes with a boldness that seemed bordering on insanity to Mollandra.

He seemed again on the point of speaking, but left it to his father, Prince Cormac, to pass judgement. 'If you would show this gentleman out and continue with your fascinating account of the Academy's progress, I'm sure I can give a good report of today's visit to my brother.'

Kindness Marta eyed Father with a focused venom that Mollandra had never seen before and hoped never to see again – a look that made her truly believe that here was a woman who had killed and endured her way through ten Academy years as one hundred became three. She gave a disgusted wave of her hand and nodded to Instructor Akki.

Father followed the instructor to the gates without a backwards glance.

'You sold yourself?' Sharp turned around while the instructors were distracted and the Kindnesses conversing with their guests. For once she actually looked impressed.

By way of answer, Mollandra handed Sharp one of the bronze marks she'd been paid. 'And now I've bought part of you, Sharp Mahalla.'

Sharp looked at the coin, a dull glint in her narrow palm. 'And what can I buy with it?'

'One tenth of a good donkey. Or, from me, anything you want. But if you purchase something I don't want to give, we will no longer be friends.'

Sharp had two looks, one diamond-hard that she used on almost everyone, and a rarely seen soft look that she used in her seductions and almost never at any other time. She used it now.

'That was a foolish thing to give someone like me, Mollandra Plight. You know how I like to spend.'

Mollandra gave a lopsided shrug to go with her lopsided smile. Sharp used up favours and goodwill with a gambler's haste. If she were ever let out of the Academy and given money, she would no doubt burn through that with equal speed. Even so, Mollandra would trust her to keep this one bronze mark. She shrugged again and turned away. She held out another of the coins to Tmanga. 'Everyone else I've given these to has died. So, better not to take it.'

Behind her Sharp snorted.

'Bek and Einsa?' Tmanga asked.

Mollandra nodded, her mouth suddenly too dry to speak. She knew Sharp would take the coin the moment there was a hint of danger associated with it. Tmanga, however, was a deep thinker.

'Was that man truly your father?'

'I had another, but I killed him.'

'This one seems dangerous.'

'You have no idea what he is.'

Tmanga took the coin. 'You will have to tell us everything so that we can be sure to do things right when we kill this one too.'

CHAPTER 32

Rue

'You told him to fuck off!'

'I know what I did.'

'But he's the ferryman! He's Death with his scythe! He's the winged ones who take the warriors straight from the battlefield! He's—'

'He's probably used to it. Dying's enough to give most people an attitude.' Rue kept to her course, putting both the river and the black sun to her back and striking out into the Badlands, an area scarred by water that never showed itself, deep gullies set around with ridges of coarse volcanic rock, all of it blowing with a black dust that made her skin hurt.

'There's nothing out here,' Senna croaked. 'I've been up high. It goes on forever. Just like this.'

'That's what they say.' Rue trudged on, her feet already sore from the sharp rocks. 'You can be a ghost two ways. When the living won't let you go they keep a shade of you on this bank of the river. A shade will stay until it's not needed any more. I don't know if the person who went over the river even knows that something stayed behind. Maybe it's just like a painting, or a reflection and the person has no real ties to it . . .' She wasn't sure if she wanted Bek and Einsa to be aware of her need, of how she couldn't let them go. If they had found something good over the river, would her cares reach out and tarnish it somehow? Or if they suffered, would it comfort them to know their spectres still owned part of her mind? 'I'm the other sort. The unquiet spirit. And I'm planning on being as unquiet as I need to be.'

'There's nobody here to care.' Senna swooped past.

Without days, without the wheeling of stars, and under the ceaseless stare of a black sun whose light seemed a kind of blindness, it was impossible to measure either time or distance save in units of pain.

In Rue's youth pain had been a frequent visitor, but a visitor nonetheless; however excruciating the wound, injury, or flat-out torture inflicted by the instructors, there would be a return to a kind of normal. Rue's youth had hauled her from the depths of agony, repaired her damaged flesh, and delivered her to another day. Some hurts were, of course, irreparable and the cumulative effects of these would remove girls from the class, leaving a few who by luck or skill or a combination of both endured.

Age had marked a slow changing of that relationship. Pain became a guest who overstayed their welcome. Pain acquired its own room, a place it preferred to be and to where it might retreat when all else was fine. And later pain became a resident, moving in for good, wandering the length of her body in search of new forms of entertainment. The sharpness of any hurt kept its edge but added to that were new notes on which torment might play a melody. Dull persistent aches, deep throbbing hurts, the crawling itch, the dry tickle, the twinge of sockets and the grind of bone on bone.

Each mile Rue strayed from the river seemed to take her deeper into the territory of pain, as if it were not the physical effort of her journey taking its toll upon her ageing body, but the very land itself. She crested a black ridge and gazed at the unending vista before her. The scream of her flesh insisted that it was this air, these rocks, this place that was hurting her and would have hurt her just as badly had she been set upon the spot by some great bird without ever once stretching a muscle to achieve the distance from the river.

'Where are we even heading?' Senna demanded, landing to peck at a pebble among the dust. The pain assaulting Rue appeared to give the crow no problems.

'Away,' Rue snapped. 'Away from the river.' She bit down on the irritation that hurting had put on her tongue. 'I don't think it matters which route I take. It's all the same.' A sweep of her hand encompassed the gullies, ridges, distant hills.

'It matters.' Bek's ghost stood close by, fainter than at the river's edge. 'It's not an easy path to walk, and it will get harder each time you walk it.' Across her phantom knuckles the girl passed the memory of the bronze mark that Rue had once given her, flipping it from one to the next in a complex shuffle. 'Why would you even do this, Mollandra? You had the coin for the ferryman. The world has never once done you a single favour. Aren't you finished with it yet? Isn't it time to leave?'

When her ghosts spoke, the bitterness that had never left Rue, grew thin, almost as spectral as the girls still frozen in their youth. She remembered them amid the nightmare of their education, where somehow they had found space for hopes and dreams, for joking, even for the love that friends should share in such hardship but seldom manage. That bitterness had coloured her vision every moment of her life, fading during the soft years she had spent hidden in the Vale but never fully absent, a wound across the breadth of her soul that refused to heal.

'Isn't it time to leave?' Bek asked again.

'I don't know.' And for a moment she truly didn't. It would be so easy to let it go. To cross the river and leave everything behind. Perhaps something better waited for her over those dark waters.

'Let her be, Bek.' Einsa sat close by on her other side. For once the girl was dry, the truth of her death left unremarked. This was the Einsa of her first year, with the rough grin, that mix of resignation and resilience she'd got from her mother. 'You know she'll go her own way. We never knew it back then, but she was always about righting wrongs. Hitting back no matter how big the bully. No point trying to stop her.'

'I'm tired.' Rue sat down too, cursing at the pain flaring from hips and knees. Now that she had someone in her corner her resolve faltered.

'You're old is what you are.' Senna stalked about, ridiculous on her crow's legs. 'You're an old woman. A toothless hag.'

'I have my teeth.' Insecurity had Rue's fingers at her lips. 'Most of them anyway.' She spat angrily. She'd thought she'd outgrown her old insecurities.

'You should have the grace to die so that the rest of us can move on rather than hang around you like some rag-tag carnival rejects. Go back to the river. Take the boat.'

Rue put her hands to her cheeks, rubbing as if she could rub away the years. She lowered them, looking closely. Bony fingers, wrinkle-clad. They weren't the hands she knew.

'Leave Sunder to someone else,' Bek said. 'He won't last forever. A hero will come along. A bigger bad. Or time will pull him down all by itself. You don't have to—'

'Sunder?' Rue remembered him. The warlord on the edge of her open grave, ready to unthrone the gods themselves. The Morrigan stalking across the dead, defying him. The boy who had so many years ago visited the Academy with his royal parents. Those years, which bore down on her so hard, seemed to have slipped from his shoulders, as if those who called him a demi-god had the right of it. 'You think this is about him?' She got to her feet with a snarl. 'I don't give a damn what the goddess wants. I was done with her the day I finished with all this Kindness nonsense.'

'What in seven hells are we doing here then?' Senna croaked.

'They killed my friends. All I want is a word with the person who made that happen, some fucking baron, Mancer wasn't it? I'll have my pound of flesh from that one and be done with it. After that I don't give a damn!'

Einsa stood up too. She held a bronze mark, edge on, between finger and thumb. 'And what if I gave you this back and told you to use it to pay the fare?' She nodded towards the river.

For a moment uncertainty chilled the blood in Rue's veins. She met the ghost's hollow gaze. 'You wouldn't do that. But if you did . . . I would take the ferry.'

Einsa shrugged. 'I wouldn't do it.' She held the coin out on the flat of her palm. 'But you could take it anyway.'

Rue turned from her and looked out across the Badlands. Somewhere out there were the caves that joined the Academy's catacombs. Hidden in the folds of death's borders were a thousand nooks and crannies through which an unquiet soul could crawl to return to haunt the living. Her pain flared in anticipation of all those miles. The untold timeless years of searching. 'Do you know the way?'

'I don't,' Bek said. 'But *she* does.' She stared at Senna.

The crow took to the air with a squawk of betrayal, evading Rue's grasp.

'Give it up!' A harsh cry from above, where Senna flew against a black sky.

Rue balled her fists. 'They killed my friends!'

'*I'm* not your friend!'

'Fine.' Rue reached into her shift and drew forth a bronze mark. One of the nine they gave her on that day of days. She held it aloft, pinched between finger and thumb, arm stretched out.

'Fine!' A dark shape plucked it from her grasp in an explosion of feathers. 'I still don't like you,' the crow's cry reached her from on high.

'That's OK.' Rue shrugged off her ghosts and set out in the direction of the caw. 'Friends don't have to like each other.'

CHAPTER 33

Rue

'Oh . . . that hurt.' Rue rolled over on the wet ground and stared up at a sky as black as the one she'd left behind, only sprinkled with stars. She pushed herself up into a sitting position. 'Dear gods, this hurts almost as much.' She sniffed. 'Did he . . . damn him. I think he pissed on my corpse.'

A flutter of wings and a nearby branch creaked under new weight. 'We're back, then. I earned my mark.'

'Damn, I'm cold.' Rue's flesh presumably had cooled to the temperature of the ground during her absence. She thought it must be the night of the same day since nothing had come to chew at her fingers yet or peck out her eyes. If the Cruelty had thought to cut off her head this return might have gone very differently. A good cremation could have sealed the door entirely. Unpleasant as Lip-Scar's final disrespect had been, it could have gone a lot worse.

As it was, with the Cruelty and his negation gone, the Morrigan's blessing, or curse, was able to re-establish itself and allow Rue to function despite fatal injuries and a distinct shortage of blood.

'Won't he just find you again?' Senna croaked from the tree.

'Depends how close he is and what I do.' Day-Father had found her the first time she'd used the power he'd raised her to inherit. The 'Ingredient' had saved both her and Sharp from the Kindnesses' elixir, but it had told the Cruelties where to find her.

'The smoke might have drawn him towards Pye, but it didn't

follow you here, and he found you anyway,' Senna cawed. 'He found you the same way the Cruelties found every other Kindness.'

'Not all of them . . .' Rue had never believed they were all dead, hunted to extinction. When she'd heard that they'd burned the Academy she'd found the nearest tavern and drunk a pint of ulik. Since it was a liquor even Ambeth drank in thimbles, she had of course thrown up, been thrown out, and ended up sleeping it off in a ditch. But for one night she had been gloriously, disgracefully drunk. And the long-dammed tears had flowed, joy, anger, shame, and sorrow all there in the mix.

When they had started tracking down every Kindness, she had been glad that she had taken her leave of the order some years previously and was already well hidden. All the Cruelties had been bred to hunt Kindnesses, but the oldest of them, the ones who had suffered through their childhoods with Rue as their leader, were better at hunting her than any other. A bond had been forged.

Despite Rue's vulnerability, her trail had been thoroughly erased at the time she had escaped her own order, and had only grown colder since. Rue had simply kept her head down and waited to see what would happen. To say she'd hoped they wouldn't find her wasn't strictly true. Part of her had wanted them to. And part of that part wanted it so she could leave the world with blood on her teeth, making the fuckers pay. And part of that part wanted it because she didn't deserve peace and because *she* was the fucker that should pay.

'So, where next?' Senna cawed. 'There was some baron . . .?'

'I need . . .' Rue clambered to her feet, wondering what exactly it was she did need. It felt as if there were too many things to say. 'To wash. Then rest. I need a roof.' She had never needed a roof when she was a Kindness. Always on to the next thing. Putting down roots had made something less of her. 'I need somewhere to regroup. They burned all my things. I need weapons . . .'

'You had weapons in that hut of yours?'

'You wouldn't believe what I had in there, Senna Weaver.'

'And you said I was just making up stories!' the crow squawked.

'You were. The fact that some of them were true was a lucky guess.' Rue turned, slowly, boots squelching in cold mud. The black forest offered no paths. She should wait for dawn but despite her pain and her exhaustion she needed to be on the move. 'You knew the way back to my body. What else have you been hiding? Lead me somewhere useful.'

The crow cocked its head, eyes catching the starlight. For a moment Rue wondered where her coin had gone but discarded the question.

'Follow.' And Senna took to the air.

Dawn found Rue emerging from the woods, having been poked and scratched by innumerable branches, tripped by every root in the forest, torn by every bramble, all while following the caw of an unseen crow somewhere in the treetops.

Senna led her stumbling into the crimson glory of a sunrise that doubtless owed much of its reach to the smoke of smouldering villages. Trailing the crow had taken away the need for choices, and in the trackless forest Rue hadn't even considered any of the alternatives. Here, with the land unfolded before her, she paused. To follow Senna was to take the Morrigan's direction, but Rue had already been treading the path of vengeance. Someone needed to bleed for the hurt that had been done to her, for Ambeth and Jayne. That's what she'd told herself, the Academy taught that lesson, but Rue had known it before she went through their gates. Age had other lessons to teach, some bitter ones, but others that were gentler, that spoke of letting go.

Rue looked to the south. She had borne three daughters. It had been a different life, an attempt to escape, to have what had been taken from her. It had been another lesson. They came together, birthed on the morning, noon, and evening of the same day. Celaeno, Ocypete, Aello. The morning child, born to greet a sunrise much like this one, was long gone, taken cruelly. The child born when the sun was at its zenith lay between worlds, her warm corpse tended by the nuns of Thellamid, or perhaps by now she had joined her elder sister. And Cela, child of the night, always the baby, if only by half a day, she had gone west.

The love of a mother for her child had been something Rue had never properly experienced until it blossomed unexpectedly in her chest when she suckled the first of her girls. It had scared her, terrified her, and that had never changed. She had given the world precious delicate things that she had to defend from the hurts and harms that lay waiting – many of them too subtle to be kept at bay with a sharp edge. She had never stopped being scared for them, but she'd found a joy there too. A delight she had never thought would be hers and that she knew herself unworthy of.

The pain of losing them had undone her. Cela worst of all because she had stalked off shouting things she couldn't possibly mean, vicious, violent words that cut so deep. Rue still couldn't think about that day or the dark paths down which her vengeance had taken her . . .

The last word of Cela had her crossing into Tavoland, back when Sunder's hands had first reached beyond his late uncle's borders to wrap around the lands where Rue now stood. Regon had fallen swiftly but the freshly minted emperor had burned his fingers when he poked Tavoland. Only now, two decades later, had Sunder returned his gaze to the west where Cela's footprints led. Long years had seen him campaign in the north and to the south, taking the kingdoms of Svellard and Kintcha. Perhaps when his empire reached the coast in all directions his ambition would be sated. Perhaps not.

Rue's eyes rested on those distant mountains, Tavoland's walls. Should she follow her daughter, look for reconciliation, even after all these years? Had age worn the edges from the hatred that Celaeno bore her? . . .

'Did you feel that?' Rue shuddered, her attention redirected.

'Feel what?' The crow landed beside her.

'That! That . . .' Something had touched her. A nothingness, sucking at her flesh like Father's fingertips. 'That . . . thing.'

The bird watched her silently.

'He's understood his mistake. He's coming after us again.'

'After *you*.' Senna didn't ask who was coming.

'Me then.' The Cruelty didn't care about the crow. Rue pressed a hand to the knife wound in her chest. She'd no desire to have the last of her blood come leaking from it as she died *again*. And her brother would be certain to finish her properly this time, whether it meant a fire or simply chopping her into pieces. 'Let's go. Quickly.'

Lip-Scar would catch them if they fled towards Tavoland where Rue's instinct pointed them. She would have aimed herself out beyond the borders that Emperor Sunder had drawn on the map, recently enough for the ink to still be wet in some cases and the ground red. But the nearby river was their best chance to outpace him, and it flowed north-east, the direction Senna was leading her.

Following the bird, Rue headed east across a bleak scrubland, striding briskly among the gorse bushes where scrawny sheep eked out an existence. Senna led her towards a lone house beside a broad river – the Wentwash. They approached along the west bank and reached a boathouse on the edge of collapse. Two skiffs mouldered away in the dank interior, one half sunk with only the prow and stern proud of the water, the other rotten but still afloat.

'We need to go downriver.' Senna perched on the boathouse gable.

Rue eyed the farmhouse, which was almost as ramshackle as the structure before her. No dogs barked. No smoke rose from the chimney. She began to uncoil the skiff's rope from the mooring post. Senna made no mention of the owners. Doubtless the crow could smell the death all around them almost as clearly as Rue could hear the corpses calling to her from within their home. Why the place hadn't been fired, she couldn't say. Perhaps the mercenaries were planning to return, or were still there.

'They might have someone in there,' Senna croaked, seeing Rue's gaze. 'Someone still alive.'

'They might.' Rue shrugged off the idea. 'No business of mine. I'm the monster here, remember? They killed Jayne. They killed Ambeth. That's what I'll have an accounting for. I'm not here to stop killing in general. People will keep on doing that long after I'm gone. It's what we're good at. Even the amateurs.' She didn't mention her brother though she could feel him hard on their heels, doubtless having discovered the absence of her corpse in the glade where he'd killed her.

Senna gave her that sideways look crows are so good at. 'In a hurry?'

'You were right all along. Is that what you wanted to hear? I'm not a good person. Never have been.'

The crow flew off towards the house. Perhaps each of them saw the other as a mirror, and not liking what confronted them they were edging each other towards a foolish act of heroism.

'Dammit.' Rue kept unwinding the rope.

By the time Senna returned, Rue had the skiff on the water, the long pole in her hands. She felt unsteady, shifting on the current, her natural balance eroded by passing decades. Water had never been her element in any case.

'Well?' she demanded of the bird.

'Empty.'

'Then for a little while longer you can hang onto the false belief that I would have helped if you'd told me different.' Rue set the skiff in motion, releasing an oath as a wobble nearly pitched her into the flow. After a while she sat down on the damp boards, trailing the pole to steer them, and letting the current set the pace. Already her brother's closeness was diminishing, like a toothache averted. The thought of her daughter diminished too, as it had so often before after innumerable resolutions to seek her out. Perhaps they'd made the cleanest cut they could, and it was better left alone. Hunting Cela down felt a selfish instinct now. And she could hardly lead Lip-Scar to her child. Then they really would see how deep his resentment ran.

This close to the Innat Hills the Wentwash ran swiftly, its current hauling them along, chewing away the miles. Senna settled on the prow, peering downriver, a figurehead for their vessel. A light drizzle fell, beading the reeds and bullrushes along the banks. The land offered from the river was rugged, more rocks than soil, dotted here and there with lone houses, occasionally a small cluster huddled together for company. None of it on fire.

'Where are you taking us, Senna?'

'I don't know—'

'You better fucking know! This ain't the direction I need to go for the baron.' When Rue spoke to Senna, the peasant she'd been pretending to be for so long infected her voice. She wondered when the pretending stopped being pretence and she actually became a peasant. 'Where're we going?'

'I don't know. I've just got a pull. Like when I led you out of the dead place. I didn't get it till you gave me that mark neither, no matter what that girl's ghost said. I got a pull. Like when birds know where to head in winter, or to find their way back to the nest. That. It feels weird and I don't like it. But that's what I've got.'

'Huh.' Rue settled back into the curve of the skiff, letting the current have its way. She wadded some old sacking in behind her to cushion the contact. 'Better lead us somewhere more useful than an old bird's nest.'

Senna hunched against the strengthening rain. 'You got a direction you like more – then take it.'

By day two the river was slower but still brisk, as if eager to be rid of the place. The land about them lay flat and dreary. Occasional hamlets seemed to have been deposited by some ancient deluge and had then decided to make a go of it anyway.

In time the Wentwash slowed again and began to wind its way into the heartland of the former kingdom of Regon, throwing wide loops across the floor of a valley carved by something greater than a river. Millennia of flooding had piled fertile soil around the river's meanderings and by the third day the farmhouses looked much further away from collapse. The spring crops showed sufficient quantity that avarice rather than desperation would prompt the harvest. They passed villages, and then a town.

Senna returned to the prow having taken wing to scan for threats and opportunities. 'You should see how these people live! All of them got cows and pigs. Better houses than mine too. Every one of them. Maybe the empire ain't such a bad thing.' She shrugged a crow-shrug. 'The emperor does all right for his people round here . . .'

'You're a loyal subject now?' Rue raised an eyebrow and resisted pointing out that ultimately it was the emperor who burned Senna's house, his purse that paid the mercenaries. If the baron hadn't been there to pay the wergild then Rue would have had to carry her demand to the capital, all the way to Sunder's doors.

'Just saying.' A crow-sniff followed. 'He looks after them. At least round here.'

'I expect you'd like him.' Rue made her own shrug. 'He always had a certain charm.'

Senna chattered out a harsh and raucous laugh. 'You don't know the emperor!'

Rue applied herself to the pole. 'No, you're right there. I don't suppose I ever did.'

As the river slowed, Rue felt the presence of the Cruelty again, pressing on her mind, not close but growing closer, his feet plotting a straighter course than the one the current chose for them. She steered clear of other craft, and even where the navigable width narrowed, the river folk gave her a wide berth.

This land had been the first prize Sunder reached for after taking his uncle's throne. It was worth noting that, in murdering his way through his own family, Sunder had broken laws that the Kindnesses were bound to punish him for breaking. Save for the predations of the Cruelties a Kindness would very likely have nipped the warlord's empire-building in the bud.

The scars of those early battles had faded and the peoples of Regon for the most part now counted themselves proud citizens of the Abronan Empire. Especially the young.

Out in the borderlands, in the hamlets and villages like Pye and Stones Corner, the peasants were more concerned with survival than with whoever nominally governed them in the name of the warlord. This Baron Mancer was the latest in a line of proxies to warm the lesser throne with their overprivileged arses. Rue hadn't even known his name until the mercenary leader had offered it up.

As far as the well-fed locals were concerned, Rue or anyone else from the Tavoland border might have come from some distant country, maybe even crossed the Narrow Sea from Gog. Traders nudged their barges clear though they outweighed her skiff a thousandfold.

Mud might have obscured the gory record of her recent adventures to a degree where the casual observer could ignore the stains, but even so, something about this ragged traveller instructed others to look away. Perhaps her own recent encounter with a far more infamous boatman still echoed around her, persuading others to avoid her even if they couldn't name a specific reason for doing so.

Maybe it was that they sensed she was being chased. As the Cruelty's presence pressed closer Rue began to pole the skiff whenever the riverbed lay shallow enough. During the long night when hunger chewed at her, she wondered if Lip-Scar might have secured himself a vessel too. How else did he continue to narrow the gap despite the river's unsleeping progress?

A third day dragged on towards evening with Rue constantly glancing over her shoulder despite her resolve not to. The Cruelty's presence throbbed like a wound now, promising that each straight section of the Wentwash would reveal him to their rear. Aside from continued flight Rue had no plan to deal with her sibling. Any fresh encounter promised a repeat of their first disastrous meeting.

And Lip-Scar would not abandon the hunt. It might have been his job to chase down Kindnesses once the order had been overthrown, but seeking *her* out, would, she suspected, be a vocation all of its own. Not so much because of the single scar she'd left on him after years of keeping him safe – or safer than he would have been without her. But because there is in some of us, those like Lip-Scar, a need to tear down any who have had power over them. Only in this manner can they imagine their pride being repaired. He would have killed Father too if he'd thought it could be done with certainty.

Fear should have chased away any appetite, but Rue's stomach groaned and demanded food. Country firesides were often host to horrific stories about what the half-dead might eat, but it was fresh bread and ripe cheese that Rue's mouth watered for. If she could let go the blasted pole that had so blistered her hands, and instead fill them with a crusty loaf warm from the oven, she would at this point keel over dead when her brother walked in, without complaint and with a full belly.

Another minor town came and went, small boys and girls chasing along the riverbank on the far side to throw stones at the 'water witch'. Their impressive stamina failed after a field or two.

'If we end up in the ocean . . . I swear—'

'If we do, I'm flying off and leaving you to it.' The bird glanced back along the river. 'Is he closer? How long now?'

'Very close.' Rue shuddered. She would take on the great ocean if it meant escaping the Cruelty. Surely, he wouldn't find her amid the infinity of wave and storm.

'The ocean don't sound too bad then, eh? Maybe you'll cross the Great Divide and find the old world. If you can't die you might make it.'

Rue raised a brow. 'What do you know about the Great Divide, Senna Weaver? Ain't you Church of Truth? Humbrold put down two jewels to float alone in the world ocean?'

Senna squawked derisively. 'Stands to reason if there's two islands there's more.' She turned her head towards the right bank. 'There! That place!'

Rue stood, cursing that every action she took these days needed a grunt or a groan or an exclamation, as if without a suitable announcement her body wouldn't bother answering the call. She steered them to the bank and grounded the skiff on a muddy beach. 'That mansion?'

'That place.'

A chill ran the length of Rue's spine. She had marched into palaces in her time. Into hovels. Once into the barracks of the Harren king's elite personal guard, the erroneously named Immortals. But this mansion reminded her of the building that had imprisoned her from small child to the day she had escaped many years later, filthy, bloody, and terrified. She had seen it from the outside for the first time that day, and the cant of its roof, the spacing and number of the pillars to the front, the way it crouched low to the ground, all were disturbingly similar to the structure standing before her in the dying light.

With a grunt of resignation Rue started up the slope. Surely, they weren't breeding new Cruelties here. She'd feel it, wouldn't she? She'd know if Mother were closeted inside like some great spider weaving the fates of children into shrouds for them to wear? She shook off her stupidity. Light was leaking through the shutters on the second floor, and on the ground floor some of the windows stood open. Whatever the place was, it wasn't a prison.

Coming closer, she noted the well-kept gardens, carving order out of the wildness of the surrounding woods. Gravel paths crisscrossed the formal geometry favoured by those with money in the west.

Two elderly women sat in the shadow of the house, both in long shawls as if feeling winter's bite even though spring had decorated the gardens with the first bold strokes of green. They looked somehow abandoned, as if waiting for someone to bring them in for the night. Both watched as Rue crossed the gardens, aiming for the doorway over which Senna had perched herself.

As she reached the heavy oak door, digging in her pockets for a lockpick that wasn't there, a voice called her from behind. 'Hey! You!'

She turned to see a burly man packed into some kind of servant's uniform and approaching at speed. Clearly whatever this place might be it wasn't one that took kindly to muddy peasants dropping by.

Rue took two paces towards the man closing on her at a jog now, his arms already extended to take charge of her. As he tried to grapple her, she made that deceptive sway she'd been taught a lifetime ago, effortlessly removing her torso from his path while leaving a leg behind.

The man went sprawling, though the impact would have broken the hip of most old women. His forehead hit the oak panels behind Rue with a resounding thud. And as he collapsed bonelessly to the ground, the door creaked open.

'What do you know? It wasn't locked.'

The presence of the Cruelty shivered through her, so close now that her wounds began to weep, the pain, absent for so long, starting to bleed from them. A spear might give her a fighting chance, and a bow of some sort could certainly bring him down before he got near enough to do her harm. Neither seemed likely to be found in the structure before her, but the odds were better than in the surrounding fields.

Without looking back, Rue pushed through and into a hall replete with upholstered chairs, delicate vases in niches to either side, plaster mouldings on the ceiling. A door to the left, a door to the right, double doors at the end, an unconscious man bleeding at her heels, and a sense of impending doom so heavy that her knees almost buckled beneath its weight.

Left! She shouldered her way into a tired-looking ballroom that would have been echoingly empty but for one old lady with a bandaged hand, twirling gently to absent music. The dying rays of the sun lanced in through the leaded glass of unshuttered windows, painting the floor in light and shadow.

'Wrong door, sorry.' Rue turned to go.

Something, some hook in her chest, deeper than the Cruelty's fear, made her glance back at the woman. Tall, painfully thin, long hair making a silver-white river between her shoulder blades. Her dress elegant, but faded like the room.

'Do I . . .?' Rue turned, stepped in, took another step, all the while ignored by the woman who danced on, captured by her own slow grace.

'No?' Rue's mouth dried. 'Sharp?'

The old woman stopped and peered at Rue, pale skin wrapped around high cheekbones, crossed by a thousand tiny wrinkles like a wizened fruit. 'I was dancing.'

'It's me.' Rue's eyes prickled. Sharp had sworn to kill her if they met again, but that was neither here nor there. 'Sharp. It's me, Mollandra.'

Sharp shook her head, a brief shiver of rejection, and returned to her dance.

Rue strode closer. 'Sharp, it's me! Molly!'

Sharp stopped again, regarding her with distaste. She sniffed – an echo of the snorts she used to be so free with. 'Molly's grandmother more like. You're too old even to be that awful mother of hers.' She turned away, raising her arms to the music that wasn't there.

'Sharp!' Rue set a hand to the woman's upper arm, shocked by the thinness she found there.

Sharp stopped. She looked pointedly at the fingers on her sleeve. 'Mollandra,' she said archly, 'was a beautiful girl. You are a dirty, malodorous peasant.' She paused. 'Where did your tooth go? Did you know you'd lost one?' She set a narrow finger to one of her front teeth. 'It's not very attractive.'

'Enough of this!' Rue moved towards the door, trying to pull Sharp with her. 'We need to go. A Cruelty's coming.'

'Did you bring Molly with you?' Sharp looked around as if there might be a child close by. 'I do miss her. And the other one. I forget her name . . . I lost them somehow. I'm not sure— Have you seen them? Molly? And the dark girl?' One finger traced Tmanga's scar on her own cheek.

'Sharp . . .' Rue's hand fell away, an awful truth starting to dawn on her. 'Sharp?' She met the confusion in her friend's eyes. 'Oh no.' She set her fingers to the old woman's withered cheek. 'How could this have happened to you?' And before Sharp could speak, a second terrible realization woke in Rue's chest, squeezing the air from her lungs so she could only whisper it. 'I've led him to you. I've led him here.' She faced the door. 'I have to go.'

But a figure in black already stood there blocking the way.

CHAPTER 34
Mollandra

Year Five

'Tell us then.' Sharp sat on the end of Mollandra's bed.

'Everything.' Tmanga from the next bed, pulled up close.

The other members of the class – fewer than two dozen of them after the elixir – shot curious glances across the dormitory but knew better than to intrude on their privacy.

Mollandra sat cross-legged, unwilling to speak though knowing she must. They were memories she had buried as effectively as she knew how, and now that they bubbled to the surface, like shrivelled corpses in a tar pit, she knew that forgetting was part of what they had taught her back in her old home.

'My family. It wasn't a normal one. I didn't know that at the time. I didn't know anything except what my parents told us.' Half of her mind was still in the courtyard, shrinking from the shock of Father's appearance.

'You had brothers and sisters?' Tmanga asked. It seemed that every acolyte had siblings, too many of them. It was generally part of the story behind them being sold to the Academy. Tmanga was a rarity having none. Sharp had eight siblings that she knew of. All of them sisters. She hadn't been the oldest or the youngest, a fact which Mollandra had felt as an ache in her chest when Sharp first told it. There should be some easy reason like that for choosing which child to be rid of.

'I did. Brothers and sisters. Too many of them—'

'We all had too many,' Sharp said. 'Except Tmanga, of course.'

'I had too many to make sense. I was the oldest.' Mollandra had been the oldest when she left, when she abandoned them. But there had been others, other Eldests, other abandonments. 'I was the oldest, but none of us was under five and there were at least two dozen children in that house.'

'That *is* too many,' Tmanga agreed.

'Were they stealing babies?' Sharp asked. 'Or were you all quins and quads?'

'Not even twins.' Mollandra shook her head. 'It was bad there. Worse than here.'

Two sets of eyebrows elevated but neither Sharp nor Tmanga called her a liar. Tmanga drew her knife as if taking comfort in the edge. 'They killed their own?'

'Worse. They hunted us. Torture and fear. We were never safe. Not when we slept. Not any time. And it was our whole world. We didn't even know there was an outside. Just walls and bars.'

Sharp's face grew tight, her eyes narrow – the look she got when she was about to murder someone.

'Why?' Tmanga asked the obvious question.

'Some people just do stuff like that.' Sharp nodded, as if agreeing with a voice in her head. 'They enjoy it. People say necromancy is evil. They'd call Undu a monster. But there are people in the city who smile and laugh and have friends and look like all the rest, yet under the skin they're filth. Demons waiting to close the doors on the world and let themselves out.'

Mollandra unclenched the fists she hadn't chosen to make. 'They had a reason. I don't properly know why, but there was a plan. They taught us things too. Fighting. Reading. It wasn't like here, more chaotic, but we had lessons to learn. And . . .' She faltered. Next to the stalking and the hunting and the hurting, next to the biting and the twisting, it seemed a small thing, but somehow it was the worst, the hardest to remember, the most difficult to speak of.

'Did he touch you?' Sharp had gone deathly still, murder trembling in her hands. 'He looked the sort.'

Mollandra shook her head. She knew what Sharp meant. 'It wasn't that. It was . . . You know the elixir?'

Tmanga and Sharp nodded rather than tell her how stupid her question was.

'They fed us . . . something . . . in the food. And you had to eat it, or Mother . . . Anyway, it made you forget things, sometimes just for a while, and sometimes it took them and didn't give them back. I don't remember being really small, not at all, not any part of it. And if the forgetting sickness got too bad, you just vanished like you'd never been. When that happened we all forgot about whatever sibling had gone under. Not like pretended to forget – it was as if they hadn't ever been. We only worked it out because my brother Strong . . .'

Mollandra's voice died in her throat. Strong. She saw him now, a shadow of himself, weak, crawling away, so thoroughly forgotten by everyone in the mansion that even their eyes couldn't help them remember him when he was right there in front of them. She understood now who the young prince, Sunder, had reminded her of.

'Your brother Strong,' Tmanga said, 'what about him?'

The ache in Mollandra's chest made it hard to speak. The prince really had looked like him. 'Strong carved his name into one of the attic rafters with a bit of tile, and part of the lettering went over something I'd written there. Something I remembered putting there the week before. So, Strong's writing must have been done later. But I didn't remember him. Still don't. Whatever they gave us . . . it took him away, stole him from all of our minds.' Only starvation had returned that scene to her, of Strong crawling away, a ghost to all of them. 'There were others taken away like that too. Maybe Father's poison wiped them out of the world entirely. I don't know . . .'

'Why would they feed you shit like that?' Sharp asked.

'Same as here. It did something to us. They're breeding a family for some purpose.' Mollandra had had plenty of time to think about it, but it wasn't until the day Kindness Marta had taken them to the deep vault and slaughtered nearly half the class with the elixir that the corner of an idea had started to intrude into the vicious circling of her mind. 'Repeat the Creed of the Three.'

'Alecto, unceasing in her anger, implacable. Her whip of fire lashes heaven. Thunder rides her rage—'

'Next,' Mollandra cut Sharp off.

'Tisiphone,' Tmanga supplied. 'She who avenges. Retribution made flesh. No door shall hold—'

'And?' Mollandra circled her hand.

'Megaera, keeper of grudges, custodian of feuds, jealous guardian of old fires. Her histories are written in bl—'

'Megaera. Memory. Alecto. Anger.' Mollandra counted them out on her fingers. 'Tisiphone, standing between them, revenge – it's a combination of memory and rage. Here they feed us the elixir, whatever it is, and it unlocks the gates to rage, and they make us angry, they make us hate.' None of them had seen a Kindness unleash the rage of the Furies but the potential hung around every one of them. It was what opened castle gates and kept the guards' swords in their scabbards. 'That stuff . . . the Ingredient . . . it changed us somehow. Father's had it too, too much of it. Nobody saw him when he came among us. He wasn't sneaking in the shadows, and he wasn't invisible either, you just forgot him from one moment to the next. Memory.

'They terrorized us to wake that power, so we would hide, and so we would forget the worst of it and not go mad. I used to feel it, like a blackness running through the middle of who I was. Father could do more than that, though. He could make things forget how to be what they were or remember it. He could make a thing rot, or make a broken chair remember how to be whole. He could make you forget how to breathe.'

'Wait.' Tmanga stood as she understood. 'You made the fire forget to burn up Sharp. That day down in the vault. That was this darkness inside you?'

'Either it made the magic forget how to work, or it just made Sharp forget to be angry. Either way, yes. I didn't do it on purpose. I don't know how to. Sometimes it's like a hunger, like a hole that just wants to swallow everything away. That's how it was when

Undu gave me the elixir. That was the first day I properly felt it here, the darkness. And then he came. Like he'd felt it too and known where I was after all these years.'

'How much do you think Marta knows? Or Undu?' Tmanga asked.

'I don't know.' Mollandra shrugged. 'They didn't give me up. But that could just be them being Kindnesses. They wouldn't let any of you go either. There was that first night we could leave and that was it. They like their rules.'

'So, are you going to tell them?' Tmanga asked.

'Fuck them,' Sharp swore softly.

Mollandra pointed at Sharp. 'What she said.'

'What if your parents come for you again?' Tmanga asked. 'Your father. That man who says he is, at least. He got in when everyone was watching. What if he does it again?'

'It's not an if,' Sharp said. 'It's a when. Didn't you look at him properly? He makes *me* look sane.'

'They'll come tonight.' Mollandra could feel it in her bones, feel her family pressing around the Academy, out there in the night, waiting, but not for too long. 'They'll come while the Kindnesses are talking about it, planning what to do.' She looked up suddenly, eyes drawn to the ceiling. 'One of them's here already. On the roof maybe.'

'Good.' Sharp stood up, knife in hand. 'I hate waiting.'

CHAPTER 35

Rue

All the insults to Rue's flesh, both the sharp and the blunt, began to cry their outrage. She fell to her knees, and focused on the effort required to draw air into her lungs, one punctured by Isik's blade.

Lip-Scar kept his place in the doorway, seeming content to let the darkness within him hurry Rue towards her third, possibly fourth, death. Sharp stood there in her faded dress, looking from Rue to the man in the doorway and back again as her faded mind struggled to make sense of the scene.

'I knew a girl called Mollandra once. Fierce little thing she was.' The old woman turned away. 'Where did I put my . . . Never mind. Is it time for dinner yet?'

The Cruelty, Rue's brother as much as Sharp was her sister, leaned against the doorpost, watching them both. As a child Lip-Scar had been forgettably average, marked only by his streak of meanness. He wasn't an impressive man either, neither young nor yet properly old, not handsome, not – despite his title – visibly cruel, just . . . forgettable. In another life he might have been one of the farmers Rue saw from the river, or the orderly lying by the door. She tried to hate him but found only guilt. He was owed his grudge, his vengeance.

'Taking . . . longer this . . . time,' Rue grunted. She wondered why.

The Cruelty frowned and, holding a hand out before him, slowly made a fist, as if crushing some invisible thing. Rue felt the black waves roll towards her, made suddenly aware of the ocean she had always been adrift in. The waves would quench whatever fire the goddess had put into her, and the truth of her wounds would kill her.

As the first pulse of darkness reached her, Rue felt its answer shudder out of her core. Her own blackness rushed out to wrestle with her brother's, one wave cancelling the other, peak to trough, trough to peak.

With a snarl, the Cruelty drew the thin sword at his side and came forward, his advance more cautious than Rue's condition deserved. She might have negated the negation that would have killed her but, weighed down by her wounds, she still couldn't get off her knees. The knife at her hip felt out of reach, not that it would match her brother's sword, even if the strength behind each was equal.

Sharp meantime had forgotten about her dinner and returned to her dancing. Her slow twirl carried her towards the Cruelty's path.

'Don't . . . don't hurt her.' Rue nodded in Sharp's direction.

Lip-Scar sneered, but as the old woman spun into him he shoved her aside without particular violence. Even so, it was enough to set her staggering, clutching one bird-like arm to her side as if fragile ribs might have broken.

Rue struggled to reach her knife with numbly disobedient fingers. She caught the hilt in an awkward grip as the Cruelty loomed over her, still too far to reach even if she could have slashed at him with sufficient speed. Sharp resumed her dance, tottering on the edge of a hip-breaking fall at each turn.

'Mollandra Plight.' Lip-Scar spoke with the soft vowels of Tandra-ah. 'You have betrayed every family you ever had. Time to—'

'Ha!' Sharp twirled past, the skirts of her dress flaring out.

Something had sprouted from under the Cruelty's chin. A dark object . . . like a handle. As he opened his mouth – shut by the flickering impact a moment before – Rue saw the bloody gleam of the blade whose hilt reached down from beneath his chin.

'No . . .' Rue raised her hand. Salvation carried no relief. She had deserved what was coming to her. She *had* betrayed every family she'd ever had. Her brother had deserved his vengeance.

The Cruelty fell to his knees facing Rue, burst veins spreading crimson in the white of his left eye. His skewered tongue twitched, but whether with threats, regrets, or apology Rue couldn't say. He keeled forward, and for a moment Rue supported her one-time brother against her chest, whispering her own apology, the one she had carried with her for a lifetime. Then finding new strength and knowing that he stood now beside a river she knew well, Rue pushed him aside and stood as his face hit the floor.

Sharp, executing yet another slow twirl, stopped on catching sight of the fallen man. 'The staff here are so lazy . . .' She looked away. 'Is it time for dinner yet?'

Trembling, Rue took her friend's hand in hers. 'How can you still be so fast? You killed him with his own dagger.'

Sharp met her gaze, eyes widening as if registering her presence for the first time. 'I'm not fast, silly. We're old and we're slow. But I was always faster than you, little Molly. And that's not going to change.'

'Sharp!' Rue reached for her other hand, finding it heavily bandaged.

'Ouch! Not so rough, Molly.' Sharp pulled the hand away.

'Yes! Molly! I knew you knew me.'

Sharp's eyes widened in confusion. 'I do? I think . . . Little Molly? You're one of the ones who work here?' She shook her head. 'You're so dirty. I should tell Maria!'

Rue kept tight hold of Sharp's good hand. They'd killed Ambeth and Jayne. It had made her angry. They'd torched the Vale, and the anger had become a flame. But this . . . she wanted to cry. Sharp Mahalla had burned so bright. She'd been destined to die a glorious death. She'd been certain to go out in a blaze of hellfire taking a hundred enemies with her, or plummet over an achingly tall waterfall in a boat full of treasure while fucking a prince, or a princess. This wasn't her. It couldn't be.

'Come with me.' Rue led her from the room, meaning to avoid the Cruelty's corpse. As she passed by, though, she both saw and sensed a trembling within Lip-Scar's body – necromancy's dark flicker.

Releasing Sharp's hand, Rue fell to the ground, pinning Lip-Scar's neck beneath her knee. Dead eyes sought hers as Rue wrenched free the dagger that Sharp had used to kill him.

The dead man's eyes widened in recognition. His tongue, wounded but released from the knife's skewer, formed a single word, rough but comprehensible, 'You!'

Rue returned the knife, this time through Lip-Scar's left eye, working the blade to ruin all that lay beyond. She searched with both her mind and her fingertips, quickly locating in an inner pocket a small piece of the void-beyond-the-river. She withdrew the jet-black finger bone, wincing at the scalding cold of it, and hastily added it to the one she had taken from Gressa, wrapping the worn strip of leather around both of them.

'Baron Mancer has a long reach . . .' Rue got to her feet, slower on the ascent than on the descent. She looked down at Lip-Scar, surprised at the deep, hollow ache in her chest. He looked older now she'd killed him. 'I'm sorry.' Too late. Too little.

Sharp had gone into the hall and was peering through the front doorway at the burly servant who lay just outside with his head reaching in across the doorstep. Rue took Sharp's hand again and steered her in the opposite direction, towards the double doors at the far end of the corridor.

'I was dancing!' Sharp protested every step of the way. 'I don't want your muddy paws on me! Let go!'

As Rue pushed into the room at the end of the hall they met two women coming the other way. Both of them appeared to be orderlies, wearing a similar uniform to the man who had opened the front door with his face. The room itself was a lounge of sorts. A score of stained armchairs were scattered across a floor thick with rugs, as if abandoned by some giant child who'd been in the act of playing house. Half a dozen were occupied by old women, several of them asleep in their outmoded finery, brooches and feathers, silver chains and poorly applied rouge, all signs of futile attempts to cling to the glamorous lives that had abandoned them.

'Senna really did bring me to an old bird's nest,' Rue muttered. 'Or a nest of old birds.'

One of the two orderlies planted herself in their way. She opened her mouth to speak.

'You!' Rue stole the woman's thunder, replacing any questioning with her own demand for an explanation. 'What's going on here?'

She had meant to ask a better question but found when the time came to make the words that she had nothing more useful to say.

Perhaps it was only that the light was better inside and that the two orderlies could properly read the warnings written over every inch of Rue, the ones their colleague in the doorway had had the misfortune to miss. Or perhaps they were better judges of character. Either way, despite the fact that both clearly wanted to have their muddy intruder swiftly ejected, they made as nice as they could. The younger, blunt-faced woman, whose bristling hair reminded Rue of a hedgehog, closed the door behind them, while the older one addressed Sharp with apparent concern.

'Lady Mahalla, are you all right?'

'Maria!' Sharp put her hands dramatically over her heart. 'I'm so hungry! What has Anton prepared for lunch?'

For a moment the woman seemed too astonished to reply. 'Maria left us some years ago, Lady Mahalla. I'm Cheva. And Anton is making stew for dinner.'

'Stew?' Sharp's face fell. She noticed Rue beside her and blinked in surprise before rallying herself. 'Do you like stew . . . Muddy? It is Muddy, isn't it?'

'Molly,' Rue said.

'Gulla, take Lady Mahalla to her chair please.' As Rue reluctantly released Sharp into the care of the chunky young orderly, Cheva looked her up and down with a disapproving eye. 'I don't know who you are, and I do know you're not supposed to be here, but you seem to have had a remarkable effect on Lady Mahalla.'

'I make her worse?'

'Worse?' The woman's brows lifted. 'She hadn't spoken for a year. Catatonia of the old, our doctor called it. Then a couple of days ago she said something that upset the other ladies, and she got up out of that chair she's been sat in most every day since she arrived here, and . . .'

'And what?'

'She started dancing. Didn't say anything else. Just dancing. All the time in the ballroom. Didn't need no music. And now she's talking about dinner . . .' Cheva shook her head in amazement. 'Who *are* you?'

'What was it that she said?' Over Cheva's shoulder Gulla seemed to be having problems sitting Sharp in her chair.

Cheva hesitated, making the sign of Ordon, father of the eastern gods. '*The darkness is coming.* That was it. Just that. We had to give Madam Robin her powders, and Juna wouldn't work any more that day.'

'Well, she wasn't wrong—' Rue broke off, raising her voice. 'You keep pushing her if you want to get stabbed, dear. Just a friendly warning. Not me. Don't look at me like that. Sharp's the one who'll stab you.'

Cheva rallied herself. 'We can't have talk like that at Marriot House. If you're not family I'm going to have to ask you to leave.' She gestured hopefully towards the doors behind Rue.

Rue shrugged. 'If she does, she does. I guess she hasn't . . .' She was going to say 'stabbed anyone since she's been here', but she knew that to be untrue. 'So, tell me . . .' She circled her hand for the woman's name. 'So, tell me, Heva—'

'Cheva.'

'Tell me who pays for "Lady" Mahalla here. Looks like it's an expensive place to stable folk who've outstayed their welcome.'

'I can't tell you that. Privacy is—'

'Privacy is all well and good, Heva, but I've killed one, possibly two, men since I got here, both times for disagreeing with me. So best not to be disagreeable, eh?' Rue gave the woman, probably twenty years her junior, her gap-toothed smile. 'Who pays?'

The blood drained from the woman's face. 'A factor from Benith Town. But I heard he works for Minor Remon.'

'Minor Demon?'

'Remon.'

'Who the hell's that?'

Despite her fear, Cheva couldn't hide her surprise at Rue's ignorance. 'Part of Baron Mancer's personal staff. Highly placed.'

'And Baron Mancer lives in . . .'

'Chaim City.' Surprise turned to shock.

Rue waved the woman away. 'Makes sense . . . Come on, Sharp. We're going.'

Sharp caught hold of one of Gulla's fingers and immobilized the hefty young orderly, putting an end to her efforts to force her into the admittedly comfortable chair. 'Go? But it's nearly lunchtime.' She frowned. 'And you look thoroughly untrustworthy. Do I know you?'

'I've got a crow that wants to meet you.'

'A crow? You should have said.' Sharp backed Gulla into the nearest chair and released her finger. 'Should I bring my things? I had some jewellery somewhere . . . And a dog. I had a dog once?'

'We can send for them.' Rue bit her lip hard. Hard enough that she could pretend that it was the pain that had made her eyes water.

'I'll need my book.' Sharp bent to recover a small black book from the arm of an empty chair. She tucked it into her skirts then turned to follow Rue.

'Oh no you don't, "my lady".' The young orderly, still unaware who she was dealing with, struggled out of the chair in which she'd been so unceremoniously dumped and accelerated after Sharp. 'You'll get back in that chair even if I have to break your other—'

The nearest object was a black porcelain vase with gilding in the form of serpents wrapping its girth. Rue's aim proved true. The vase shattered on the woman's forehead and the bridge of her nose. She staggered back a good ten steps before collapsing into the chair she'd so recently left. One old lady in an armchair close by started applauding as if at the theatre.

'Come on.' Rue pushed the doors open.

'Holy Ordon!' Cheva followed them into the hall. 'That's Meccom! Is he dead?'

'Not at all,' Rue lied. Her dead-sense told her that the man had given up his struggle for survival while they were in the lounge. 'He's just resting.' She tugged Sharp after her. 'Get up, Meccom! You can see us off the property.' With a surge of necromancy she stood the orderly up and turned his back on Cheva. 'The man in the ballroom though, he's definitely dead.'

'Oh my!' Sharp looked through the ballroom doorway as they passed. 'How did that happen . . .' She pulled away from Rue and danced off towards the Cruelty.

'Sharp! Come back. He . . . he's . . . probably sleeping or something. Leave him be.'

Sharp, who had bent over the corpse, straightened, holding the man's sword. 'He said I could have this.'

Rue blinked. 'All right.'

The door opposite opened and two old women peered out, one rotund in a great tent of a dress, and another almost as tall and thin as Sharp.

'Whatever. Hurry up.' Rue needed to get out before the whole household came to see what was going on. They might have guards somewhere if all their charges were rich.

'How exciting.' Sharp hurried back, twitching the narrow blade, making the point dance. 'An adventure!'

They followed the dead orderly out into the thickening gloom.

Senna swooped down from a gable overhead and landed on a statue of some minor godling pouring water from an urn. 'Who's your friend?' she cawed.

Rue realized she'd lost hold of Sharp's hand and turned to see her standing in the doorway with Cheva and various residents starting to crowd at her back. She'd stuck her rapier point first into the gravel and was digging in her dress in a most unladylike way as if she'd dropped a crust down her front.

'She's the one you brought me here to find,' Rue said.

Senna cawed. 'Really? I don't think so . . .'

Sharp, outlined in the glow of two lamps brought out from the drawing room, concluded her search and withdrew her hand with a triumphant 'Ah ha!'

'Ah ha,' Senna croaked. 'That's what brought me here.'

Sharp held up a bronze mark between finger and thumb. She'd finally found it nestled in the pages of the book she'd fetched. 'This! You gave me this! You're Mollandra Plight!'

'Yes!' Rue's grin was so fierce it hurt her cheeks. 'I did! I am!'

Sharp snatched up her sword. 'Fucking Mollandra fucking Plight. Prepare to die, bitch!'

CHAPTER 36
Mollandra

Year Five

Mollandra could sense the intruder above her on the roof of the Academy, just as, long ago, she had started to be able to sense Night-Father when he hunted. There was a familiarity to the contact, a certainty that they felt her presence just as she felt theirs.

Day-Father had sent Milk-Eye up the chimney after Mollandra when she made her escape bid. Had he sent her again? Would he send all of her one-time family to drag her back to him? What madness must it take to reach into the Kindnesses' home and claim what was theirs?

'We could just barricade the doors and let the Kindnesses take care of it.' Tmanga was terrifyingly practical at times.

Mollandra shook her head. 'Not one of them saw Father even when he was right out in the open.'

'If he starts kicking the dormitory door in, they probably will.' Tmanga got to her feet, raising her voice to address the other acolytes. 'Block that door, ladies, or we're all going to die, Mollandra's daddy's about to arrive.'

'Sounds like a Mollandra-shaped problem to me,' Freeda glanced up from her bed without enthusiasm.

'Why would he kill the rest of us?' Lurgan at least seemed worried.

'You saw what he looked like.' Sharp drew her knife. 'He'll slice your belly just to hear the splat of your guts on the floor. Same as I would. Same as I will right now if you don't get moving.'

The girls hurried to block the door, even Freeda. Whether they were more scared of Sharp or of the visitor wasn't clear. They moved beds, breaking splinters from the bed planks to use as wedges.

The intruder didn't feel like Father, but Mollandra let the idea stand. They had all seen him and understood the threat, or at least felt it crawl over their skin.

As the acolytes worked, Mollandra became aware of more intruders, many more. None of them felt like Father had, these were smaller vortices in the void, carrying some of his terror but less paralysing, at least singularly. Still, if there had been somewhere to run to, Mollandra would have run.

With the beds bracing the door, the acolytes readied their weapons. All of them had daggers of one design or another, save for Loom, who favoured a weighted club ever since taking the elixir. She'd surprised everyone by recovering from the burns but the damage to her hands meant she wouldn't last long now. Not that any of them looked like lasting long.

The handle moved silently. Normally it squeaked and the acolytes liked it that way. Whoever was outside had used strange magics to swallow the sound – that or simply injected oil into the mechanism.

Mollandra watched, entranced as the handle moved up and down. The first of them to arrive had been joined by three more. Five new ones moved up the corridor to join those already there: she could feel their presence like fingertips pressed to the surface of her brain. More came hurrying in bursts of movement, keeping close to the walls, like cats or rats.

These were her brothers and sisters in the life she had escaped. The children she had abandoned to their fate. Little had scared her since she joined the Academy. She had thought that part of her had been broken, the capacity for terror burned out of her at unknown cost. But she found herself trembling now, frightened to see what Mother and Father had wrought of the children she had left behind. Frightened of the creatures they had twisted her siblings into. And terrified not so much of their rage or of their hatred, but of the hurt and accusation she might find in their eyes.

The handle turned again, accompanied by a muffled thud. Twice more, slightly less muffled each time.

'We could scream,' Sharp suggested, seeming more amused than scared.

Nobody bothered replying. Night screams were part of the Academy, part of the system by which one hundred became three. No one would come running.

'An instructor will come to look for us in the morning.' Tmanga sat back on her bed, anticipating the wait.

Boom!

The door shook under the coordinated impact of multiple bodies. The acolytes threw themselves against the stacked bedframes, bracing the timbers.

BOOM!

Another blow, this one jolting through the bed that Mollandra had set her shoulder to. Sharp came to stand beside Mollandra, not helping, as if she'd rather those outside were permitted to come in and debate the matter with her. Tmanga joined them, also not helping to support the defences.

'The wedges will hold. You can't get enough bodies against that door to bludgeon it open. If they'd brought axes, that'd be a different matter.'

Mollandra continued to lean against the stacked beds. 'They'll have brought something.'

Even as she said it, she sensed the invaders stepping back from the door, organizing themselves in some manner. The swirling darkness that she could somehow see in place of each of them, even through wood and stone, seemed to align, the vortex of each matching those around it.

'It's happening now . . .' In Mollandra's mind it was similar to the thing that Undu had taught them only months before in the stench of the catacombs. Though neither she, Sharp, nor Tmanga had any great skill when it came to necromancy, they could within their trio combine their strengths in a manner that was greater than mere addition.

This joining proved far from easy and Undu had titled their efforts 'pathetic', but they had accomplished feats far greater than any of them could have managed alone. The key came down to trust, Undu said. Since the only place true trust had even a slight chance to exist inside the Academy was within the confines of a trio, these bonding efforts could never involve more than three acolytes. This limit clearly did not apply to those who had come for Mollandra.

'Something's happening . . .' Gola, the largest and strongest girl in the class – at least of those still alive – stopped straining to hold the door.

All of them could feel it. Something wrong, some kind of offence against nature, dire as necromancy but different, unknown. The door looked changed somehow.

'The hinges.' Mollandra spotted it first. Rust bloomed across the old iron, bubbling up like a pot boiling over, the corrosion eating deep into the metal. Rust flowered and collapsed, flowered and collapsed, raining red to the floor.

BOOM!

The bodies hit close to the hinges this time and the beds, positioned to prevent the normal opening of the door, slid back several inches as the door came out of its frame. Dirty arms reached through the gap, pushing at the obstacles.

Sharp was the first to act, stretching through the forest of legs to jab her knife blade through a reaching hand. Other acolytes followed but the weight of numbers outside drove the now-unstable blockade back, along with the girls trying to support it.

The children spilling in were younger than Mollandra, some just a year or two shy of her fifteen years, most around twelve. In the rush, she didn't recognize individual faces, but she recognized the ragged mass of them all together, she recognized the smell of them. She had once been part of that terrified, terrifying mass, hounded through the dark spaces of the manor as her parents beat them into something new.

Mollandra's former siblings broke through the barricades in an awful silence. Some among them were too small to have been part of the family back when Mollandra escaped. They came on, giving no voice to their intentions, giving nothing back to the acolytes' angry challenges. The determination on their grubby faces held no anger; if anything it was closer to desperation. They held their blades close in the manner Father had instructed them, thin razors best suited for cutting throats and slicing flesh. The combat they'd been taught, Mollandra now understood, had been focused on ensuring their enemy died, with little care for their own survival. Accepting the opponent's sword or knife in the guts was a tactic that could be used to trap the weapon and allow them to get close enough to open an equally grievous wound in reply.

'You don't need to do this,' Mollandra shouted. She had been their leader. Cared for them. Protected them. Abandoned them. Just as, in the end, Strong had abandoned her. But Strong was forgotten and she—

'Just her!' The reply, also shouted, came from the corridor beyond. 'Just her! She's all we want.'

Many of the acolytes backed off at that. Jemna, too slow, went down under three of the children in a flurry of blades. It didn't look like any of them would be getting up again with much blood left, but the numbers were with the intruders and against those still standing with Mollandra.

Scab, the first boy to reach Sharp, got a slash across his face from one corner of his mouth to the corner of the opposite eye. Even so, he nearly managed to grapple her. She twisted away, slicing a small girl's shoulder and kicking a larger one to the floor.

Tmanga caught a boy's wrist, broke his arm, and shoved him before her like a shield, stabbing at anyone who came around the sides. Mollandra recognized him as Grumble. His complaints tonight would be short-lived.

Mollandra climbed the unstable pile of beds. Over the past months she'd fashioned a small collection of darts from scavenged nails and timber, making weapons much like the ones Kindness Terra had trained them on.

She hesitated a moment, but just one moment. She couldn't let the others fight this battle for her. With a curse she let fly with one of her projectiles, launching it at the head of a boy she didn't recognize. Another followed, and another. Throwing them from the shifting stack tested her balance but she managed to hit only her old brothers and sisters rather than her classmates. Even without piercing the eyes and throats she was aiming at, a dart in the cheek or shoulder could hardly fail to distract.

Brooth looked about to take a knife in the face when her attacker was hauled away by another of the intruders. This unlikely saviour, already perforated by several chest wounds, fell on his former friend, throttling her. Mollandra noted gratefully that Brooth had chosen a good time to successfully animate her first corpse. She flung the last of her darts to inconvenience an attacker running at Brooth's undefended back, finding an eye for the first time.

In the heat of battle there wasn't the time to care about who these others had been to her. The fight proved swift and gory, and promised to be short. Those standing with Mollandra were going to lose before an audience of those who'd rejected her and now pressed themselves to the walls, pretending not to be there. There would be more dead intruders than dead acolytes, but Mollandra would end up among the fallen, or worse, captured.

Mollandra leapt from her 'castle' before it fell. In the moment she felt no fear, only anger that they had found her and brought her family's sickness among those she considered her true sisters. The Academy had blunted her concern for the business of sharp edges, furious combat, and even for dying.

She crashed into the melee, taking two of her siblings to the floor, locking her legs around the neck of the smaller boy while stabbing the larger girl with precision wherever the opportunity presented itself.

Skill, speed, determination, these are all important in a knife fight, but they were a currency filling pockets on both sides of the battle, and in the end numbers tell. They always do when it boils down to arm and blade, muscle and flesh, blood and bone.

Mollandra never felt the knife go in, but over the next handful of heartbeats she understood that her strength was leaving her. She ended up on her back, straddled by a fair-haired girl with pale eyes who might have been her twin save for the two years or so between them. Mollandra recognized the girl's piercing scream as much as her face. Years ago she had given the girl her name: Shrill.

They fought for control of Shrill's curved blade, a straining battle taking place no more than two inches above Mollandra's throat. A contest of strength that Mollandra was losing with each pulse of her traitor heart as the blood pumped out of her.

The razored edge touched her neck. It bit. It bit deeper. Had there ever been a time when Mollandra would have welcomed the fabled rage-storm of the Kindnesses it would have been then. But Mollandra, staring up into what was so nearly a mirror of her own face, could find neither hate nor rage. She hoped Shrill, now out in the world, would run from the mansion, far and long, and never look back.

The wave of heat that curled Mollandra's hair into tight spirals on her left-hand side did far more damage to the girl engaged in the act of cutting her throat. Centred in the blast, the girl's hair and rags burst into flame, her skin shrivelling, splitting over her muscle. A scream of epic proportions accompanied the detonation, and as she came into view Sharp was still roaring.

Both Sharp's knife hand and the empty one were wreathed in fire. She struck one scorched intruder an open-handed blow as she passed him, the force somehow ripping off his head. The decapitated torso flared like an oil-soaked torch.

The girl astride Mollandra stayed there, frozen in shock or paralysed with pain, until Sharp stabbed her in the stomach, lifting her bodily into the air and casting her over one shoulder to the floor behind.

Mollandra struggled up, bleeding heavily, and watched Sharp stride among the burned attackers, dispatching them with fiery blows.

All around, the acolytes not too busy dying or being dead, struggled up to stare in wonder at Sharp's holy fury. Tmanga, her other cheek sliced in a wound that might match the one that gave her her livid scar, crawled painfully towards Mollandra. An injured intruder made a lunge at her, but a dead one caught their wrist and dragged them into a silent grapple – Brooth's work, no doubt.

'Sharp'll burn too.' Tmanga's voice sounded wrong, her open cheek making it hard to understand. 'She would . . . never have survived the vault without . . .' The girl slumped to the floor. Not dead. Mollandra would have felt that. Surely.

Those of the intruders who could run, did so. A tall girl lingered at the door, hauling away any who showed an inclination to stay. The girl's gaze met Mollandra's for a heartbeat. One eye reflected Sharp's fire, the other, milky, glowed with the light.

Sharp, cutting her way through the remainder of Mollandra's family visit, was now swathed in pale flame. She glowed beneath her skin, bright fracture lines shining through the thinness of her flesh.

For her part, Mollandra could hardly keep her feet, swaying as badly as when she had been poisoned in Instructor Jane's class. As she tried to gather both her strength and her courage, the last two intruders still in the room and on their feet backed towards Milk-Eye at the door. Sharp was too close for them to turn and run. Their rags were smoking in places and scarlet burns marked their arms. Mollandra had named them both: Lip-Scar and Runner.

She hadn't even liked Lip-Scar, and Runner had earned his title for cowardice, though he had proved useful and even brave in later years. But to watch Sharp destroy them, under Milk-Eye's horrified gaze, was more than she could bear.

Mollandra tried to throw herself at the backs of Sharp's knees, but her own legs betrayed her, and she fell short, sprawling to the stone. Sharp, in the grip of her rage, hurled herself at Milk-Eye and the others. In that moment darkness pulsed from Milk-Eye's outstretched hand, snuffing Sharp out like a candle flame. The act seemed to surprise both of them equally. A laugh burst from Sharp as she sank to her knees, then slumped to her side. For a moment it looked as if Lip-Scar would step forward to stamp on her head, but other acolytes, emboldened by Sharp's performance, were moving forward to claim part of the victory.

Milk-Eye's hand snatched Lip-Scar back. She pulled him away, following the sound of Runner's rapid retreat.

CHAPTER 37

Rue

Sharp stood in the gardens of the mansion in which she'd been left to rot alongside a few dozen old women whose wits had leaked from their ageing skulls. The rapier she'd claimed from the dead Cruelty was now levelled at Rue's heart.

'You don't want to kill me, Sharp.' Rue felt this was probably untrue but decided it was worth saying even so.

'I'm very angry with you.' Sharp's anger had always been a scary thing to witness, and from the pointed end of her blade it proved considerably worse.

'I had to leave.' Rue hadn't been fully trained to use the powers of a Cruelty, but the Ingredient, the black remnant of Megaera's earthly form that her parents had hidden in their food, still laced her flesh. In the past she had made people forget inconvenient truths or remember helpful lies. Grievances, though, seemed to thrive on the power rather than be erased by it. It appeared that the Cruelty had inadvertently woken the memory of their falling-out more than thirty years previously. 'I couldn't stay. You know that. Nothing we were doing was right. None of it was for us.'

'You shouldn't have run. We would have protected you.' Sharp moved with terrifying swiftness, the point of her sword pricking the soft hollow of Rue's throat. 'We. Were. Sisters.'

Rue felt the old anger catching light. 'You! Wouldn't! Listen!'

'We were a three. You gave me your coin, Mollandra. How could you walk out and leave us to die?' Sharp held the blade steady, the tremor in her voice not reaching her hand.

'You could have given the coin back and asked me to stay. You knew I have to go, but didn't do that.' Rue closed her fingers around the blade. 'And the Cruelties didn't move on the Academy because I quit our trio. That was years after.'

Senna flapped over them, cawing.

'That your crow?' Sharp's gaze stayed locked on Rue.

'Sort of.'

Senna cawed her outrage.

'It's stupid.'

'Agreed.'

'I'm angry with you.' Confusion crept into Sharp's eyes. 'I don't remember . . . yes! You abandoned us. We were the three who are one. You abandoned both of us.'

'I'm sorry.' Rue really *was* sorry, though she would do it again.

'I'm sorry too.' The steel bit deeper. 'But there are rules. Lore. I have to kill you now.'

Rue could see a new clarity in Sharp's vision. She was a heartbeat from death. Three at most. She forced the darkness to flow. Since the Cruelty had killed her it had become easier to release what they had put in her. Not as easy as biting off your own finger, but easier than it had become over the years as age wrapped itself around her. She couldn't dull the memory of Sharp's grievance against her. This power was Megaera's, and the keeper of old grudges would not suffer such a trick to be played with her mastery of memories and time. Instead, Rue woke within Sharp an older need for revenge, a desire for retribution that ten years of instruction had long ago twisted into a kind of love for the Academy and all its creed. Rue took hold of the hatred they had once shared for the Academy and the horrors it had inflicted on them. She grasped it in both hands and set it on fire, overwriting Sharp's current anger.

'Oh, those fuckers . . .' Sharp lowered her sword. 'We should go and get them.'

'I think most of them have already been got. But let's give it a go.' Rue turned and set off back towards the river.

'I'm still angry with you too,' Sharp said, following. 'Whatever your name is. But . . .'

'The enemy of my enemy is my friend,' Rue replied over her shoulder.

'Bugger that,' Sharp spat. 'But you kill the biggest bastard first. That's what they taught us.'

Senna waited for them perched on the prow of the skiff.

'It's going to be cosy,' she croaked.

'Won't be for long.' Rue took the tie rope, ready to pull the boat back into the water. 'Chaim City's, what? Twenty miles downriver? I need to find this Minor Remon, and I can't just leave Sharp to wander.'

'Who and who?' Senna croaked.

'Her.' Rue nodded to Sharp who was still standing at the edge of the grass, prodding the mud ahead of her with the Cruelty's sword. 'And some bureaucrat who, conveniently, works for the very baron I plan to prune from the nobility.'

'Why see this bookkeeper?' Senna asked.

'She's the one who put Sharp in that place.'

'What's she going to do with a demented old biddy?' Senna asked. 'Didn't she put her there so they could keep an eye on her instead of having to do it herself?'

'Well . . .' Rue didn't like where the conversation was heading. 'Just come over, Sharp. It's only mud. It doesn't bite!' She looked back at the crow. 'Well, I want to know why . . .'

'Because she's lost her wits. Happened to Bessy Grain, you remember? Her son let her roam, and people kept bringing her back, until they didn't. Probably fell into a river or some such. It's a kindness really or you'll just end up trying to spoon food into them quicker'n they can drool it out again. Keep 'em too long and you've got an oversized, wrinkled old baby whose arse you have to wipe. You should just let this one—'

Senna took off with a squawk, leaving a feather spiralling where Rue's fist passed. Everything the bird said was true, for all that Senna had been an old biddy herself and prone to mixing up the names of her grandchildren. 'She's getting better!' Rue shouted. 'They said I'm making her better!'

'Who is?' Sharp climbed barefoot into the moonlit skiff, her shoes and stockings sucked off her by the mud.

'Sounds like she should stay with you then rather than some minor demon!' Senna cawed overhead.

Sharp sat in the skiff while Rue squelched around in search of her footwear. She started to sing some children's rhyme about row-row-rowing your boat, all the while tapping out the rhythm on the gunwale with the blade of her sword.

'She can't stay with me.' Rue tossed both shoes and the lone stocking she had been able to find into the boat, all of them thick with mud. With a grunt of effort she tried to shove the loaded skiff into the water. It seemed easier than negotiating Sharp back out of it again. Fortunately, the skiff shifted. She splashed after it through the icy water, got in, took hold of the pole and manoeuvred them into the current.

'I'm cold.' Sharp sniffed.

Rue realized she should have brought blankets from the mansion's parlour.

'Bring me my slippers. And some candles. It's terribly dark in here.'

'We're in a boat, Sharp.' Rue kept her voice soft, suddenly overburdened with sympathy for her friend's confusion, hurt constricting her throat and prickling at her eyes.

'You might be. I'm certainly not. I don't like boats at all.' Sharp looked around as if the starlight were insufficient to break the night's blindness for her. 'And my feet are cold.'

'We'll find somewhere,' Rue promised. 'Somewhere with a bed.'

'One bed? I'm not sharing,' Sharp declared, the shiver in her voice could have been cold or revulsion. 'You're very old. So no thank you. Not even in the dark, with a bag on your head.'

Rue barked a laugh. Age might have blunted Sharp's mind, but her tongue still had edges. 'Two beds, Sharp dear. Two beds.'

Rue kept them on the river for a couple of hours, enough to put some space between her and the corpses left in their wake. She focused on the water, cautious in the dark, letting Sharp's complaints and musings flow over her. She wanted to ask questions. Questions about who had survived and who hadn't. Which of her few friends had been moved into the 'lost' column, and which, if any, remained in play. But Sharp's answers couldn't be trusted and wouldn't help one way or the other.

For a while Sharp pretended to read her book despite there not being the light for it, talking all the while. The book turned out, disappointingly, to be a copy of the Creed, probably illegal now and liable to get the owner burned along with it.

Sharp's rambling discourse resurrected acolytes who had been dead forty years and more, touching off memories Rue had been glad to forget. It seemed that her friend's years-long catatonia had been replaced by something very different, the deep pools of her mind stirred up by the Cruelty's power and Rue's answer to it. Her discourse never followed a single path for long, though often it would cycle around the same two or three questions many times, as if the passage of a few hundred yards of riverbank had wiped the fact she'd already asked them from her mind. New memories, observations, and points of discussion bubbled up periodically, given voice as they appeared in Sharp's broken thoughts. It was as if someone had shattered the woman Rue had known and thrown the pieces into a boiling pot in whose churn they would appear without sense or order.

'It's funny but sad,' Senna said from her place on the prow, an ill-omened figurehead.

'Mostly sad.' Rue watched her friend, the planes of her face caught by starlight, back straight, head erect, still holding on desperately to her pride, to her dignity, amid the confusion. 'Mostly sad.' She let out a long slow breath, willing the hurt to leave with it. *How did this happen? How did we get like this?* she wanted to ask but would not, because it was too cliched, the answer too obvious. They had met as children, and the years had washed over them, and somehow, against all odds, they were still here. And wasn't that what every old person thought and felt? A constant astonishment at the change around them, and at the change inside, just as swift and just as thorough, and at the things that had not changed – those most of all left the bitter-sweet cuts on the soul.

'How about there?' Senna pointed her beak at a farmhouse not far from the river, dark but with a thin coil of smoke still escaping one chimney, made silver in the silver light.

They slept that night in the stables by the house, Rue too tired to argue with the tenants. Sharp got the largest and deepest pile of hay, complaining all the while about it scratching, and Rue the smaller, nibbled at throughout the night by an old mule with a seemingly bottomless appetite.

Only when wrapped in a malodorous horse blanket and having dipped all her toes into the well of sleep, did Sharp ask a question that reached beyond the circling of her wandering mind.

'You had children, Mollandra?'

'I did.'

'Girls.'

'Yes.'

'Three of them.'

'Triplets.'

'How are they?'

'One dead, another hopefully dead, and the fate of the third I don't know.'

Sharp fell silent after that, and Rue lay staring at the darkness, thankful for the questions that her old friend hadn't asked.

Rue chivvied Sharp out of the cottage at dawn, tipping the remainder of her coins into the hands of a wide-eyed farmhand named Arthur Dun while his comely wide-eyed wife, Martha, watched on.

'It's too much, ma'am.' Arthur had upgraded her from 'muddy vagabond' to 'ma'am' when the daylight revealed Sharp's soiled finery and by association conferred some degree of respectability onto Rue. He looked ready to call her 'highness' as he stared at the modest pile of copper bits and the two silver crowns in his broad palms.

Rue shrugged. 'Give us some bread and cheese to take with us if you're feeling guilty.' It was the last of what she'd kept in her pouch along with the weed for her pipe. She was sure the mercenaries would have taken it after killing her, but it had been small change as far as Gressa and her lieutenants were concerned, not worth bothering with as they'd searched her for clues to her purpose.

'Who are these people?' Sharp wandered out into the muddy yard in her muddy shoes, frowning at the ducks. A skinny dog ran up barking. Sharp fell to her knees before it, unleashing an awful growl and the hound reversed course in a remarkably small space, tearing away with its tail between its legs and yipping in terror. Sharp stood up awkwardly, laughing before noticing the filth on her dress. 'And why is everything so dirty?'

Half a day on the river and an afternoon's walking brought them through the wagon-choked One Line Road to the western gate of Chaim City. While still on the boat Rue had stolen Sharp's sword from her, poking the blade through her own smock in such a manner that her pocket concealed the hilt. She had foreseen problems if the guard at the city gates spotted the weapon in the possession of an old woman. She also had foreseen problems with Sharp murdering the first person to jostle her.

In the end, nobody cared about two old women entering the city. The guard waved them through without a first glance, let alone a second.

'Instructor Maggery would be proud of us,' Rue muttered. Maggery had always been critical of Rue's efforts when it came to disguises. 'We've finally perfected the old woman look, albeit by becoming old women.'

Together they pressed on through the crowded high street. Ahead of them the castle loomed on the outcrop of rock that long ago brought the first wanderers to a halt at this particular bend in the river and encouraged them to stay. As the emperor's new governor of Regon, the baron had had several choices when it came to setting up court. The last incumbent had taken the citadel in Ryecrest, but Chaim City lay closer to the border with Abrona and the emperor's palace. Better to stay as near as possible to the heart of things. The baron had almost certainly never been within a day's ride of Pye or any of the other hamlets burned on the Regon–Tavoland border to justify the war he wanted to start.

'Keep close to me!' Rue took hold of Sharp's hand the second time she got separated and hauled her on despite her protests that she was shopping and didn't need a guide.

More than a decade had passed since Rue had troubled herself with cities and all their complications. The stink and the noise brought it all back quickly enough though, and soon she was deploying her elbow to good effect. She spotted a side street whose hanging signs offered what she sought.

She dragged Sharp out of the high street's flow.

'Don't.' Rue stared down a ragged child who'd been in the act of reaching for Sharp's non-existent pocket. 'First: it's a dress. Second: if she'd seen you before I did you'd be missing fingers.'

The girl scampered off, blowing a raspberry, ignored by Sharp who stood blinking at all the signs.

A few dozen better-dressed citizens roamed the narrow street under the watchful gaze of guards set at the doors of each establishment.

'Darkmon and sons. Fine silver—'

'Come on.' Rue jerked Sharp along. 'We need a jeweller.'

Sharp shook her hand free of Rue's. 'You are a very rude and rather dirty—'

'Enough of this.' Rue took the hand back, dredging up the awful blackness inside her once more, suffering as she pulsed it through Sharp. 'You *know* me. You *know* this.' She focused the power on Sharp's memories of their past, trying to open the doors that this age-wrought illness had closed across her friend's mind.

'. . . Mollandra . . .?'

'Yes.' Rue spotted a gemsmith's. This far from the town centre, half the establishments, even on a well-heeled street sporting silversmiths and gemsmiths, bought much of their merchandise off those who thieved it from the gentry living closer to the seat of power. It was the sort of halfway place Rue needed. At a wholly legitimate jeweller's, even with Sharp's faded elegance, any deal of the sort she was about to make would end with them in a cell.

'Focus now. I'm going to need you to sell something.'

'Sell what? Where are we?' Sharp looked around curiously, just as she had been, but with a different light in her eyes.

Rue stopped outside a silversmith's, the third the street had offered them so far. She knelt with a groan next to the scraper set by the door so that people could remove the mud from their boots before entering. Doing her best to shield her activity from prying eyes she pulled the necklace of clay beads from around her neck. It had a sturdy cord, but she still considered it a miracle she'd managed to keep it through all her recent beatings.

She set one of the beads on the scraper's support. 'Not too hard . . .' and hit it with the hilt of her knife '. . . not too soft.' The bead broke into several pieces, revealing a brilliant diamond almost the size of her smallest fingernail. She swiftly pocketed the gem before fastening the necklace back around her neck, five beads remaining.

She prodded Sharp across the street to the gemsmith's.

'Do not lose this.' Rue presented the diamond to Sharp.

'Sparkly!' Sharp promptly took it between finger and thumb. '*Don't* lose it?' She splayed her hand, turning it this way and that.

'Where . . .' The gem had vanished. 'Dark gods, Sharp!' Rue bent, staring at the flagstones for any sparkle.

'What's this?' Sharp reached behind Rue's ear and produced the diamond. 'Lose it? You have me confused with someone else, my dear Molly.' She sniffed. '*You* may have let yourself go, but I . . . am still sharp.' And, so saying, she stalked past the burly fellow at the door and into the shop.

Rue followed, praying that this spark of her old friend would catch light and summon her from the darkness of her mind.

The shop's interior suggested an establishment that sold to other merchants, artisans, and the like, rather than the intended wearers of its goods. Dimly lit and walled with innumerable tiny drawers, all secured by locking bars, the place smelled faintly of pipe smoke and old leather. A scrawny man wearing a white-ish apron over a black tunic emerged from a doorway at the back, and eyed them both with suspicion.

'Can I help you?' he asked in a tone that very much suggested he could not.

'I have a diamond!' Sharp announced, holding it up, before seeming to run out of purpose.

'That she wants to sell.' Rue nudged her. Sharp's participation would ensure a better price. She at least looked as if she might legitimately be selling off the remnants of her estate to fund her decline. In Rue's hands the gem would clearly be stolen property and subject to all the discounts expected. In fact, the doorman might be called in to take it from her, given that she looked incapable of putting up a fight and was certainly not going to be taken seriously if she reported the theft.

Even with the gold now filling her pockets from the sale of her gem, Rue knew that the path to the castle would require a number of steps. The social ladder can be scaled at speed, but seldom can it be leapt in a single bound. A peasant with ten times the cost of a fine new set of clothes from the most exclusive tailor in the land will still not get past that tailor's threshold. They would need to be so loaded with gold that they could hardly walk in order for that 'exclusive' to be overcome along with the damage to the merchant's reputation.

While Rue fretted and paced, Sharp seemed quite delighted by the process of buying Rue three successively grander sets of clothes, with a bath in between set one and two. Each change of garb was the price of entry to the next stage. Sharp herself upgraded in a single step, from her faded and outdated finery to vivid, contemporary plumage that would see her through the doors of any house in the city.

Rue's diamond had emptied the strongbox of the gemsmith, and even with a smaller, less finely cut ruby added into the exchange, the man had still come away with a bargain the like of which he'd never seen.

The price hadn't surprised Rue. The diamond had once hung on the forehead of the Taveen empress as part of a constellation set in white gold, and even with the woman's fatal transgressions it would have stayed in that dynasty for generations. Power, however, not only corrupts souls but clouds judgement, and the dynasty had ended on that day of retribution as the empress's sons sought to debate with a Kindness rather than wrestle over the inheritance she had delivered into their laps.

Baron Mancer's castle, a single large keep, crouched at the centre of the city, its walls of undressed stone rubbing elbows with works of architecture in which every modern sensibility found expression in arch and column and portico. The castle, however, had remained as a brutal reminder of times when neighbours might smile and make nice but should never once turn their backs. An uncompromising pile of bedrock that might resist even a Kindness's wrath. If King Handelf had taken heed of that reminder then the armies of his grandson, Sunder, might not have invaded from Abrona twenty years ago and stolen his kingdom from him.

Staring up at the walls, Rue found she had company. Sharp had moved in beside her and was studying the ancient blocks of stone. 'We don't have to climb?'

'No, dear.' Rue's climbing days were behind her. The days when her lean form could hang from fingertips dug into a crevice seemed a dream now.

'Will this baron be enough for you?' Sharp asked. Sharp who never had enough of anything, vengeance or violence, laughter or lovers.

'I think so.' In truth Rue hadn't anything else to do. She feared success as much as failure. If she tore out the baron's heart, what then? She would be alone with herself once more. 'The debt will be settled.' That was the Kindnesses' way. There had to be an end, a bill that could be paid. If for no reason other than to free them up to punish the next crime.

'It had better be. You know who would be next.' And in her moment of clarity, Sharp had cut to the truth of it. There was a hand behind Baron Mancer, and that hand belonged to Sunder. The same Sunder that they had challenged at the height of their powers. The same Sunder in whose path the Morrigan had attempted to set Rue once again.

There was a time when Rue had found the emperor-to-be so familiar that she had been convinced her brother Strong had been stolen from Sunder's family. She had wondered if somehow Mother and Father had managed to take a royal child from its golden crib. To what end they would then poison and torture him, she couldn't say at the time, but there seemed a real possibility that Strong could be Sunder's true brother, perhaps even his twin, for they had surely been born in the same year.

'We won't be calling on the emperor, Sharp dear.' Rue felt the tension leave her friend, and perhaps the clarity too, as the old woman slumped and turned away from the wall.

Rue had many reasons not to pursue Sunder. The suicide that taking on the baron was was as glorious or perhaps inglorious an end as she desired or deserved. Even under the Creed, Sunder's hands could be considered clean where Jayne and Ambeth's deaths were concerned. Indeed, all of Pye was beneath his notice. He gave the direction of travel, but the baron chose the methods, and the baron's minions executed the plan.

As important as any of those reasons though was that Rue did not like to be pushed, or steered, or told. She had had her fill of those things in the Academy and before that in the mansion. The Furies, whose poison burned in her veins, and the Morrigan were just two faces of a coin of very many sides. The bitch goddess was that coin. She whose hands were never still, spinning so many webs, trimming the cords of fate, weaving a tapestry on her loom wherein all stories were told. Rue didn't know if she could beat the goddess, but with death just a step away, she might yet turn from the paths laid out for her. Win or lose though, she would make the three-faced-one, maiden, mother, or crone, work for it.

The last reason for leaving Sunder alone, and not the least, was that the man scared her.

Sharp allowed herself to be towed towards the main entrance where portcullis teeth fringed a stone arch wide enough for wagons to pass each other without scraping the stonework. As the shadow of the walls fell upon Rue she felt a familiar ache.

'He has a sorcerer.'

'Damping shield. Quite strong,' Sharp said in a rare moment of clarity.

'It's been a while since I felt one.'

'One what?' Sharp frowned as if Rue had made an improper suggestion, then looked behind her as if someone might have pinned a tail on her.

Rue shook her head. Most of the nobility had employed a sorcerer back in her day, and she had in her arrogance imagined that they were trying to save themselves from the justice of the Kindnesses. A damping shield could hide all manner of sins and also made it harder for a Kindness to work any magics they might have.

The sorcerers had of course been part of the largely ineffective defence against those who survived the Academy, but the fact that they remained even now showed that the nobility's worst enemy had always been the nobility.

A silver coin saw 'Lady Mahalla' and her companion past the gates and into the office of the assistant chamberlain in whose custody a great tome of appointments lay neglected on an implausible acreage of polished oak. More silver kept the covers closed and saw the old ladies escorted across the courtyard once more to another, larger door.

Senna dropped from the sky as if she'd forgotten she owned wings. She hit Rue's shoulder with an impact that bird bones were not shaped to absorb, nearly failing to find purchase. Saved narrowly from a further tumble to the flagstones, she cawed loudly.

'Not in my ear!' Rue raised a hand to swat the crow.

'There's something wrong with the air,' Senna protested.

'Sorcery doesn't agree with you. That's all it is.' Rue scowled. The strength of the disruption charms didn't bode well. She already felt the ache of her wounds. 'Shit on me and I'll wring your neck.'

Senna released a more subdued caw from one end, and nothing from the other. With any luck, the sorcerer had laid their enchantments and moved on, returning only periodically to maintain them. With no luck, they'd be here, waiting.

The guardsman assigned to them opened the door and, relinquishing his responsibility to a liveried underling, retreated with a suspicious glance at the crow.

'You can't bring that bird in here, my lady,' the young woman standing in their way declared.

'Can and will.' Rue pressed a silver crown into her hand.

More bribery saw them through a series of doors, up a flight of stairs, and into another office.

'Visitors, Master Percival.' With this briefest of introductions, the latest servant retreated at speed, closing the door behind him before anyone asked him to explain why he'd delivered two old women into the heart of the keep.

'Lady Sharp Mahalla is here to see Minor Remon.' Rue offered the chamberlain her best smile, keeping her lips together to hide her missing tooth.

'And does Lady Mahalla have an appointment?' The official pretended to consult the book lying open before him on his desk.

Rue, having purchased her way this far, felt that while bribery might still be an option, the depth of the man's frown seemed to call for a different approach.

'Through there, are they?' Rue looked pointedly at the grand doors to the left of the chamberlain's reception chamber.

'I'm sorry, madam, but Minor Remon really can't see anyone without an app—'

Rue leaned forward and dragged the leatherbound tome to her side of the polished desk. She glanced at the exposed pages without bothering to rotate the volume.

'Yes, I see. Quite the oversight.' She shut the book and the clap of it closing echoed around the vaulted chamber. 'Perhaps I need to amend the record.' She straightened, lifting the heavy book.

'Madam! I must insist . . .'

As Rue walked purposefully around the table, the man, taller, heavier, and younger than her, stood hastily from his well-upholstered chair and backed in the other direction.

'Master Percival.' Rue strove to sound concerned. 'It *was* Percival, wasn't it? Yes?' She reached his now-vacant chair. 'I'm just a frail lady in the winter of her years.' She sat in the chair and set the book down. 'I've never used a book to kill anyone.' She took the quill from the inkpot and opened the ledger again. 'You've nothing to fear from me.'

As Rue started to append Sharp's name to the appointment list, Master Percival found his voice and at least one of his balls.

'Now listen here!' He returned at speed before pulling up with a sudden yelp.

'Sharp, however, you should fear. I've personally witnessed her kill three men and a cow . . . it was a cow, wasn't it?'

'Donkey,' Sharp said. She twisted Percival's arm further up behind his back. 'I'm not proud of the donkey.'

'Killed three men and a donkey with a book . . . Sharp had the book, not the donkey. I'm sorry if that wasn't clear. And it wasn't *that* big a volume. About this size.'

'Iron-bound,' Sharp said as she steered Percival towards the double doors.

'Iron-bound! Yes.' Rue shook her head. 'How do you remember that when you can't remember my name from breakfast to lunch? Or what we're doing here for longer than it takes me to explain—'

Sharp accelerated Percival across the last few yards, using the allied principles of leverage and pain rather than brute force. She also caused him to bend forward, resulting in him hitting the doors head-first.

He collapsed immediately, any groan lost in the boom as the doors shook.

'Well! What do you know?' Sharp looked over her shoulder at Rue. 'Locked.'

CHAPTER 38

Mollandra

Year Five

'You want me to eat brains?' Tmanga narrowed her eyes, peering first at Mollandra and then at the crinkled grey mass in her cupped hands. It was hard to tell which she was more suspicious of. 'Cold brains?'

'They're actually pretty warm.' Sharp licked the finger she'd poked in to test them.

Tmanga wrinkled her nose. 'Is there nothing you won't stick your fingers in?'

Sharp sucked the offending digit by way of answer before turning to Mollandra. 'Explain it again but make sense this time.'

Mollandra took a deep breath and sighed it out, wincing at the pain from her tightly bound stab wound. Clear fluid dripped between her fingers, the room stank of death, and Brenna's cries of pain set her teeth on edge. 'Why did I just have to stitch up your face, Tmanga?' Mollandra realized that she had been in denial about the power of denial. She was amazed that the pain from the girl's freshly sliced cheek wasn't a constant reminder of what had happened. 'How do you think Jemna and Takki ended up dead? Why is Brenna gut-stabbed? Why are half the beds charred, the room full of smoke?

And – this is the clincher – why are there nearly a dozen dead children scattered around, half of them with their faces burned off?'

'It is a bit smoky.' Sharp nodded.

'What children?' Tmanga looked left and right, failing to see at least eight of them.

'Focus!' Mollandra would have grabbed them both again but shaking hadn't worked, and now her hands were full of Grumble's cooling brain. 'What about Jemna and Takki?'

'They fought?' Sharp shrugged.

'They were in a three!'

'Over Brenna!' Tmanga said, triumphantly. 'Jemna was sweet on her for sure.'

'This is how it works.' Mollandra spoke slowly and clearly, holding Tmanga's gaze. 'When they die, you forget them. It's how the Ingredient works.' Milk-Eye's burst of darkness might have played a role too. Even Mollandra's memory of those moments was fuzzy.

'There are bodies on the floor? Corpses only you can see? Just you?' Tmanga frowned, concentrating. Sharp, on the other hand, had wandered off to see Brenna.

'Because they fed me the Ingredient when they had me. These were my family that attacked us. Part of it anyway. I thought my parents would come but . . .'

'So, why am I looking at . . . that . . . goo?' Tmanga wrinkled her nose.

'It goes to the brain. It has to. Look, you can even see little black flecks . . . The elixir, I think that ends up in the heart, but the Ingredient, that's all about the mind. See what it's done to yours!'

'You're telling me the floor's covered in bodies?'

'Yes.'

'That I can't see?'

'Yes.'

'Invisible bodies? Won't we all keep tripping over them? They're just going to lie there until they rot away and leave us kicking the bones about?'

'I don't know,' Mollandra admitted. 'And they're not invisible. You just don't see them. It's complicated. You're all stepping over them without remembering it the next moment.'

Sharp returned unexpectedly, throwing an arm over Mollandra's shoulders. 'Is this a trick, Mollandra? You're getting us to eat brains for a joke? If it is, congratulations. It's only taken five years, but you've developed a sense of humour. Which makes precisely two of us in this place. Treecie was funny too, but you killed her, so . . .'

'Just eat the fucking brains, all right?'

'Why would it even work?' Tmanga asked.

Sharp elbowed her aside and gouged out a lump of the slimy mess, holding it quivering in the palm of one hand.

'Not too much – it's dangerous.' Mollandra wanted to open their eyes, not lose them both. In sufficient quantity the Ingredient could wipe them from the world's memory.

'You're not going to eat that.' Tmanga stared.

'It's how they did it to her. They fed it to you, yes?' Without waiting for an answer, Sharp crammed the stuff into her mouth, chewed briefly, then swallowed. 'Needs salt. I've had worse in this place.'

'Your go.' Mollandra thrust the remainder at Tmanga.

'I'll wait to see whether Sharp—'

'Wow! So many bodies!' Sharp stared around the room, eyes wide.

'You're lying, aren't you?' Tmanga scowled.

'You'll never know if you don't eat up.' Sharp focused on a piece of empty floor ahead of her. 'This one's missing a head!'

Tmanga huffed out a breath and took her own lump, smaller than Sharp's. She nibbled on it at first, then retched. 'Sharp . . . you lying cow . . . this is the worst thing I've ever tast—' She retched again. Scowling her determination, she began pushing the rest of the stuff into her mouth, small grey lumps rolling wetly down her chin as she screwed her lips up and swallowed.

Tmanga bent double, holding onto her belly for several long moments, before straightening, still with her lips pursed in disgust. 'Oh, you bitch! Sharp! Come here!'

And just like that the pair were chasing all over the smoke-laden dormitory, skipping over dead children, vaulting charred beds, paying no heed to the corpses of their classmates.

Mollandra watched them for a short while. It seemed that a kind of madness descended when memory and reality disagreed so thoroughly. To make sense of such discord required the kind of logic exercised in dreams.

She knelt by the nearest corpse, a girl a few years younger than herself, her chest a charred ruin from which blackened ribs reached, guarding the crater of her heart. A victim of Sharp's holy wrath. Had this been one of the sisters she had run from Mother and Night-Father with? She couldn't tell. There were new ones here, added after her escape. The girl's pinched, pale face held something familiar, but perhaps it was just echoes of the same horror she saw beneath her own reflection. Sharp's laughter cut against Mollandra's sadness. There was no victory here, just sorrow and guilt. It had been her escape that had caused all this.

Would more come? Would Father and Mother descend on the Academy? Mollandra glanced towards the door for the twentieth time since the attack ended. Surely the Kindnesses would come. They must have sensed Sharp's rage? Unless, somehow, the intruders had shielded it with the null aura that surrounded them . . .

'Wait!' Sharp stopped suddenly in mid-chase.

Tmanga crashed into her back. 'What?'

'There really are bodies . . .' Sharp's eyes moved from one to the other.

'You remember killing them now?' Mollandra stood, holding her side.

Sharp's smooth brow, rarely bothered with frowns, now furrowed. 'Maybe . . .'

'How about you?' Mollandra confronted Tmanga. 'You can't see this?' She crouched and lifted a dead boy's hand to wave at her friend. 'Nothing?'

'I see them.' Tmanga nodded. 'It's like those drawings Kindness Marta showed us in Creed. You see them one way, then you see how they can be a different thing, and the first way of looking at them is gone. Illusions.'

'We need to get rid of them,' Mollandra said.

'What for?' Sharp flomped back on the bed. 'The servants will do it.'

Tmanga turned the nearest invader over with her foot. A boy not more than ten, still clutching both his knives. 'Because if

Kindness Marta thinks Mollandra is drawing this sort of trouble she'll probably just kill her. They kill nearly a hundred girls a year in this place for no good reason. You think they'll hesitate if they actually have a reason?'

'So, what do we do? Pile them in the corner and throw a blanket over them?' Sharp snorted. 'They smell bad enough already. We can't turn our dormitory into the catacombs.'

'Whatever we do, it needs to be quick. The forgetting comes after the eating.'

'There must be a dozen of them.' Tmanga rolled the child over again, hiding his face. 'We'd have all been dead if Sharp hadn't raged.'

'I did rather save the day.' Sharp inspected her hands as if looking for charred patches or perhaps a lingering flame.

It hadn't been the grand full-blown rage of a legendary Kindness, but it had certainly been beyond expectation for any acolyte. By saving Sharp in the vault Mollandra had left her far more dangerous than she had been before. A volcano ready to erupt.

'We can't carry them,' Mollandra said.

'Carry them where?'

'To the catacombs. It's the best place to hide them. Among the dead. But there's too many. Even if we could get the others to help. And they won't even admit that there *are* any bodies unless . . .'

'Unless you convince them to turn cannibal first,' Tmanga said. 'And why should they? If the Kindnesses get rid of you it improves their chances.'

'We'll walk them there on their own feet,' Sharp announced.

'You can't get a corpse to do much more than twitch.' Mollandra had never seen Sharp raise the dead much beyond a slouched sitting position.

'But I'm feeling good today. Different. That energy . . .' Sharp's gaze returned to her hands. 'It's still echoing inside me. It could help. If we're quick. And besides – these ones are still warm.' She licked her fingers rather unnecessarily.

'She's right.' Tmanga nodded. 'The quicker we do it, the easier it will be. And if we do it as a three . . .'

The Kindnesses had shown that whatever power the goddesses

gave them would double if two joined together in the effort, but if three were to join, the power far more than tripled, scaling beyond what a whole class might achieve in total. The difficult part was, of course, the joining. It required trust in a place that would slit trust's throat in a heartbeat. More than trust, it required understanding, which is something different and perhaps deeper than friendship.

Mollandra took Sharp's hand. Understanding Sharp wasn't hard, up to a point. She was an elemental creature, pure as a cat, transparently selfish, recklessly violent. But fathoms down a secret self lurked, a different kind of soul that seldom spoke but with a conscience and faithfulness that might colour what lay above if stirred with sufficient vigour.

And Sharp herself showed an unexpected ability to cut through pretence and to know by instinct, rather than by intellect, what was true about a person and what was not.

Tmanga, on the other hand, was the weakest link in their chain of trust, the stumbling block when it came to unlocking the power of their trio. Tmanga might be flesh and blood, but she was also one secret wrapped around another, wrapped around another. Where the horror of Mollandra's past had armoured her against the new terrors of the Academy, and where Sharp's endless shallows had kept their training from touching her too deeply, it was for Tmanga her privacy that had kept her sane. None of them had seen her true self and all of them knew it. The instructors had sought to break her but had never done more than scrape away a new layer.

Mollandra laced her fingers with Sharp's much more pale ones. She grasped Tmanga's hand, much darker than hers, and extended both arms towards the dead. She summoned Sharp onto the backs of her eyelids, flaming and glorious as she had been in the rage whose afterimages had so recently faded. She painted Tmanga over Sharp, watchful, knowing, calculating. She placed herself in their hands more fully than merely locking fingers.

Their trio had never properly interlocked, and the fact that none of the others in the class had either was cold comfort. The barriers that had kept them apart, barriers of mistrust and fear, were the same ones that had kept them alive for nearly five long Academy years. They lived in a place that punished any square inch of flesh left exposed, and yet to make a trio function they had to do so much more than temporarily lower their guard.

They had worked on it, though. Mollandra had saved Sharp from immolating in her own fire. Tmanga tried to show that something more human lay behind her shields. Sharp still had her edges, but was more likely to cut herself than to cut Mollandra or Tmanga.

Strength and focus built then built again, as if their power was a ball passed between the three of them, back and forth at ever faster speeds, daring any of them to drop it. Their joined potential passed beyond any effort that they could make alone, surpassing the sum of such efforts. The rate of increase was slowing, the game of passing becoming ever more difficult, the burden heavier and harder to hold.

The deaths echoed all around Mollandra. Her own blood loss had taken her closer to the river. Faint, very faint, but louder than she had ever heard them. The volume of the corpses' discontent swelled as she heard with Sharp's ears too, then again as Tmanga's senses joined hers. All around them dead hearts strained to beat, some still twitching. All around them flesh that had been too young to die listened in vain for the commands that would never come. At least not from the owners of that flesh.

Will stacked upon will, purpose on purpose, desire on desire. Mollandra didn't need to open her eyes to know that the bodies had begun to stir. Not just one or two, but all of them, limbs starting to reach with the urgency of their last moments, violence shuddering through them, their anger like that of Lucia Aqualas Divinanar, ready to fill each of them till their skins burst. The danger and the skill concerned the twisting of that spigot connecting the deadlands to those of the living. Too small a turn and the departed would barely twitch in death's consuming sleep. Too great and their rage – always the first emotion to return – would pour through, creating new foes every bit as dangerous as the ones the acolytes had already fought.

A new idea found root in Mollandra's head. Might they turn these creatures on those who had for years tortured and killed their charges? If the instructors and Kindnesses couldn't see the children of the manor, who knew what could be achieved? But on reflection, it seemed more likely that the erasure impacted those closest to them at the time of death and might have had no effect at all on the wider population of the Academy.

Tmanga provided the judgement so absent in Sharp and so conflicted in Mollandra, filtering through just enough anger to animate limbs and restore the instinct to put one foot in front of the next to keep from falling.

The trio's building strength plateaued, far shy of the multiples the Kindnesses promised. They hadn't yet reached ninefold their separate strengths, certainly not twenty-seven times, but it had been enough.

Slowly, leaving the fallen acolytes in place, the trio led the way out of the dormitory holding hands and the dead children followed in a stumbling parade.

'Over the wall,' Mollandra muttered.

It would send more of a message, and besides, there were more doors and gates between the dormitories and the catacombs.

The parade of intruders shambled on, some horribly maimed, one with her head cracked wide, others with a single stab wound. Along the corridor, past three other dorms, up stairs, another corridor, more stairs. A door whose lock the children from the manor had already defeated on their way in, and onto the windswept roof.

Mollandra, Sharp, and Tmanga tumbled the dead over the parapet, releasing them from the bondage of necromancy as they fell. A lone crow looked on. There would be more soon. Mollandra winced as each corpse thumped the ground far below, feeling anything but victorious. Most of the children had been at the mansion when she was. They had followed her lead, and the unspoken bargain had been that she would look after them, never abandon them, never flee her family.

The bodies hit the rocks where the waste from the privy pipes splashed. It wasn't, Tmanga explained, an act of disrespect but to disguise the stench as they rotted.

'I mean,' said Sharp as they returned to the dormitory, 'there's a bit of disrespect in there too. The fuckers came to our house!'

'They were my family. Our parents, they forced them to do it. The same way the Kindnesses force us.'

Sharp snorted. 'You *were* there when Old Mary told us how babies are made, weren't you?'

'Yes,' Mollandra said, defensively. 'The man puts his—'

'Not the quick bit,' Tmanga joined in. 'The slow bit.'

'Three quarters of a year,' Sharp said. 'No way one woman squeezed out so many in such a short time.'

Tmanga led the way down the stairs. 'I thought you understood this, Mollandra. Those can't have been your true parents.'

Mollandra nodded. She supposed that the fact she was given to the mansion's family rather than stolen by the monsters who ruled it was one of the secrets they would need to share if they were ever to combine fully as a trio. But not today. For today at least, for a little while longer, let them think of her as someone who would need to be taken and not someone who was discarded.

Honesty. Sometimes Mollandra felt she'd rather take a knife to the guts than surrender the truths of her life. She knew that the three of them had nearly failed to animate their attackers' corpses. If there had been just a few more of them, or if they had been just a little older and less full of life, or if they had been a little less angry . . . 'If we don't join better, we're never going to leave this place.'

'It's true,' Tmanga acknowledged, pausing on the stairs without looking back at the other two. 'It's also not something I know how to do.'

'Maybe . . .' Sharp looked speculatively from Tmanga to Mollandra.

'No, Sharp.' Mollandra shook her head in exasperation. 'It's not that kind of closeness we need. It works for some trios, but that's not what ours needs. And besides,' she spoke over Sharp's protest. 'Sharing a bed isn't closeness at all, not when you do it. It's just fun. A kind of sport. And you know it. What we need is honesty.'

'So, be honest with us then,' Sharp challenged, as if she knew that while Mollandra's secrets were not so obviously there as Tmanga's, she too dragged them behind her like anchor stones bound in many chains.

'I . . .' Mollandra shut her mouth and passed Tmanga to take the lead.

The stairway still smelled faintly of char, drops of blood visible here and there on the steps. Mollandra slowed to a halt. 'I think . . . every child imagines at some point that they've been stolen away from their real life.' She spoke hesitantly. More nervous than before any fight with sword or spear under Kindness Terra's scrutiny. 'Every child imagines that they're special, chosen, and that the terrible people steering their lives away from what they were supposed to be, those people have somehow replaced the wonderful parents that were taken from them.

'A lot of my brothers and sisters said that, but I think it happens in softer lives too. Children whose only hardship is the disappointment of not being a prince or princess imagine their dull peasant parents are simply guarding them until the day that the king and queen come to explain the ruse and make everything better.

'But yes,' she raised her hand against a repeat of the logic. 'Yes, we were too many and too different to have the same mother. The two monsters who raised me were not my true parents, and I'm glad of it, though my true parents were not good people. Even so, born or made, I'm a monster now. And that's enough honesty for one night.'

Without looking back she carried on down the stairs.

CHAPTER 39

Rue and Sharp stood over the unconscious chamberlain whose name they had both forgotten. The iron-bound door that had resisted the man's involuntary headlong charge remained closed and locked. If this 'Minor Remon' who had organized Sharp's care at the mansion by the Wentwash was inside, they were showing no inclination of opening up for unannounced visitors.

'Where are we?' Sharp looked around speculatively.

'Baron Mancer's keep.'

'Why?'

Experience had taught Rue that if she answered enough of Sharp's questions she would find herself back at the start, repeating the cycle. 'I'm not entirely sure myself. I suppose I was hoping that if I murdered him I'd feel a bit better about the whole dying business. I'm not so sure I will, but I'm still ready to give it a try.'

Sharp nodded thoughtfully. 'It's quite clean.'

'When did you start worrying about dirt, Sharp?' The old Sharp . . . the young one . . . had never been so fastidious.

'Tmanga said it was a whatchamacallit – a metaphor – for guilt. The whole clean . . . thing.' Sharp mimed washing her withered hands.

'Oh, so you remember Tmanga all of a sudden?'

'Who?'

The doors to the main corridor opened, saving Rue from

answering. Five figures blocked the doorway, two guardsmen still pushing the doors wide, two black-clad men with crossbows trained on the women, both wearing black leather facemasks, and in the middle, a slight individual in a blue robe.

'My name is Minor Remon,' the robed figure said in a voice that sounded neither male nor female, a crop of short black hair steered Rue towards male, but the band of embroidered gauze bound across their eyes was a more delicate touch. Smooth skin and the absence of grey put them in their thirties.

'I remember you!' Sharp pointed at the Minor.

Rue puffed dismissively. 'You don't remember what we ate for breakfast.'

'I do!' Sharp insisted. 'Bacon. And this Minor person ... I remember.'

'It was porridge, and the Minor here put you in the place I found you—'

'No, before that! I remember ...'

Minor Remon raised a hand to indicate that they should proceed along the corridor before them. 'The baron will see you now.'

'I was going to speak with you first, then move on to the baron,' Rue said. 'Why are you paying Sharp's board at that rather elegant graveyard by the river?'

'I'm afraid that the baron's business claims precedence over any other.' Minor Remon gestured again to the corridor, inviting Rue and Sharp to precede the escort.

Rue shrugged. 'It is his keep, I suppose. We'll talk later, young ... Minor.'

She took Sharp's hand and led her from the room.

The armour of the Kindnesses had ever been their reputation. The order produced dangerous warriors and assassins but, apart from a small number of well-documented cases, it did not make them superhuman. It was the fear that they might turn out to own extraordinary powers that had kept every common guardsman, roaming knight, or local bravo from unloading a crossbow into the back of a Kindness's neck. Also, the certain knowledge that even if it worked, many more Kindnesses would soon arrive seeking vengeance.

Walking in front of the Minor's crossbowmen, with the Minor bringing up the rear, Rue knew that such protections had long ago worn thin.

Senna rocked quietly on Rue's shoulder, ignoring several chances to fly away through high windows. She appeared to have more faith in Rue than Rue herself did. Rue had no great plan for besting a mighty lord in the heart of his domain. All she knew was that she had nothing left in the world that she wanted to do more, no person that she would rather die beside than Sharp, and an arrogance born of a life which, while hardly charmed, had shown her many opportunities to depart it over the years and yet still couldn't shake her.

'Where are we going?' Sharp asked.

'To a reckoning, Sharp dear. To a reckoning.'

'A reckoning?' Sharp clapped and grinned, and a spark of her old fire lit her eyes. 'Oh, I like those!'

Rue walked through the great halls and chambers of the baron's keep, not needing to be directed. The path to power announced itself in the grandeur of the doorways and the width of the staircases. She wondered if these would be her last steps. If her body would be carried from the place, discarded with Sharp's as so much garbage, old bones for the rats.

It felt a small end to what had been at times a large life, the path behind her at once both achingly long and shockingly short. She remembered the woman beside her as a wild-eyed child, and surely it had been only yesterday. But there had been so many yesterdays. Enough to drown in. And so many *had* drowned.

'You never once met a kind person,' Senna crooned by her ear, the soft warbling that crows reserve for when they are among their own.

'Bek was kind,' Rue muttered, thinking it an odd conversation to have with a crow at any time, more so when the crow was Senna Weaver, and especially so when they were marching towards what was commonly known as 'certain doom'. None of the others seemed aware that the bird's talking was anything but meaningless noise.

'From a grown person. You never once had a drop of proper kindness in your life from the people who should have given it to you.'

'What would you know?' Rue muttered, even now embarrassed to be thought mad, even by the people who were going to kill her.

'I've flown back and forth from death to life. You think I can't fly to other places? To other times? I watched you at that academy. The day you entered. The day you left. The years between.'

Rue gave her passenger a sideways glance. The crow's eyes had turned to a luminous, hazy grey. She felt that she remembered those eyes, though she couldn't say from where or from when. It no longer sounded like Senna, or rather it did, but a different Senna, one who might have been but never was. Rue supposed that everyone, including herself, was just the might have been that got to be. She'd often wished to be someone else, which was, she understood, a foolish wish. But to be herself but different – that held meaning, it could have happened, given a different life.

'You can fly through time now?' Rue hissed.

'It's not so hard. Maybe every crow can. We can't change it though. Nothing can.'

'Good.'

'Good?' Senna croaked.

'If it could be changed it wouldn't ever mean anything.'

'What would you say to her?' Senna crooned. 'To Mollandra back then. Back in the crow tower?'

Rue shrugged. 'If it couldn't change things, why say anything at all?'

Senna made no reply.

'I'd tell her what she knows already. To fight. To never give in. To protect her friends because she won't have many, and to avenge them when they're gone. I'd tell her that she'll never be rid of the anger they put in her. So, she might as well use it. I'd . . . ' Rue pressed her lips together, remembering when she had heard her own words across the gulf of time. Senna had been right. It hadn't changed anything.

The bird on her shoulder cocked its head at her and its eyes darkened, returning to normal. Rue tried to imagine who might truly be watching her through those twin drops of midnight. Was the crow still in there? Did the Morrigan watch too?

'You watched me? All those years?' Rue didn't know how she felt about that. If Senna wasn't lying, then the crow had seen more of her childhood than any of her parents, the false and the true. There had always been crows at the Academy: the place stank like a charnel pit. A single crow could have watched her unobserved from among the many, following through all the days of her life. At least they could have once she'd wriggled out of the mansion's chimney, born back into the world, soot-black and full of terror. What had happened beneath that roof was beyond even Senna's vision, shared only with those who had suffered beside her.

'Sharp and Tmanga were bad friends,' Senna said.

Sharp was glancing at the crow now, not seeming to understand what was being said but made curious by its warbling.

Once, Rue would have defended Sharp and Tmanga vehemently, and later, she might have agreed with Senna's judgement. Now she saw both sides. 'They were as good as they knew how to be.'

'You deserved more.'

And Rue, who always had a sharp answer for pity, and had been marching clear-eyed towards her death, faltered beneath the weight of this simple truth. The soft pain in her chest, so different from any wound, made her throat constrict, her voice tremble, as if she were a child instead of an old woman, harder than nails. She gathered herself. 'Fuck you.'

At last, they reached tall doors scrolled with elaborate ironwork, guarded by so many swords that only the baron could wait beyond. They would die with, or at the hands of, this stranger. There could be no escape. Rue wasn't sure how she felt about that. Was it better to fall to a stranger? Live long enough and strangers were all that were left . . .

The doors opened noiselessly on oiled hinges and once more Rue was striding unopposed into a seat of earthly power, facing a ruler beneath their own roof. The old days echoed in her footfalls. Perhaps to the callow youths arrayed in the finery of their master's armour standing around the pillared chamber it seemed that two old women had hobbled into view. But *perhaps* they would learn today that although age might twist people in its grip, that too might be an ordeal that, like the work of the Academy, revealed strength.

Sharp tugged at her sleeve. 'I need the privy.'

Or perhaps not.

'Watch for the sorcerer,' Rue told Sharp without great hope.

They walked on with the Minor and four well-armed men at their backs. Rue passed ten pairs of pillars, each sporting burning sconces. On the walls hung towering portraits of barons past, paintings Baron Mancer must have installed after the emperor had granted him the keep and what it kept. Here and there stood tall mirrors, presumably for the baron's vanity.

The Cruelty's thin sword slapped against Rue's leg within the confines of her long skirt. Slowly, the figure against the far wall came close enough for detail. Baron Mancer sat on a throne as uncompromising as his keep, a block of unadorned stone, shaped only roughly into a recognizable seat. In contrast, the baron's robes showed every ostentation that gold could furnish this far from the heart of the vast empire Lord Sunder now rested his heel upon.

'A toad in peacock's feathers.' Sharp's tongue found its edge again.

Rue snorted. However expensive the vivid embroidery, its colours clashed, and the fine linens stretched across a body gone soft in its decline. Grey curls edged a circlet of silver and diamonds.

'This won't do at all!' Rue declared as she approached the baron's dais and two tall men-at-arms moved to halt her advance. 'I came for a proper reckoning. With Baron Mancer. Not with some ageing man-baby crouching on the throne at the arse end of a failed dynasty gone rotten with inbreeding. It can't be you I'm looking for?'

In the silence that greeted Rue's question Senna took to wing, flapping noisily across the hall to rest on a marble bust set above the exit. Rue recognized nothing of her enemy in the man before her, but she was familiar with the sneer that now spread across his corpulent face. She had seen it imposed on the blunt features of Senna Weaver's son. And she saw now what she should have seen – would have seen when she was younger – the man's left hand was of immobile silver where the other had formed a fist. She knew then for truth what she had suspected based on lessons Kindness Undu had long ago scored across her soul. She understood how the man's sneer had crossed so many miles to find her.

Baron Mancer lifted the silver hand now, turning it to catch the light, as if announcing himself in a way that no throne or crown ever could. 'You'll regret those words, old woman. You'll come to know me better as we explore the thresholds of your pain.' A fleshy, wet smile accompanied the promise. 'I already know all about you, Mollandra Plight, last of the Kindnesses—'

Sharp gave an annoyed cough. The baron ignored her.

'—late of the hamlet of Pye. Ten years hiding in a peasant's hovel. An inauspicious footnote to your order.'

'They were never mine,' Rue snapped. 'I'm here for Ambeth Potter and Jayne Clay. They were dear to me, and you owe me for their lives. I am here to claim seven ounces—'

'Lies!' Mancer barked, standing unexpectedly from his throne, a rising wave of flesh, a thick gold chain spilling down his chest. 'You're working for Tavoland! Trying to stop Emperor Sunder's advance.'

'I don't give a damn about any emperor. I'm here for Ambeth—'

'Put them in chains!' Mancer waved his guards forward.

'I bring the oldest lore.' Rue raised her voice but didn't shout. Even so, it was enough to stop those advancing on her in their tracks. 'I am she the gods fear.'

Rue opened her mouth to speak the rest, but Sharp's voice surprised her. 'My sisters walk ever by my side.' She said the words without heat and yet the hairs on Rue's forearms rose as chills ran the length of her. 'Stand aside or be forever accursed.'

Rue glanced towards her friend and in that moment it seemed that the Morrigan stood where Sharp had been, or rather, that the goddess who had evicted her from the grave had been Sharp all along and had walked beside her for most of her life.

In the next instant it was just her friend: old, frail, and mean as a knife in the ear. Rue considered drawing the sword from beneath her skirts and handing it to Sharp, but reasoned it would get her killed.

The first two guards were close and closing. Rue ignored them, focusing instead on her awakening in the open grave outside Stones Corner. The pressure between her shoulder blades returned – the goddess pushing her back into life. The triple-goddess had touched her, filled her with power and purpose, neither of them Rue's own. Rue needed one now, if not the other. She needed that promised strength.

And now she felt it, something of the Morrigan burning cold through her veins.

'No!'

The first man tried to lay hands upon her, and she punched him. The blow should have broken the brittle bones of her fist. Instead, his head snapped to the side, spraying a crimson cloud. Something rattled against the nearest pillar, a hard rain falling. Teeth, they bounced off the stone to skitter across the polished floor.

Before the guard's body hit the flagstones Rue had her leather wrap in hand. She took out the shorter bone, the black relic she'd removed from Lip-Scar's over-lively corpse. 'Distal phalanx, I believe.' Instructor Jane had taught them that in torture class. She'd taught them the name of every bone in the hand and how to break it.

Beside her, Sharp stamped disdainfully on the back of the neck of the second man-at-arms who had somehow ended up face down on the floor. A dozen more armoured figures closed in from all sides.

Rue broke the black bone using only her thumb and the goddess's strength. The shock of unleashed necromantic power left her shaking like a leaf on a branch. On the dais, the baron screamed in agony, a shrill cry that seemed too high to have come from such a chest. For a moment every guard turned to look at their master in confusion, ready to gain his side and defend him.

In his distress, Baron Mancer ripped the silver hand from the stump of his left arm, clutching the wrist below the missing flesh as if to choke off the pain. He had sacrificed his hand, and a work of necromancy, far beyond any Rue might achieve, had bound those bones to him, regardless of distance, so that with them in the keeping of his servants he might keep in touch with the progress of his plans.

The baron had struck Rue as a soft, spiteful blowhard, not the sort to endure pain when others might suffer in his place. But the evidence spoke for itself. The hand was gone, the bones scattered. His power had cut both ways, though, leaving him vulnerable.

Rue threw the bone fragments to the floor, and Mancer, gasping his agony, put the raw flesh of his stump to his mouth as if to suck the injured fingertip. He found nothing, overshooting his mark.

The guards drew their steel, a common agreement that the time for polite treatment of captives had passed. Whatever strength the goddess had given her, Rue noted that the man she had punched still had his head on his shoulders, and that it was in no way sufficient to cut down a dozen court guards, let alone the others who would surely follow in their footsteps.

For her part, Sharp had commandeered a sword from the man she'd felled and stood ready to teach the latest generation a pointed lesson in how to die.

'Metacarpal.' Rue took the second, longer bone in both hands, ignoring the guards and the cold, sick searing of the blackness against her skin. She snapped it. This second blast of released necromancy ran through her in a cold thrill, its power almost more than she could bear. The surge lent new strength to her half-dead body and sharpened her senses. Both the guards at her feet died in that instant. She felt their souls dragged away through the thinning barriers to the underworld, and their deaths sang to her.

The first bone had given the baron the same pain on being broken as if it were still within his living hand. The second though, thanks to the baron's own actions in pressing his stump to his mouth, would rightly now occupy a position deep within his skull, and the effect of breaking it was magnified far beyond expectation. Rue's hope had been to hurt him, to make him suffer as her friends had suffered. A price extracted for his crime – perhaps not the full price, but payment even so. Instead, with an inhuman cry, the baron fell stricken from his throne, hitting the steps like a dead thing, with no attempt whatsoever to cushion his fall. She sensed his death, tasted it bitter on her tongue.

Rue felt nothing, just the emptiness where something should be. She looked around. 'Nobody else has to die.' It was, Rue reflected, unfortunate for the two men dead at their feet that they had not been people she cared about. They had died because she was angry that Jayne and Ambeth had been killed. And in truth, she'd been angry about young Soosa too, and Senna's boy and grandchildren ... everyone in Pye ... The dead guards were probably of no less worth, had lives, families, childhood memories, but the fact was that people cared about those the world put in front of them, and the rest became a background. Would the world be a better place if everyone cared for everyone else? Yes. Was it like that? No. Rue knew that she was not now and never had been a good person. And yet she found herself acutely aware of the two men dead at her feet. Her necromancy told her the truth of the three deaths beneath the baron's roof, but she felt them more deeply than that, at least the absence of the two guards. And she found herself surprised, her appetite for more entirely gone. 'Nobody else has to die,' she repeated, more quietly but with greater passion.

Perhaps echoes of the Kindnesses' reputation, combined with the sudden agonizing death of their liege lord, returned the guards' swords to their sheaths. Or maybe it had been the distant look in Sharp's eyes as she pondered the deaths of their companions, clearly not giving a damn whether the rest of them came at her or not. Either way, a dozen armoured warriors whose skills had earned them a place in the baron's personal guard now slunk away without recrimination, unable to look at their fellows or the body of their employer whose blood was even now trickling slowly down the steps of the dais.

'Where are they going?' Sharp asked. 'I thought we were having a reckoning ...'

As the baron's defenders retreated beyond the pillars, Rue saw that by the door the two masked and black-clad men had fallen to their knees, clasping their heads in pain, crossbows discarded on the floor. The other two guards were looking uncertainly at Minor Remon for instruction.

A single clap rang out as the Minor's hands met. 'I didn't think you could do it. I really didn't. She said you would, but I didn't believe her for a moment.'

'Run away.' Rue made a shooing motion with a confidence she didn't feel. Something in the way the Minor stood told her there wouldn't be any running. At least, not away ...

'That sorcerer hasn't shown up yet,' Sharp remarked absently.

'Nasty, tricksy things, sorcerers. Not as bad as Cruelties, mind, but those bastards were bred to kill us. I remember back in—'

Rue raised a finger to her lips.

Minor Remon's hands were behind her head now, her fingers on the knot of the gauzy fabric band tied across her eyes. The cloth fell away and despite herself Rue stepped back under the weight of recognition. Every flame in the hall seemed reflected in the one hazy eye. The other swallowed the light, its stare dark and even.

The damping shield snuffed out, as if with the unmasking. It had of course hidden the Cruelty's presence. Even the bond that now stretched clear and taut between Rue and the sorcerer before her. Heart to heart. Head to head.

'Milk-Eye.' The name seemed as silly for a grown woman as Lip-Scar had for a grown man, but Rue had no other. And in all the long years since they had been children together in the Tandra-ah mansion, there had been no Cruelty more savage in the prosecution of their task. No Cruelty to slay more Kindnesses. 'Milk-Eye,' she repeated. Her sister-from-the-dark. Seemingly unburdened by the age that weighed so heavily on Rue's shoulders. Milk-Eye with guards at her back, and Rue with no one to stand by her, save a broken-minded Sharp.

CHAPTER 40

Mollandra

Year Six

'Do this or you die. Do that . . . or you die. How about you fucking die for no reason today?' Mollandra strode before Sharp and Tmanga in the freezing bell tower as if she were an instructor and they the pupils. 'That's how they train us. That's how we've lived. Well today it's my turn! You two are going to do this or we all die. I swear it by the dead gods and the dying.'

'You're going to kill me, little Molly?' Sharp grinned her dangerous grin. She sat to Mollandra's left on the ledge, with the drop beneath the great bell just an inch from her left hip. 'You know you're our weakest link? You do know that, don't you?'

'She's not.' Tmanga sat cross-legged and to Mollandra's right, hidden from Sharp's view by the bell's bronze immensity. She spoke quietly but as ever she fitted her words neatly into a quiet space so that she was heard.

'What?' Sharp made to stand. 'Everyone knows I could beat her in the Wound Garden.'

'Sit down. Mollandra's our strongest link. Always has been. And life won't be offering you many duels, Sharp. If Mollandra comes for you, you won't see it. Be thankful she's your friend.'

'Fuck you.' Sharp wouldn't have taken it from anyone but Tmanga. But she sat down.

'Mollandra's exactly what Kindness Marta is looking for. Terra wants warriors, and Undu wants necromancers, but that's why Marta is in charge. First among equals. She's looking for survivors. Mollandra's karren grass in the wheat. When the blight comes, or the hunger-bug, and the wheat gives up, she'll be left. It's not something this place put into her – it's something they can't take out. My cleverness, your speed, they'll take us a long way. But if you bet against Mollandra here not still marching along the path when we've both fallen to the side . . . well, chances are your money's lost. Let her speak.'

Mollandra blinked. Tmanga had never said anything like that about her before. Tmanga had seldom said as much about anyone or anything. Mollandra gathered her thoughts and stopped her pacing at a spot where she could see both girls.

'We're all going to die if you don't do what I say. We'll die because Brooth, Brenna, and Kaya will be the Kindnesses for our year. None of them can beat any of us at anything of consequence – except Brooth with her corpse-work – but when they're a three they can crush us. They trust each other.'

'I trust—'

'They're . . . friends.' Mollandra cut across Sharp's protest, her throat constricting with unexpected emotion. 'You trust us with your life because it's something you don't give the slightest shit about, Sharp. And neither of us know *why* that's the case. If I believed you're as endlessly shallow as you make out, then perhaps it would be all right. But I don't.'

'It's not like *you* tell us anything,' Sharp snapped, her humour gone. 'Five years. Five fucking years of murder and torture and sheer fucking hell, and it takes that madman actually walking in through the gates before you say a word about the craziness that drove you here. You SOLD YOURSELF. You didn't think that was worth mentioning?'

Mollandra set both hands to the cold bronze before her and leaned her weight upon it. The bell gave by degrees. 'But I *did* tell you.'

'Eventually.' Sharp snorted. 'If "Daddy" hadn't come calling we might have been old ladies before you told us.' She laughed, and Mollandra, thinking it must be at the idea they would ever be old, joined in despite herself.

'I'm angry.' Mollandra fixed her gaze on the dark drop that her toes overhung, a space the bell's retreat had made wide enough to swallow her. She spoke in a low voice and the wind carried it away through the perforated stone enclosing the tower top. She half-hoped the wind would keep what she said from the others. Even though the whole thing had been her idea, her demand. 'I'm so angry. All. The. Time. I'm worried that this anger might be all I am, not just the sea I drowned in. I'm worried that even if none of this had ever happened to me, I would *still* be this rage and nothing else. And you, Tmanga, you make me feel worse every day I'm with you – you're like that hole the Tallowmen throw their curses into on strips of lead – you give nothing back. Not even the Academy can ruffle your feathers, and I don't know how that's possible. How haven't they broken you like they broke every other child that ever came through their gates? Sharp and me, we were in pieces before we ever came here. But you. You're whole. Complete. Not so much as a crack. Nothing for us to hang onto you by, not even just by our fingernails.

'And if the Academy couldn't break you open, then I have to. Otherwise you'll never let us in. And, yes, you might die with all your secrets intact. But you'll still die. And so will Sharp and I. Because we're not a three. And we need to be.'

Mollandra closed her mouth and listened. Waited. The wind hissing through the tower's irregular gaps, sighing in many voices. The red light of the setting sun, cast in sharp-cornered glory across the gentle bronze curve. The fall at her toes and the great silent tongue of the bell. Mollandra felt herself at the top of more than one fatal fall, with Sharp's narrow hand and Tmanga's broad one pressed to her spine, high up between the blades of her shoulders.

The cawing of a crow, shockingly loud, surprisingly close at hand, broke the silence and startled Sharp into speaking. 'I don't want to tell you.'

The strain in Sharp's voice was as if she were lifting a weight beyond any dared before. She hit the bell with enough force that Mollandra felt the pain, though the bronze swallowed it all without comment. 'I don't want to tell my story, even to you, because it's small and dirty and so fucking ordinary it bores even me even as it's making me cry. Is that what you wanted? To break me down, make me dull and stupid just like everyone else? You need my tears before you'll believe I'm real? 'Cos I won't do it. Not even for Mollandra-fucking-Plight.' She held Mollandra with a stare that had murder in it, and fire, perhaps that of the dying winter sun, or perhaps the flame they'd put in them deep down in the vaults, the inferno every Kindness carries, and few can release.

'You will,' Mollandra said, and if not for Tmanga who had circled the walkway and come to Sharp from the other side, they might have fought, or burned there together, a funeral pyre in that high tower, red tongues licking through the cut stone and the great bell falling to strike the floor far below with its final exclamation.

'You must.' Tmanga took Sharp's arm, closing her hand over the girl's pale fist.

'You know what it is. My story happens all the time, out there.' Her head jerked towards the city and ten thousand tiled roofs beneath which the human saga played out, variations of the same theme on so many different stages. 'I don't even . . .' Sharp always kept an edge on her tongue, but the words she applied it to were few and simple, sufficient for the facts of her pain but incapable of expressing the subtle ruin they had wrought upon her, blood to bone. 'Things like this . . .' Sharp shook her head, as if hoping the red foam of her hair would sweep forward to hide her.

Mollandra's breath caught on the ache in her chest. The first prickle of tears. She had asked for truth, demanded it, and now she wanted to stop her ears.

Sharp continued in the monotone that sounded nothing like her. 'You had it easy, Mollandra—' She bit her tongue. 'Not easy. No. But at least it was special.' She shook off Tmanga and took both Mollandra's hands in hers, staring into her eyes, imploring, almost pleading. 'At least it was . . . unique. Nobody would ever look at it and see no problem, nobody would just shrug and turn away. They wouldn't say, "that's just life" or that it "happens on every street".

They'd be horrified. They'd shout. Get the pitchforks and the torches. They wouldn't tell you to shut your mouth, say you were lying, then sell you so you wouldn't carry on making a scene.

'I mean . . . it's a crime on the Kindnesses' books. They've killed kings and princes over it. Nailed their manhoods over their golden doors. But on the way to those palaces they hardly walk down a street where . . . and they do nothing.'

Sharp held Mollandra's gaze the whole time, showing her no mercy. The fire in her eyes flared and guttered and fell to hot embers but all their tears couldn't put it out.

'Thank you.' Mollandra had nothing more to say in the face of an evil so deep and so old and, as Sharp had said, so terribly, wrongly ordinary. Innocence and vulnerability were the world's tinder, and trust too thin a shield to keep them from the flame.

'It's not enough,' Tmanga said, dry-eyed.

'What?' Mollandra turned angrily on the girl. Sharp would rather have literally sliced herself open than have opened in the way she just had. 'How is that not enough?'

'How can we kill them unless we know their names?' Tmanga replied.

Sharp laid her head on Tmanga's shoulder. 'I'll give you one name. The worst. The rest I'll kill by myself.' She paused, opened her mouth to speak, winced in pain, frowned, and sealed her lips.

'Tell us.' Mollandra's nails dug into her palms. 'Say it.' Having told some of her own story, she knew now that speaking the name aloud, no matter how painful, would draw some of the venom from it.

Sharp gritted her teeth. 'Matrin.' She whispered it. 'Matrin Smith.' She gave a shocked laugh. 'I told you it was pathetically ordinary.'

'When we leave this place we will kill anyone guilty of high crimes, no matter how low they lie.' Tmanga spoke without anger, only certainty.

'We will.' Mollandra nodded. She paused, looking at Tmanga, still by Sharp's side.

'She wants you to blub now,' Sharp said. 'Bare your soul so we can be a three.'

Tmanga pursed her lips. 'You assume I've been holding out on you both. You think that where Sharp's shallows hid such depths, my silences are full of secrets.' Her smooth brow furrowed. Tmanga so rarely frowned that Mollandra could imagine her older than Kindness Marta with no more wrinkles than a still pond. 'My parents sold me here. I was their only child, and they were not poor. I dreamed that first night that as they walked away from the Academy's gates my mother scattered those coins by the roadside, like sowing corn, as if she wanted to be rid of every part of me.

'I blame her of course, and my father who let it happen – he was always a weak man – but the idea and the insistence, that was all my mother. I blame her but I'm not angry with her.'

Mollandra had never seen Tmanga angry. It was part of the reason that she had never been able to fully trust her.

'I'm angry for you,' said Sharp in a tone that suggested she had heard the story before.

'My mother wasn't cruel. She just didn't . . . care. At least not as much as other people do. And that was the problem. She saw the same thing in me, just more of it. She knew I didn't love her, not like children are supposed to love their mothers. And she didn't love me as much as she should. That bond, the one that will pull a mother into the fire if you throw her baby into the hearth . . . she never felt that. I guess I made her feel guilty.

'It annoyed her. We argued, or at least she did. The more silent I was the more she raged. She did this.' Tmanga touched the pink scar she'd brought with her to the Academy. 'None of it was anything to me. Just weather.' She frowned that un-Tmanga-like frown. 'You know, until I came here, and they started trying to kill me . . . I don't think I'd ever felt anything. Not really. Everything had been so . . . flat . . . before that. I found out that even terror is better than nothing.

'I'm exactly the sort of monster they're always looking for. I couldn't have been a part of the world. I would have just lain down and starved. Or done terrible things. At least this way there will be a reason for those terrible things . . .' Her dark eyes found Mollandra's. 'It's not what you want to hear, but it's the truth. The Creed has given me direction. This place, horrific as it is . . . I wouldn't leave it. And this, right now.' She gestured between her heart and Mollandra's. 'It's as deep as I go. Sharp's not the shallow one. It's me. Ankle-deep. I've spent my life watching, never properly taking part, standing to the side, not feeling the highs or the lows.'

'It sounds lonely,' Mollandra said. She'd known it, really, that Tmanga had always stood apart from them.

'It's what I know. What I am. We can't change our natures. The Kindnesses understand that. They know that all they can do is reveal what we are.' Tmanga shrugged. 'I'll promise to stand with you both. To die with you both. To serve the Creed. But I can't ever love you.'

'And if I died tomorrow?' Mollandra asked, somewhere between hurt and disbelief.

'I would avenge you.'

'Because of the Creed?'

'Because of the Creed.'

'But how would you feel?' Mollandra asked.

'I think . . .' Tmanga rubbed at the cheek scar her mother had given her. 'I think . . . nothing. But you'd have to die for me to be sure. Maybe I'd surprise myself and be sad.'

'She'd be sad.' Sharp took hold of Tmanga's arm. 'But not as sad as if *I* died. She loves us both.'

'I do not.'

'She just thinks she doesn't.' Sharp nodded confidently. 'She's not lying. Just wrong.'

CHAPTER 41

Rue

'Eldest.' Milk-Eye nodded her acknowledgement of Rue. 'When Mother dealt the baron his hand in the game – forced it on him really' – she circled her left wrist with the fingers of the right as if to pinch it off – 'it was in order that he use it to seize power. I am impressed that you turned his own hand against him so effectively.'

Mention of Mother put a chill into Rue. She wanted to ask how long ago this plan had been laid, how long ago the baron had been maimed. Mother had been dead for many years, surely?

She felt snared now in a way that even Milk-Eye's appearance hadn't made her feel. There were plans here decades and more in the making . . . 'You! *You* put Sharp in that place!'

'A lure for you, Eldest. You were a long time coming. I'd lost faith that you would. I thought you'd abandoned your new family as completely as your old one.'

'You're so young.' This talk of new and old had brought Milk-Eye's age into focus. 'So many years thrown away . . .' Without time's tether the girl was a floating point, trapped in an endless now. Rue had cursed her age more in the last few days than in the previous ten years, her weakness highlighted at every turn. But without the foundation of memory she wouldn't have cared about Jayne or Ambeth or even known Sharp or felt the bonds they'd earned after the Academy.

'You threw us *all* away, Eldest. All our years.' The woman, who

Rue recognized only from the peculiarity that had named her, sneered. 'What do you care whether we keep our years or cast them aside?'

The truth of it lay beyond words. She could say that she had also been a child. That both of them were victims. That if Milk-Eye had held tight to her experience then age would have taught her perspective too. But there was no home for these words behind those mismatched eyes, so Rue answered with a question.

'If Sharp was bait, who was watching her?'

Sharp, hearing her name, looked up in confusion, no recognition in her face. 'Me?'

'Who was watching her?' Rue continued. 'And why didn't they close the trap?'

Milk-Eye nodded to the masked figures left and right, only now starting to stand, having rid their minds of the echoes of the baron's death. Concentrating on the pair, Rue could now sense beneath the damping shield traces of the bones they carried, the baron's fingers, linking them to his corpse. She sensed the Ingredient in them too – a new generation of Cruelties.

'When they saw you were heading in the right direction, they followed you here. No need to step in. You were in the baron's grasp for a long time before you . . . broke it.'

Milk-Eye watched her, half-amused. Savouring the moment. Watching different levels of understanding surface on Rue's face.

Rue needed help and she knew it. Without Sharp she had no chance at all. Even if she were to regain her friend, a three-legged donkey in a thoroughbred race would have better odds. But at least she wouldn't feel she was dying alone, unwitnessed.

Megaera's poison, whatever it was they'd fed Rue – scavenged from the Fury's earthly remains – had allowed her presence to stir Sharp's depths, bringing her part way out of the catatonia age had mired her in. But she needed more and she had never been trained in the subtleties of that power. Rue had fled too young to learn the Cruelties' craft.

She needed something more than the ability to dredge memory from the darkness or press it back into black oblivion. In the face of this disease, that was too blunt a weapon. She needed something . . .

sharp. Something personal and so deep that it would bring up with it the delicate webs of recollection that constituted her friend's being.

'I'm sorry, Sharp . . .' Rue moved to her friend's side. 'But I need you.'

Sharp's confusion deepened. 'It must be time for dinner by now. Where's Maria?'

Rue pushed forward with the darkness even now unwrapping from her bones. She needed an arrowhead, though. Something to pierce deep and open the way.

'Matrin Smith.' She whispered the name, just as Sharp herself had whispered the man's name at seventeen when she shared her deepest and most secret hurts a lifetime ago and a world away.

A soft cry of hurt escaped the old woman, and she staggered. Rue caught her arm, pouring in Megaera's power.

'Matrin Smith.' Rue spat the name now. 'Remember how we killed him? The three of us?'

'I . . .' Sharp straightened. 'I do.' Her face hardened. Her gaze became focused. She shook her arm free.

'I remember this one.' Sharp stepped past Rue, pointing with her sword at Milk-Eye. 'I told you that I knew her! The eye-girl. Came to our dormitory with a bunch of stabby children.' Sharp nodded. 'I burned them all up. We threw them off the wall. Down where the shit goes. She ran away. Now she's back to finish it.'

How much she'd been able to restore to Sharp Rue had no idea, but she clearly had more of her friend with her than she had moments before. Rue narrowed her gaze at Milk-Eye. 'Sharp's right? That's what this is about?'

Milk-Eye looked surprised, as if she hadn't imagined that there would ever be any doubt about that, of all things. Somewhere far away a bell began to toll, though whether to raise the alarm or to note the baron's passing, Rue didn't know.

'Of course that's what this is about. *You* might have grown old and forgotten what you did to us. You might have hidden yourself away in some pigsty village and played nice with the peasants. But *I* didn't, *we* didn't, the ones you left behind. Father and Mother taught us all about memory, sister. We forget our years but never the wounds we're dealt.'

Beside Milk-Eye, the masked Cruelties had recovered and brought their crossbows to bear once more. Rue knew she should have attacked when they were weak, but somehow she didn't think Milk-Eye had nursed this grudge for half a century only to end it with a bolt to the stomach. She'd want a more personal revenge.

To Rue's despair, her own back-up, Sharp, seemed to have forgotten about Milk-Eye and the others entirely. Instead of watching them, she stared at her reflection in the various mirrors around the walls, swaying this way and that for a better angle.

One of the crossbow men, with exaggerated motions, drew a bead on Rue's head.

'Kill me then. If that's what you're here for.' Rue raised her eyebrows at the man aiming his weapon, and touched a fingertip to her forehead, daring him to loose the bolt. She snorted at the thought they might call her bluff. Sharp, thinking the same thing, or perhaps remembering a joke from thirty years ago, laughed, sounding unaccountably young.

'Time hasn't healed me.' Time had told her that truth itself. Something as small as a slap could echo through decades. Rue knew there had never been any chance to recover from what they did to her. 'I am what they made me.' She caught sight of herself in one of the mirrors on the wall: a used-up old woman, or in the next moment, a queen on her throne of bones, and a heartbeat later, both at once. She would have liked to meet the Molly who might have grown into the old woman she'd been pretending to be. But that was another life, another Earth, another story. 'I'm a toxin, a wound in the world . . .' Time had soured her rather than healing. Rue knew herself a crack that ran through things, breaking them. That same crack had run from her, through her children, fracturing any love before it flowered. She met Milk-Eye's fierce regard. 'Kill me then. Lip-Scar knew how to do it. There's nothing but old magic and stubbornness holding me together.'

'That would be too easy. They call us Cruelties after all. First we destroy what you love. Your precious peasants. Their dung and straw huts. Your friends—' She raised her hand and one of the crossbows jolted with the release of its bolt.

Sharp, whose swaying fascination with the mirrors had yet to cease, flinched only when the bolt shattered on a pillar behind her.

'Ouch!' Her hand went to the crimson rawness where the very top of her left ear had been. Her cry, more one of outrage than of pain, coincided with Rue's own strangled 'No!'

If Rue hadn't seen Sharp in so many fights, she might have imagined it an improbable accident, and dismissed the idea that any human could dodge a crossbow's bolt. As the second crossbowman raised his weapon to his shoulder, she knew with grim certainty that such overconfidence would not be repeated, and that even in her prime Sharp could not have sidestepped a chest shot at such short range.

Desperation can flower in a heartbeat. A prayer, as long as it is wordless, can be thrown nearly as swiftly. Rue found herself gripped by unexpected terror.

Almost before the bucking of the second bow, Sharp staggered backwards, clutching her side. 'Oh, you cunts!'

The first of the masked Cruelties closed on her, and having underestimated Sharp for the second time, found himself impaled on her blade. He stepped back, blood jetting from the wound in his chest, and collapsed to his knees. For her part, Sharp straightened and with an oath pulled out a small black book from her waistband. A single lazy drop of blood fell from the tip of the bolt protruding from the back cover.

'The Creed?' Rue shook her head. 'You're trying to tell me the fucking Creed saved your life?' She felt the Morrigan's hand all over this. The intervention she had begged for in one broken moment, made wordless promises for. But the Creed, though bound in leather and thick with hypocrisy, was surely insufficient to arrest the death that had so pointedly rushed towards Sharp's vitals.

Sharp, still holding her sword out before her at arm's length, gave a wild laugh and shook the book open. The bolt also transfixed the bronze mark that she had kept sandwiched within the pages. The coin Rue had given her a lifetime ago.

The second of the masked Cruelties closed on Sharp, more cautious than his friend, who chose that moment to complete his journey to the ground. Sharp, perhaps focused by the pain or the remnants of whatever luck the Morrigan had bestowed on her, squared herself to meet his advance.

Rue had seen Sharp bested with the knife as a child. Only by Wenda though. And Wenda had been something of a phenomenon with a short edge. Rue had killed her by seizing her moment rather than through dagger skill. With a sword, though, particularly a long, light blade, Rue had never seen Sharp's equal.

Tmanga had been right: life would not present any of them with many duels, neat little contests on level ground where a honed skill could shine. But Sharp had waited for a long long time, and here was a duel.

Blades touched, a ringing engagement, the young man's boots scraping the floor as he sought position. Sharp, for her part, stayed still. Her blade might gleam but her skill lay as rusty as her strength. She turned the Cruelty's query aside, understanding as she did so quite how much she had lost.

She stepped back, holding up her left hand, long fingers bloody. Still straight, but withered. 'I was never meant to grow old. It's a cosmic joke. Look at me!' A glance at Rue. 'What happened to us, Molly?' She beat down the attack the Cruelty launched as she turned her head, not even looking at him.

'Don't toy with him,' Rue advised. 'He'll wear you out.'

'Him?' She flashed her teeth. 'We can keep his mask after he's done. Might come in handy. Better than a bag on your head in any case.'

The Cruelty came on, fast and fierce and measured, natural skill evident on top of years of practice. Sharp contained him with taps, with tricks, with experience, with the memory in old muscles, never once showing the breath-stealing speed that had won her fame.

She faltered, flesh unequal to the demands she made upon it, and he cut her, slicing through the expensive dress from elbow to shoulder, cutting rich brocade, plush velvet, pale skin. If it had been her sword arm that would have been the finish.

Sharp swore, filthy as ever, 'Whore's teats!' But even as blood soaked her sleeve she didn't advance, didn't hurry. She anticipated his feints, anticipated his pride, killed him when, for just a moment, he overreached. He didn't die then, of course, but the cut tipped the scales, the second and third tipped them further, and the fourth spilled their contents across the floor.

'Ewww.' Sharp had always complained about the messes she made. Guts most of all.

Milk-Eye raised a brow. The two guardsmen who had helped escort Rue and Sharp from the Minor's office had slipped away while Sharp was killing the Cruelties. 'The training lacks its old bite since Father . . . left us, but I still would have bet on Jasper or Samd to take down this dried-out old stick. When I left her in that place she could barely feed herself . . .' She smiled, a cruel thing that Rue felt had been made for her, perhaps crafted over years. 'Still, what's been given can be taken away.'

Milk-Eye extended her arm, hand clawed, and the darkness pulsed. Rue felt her wounds twinge with wakefulness, growing damp with their lust for life, even though she wasn't the target. Sharp crumpled, as if every drop of the vigour that had animated her was now spilling from her faster than the blood from her arm, faster than the guts that Jasper or Samd still grasped at had slithered from what was left of his belly.

'That's more how I remember you.' Milk-Eye deployed the razor of her smile once more.

Sharp, trembling and vacant now, clutched her sword with both hands as if it were all that kept her upright. She panted, cheeks hollow, lips bent around her gums as if she were toothless.

Rue stepped towards her friend with empty hands.

'Stay where you are!' Milk-Eye shouted. The blackness – unseen and all the darker for it – pulsed around her fingers and the pain of the wounds that the Morrigan's curse, or blessing, had kept at bay, blossomed through Rue, staggering her.

Milk-Eye advanced on Sharp, ignoring her fellow Cruelties, the dead and the dying. 'You want to help her? Her? Where were you when *we* needed you, Eldest?'

Somehow the weight of that name, *Eldest*, was harder to carry than all the hurting of her flesh. She had traded 'Eldest' for 'Mollandra', or perhaps reclaimed it, but she'd worn the name 'Rue' far longer than any other. She had taken it in place of the mourning she had found herself unequal to and had instead worn her grief as a name.

'Don't hurt her!'

And though Milk-Eye sneered, thinking it was Sharp that Rue sought to protect, in truth she meant both of them, both of them right now; and both of them as children torn from their innocence.

'Don't hurt her!'

Milk-Eye held her sword ready now, understanding that Sharp's threat lay in her limbs as much as her mind, knowing that the fog in which the woman drowned could still be parted by the hooks of muscle memory, allowing sudden danger to emerge. The younger woman closed on the older one as one might disarm a trap, the mechanism understood but filled with coiled potency that would punish any slip in concentration.

A crow's caw rang out in Baron Mancer's hall: Senna, forgotten on her perch upon the bust above the door. The cry came again, dark and bitter and old as winter. It shivered through Rue, shaking thoughts and memories loose from their moorings.

Recollection bore down upon Rue to add to the weight of her names, to the burden of her pain and of the years and of the guilt that hung about her neck. There had been a garden, a night garden, never seen and yet it had held their hearts. Toadstools in the dark, decorated with spring's petals: Tune's gift to them. Known only by fingertips. Such a small thing, so tawdry and inconsequential, yet so precious to three children drowning in their pain.

'Don't. Hurt. Her.'

Memory beat at her. There had been a three, forged in the sharing of hardships and horror and the banter of young girls and sealed in an exchange of secret weaknesses around a great tongue that might toll but never tell. 'Don't . . .'

The cause that had brought Rue to this ruin, an accounting for old new friends, for Jayne and Ambeth, was both true and a lie. She had held them dear, but those bonds were echoes of older, deeper ties that bound bone to bone, heart to soul. The twists and turns of a childhood might be random, windborne chance, petty, predictable, unspecial, freighted with neither destiny nor grand design . . . but these had been *her* twists and turns. Fate had furnished her with Sharp and Tmanga. At the beat of a sparrow's wings she might have found other friends, a different life . . . She had not. The Furies, the Morrigan, every shadow and reflection of the triple-goddess could go hang. *This* was her holy. This her faith.

She straightened, shrugging off the pain through no magic but her own fire.

'No!' Her denial shivered through the hall making a dance of every flame.

As she turned, Rue now wore her curse black across her face, a crow's wings spread wide, the whites of her eyes bright in the darkness that curled around the sides of her head. She stood, reflected in many mirrors, hardly knowing in that moment which of them might be her true self.

Milk-Eye held Sharp's gaze now, covering with one hand the old fingers wrapped around her sword hilt, and with the other, aiming her blade at the Kindness's heart.

Rue ran her fingers into the grey nest of her hair, and in the slow pulling of both hands down across the time-ravaged ruin of her face, she drew forth the poison she'd been fed. The gift, the curse, the Ingredient. Particles of a fallen goddess, or at least the body that the goddess had worn during many lifetimes of men. The Ingredient that had stayed so stubbornly within her as a child was easy to release now. All that had ever been required was to understand its power – that it was a strength in and of itself, a sprinkling of divinity.

Power is hard to surrender at the best of times. In the worst of times most would sooner shrug off their skins than relinquish the strength that might save them. That was the hard part. Not the tearing of its eidolons from her mind. The Ingredient had been impossible to reject as a child, but now she knew its power, the physical act was easy: it was the sacrifice that was hard.

Rue flung it from her in two handfuls. What struck Sharp held memory and purpose and one small but vital blind spot.

What struck Milk-Eye carried forgetting.

Both of them fell back, crying out in shock. Milk-Eye to her knees in the blood of her brothers.

'The hell?' Sharp looked up, bright-eyed, the black of the

Ingredient sinking beneath her pale skin, running into her eyes like tears uncried. Without the trace that already lay within her from that day far back in their childhood Sharp would not have withstood the invasion. But what she had once consumed, combined with the long years in between, now acted as a lodestone drawing the rest within.

She would never wield this power as one raised on it by degrees through a mockery of a childhood, but even this small fragment of the mind of Megaera would brook no unchosen forgetting. The trace had sustained her even in the depths of her disease. It had echoed with Rue's approach, returning some faculty, and now Sharp stood returned, as if dementia, that cruel goddess, had never once laid a finger upon her.

Sharp looked around her, at the bloody sword in her hand, at the dead men by her feet, the baron broken on the steps of his dais. Her confusion was no longer that of a crumbling mind but of a sleeper waking to inexplicable discoveries. Not once did her swinging gaze catch on Rue. Nor did it find Milk-Eye, who rested on all fours now, still struggling with the invasion of her mind.

Sharp, blind to the presence of Rue and the surviving Cruelty, and feeling the pull of the purpose Rue had thrust upon her, strode towards the throne, her energy at odds with her age-wrought delicacy. She tore the golden chain of office from Baron Mancer's neck, pausing to study the sigil.

Armed with new information, plus a source of funds, she walked towards the main doors.

Sharp passed both Milk-Eye and Rue without a glance, and though Milk-Eye raised her head as the Kindness swept by, she saw nothing. Rue had made strangers of the two of them, removing each from the other's consideration and expunging them from their memories of the day. They could live as so many in the city did, separate yet together, wrapped in their own lives and blind to almost all they shared the streets with.

At the entrance through which they'd so recently come, Sharp paused, remembering her wound, and bound her arm with cloth torn from her skirts. She stood for a long moment, hunting the pillared hall for something, staring through Rue and through

Milk-Eye as the woman struggled to her feet. Seeing nothing, Sharp shrugged, frowned and carried on her way, pushing her sword through the belt of her dress, smearing the costly fabric with crimson. Before vanishing down the corridor she began, improbably, to whistle.

Rue had placed in her old friend the imperative to seek out any surviving Kindnesses and use her new ability to sense the approach of Cruelties to protect them. So, by most standards, Sharp was off to a particularly bad start, walking away from a much-weakened example of what she was to safeguard. But Rue only smiled as the echoes of Sharp's tune died into the distance.

By reducing both Sharp and Milk-Eye to blurs on the periphery of the other, Rue had saved them from each other, at least for now. Leaving just her to pay the price.

'What did you do?' Milk-Eye stared around in suspicion. 'You did something.'

Sick as she already was with the Ingredient, Milk-Eye was far less susceptible to the manipulations Rue had used on Sharp. Apart from blinding her to Sharp's presence, Rue's sacrifice had only added to Milk-Eye's power. And the burning eye she now turned on Rue held not an ounce of gratitude.

CHAPTER 42
Rue

'You left us.' Every rigid angle echoed the accusation. Milk-Eye hunched against an old unhealed pain, ready to strike. 'You left me.'

'I'm not a good person.' Rue kept all passion from her voice. 'I never have been.'

'I was there. Right below you!' In her face the desperation of that child could be seen, there among the lines experience had drawn. 'You could have reached down.'

'And I didn't.' Rue would sully neither her own tongue nor Milk-Eye's ears with the word 'sorry'. Instead, she opened her arms, showing her wounds and her blood. 'But I'm here now, and you should strike your blow.'

When she was young, when she had been Eldest and Mollandra, Rue had imagined that as you grew old, as your grip on life began to loosen, nail by nail, finger by finger, it would become easier to let go. Pain would become a blurry thing, just as vision failed and taste dulled. The truth was that death had always seemed an approaching fire, and whatever a person's age they felt that heat and struggled all the more as it drew closer.

Rue, in spreading her arms before Milk-Eye's blow, hadn't lightly surrendered the tail end of a long life. She had faced the flames and offered the price her guilt had demanded. Without the passion and blinding speed of the fight, the bright blade in Milk-Eye's hand looked all the more terrifying, and Rue flinched before it as she had not before the swords of Isik's mercenaries nor beneath Gressa's glowing iron.

Soldiers from the garrison began to pour into the baron's hall. The sharp sounds of order being imposed could be heard above the tramp of booted feet.

Rue scanned the soldiers piling in, some half armoured, some missing their spears and helms, hair awry as if just roused from sleep. 'Do it now, or lose your moment.'

Milk-Eye's face tightened as if anticipating a blow. The milk of her clouded eye bloomed crimson, as if drops of blood were falling into the whiteness. A red hue like that of stained glass, lit from behind by a summer day, glowed within it. 'I see you, Eldest.' Her voice fell through the octaves to a croaking whisper.

'No?' Rue stepped back, her arms falling to her sides. She knew then another moment of true fear, deep as that felt when Sharp was going to die, but of a very different flavour. 'No?' It was a trick. Imitation.

The glow from the Cruelty's bloody orb intensified, sucking the life from the flaming sconces, and it seemed also that the daylight from many high windows failed as if a storm cloud swallowed the sun.

Far above Rue, wings flapped, and Senna's wild cawing grew faint.

Milk-Eye raised her hand and the weight of Rue's many wounds took her to the ground. Soldiers crowded in from every side.

'Bind her. Bring her.' The voice that came from Milk-Eye's throat was one she had never owned.

Rue didn't allow herself the indignity of struggling. She had surrendered her defence against the Cruelties' power, and by mistake or design the Morrigan's gift was helpless before it. In truth, the darkness in Milk-Eye was just another aspect of the triple-goddess's strength. And since one person making war upon themselves was human nature, old as hills, deep as hunger, then no eyebrows should be raised at one aspect of the triple-goddess fighting another.

Four soldiers brought Rue along behind Milk-Eye, carrying her by her arms and legs, her spine skimming the flagstones. Four more followed.

Rue didn't struggle because it would be useless to do so, but every fibre of her wanted to fight. Screams demanded release. Her hand ached for the sword beneath her skirts. The voice had been one she'd not heard in half a century save in nightmares throughout her time within the Academy, and still sometimes beneath the moon or beneath the shingle roof of her peasant hut, an old woman haunted by a child's terror.

She had imagined Mother with both fathers, Night and Day, mouldering in a grave, their war against the Academy long since won. The alliance they'd had with the warlord was ancient history now. Sunder had claimed the Cruelties for his own – and perhaps they had always been his in some sense. The uneasy alliance he had entered into with Mother and Father had seen them edged out of their own family, undermined by princely power and the ability to navigate the seas of the real world rather than of a bricked-up mansion. It must have taken nerve though. And strength. And it had most definitely taken something more to resist the tricks of memory at their disposal.

Soldiers of Cessation Emperor Sunder had named Rue's former brothers and sisters, though 'Cruelty' was too fitting to leave the common lip. His soldiers' role was to root out sedition. Also, to cow any challenge from what remnants of conquered nobility survived amid the sprawl of an empire so fresh that much of it was still bleeding. Hunting a handful of Kindnesses in hiding was very low down the list. Mere chance had picked the Vale, and placed Pye among the villages that needed to burn so that a new invasion might wear the oh-so-thin robe of legitimacy. But for that misfortune Rue's gentle slide into antiquity would have seen her buried in the garden behind her hut after a peaceful decline.

But what had looked at her out of Milk-Eye's face had struck too deep a chord to have been theatrics. Even now, Rue could see Milk-Eye bend her head and press a hand to her brow as if trying to squeeze away an agony, as if a spike had been driven into her brain.

They passed unchallenged through the chaos of the baron's household, the news of his demise having spread as fast as his fleeing bodyguards. Servants ran hither and thither, some clutching stolen vases, silver candlesticks, wine from his cellars, other staff in pursuit, shouting about consequences. Some sentries had joined in with the looting, and were draped in stolen tapestries, while those whose sense of duty ran deeper stood their ground and doled out the justice of fist and boot.

Milk-Eye led the way down one flight of stairs, then another. Lanterns punctuated the journey along corridors and through chambers where winter's chill still lurked, and dampness glistened on brickwork older than the castle above.

More stairs, these a spiral, sharp edges striking Rue's back every few steps. Decay hung here in the cold air around the central column as they circled down into the darkness. No lamps had been set, no brave little flames danced in wall sconces. Milk-Eye held the only light, a storm lantern, filigreed brass glimmering in the reflection of its own glow from wet and curving walls.

They reached the catacombs, passing through an arch framed by twin angels of death, their stone faces half flesh, half skull, divided vertically along the bridge of the nose, like the ancient goddess, Hel.

The soldiers' boots rang on the stone, shocking the silence and returning in many-tiered echoes. Milk-Eye led them through the vaults, the statues of lesser kings and queens looming out of an ancient night to wear the lantern's glow before the darkness swallowed them again.

Further on, the masonry grew more crumbled, some fragments scattered on the floor, and the drip of water counted out the years, stacking one century on the next.

'Here. Hold her fast.' Milk-Eye came to a stop beside a tomb whose heavy top slab had been shattered by the fall of a block from the ceiling.

Draperies of rotting velvet curtained the alcove, held back by tarnished silver cords. A large cauldron of blackened iron stood to one side of the broken tomb, its yawning mouth hip-high and wide enough to swallow a large sow whole.

Rue tested her strength against that of the men holding her limbs. She'd seen the cauldron once before. Mother had dragged her to her bone-strewn nest in the deepest of the mansion's cellars. The cauldron had rested there amid the mouldering skeletons and when Mother had laid her hand upon it the iron had lit with the same light that shines upon the last river, its rim heavily wrought with coiling vines, black grapes, glaring boars' heads, wheatsheaves and other symbols of plenty.

The soldiers felt *her* approach at the same time Rue did. Free now of the Ingredient there was nothing in Rue to tremble in anticipation. Sensibly, the men fled. Even without a light to guide them to the surface, not one of them felt that the darkness held greater horrors than that dry rustle behind shattered teeth of stone.

Rue managed to sit up, and watched as Mother clawed her way, hissing, into the light. Rue had never seen the creature they'd called Mother by anything other than blindsight, the woman limned by the non-illumination of her own being. Now, for the first time Rue saw her, licked by the light of Milk-Eye's lantern.

How someone so obviously broken could show no identifiable break Rue couldn't say. Mother seemed unchanged by fifty years and more. The same gaunt limbs, and a wild, straggling explosion of hair, revealed by the fire's light to be black but edged with grey. The rags that hung from her were so far gone that it was impossible to say if they had once graced a queen or a farmgirl.

'Eldest.' Her slithering voice the same that had haunted the mansion's cellar. 'My child.'

'I was never yours. You stole every child you ever twisted. Stole or bought.'

'I have missed you. You were always my favourite.' Mother climbed out of the tomb. It was her movements that marked her as something other, as if, though her body were human, what animated it was something very alien.

Rue struggled against her weakness and against her pain, at last wrenching the sword free from her skirts. The same narrow blade that Lip-Scar had carried, and that Sharp had killed him with. 'I'm not a child.' Planting the point of her blade on the stone floor, she used the sword to help her stand. 'I'm older than you because I hold my years inside me. You, you're just a moment in time, a collection of wounds you can't let go of.' With her endless forgetting, spilling time from her shoulders as if it were no more than rain, Mother seemed a far smaller figure than the one Rue had carried with her for so long.

'So proud,' Mother whispered. 'We were always so proud of you.'

'How can you serve this?' Rue turned her head to Milk-Eye, gesturing at the monster in front of them. 'If you'd kept what life taught you, you'd see her as she is. You'd see how pathetic the creature that stole us truly is. If not for the awfulness of her crimes you would pity her.'

Mother's hiss at the word 'pity' carried a dangerous edge. 'We need you, Eldest. It was always our plan. You the strongest. You the warrior. Sunder would never have treated us so with your strength still in our family.'

'Family!' Rue barked a laugh decorated with a dark spray of blood, halted by a chest full of razored pain. 'Family?'

'You'll come back to us now. You were our first. We fed you first. Gave you the finest of Megaera's feast. Throw away this useless age you wear. With you on the field the throne can still be mine. Ours.'

Rue wiped the blood from her mouth with the back of her hand and showed her teeth. 'It was the Academy that Father wanted to bring down. But it's hard to stop, isn't it? Once power's been taken, it hurts to let it go.' She spread her arms, wincing. 'Look at me. The poison you put in me is gone. I found a way to spit it out.' Rue pointed at Milk-Eye. 'She has it now. Make her your champion, to fight your battles if you must. Leave me out of it.'

Mother turned her hollow gaze on Milk-Eye. 'What have you done?' There was horror in her voice.

'All I need from you, "Mother", is seven ounces of gold, and I'll be on my way.'

'Seven o— What madness is this?' Ghost-eyes found Rue again, haunted and haunting.

'Seven ounces of gold,' Rue repeated. 'For the deaths of Jayne Clay and Ambeth Potter. It's the lowest tariff on the Kindnesses' books, three-and-one-half ounces, the least that can be paid in wergild for a life. For a prince it would cost a thousand ounces to wipe the slate clean. It's old lore. Megaera and her sisters held to it. The baron was your creature. This debt is yours.'

'Ah!' Mother raised a crooked stick of a finger and bent her head. 'Ah ha ha!' Her face snapped back up. 'Eldest is still in the game. Still fighting. Still the warrior she pretends has gone.'

'Seven ounces. Why does no one—'

Mother extended an empty hand, palm up. She clenched her fingers like a trap closing on prey, and with a cry, Milk-Eye fell to her knees. 'This one was always weak. She can no more hold what we gave you than a cup can contain an ocean.'

Milk-Eye uttered a strangled sound, her good eye turning black, her white one shading through the greys, darkness painting every vein in her throat like the rising limbs of a winter-bare forest.

'What are you doing?' Rue took a half-step towards Milk-Eye.

'Killing your sister, of course. So you can have your power back. Then I'll teach you to use it, and we can forget all the unpleasantness that has passed between us.'

'She's not my sis—' But Rue could see it didn't matter. Milk-Eye's mouth opened in a scream though no sound came, just a misting of blackness, the Ingredient being drawn from her mind.

The fire that the Kindnesses had put into Rue as a child had burned for a generation and if her anger had been given unfettered access to it, she might have incinerated half the cities on the island before she consumed herself in the rage-storm. What the Kindnesses had given her in the elixir had been wrapped within what the Cruelties had given her in the Ingredient. Megaera's blessing shielding her from Alecto's gift, and perhaps it had been Alecto's fire that had kept her from being seduced by Megaera's darkness.

That protection had gone now. Milk-Eye's silent scream could have ignited the spark of Rue's anger by itself. The betrayal on her face, echoing what had been there when Rue had abandoned her as a child, fanned those flames. What brought it roaring from her skin was Mother's angular horror, her brew of hate and madness, and that twisted love of hers, which was worse than both together.

For a moment every small stone, each unanchored hair, rose unchecked by the world's pull. The catacombs drew their breath, leaving an airless silence to anticipate the flames' crackle. And in the instant of Rue's breaking cry, the wind howled in, swirling a spiral inferno to taste the stones above her.

Mother's darkness swatted down the firestorm in the same heartbeat. 'Foolish girl!'

The Furies' strengths had worked together, Alecto the starter,

Megaera the finisher, Tisiphone standing between her sisters, the bridge that joined them. The Cruelties were a force fashioned to undo the Kindnesses and their Academy. Rue had never believed her rage would overwhelm the deep well of Mother's darkness. She had only needed a distraction, but even as she reversed her blade, setting the point to her chest in the moment that Mother's attention left her, the monster had her in focus again, reaching to stop her.

Senna arrowed out of the darkness, swooping beneath a stone arch, an explosion of feathers in Mother's face. Stabbing beak, small sharp claws. Mother snatched the crow away, slamming the crushed carcass aside. It fell soundlessly into the cauldron's maw.

But the moment Senna had purchased proved sufficient. Lip-Scar's blade transfixed Rue, cold steel thrust through her chest. Through her heart. Not even the Morrigan's enchantment could enter Rue's heart uninvited. And it would not sustain her past this wound. She fell like a hewn tree, her gaze on her sister.

Mother couldn't kill Milk-Eye now. Not when she'd lost her prize. The monster released Milk-Eye, instead throwing herself at Rue and catching her in emaciated arms just inches from the ground.

'You stupid child!' Blackened teeth, a dry tongue, the enfolding tomb-stink.

Rue twisted her lips in a fierce grin then rolled her head back, listening for the flow of the river that she was ready now to cross.

Mother clutched Rue to her chest, strong in her madness. 'The burden's on your sister now.'

Rue could no longer steer her gaze, but she could see Milk-Eye flinch.

'If not our first-born then the second true-born.'

Milk-Eye shook her head, more scared than when Mother had started to kill her.

'The rest were stolen, but you three, Eldest . . .' some mockery of grief shuddered through the monster's skeletal chest '. . . we should never have left you with a foster family. Your father didn't listen.' Her voice began to fade behind the rushing whisper of a black river. '. . . Keep them with us . . . fruit of my womb . . .'

CHAPTER 43
Rue

'No!' Rue reached out towards her sister and her fresh betrayal, only to find herself stretching towards the retreating shore of the river.

Somehow, she was already on the ferry, gliding across the racing waters, though the ferryman kept just one hand on his pole.

'But I didn't . . .'

She saw her bronze mark resting on the bones of the ferryman's other hand. To take your own life was to place the money in his palm. That was what the rhyme said, albeit a grim doggerel for children.

Rue opened her mouth to protest but no words came. Instead, she choked on the sudden memory of Mother's last words to her. True-born, fostered out. That Mother and Father, Night or Day or both of them together, were her actual parents was not a fact that wanted to remain inside her. She fell to her hands and knees on the planked belly of the boat retching as if to vomit so deeply that even truth might leave her.

The man she had killed after all his crimes against both her and Bek was not her father, not her blood. She had cut his throat after the depth of his betrayals had broken both her mind and spirit. Patricide could be struck from the list of her sins. But it meant that Bek had never been her blood either, and that felt a greater loss than anything she might have gained.

She retched again, more violently. Her mother could not have been that witch in the basement. Her father could not have been the spider in the parlour, the ravening wolf who ran the halls. She had known herself to be evil, to have been polluted by experience, but now, in the moment of her death, to be told she had sprung from so foul a source, and to carry that curse across the river with her . . . it was too much.

The termination of a black thunderbolt against the planking in the bows shook her from her anguish. The new arrival missed the water by a foot at most, and Rue by inches.

'Senna!'

The bird lay stunned in the confusion of its own feathers.

Senna lifted her head unsteadily and gave a low caw. 'Who followed who this time?'

Rue heaved herself up using the side of the boat. For a moment the receding banks distracted her. A knotting of the half-light had caught her eye, there, higher up where the bank stepped towards the Badlands and tangled thorns grew in leafless profusion. 'I'm not sure . . .'

The knot in the light became a swirl, sweeping darkness into its gyre beneath the black sun's eye. The thorns leaned this way then that, caught in a great wind, stones and grit flying. Even across the expanse of water Rue heard the squall's fury, though no hint of it stirred the air about her.

'Mother . . .'

The creature dropped from the heart of the gyre and the wind blew itself out as swiftly as it came.

'That's really your mother?' Senna hopped onto a bench, dishevelled such that one might think she'd wrestled a cat and lost.

'I don't . . .' But it felt true. Horribly true but true nonetheless.

'Can she come after us?'

'That I don't know.' Rue gripped the ferry's edge. 'I hope not. But I wouldn't put it past her.'

The boat's speed had reduced Mother to a dot, one that would have been invisible save for the knowing that she stood there, stark and irreducible.

In her life Rue had held many riches, but she had had few things that were precious to her. In one tiny, private corner, deep and hidden, Rue kept the memory of an unseen garden, a pathetic collection of mushrooms, shared first with Milk-Eye and then with Tune for the gift of the petals that had decorated them. It was both pathetic, a child's dream, and yet incalculably dear to the old woman who visited the memory often, even in her final years.

A second precious thing that she had kept was the knowledge of Bek as her true sister. And now that had been ripped from her. She was the product of monsters. Milk-Eye her sister – and one other, a third – perhaps it had been Lip-Scar. Perhaps one of those others she'd killed and she had merely swapped patricide for fratricide. Either way, it had hollowed her. If the strength of this body she'd been given for the afterlife matched those of her emotions, the boat's gunwale would have been reduced to splinters where her fingers gripped it.

The crunch of the prow against gravel, and the sudden deceleration took Rue by surprise. Save for her tight hold of the wooden edge, born of an entirely separate concern, her arrival on the shores of the Underworld would have been head-first, flat on her back, mouthing obscenities.

'Where to now?' Rue turned to the boatman whose only reply was to indicate with a sweep of his bony hand that she should leave the ferry.

'Is this because I told you to fuck yourself last time?' Rue shook her head and clambered onto the shore. She was careful not to touch the water. Some things even the dead fear.

She stood, bare feet on the grit, looking ahead into the gloom. The river ran more slowly here, and although it had seemed straight on the far side, on this shore it appeared that she was on the inner curve of some great meander. Her naked body was neither young nor old, and her injuries were gone. As Senna took to the air, squawking, Rue clothed herself by force of will, choosing her peasant smock, wool stockings, and a thick coat rather than the newly purchased finery she had died in. She had better memories of the years she'd spent penniless, battling only the seasons and the soil.

'Time to see what's next.'

She climbed the bank's slope without her habitual complaints. Age had left her. It had leaked from her joints, unbound her chest, taken with it the blur in her eyes and the fog in her mind. The absence of that weight of years was a kind of euphoria and Rue resisted the urge to whistle as she strode ever more confidently up the broken ground. If not for the parting memory of Milk-Eye's panic and the understanding that of all her false sisters, it had been her true one she'd first betrayed, Rue might have thought herself in the borderlands of paradise. Youth, it seemed, was a drug she had forgotten during the course of its slow weaning. But returned at a stroke it felt like intoxication.

From the far bank the Underworld had loomed like an approaching dust storm. From this side of the river, mystery replaced that threat of violence. It seemed that a great fog swelled above the shore, filled with the glow of many lights, some static like distant stars, others drifting like fireflies in the air.

There was in that luminous unknown a great promise coaxing its echo onto Rue's lips, placing onto the tip of her tongue answers that need only be spoken. Premonition trembled in her. The life that she had been torn through, left scarred by as if it were the densest thicket of thorns, that life could be shrugged from her shoulders like discarding a worn-out cloak, and in its place . . . *better*. She had had the potential for so very much more. That small child, that little girl, that young woman, all of them could be reborn into her past, and loved as they should have been.

All of it waited for her. All of it lay just beyond sight, needing only for her to truly want it and, in that wanting, be revealed.

As Rue crested the bank, two figures were emerging out of the mists. Bek and Einsa came trailing curling tendrils of fog. She recognized them though they were no longer children, but of indefinite age now: Bek free of the wound that had killed her, Einsa dry at last. These were not the ghosts of her memory, but the spirits of the friends she'd lost. As she ran towards them the chains of bitterness that had bound her since their deaths fell away.

There was in that three-way hug a comfort and a joy that Mollandra had always ached for, one that had never been found in the arms of her true mother or the false one. It was, she thought, heaven encapsulated in a moment.

'All right, all right . . .' Einsa rumbled, pushing them both from her and rubbing at the damp patch Mollandra's tears had left on her tunic. 'Let's not forget the message.'

'Message?' Mollandra pressed the heels of her hands to her eyes, wondering why her nose still ran in the afterlife.

'Message.' Einsa nodded.

'From Aello.' Bek wiped her eyes.

'Aello?' Mollandra said the name to shield herself from what was to come. Aello had been the first of her daughters to enter the world, arriving with the dawn, with Ocy born at noon and Cela coming at sunset.

Aello, always first, had been the first to die too.

'Of course Aello.' Bek rolled her eyes. 'She's waiting for you, back there.' She nodded her head towards the glowing fog. 'But she needs to stay where she is so that Ocy can find her.'

'Ocy?' Mollandra repeated.

'I'm guessing it was a blow to the head that killed you,' Einsa said. 'It's the only way to explain the stupidity.'

'Ocy's still alive?'

'Well, if you can call it that.' Einsa shrugged.

Bek pushed the larger woman aside. 'Ocy has a foot both sides of the river. It means she can tell Aello what Cela's up to.'

'And?' asked Mollandra helplessly. 'What is Cela up to?'

'It's not good.' Bek twisted her mouth and sucked a breath in over her teeth. 'The emperor's coming for her.'

'Sunder?' Could Rue not escape the Morrigan's games even on the far shore of death's river? 'Emperor Sunder?'

'Yes.'

'My little Cela?'

'Yes.'

'What in the world would an emperor want to go chasing Cela for? Baron Mancer's just started a new war for him to play with. Hasn't he got enough on his plate invading Tavoland? King Armand's widow . . . whatshername . . .' Mollandra snapped her fingers. 'They call her the Battle Queen. She'll keep him busy.'

'Exactly.' Bek nodded.

'Exactly what?'

Bek took Mollandra's hands. 'Cela's the Battle Queen. You didn't know?'

'Oh fuck.' Mollandra shook Bek off. 'I've got to go back.' Cela might hate her, but you couldn't leave your child, not with High Cruelty Sunder and all his iron might swarming across the borders.

'She didn't get to be Battle Queen without learning a thing or two about winning,' Bek said. 'She's tougher than you give her credit for.'

'You don't know Sunder like I know him.' Rue felt that old fear, the fear she'd learned the first time she went up against the man, but now multiplied many times over when she thought of what he would do to her child.

'Maybe that's because you never told us,' Einsa said gruffly.

'He . . .' For the longest time Rue thought Father must have stolen Strong from some royal crib, and that he might even have been the true Sunder's brother. Back then, she'd hoped that he really had escaped the mansion even though that would mean he had turned his back on her and broken all his promises, including the one he carried in his very person. She'd hoped that he would somehow return to his true family and be accepted into the warm luxury of their lives. 'He killed . . .' But Strong had never been part of Abrona's royal line. He had crawled from the mansion choking on a dose of the Ingredient higher than anyone had ever survived, perhaps as much as Father, or even Mother, with only his youth to keep it from twisting him, at least on the outside.

'I thought he was good.' It had been a child's notion, she knew that, but even now his memory wore the glow of the hero's robe she'd placed around the wideness of his shoulders. He had been her standard for hope and truth and goodness in the world. When she had abandoned the others she had betrayed his memory, and could find within herself no forgiveness for that crime.

But Strong, whether twisted by his final dose of the Ingredient, or whether always a false idol, had taken a darker path even than Rue had. With Father's invisibility he had killed the true Sunder and taken the boy's place. He had made the prince's noble parents forget the face of their own child and accept him as theirs. Every member of that household found themselves nudged into a new truth.

'I thought he was good. I was . . . wrong.' Rue met her friends' gaze. 'I need to stop him.'

'Well,' said Einsa. 'You could try. But you might be better off running because—'

Mollandra spun on a heel, took one stride towards the river and stopped.

'—because there's that,' Einsa concluded.

Across the river's flat swirl something reached, a dark claw, smoke blooming like blood drops in a glass of water, and in the midst of it all, borne by the chaos and lined in her own non-illuminating light, came Mother.

Acknowledgements

As always, I'm very grateful to Agnes Meszaros for her continued help and feedback. She's never shy to challenge me when she thinks something can be improved or I'm being a little lazy. At the same time her passion and enthusiasm made working on the story even more enjoyable. Agnes is now a fantasy author herself – check out her work under her pen name Mitriel Faywood.

Thanks to Jason Thompson for independently proofreading the manuscript. And I should also thank, as ever, my wonderful editor, Jane Johnson, for her support and her many talents, Natasha Bardon, Chloe Gough, Sian Richefond, and the design, sales, marketing, and publicity crews at HarperCollins. And of course my agent, Ian Drury, and the team at Sheil Land.